The Hidden Force
Library of the Indies
E. M. Beekman, General Editor

THE HIDDEN FORCE

Louis Couperus

Translated by Alexander Teixeira de Mattos

Revised, edited, with an introduction

and notes by E. M. Beekman

The University of Massachusetts Press   Amherst 1985

Preparation and publication of this work were
supported by the Translation and Publication
Programs of the National Endowment for the
Humanities, the Foundation for the Promotion
of the Translation of Dutch Literary Works,
and the Prince Bernhard Fund, to whom acknowledgment
is gratefully made.

The Hidden Force was originally published in
Dutch by L. J. Veen (Amsterdam, 1900) under
the title *De Stille Kracht*; the first English
translation by A. Teixeira de Mattos was published
by Jonathan Cape (London, 1922) and by Dodd,
Mead and Company (New York, 1924).

Preface, introduction, revised translation, notes, and glossary
copyright © 1985 by
The University of Massachusetts Press
Printed in the United States of America
LC 84–16208
ISBN 0–87023–465–X

Library of Congress Cataloging in Publication Data
Couperus, Louis, 1863–1923.
  The hidden force.

  (Library of the Indies)
  Translation of: De stille kracht.
  Includes bibliographical references.
  1. Beekman, E. M., 1939–   . II. Title. III. Series.
PT5825.S7E5   1985   839.3′135   84–16208
ISBN 0–87023–465–X

Contents

Preface to the Series

This volume is one of a series of literary works written by the Dutch about their lives in the former colony of the Dutch East Indies, now the Republic of Indonesia. This realm of more than three thousand islands is roughly one quarter the size of the continental United States. It consists of the four Greater Sunda Islands—Sumatra, larger than California; Java, about the size of New York State; Borneo, about the size of France (presently called Kalimantan); and Celebes, about the size of North Dakota (now called Sulawesi). East from Java is a string of smaller islands called the Lesser Sunda Islands, which includes Bali, Lombok, Sumba, Sumbawa, Flores, and Timor. Further east from the Lesser Sunda Islands lies New Guinea, now called Irian Barat, which is the second largest island in the world. Between New Guinea and Celebes there is a host of smaller islands, often known as the Moluccas, that includes a group once celebrated as the Spice Islands.

One of the most volcanic regions in the world, the Malay archipelago is tropical in climate and has a diverse population. Some 250 languages are spoken in Indonesia, and it is remarkable that a population of such widely differing cultural and ethnic backgrounds adopted the Malay language as its *lingua franca* from about the fifteenth century, although that language was spoken at first only in parts of Sumatra and the Malay peninsula (now Malaysia).

Though the smallest of the Greater Sunda Islands, Java has always been the most densely populated, with about two-thirds of all Indonesians living there. In many ways a history of Indonesia is, first and foremost, the history of Java.

But in some ways Java's prominence is misleading, because it belies the great diversity of this island realm. For instance, the destination of the first Europeans who sailed to Southeast Asia was not Java but the Moluccas. It was that "odiferous pistil" (as Motley called the clove), as well as nutmeg and mace, that drew the Portuguese to a group of small islands in the Ceram and Banda Seas in the early part of the sixteenth century. Pepper was another profitable commodity, and attempts to obtain it brought the Portuguese into conflict with Atjeh, an Islamic sultanate in northern Sumatra, and with Javanese traders who, along with merchants from India, had been the traditional middlemen of the spice trade. The precedent of European intervention had been set and was to continue for nearly four centuries.

Although subsequent history is complicated in its causes and effects, one may propose certain generalities. The Malay realm was essentially a littoral one. Even in Java, the interior was sparsely populated and vir-tually unknown to the foreign intruders coming from China, India, and Europe. Whoever ruled the seas controlled the archipelago, and for the next three centuries the key needed to unlock the riches of Indonesia was mastery of the Indian Ocean. The nations who thus succeeded were, in turn, Portugal, Holland, and England, and one can trace the shifting of power in the prominence and decline of their major cities in the Orient. Goa, Portugal's stronghold in India, gave way to Batavia in the Dutch East Indies, while Batavia was overshadowed by Singapore by the end of the nineteenth century. Although all three were relative-ly small nations, they were maritime giants. Their success was partly due to the internecine warfare between the countless city-states, princi-palities, and native autocrats. The Dutch were masters at playing one against the other.

Religion was a major factor in the fortunes of Indonesia. The Portu-guese expansion was in part a result of Portugal's crusade against Islam, which was quite as ferocious and intransigent as the holy war of the Mohammedans. Islam may be considered a unifying force in the archi-pelago; it cut across all levels of society and provided a rallying point for resistance to foreign intrusion. Just as the Malay language had done lin-guistically, Islam proved to be a syncretizing force when there was no united front. One of the causes of Portugal's demise was its inflexible antagonism to Islam, and later the Dutch found resistance to their rule fueled by religious fervor as well as political dissatisfaction.

Holland ventured to reach the tropical antipodes not only because their nemesis, Philip II of Spain, annexed Portugal and forbade the Dutch entry to Lisbon. The United Netherlands was a nation of mer-chants, a brokerage house for northern Europe, and it wanted to get to the source of tropical wealth itself. Dutch navigators and traders knew the location of the fabled Indies; they were well acquainted with Portu-guese achievements at sea and counted among their members individu-als who had worked for the Portuguese. Philip II simply accelerated a process that was inevitable.

At first, various individual enterprises outfitted ships and sent them to the Far East in a far from lucrative display of free enterprise. Nor was the first arrival of the Dutch in the archipelago auspicious, though it may have been symbolic of subsequent developments. In June 1596 a Dutch fleet of four ships anchored off the coast of Java. Senseless violence and a total disregard for local customs made the Dutch unwelcome on those shores.

During the seventeenth century the Dutch extended their influence in the archipelago by means of superior naval strength, by use of armed intervention which was often ruthless, and by shrewd politicking and exploitation of local differences. Their cause was helped by the lack of a cohesive force to withstand them. Yet the seventeenth century also saw a number of men who were eager to know the new realm, who investigated the language and the mores of the people they encountered, and who studied the flora and fauna. These were men who not only put the Indies on the map of trade routes, but who also charted riches of other than commercial value.

It soon became apparent to the Dutch that these separate ventures did little to promote welfare. In 1602 Johan van Oldenbarneveldt, the Advocate of the United Provinces, managed to negotiate a contract which in effect merged all these individual enterprises into one United East India Company, better known under its Dutch acronym as the VOC. The merger ensured a monopoly at home, and the Company set out to obtain a similar insurance in the Indies. This desire for exclusive rights to the production and marketing of spices and other commodities proved to be a double-edged sword.

The VOC succeeded because of its unrelenting naval vigilance in discouraging European competition and because the Indies were a politically unstable region. And even though the Company was only interested in its balance sheet, it soon found itself burdened with an expanding empire and an indolent bureaucracy which, in the eighteenth century, became not only unwieldy but tolerant of graft and extortion. Furthermore, even though its profits were far below what they were rumored to be, the Company kept its dividends artificially high and was soon forced to borrow money to pay the interest on previous loans. When Holland's naval supremacy was seriously challenged by the British in 1780, a blockade kept the Company's ships from reaching Holland, and the discrepancy between capital and expenditures increased dramatically until the Company's deficit was so large it had to request state aid. In 1798, after nearly two centuries, the Company ceased to exist. Its debt of 140 million guilders was assumed by the state, and the commercial enterprise became a colonial empire.

At the beginning of the nineteenth century, Dutch influence was still determined by the littoral character of the region. Dutch presence in the archipelago can be said to have lasted three and a half centuries, but if one defines colonialism as the subjugation of an *entire* area and dates it from the time when the last independent domain was conquered—in this case Atjeh in northern Sumatra—then the Dutch colonial empire lasted less than half a century. Effective government could only be claimed for the Moluccas, certain portions of Java (by no means the entire island), a southern portion of Celebes, and some coastal regions of Sumatra and Borneo. Yet it is also true that precisely because Indonesia was an insular realm, Holland never needed to muster a substantial army such as the one the British had to maintain in the large subcontinent of India. The extensive interiors of islands such as Sumatra, Borneo, or Celebes were not penetrated, because, for the seaborne empire of commercial interests, exploration of such regions was unprofitable, hence not desirable.

The nature of Holland's involvement changed with the tenure of Herman Willem Daendels as governor-general, just after the French revolution. Holland declared itself a democratic nation in 1795, allied itself with France—which meant a direct confrontation with England —and was practically a vassal state of France until 1810. Though reform, liberal programs, and the mandate of human rights were loudly proclaimed in Europe, they did not seem to apply to the Asian branch of the family of man. Daendels exemplified this double standard. He evinced reforms, either in fact or on paper, but did so in an imperious manner and with total disregard for native customs and law (known as *adat*). Stamford Raffles, who was the chief administrator of the British interim government from 1811 to 1816, expanded Daendels's innovations, which included tax reform and the introduction of the land-rent system, which was based on the assumption that all the land belonged to the colonial administration. By the time Holland regained its colonies in 1816, any resemblance to the erstwhile Company had vanished. In its place was a firmly established, paternalistic colonial government which ruled by edict and regulation, supported a huge bureaucracy, and sought to make the colonies turn a profit, as well as to legislate its inhabitants' manner of living.

It is not surprising that for the remainder of the nineteenth century, a centralized authority instituted changes from above that were often in direct conflict with Javanese life and welfare. One such change, which was supposed to increase revenues and improve the life of the Javanese peasant, was the infamous "Cultivation System" (*Cultuurstelsel*). This system required the Javanese to grow cash crops, such as sugar cane or indigo, which, although profitable on the world market, were of little practical use to the Javanese. In effect it meant compulsory labor and the exploitation of the entire island as if it were a feudal estate. The system proved profitable for the Dutch, and because it introduced varied crops such as tea and tobacco to local agriculture, it indirectly improved the living standard of some of the people. It also fostered distrust of colonial authority, caused uprisings, and provided the impetus for liberal reform on the part of Dutch politicians in the Netherlands.

Along with the increased demand in the latter half of the nineteenth century for liberal reform came an expansion of direct control over other areas of the archipelago. One of the reasons for this was an unprecedented influx of private citizens from Holland. Expansion of trade required expansion of territory that was under direct control of Batavia to insure stability. Colonial policy improved education, agriculture, and public hygiene and expanded the transportation network. In Java a paternalistic policy was not offensive, because its ruling class (the *prijaji*) had governed that way for centuries; but progressive politicians in The Hague demanded that the Indies be administered on a moral basis which favored the interests of the Indonesians rather than those of the Dutch government in Europe. This "ethical policy" became doctrine from about the turn of this century and followed on the heels of a renascence of scientific study of the Indies quite as enthusiastic as the one in the seventeenth century.

The first three decades of the present century were probably the most stable and prosperous in colonial history. This period was also the beginning of an emerging Indonesian national consciousness. Various nationalistic parties were formed, and the Indonesians demanded a far more representative role in the administration of their country. The example of Japan indicated to the Indonesians that European rulers were not invincible. The rapidity with which the Japanese conquered Southeast Asia during the Second World War only accelerated the process of decolonization. In 1945 Indonesia declared its independence, naming Sukarno the republic's first president. The Dutch did not accept this declaration, and between 1945 and 1949 they conducted several unsuccessful military campaigns to re-establish control. In 1950, with a new constitution, Indonesia became a sovereign state.

I offer here only a cursory outline. The historical reality is far more complex and infinitely richer, but this sketch must suffice as a backdrop for the particular type of literature that is presented in this series.

This is a literature written by or about European colonialists in Southeast Asia prior to the Second World War. Though the literary techniques may be Western, the subject matter is unique. This genre is also a self-contained unit that cannot develop further, because there are no new voices and because what was voiced no longer exists. Yet it is a literature that can still instruct, because it delineates the historical and psychological confrontation of East and West, it depicts the uneasy alliance of these antithetical forces, and it shows by prior example the demise of Western imperialism.

These are political issues, but there is another aspect of this kind of literature that is of equal importance. It is a literature of lost causes, of a past irrevocably gone, of an era that today seems so utterly alien that it is novel once again.

Tempo dulu it was once called—time past. But now, after two world wars and several Asian wars, after the passage of nearly half a century, this phrase presents more than a wistful longing for the prerogatives of imperialism; it gives as well a poignant realization that an epoch is past that will never return. At its worst the documentation of this perception is sentimental indulgence, but at its best it is the poetry of a vanished era, of the fall of an empire, of the passing of an age when issues moral and political were firmer and clearer, and when the drama of the East was still palpable and not yet reduced to a topic for sociologists.

In many ways, this literature of Asian colonialism reminds one of the literature of the American South—of Faulkner, O'Connor, John Crowe Ransom, and Robert Penn Warren. For that too was a "colonial" literature that was quite as much aware of its own demise and yet, not defiantly but wistfully, determined to record its own passing. One finds in both the peculiar hybrid of antithetical cultures, the inevitable defeat of the more recent masters, a faith in more traditional virtues, and that peculiar offbeat detail often called "gothic" or "grotesque." In both literatures loneliness is a central theme. There were very few who knew how to turn their mordant isolation into a dispassionate awareness that all things must pass and fail.

E. M. Beekman

Introduction

It is impossible to be concise about Louis Couperus's literary achievement, nor would such an attempt be warranted. Couperus (1863–1923) is one of the great writers of Dutch literature and one of its classic novelists. He and Multatuli were major innovators of Dutch prose, and Couperus's inspiration was anything but typical of the prevailing norm. He contributed five masterpieces to the development of the Dutch novel, including *The Hidden Force*, which doubles as a major work of Dutch colonial literature. Hence, it seems reasonable that a consideration of the present text should be attempted with at least some indication of the larger perspective.

Couperus was of two minds about what he discerned in both himself and the world at large. He lived among and wrote about opposing forces which seldom responded to conciliation. What is important here is his experience of the dichotomy itself. While awareness of disjunction is almost a commonplace of the romantic imagination, and Couperus was most definitely a Romantic, it is also a prominent feature of Dutch colonial letters. One should be able, therefore, to illuminate the general nature of that literature by discussing the specific example of *The Hidden Force*.

The Couperus family had deep roots in colonial society.[1] Louis Couperus's great-grandfather, Abraham Couperus, went to the Indies in the latter half of the eighteenth century. While the Dutch still controlled Malacca he acquired a fortune there and became its governor. He married a local woman from a respected family—Catharina Johanna Koek—whose grandmother was a native Malay. After he moved to Java, he continued his impressive career in the colonial civil service and became a friend of Raffles, who ruled Java during the British interim government from 1811 to 1816.

John Ricus Couperus, the writer's father and Abraham Couperus's grandson, was born in 1816 in the colonial capital, Batavia, and, as was customary, was sent to Holland for his secondary and graduate education. He acquired a law degree from Leyden University and returned shortly thereafter to the Indies where he embarked on a distinguished career in the colonial judiciary. While living in Batavia in 1847 he married a woman from an aristocratic family, Catharina Geertruida Reynst, whose father had been a vice president of the powerful Council of the Indies as well as an acting governor-general. The couple had eleven children. John Couperus retired officially in 1862 and went back to Holland to live in The Hague, the city preferred by most retired colonialists. Three children were born there, of whom two died, as did one older daughter. The last child (the fourth son), born one year after his father's retirement, was given the names of his three dead sisters: Louis (after Louise), Marie, and Anne.

Throughout his life, the fortunes of Couperus's family remained inextricably tied to the colonial Indies. They owned a coffee plantation in Java, called Tjikopo, and most of Couperus's brothers and sisters spent the greater part of their lives in the tropics. The men maintained the family tradition of pursuing the "gold braid" of colonial officialdom, and the women married only those men who were on a par with their brothers. Couperus wrote later that there were "two brilliancies in Java, two things that bedazzled": the gold of the sun and the gold braid of the civil service (12:229).* But only he saw a choice between what E. M. Forster once specified as the "opposition between two cosmogonies, the spontaneous and the administrative, each with its rival conception of civilization."[2] Couperus's father was forced to acknowledge that his last son would never enter the paternal world of the gold braid (7:534). But even as a denizen of what was considered the inferior domain of letters, Couperus could never ignore the powerful influence of the Indies.

As the Benjamin in the family of a retired and middle-aged father, Louis Couperus grew up in a world of women. From reminiscences he wrote later, one gets the impression that Couperus felt he was an only child (3:16). Like Forster, Couperus was "royally favoured"[3] and doted on by his mother and sisters (9:605). He was a fragile, pampered boy who was constantly fussed over because of his delicate health. Though catered to without restraint, he was not allowed to play outside because it was thought that children of good families never indulged in such a rough pastime. He had to content himself with a fantasy world to ward off boredom.

Couperus described himself as having been a "weak, soft child" who was quiet and content to be by himself. The male world of his father always "remained somewhat at a distance," while he felt "safe and warm" in the feminine world of his mother, assured "that she would always protect" him. This strong bond with his mother never weakened. After her death he experienced her absence as intensely as he had relied on her presence in his childhood (7:666–67); one possible

---

*References for quotations from Couperus's work are given in the text and refer to the collected works: Louis Couperus, *Verzameld Werk*, 12 vols. (Amsterdam: Van Oorschot, 1952–1957). I have tried, to some extent, to maintain the highly idiosyncratic style.

reason for his subsequent marriage was to insure himself of a maternal substitute.

His childhood was only marred by a sense of loneliness and fear. "Because . . . I was a scared child: I was scared of dark staircases, I was scared of bearded men, I was scared of murderers and especially of tigers, and I was very scared of ghosts" (7:667). The sensation of dread was aggravated in the Indies when, as a boy of nine, he accompanied his parents to Java. Couperus made a distinction between being afraid and experiencing dread, always referring to the latter as "Angst."

> Later the child knew Angst in the mysterious Indies. . . . Do you know the tropical hour of dusk, brief but shudderingly fearful, when all sounds suddenly fall silent: the shuddering, fearful pause, when from among the foliage of the *waringin* trees stare pale ghost-faces. . . . In the shadows of the dusky gardens lurk coiling pythons and in the shadows of the large houses, where not all the lamps have been lit yet, shuffle white shades along whitewashed walls. . . . It is the moment when the spirits accompany you along the covered pathways which lead through the gardens to the large bathrooms. . . . Don't take your second bath so late. . . . It is the moment when the black shades dance along the jet-black tar-edges of the large bathrooms and gray away between the large martavans (a large jar). . . . The martavans themselves have become large gnomes. . . . When the child had to stay after school and was forced to take his second bath very late, he would pour the water over his trembling body while the black shades danced all around and above him three bats flappered in threatening circles. (8:376)[4]

Couperus's father had decided to return to the Indies in 1872 in order to help his grown sons find their way into the official hierarchy and to oversee the family property which was threatened by new agricultural legislation. They lived in a large house on the main square of Batavia (Koningsplein) in a manner far more expansive and opulent than they could have afforded in the Netherlands. Couperus was nine when they arrived and fifteen when they returned to Holland in 1878, this time permanently. These tropical years of puberty were a crucial, happy period. He lived like a princeling in an environment that, both in a physical and in a psychological sense, had more space, was more enticing, luxurious, and sensuous, and offered far more freedom than Holland ever could. The resonance of this life was symbolized by the sun, and it never lost its luster for the rest of Couperus's life. "What I found so marvelous was that the sun shone. The sun, that was something improper, something hidden in Holland, even if the sun did shine during the summer! But a steady sun, that was something divine! A child does not suffer from the heat and I, I adored the sun. The sun was like a god to me. The sun in the blue sky seemed God himself, at the very least his eye! The sun was a god, and the moon was his wife!" The sun was not only the generative heat that warmed the land and his imagination, it also made Couperus discover his sexuality, though this had to be kept a secret from his parents (7:672; 3:171): "there was something that was good for me in the Indies: I felt myself ripen like a little green fruit" (7:671).

This may seem perfectly natural to us, but it wasn't natural in the last quarter of the nineteenth century, particularly in northern Europe. Couperus had matured more in those five years in the tropics than he would have in a period twice that long in The Hague.

> I thought that Holland was terrible. I believe that every Indies child that comes to Holland must experience the same thing. The smaller house, the hole of a garden, no carriages and no horses . . . two maids and a man-servant instead of thirty servants: I thought it was terrible, didn't understand it, thought that my parents had been ruined, and didn't want to believe that this was not true at all. And at school . . . all the boys had an odor: I thought that they didn't wash themselves, and passionate dramas were out of the question: no one spoke about women, they weren't in love with girls, and nobody had an intimate friend. I looked down on them with disdain and thought that they were just "kiddies," very dull and boring. (7:673)

This profound experience of dislocation is fundamental to Couperus as a man and as a writer. Even as late as 1915, when he was past fifty, he still admitted that when he returned to the city of his birth, he felt "like a tourist, like a foreigner who speaks Dutch remarkably well. . . . It does appear that I am a Dutchman, yet this still seems strange to me at times. It seems that I was born a citizen of The Hague, but I can't always believe it. Just as everything else is contradictory and dualistic in me, so too are these feelings always divided and double" (9:606, 611, 605). The average British tourist would know more about Holland than he did: "I know Siena better than Gouda or Doetinchem; I know Capri better than Marken (where I've never been); and Michelangelo is more familiar to me than Rembrandt" (9:604).

This alienation is shared by most colonial authors; Rob Nieuwenhuys, for instance, who wrote an important essay entitled *Between Two*

Fatherlands (*Tussen twee vaderlanden*, 1959), or Kipling, who felt that England was "the most wonderful foreign land" he'd ever been in. And if we identify the Indies as representing solar freedom and Holland as hibernal constriction, we have the first variation on this cantus firmus of antithesis: the opposition between summer and winter. One will find a symbolic corollary in Henry Adams's description of the New England climate: "Winter and summer were two hostile lives, and bred two separate natures. Winter was always the effort to live; summer was tropical license . . . summer and country were always sensual living, while winter was always compulsory learning. Summer was the multiplicity of nature; winter was school."[5]

This antithesis can be further amplified by matching the Indies and summer with Freud's licentious id, and Holland and winter with the restrictive superego. The first set would coincide with the feminine world of the mother, and the second would reflect the male world of the father. The first would correspond to the Orient, to Asia, while the second would concur with the hostile arrogance of Western civilization. It was the conflict between these irreducible opposites that energized Couperus's art.

Back in The Hague, the adolescent Couperus proved to be an indifferent student. He failed his exams again and again and his father despaired about his prospects for a career in the colonial civil service. The son veered more and more to artistic interests and finally succeeded in acquiring a degree which certified him to teach literature and language, though he never used it.

Couperus made his literary debut in 1883 with exotically romantic poems, overblown and highly artificial. At the age of twenty-one he published his first book, a collection of poems, in 1884. Four years later he became famous with his first novel, *Eline Vere*. This is the story of the demise of an extremely sensitive and overly refined young woman in the upper-class milieu of nineteenth century The Hague. Some of the themes in *Eline Vere* remained constant in Couperus's work, such as the opposition between a refined and lyrical sensibility and the realistic world of practical sense, the imagination versus the lethal weight of quotidian reality, the impasse of loneliness, the delights of passivity, and the inexorable weight of fate.

Louis Couperus was also, of course, a product of his age. In terms of literary history he displayed affinities with the fin-de-siècle literature of the final two decades of the nineteenth century, that concluding episode of literary Romanticism also known as "decadence." The latter term is bothersome because of its negative connotations. It is an easy weapon for those who want to strike out at contrariety. If such a great poet as Baudelaire is explained away by simply labeling him "decadent" then one must register dissatisfaction with the critical norm. That norm one will find discussed with skill and erudition by Mario Praz in *The Romantic Agony* and more recently by the French scholar Jean Pierrot in *The Decadent Imagination, 1880–1900*.[6] There is no space here for exhaustive analysis, but one can state with some justification that in his art, Couperus subscribed to conventions that, superficially, are said to be typical of "decadence": exoticism, eroticism, aestheticism, deliberate artificiality of style, the glamour of gloom, yearning for a distant past, predilection for legends and myths, and a preference for whatever was illicit at the time. In his personal life one will be struck by other forms of deliberate aestheticism—his dandyism, his sartorial disdain for the ordinary, his aristocratic disassociation with the common man, and his unabashed elitism. This was no mere indulgence of the moment and Couperus never significantly modified any of these habits throughout his life. But he paid a price. He was caricatured by his numerous detractors as an effeminate fop who was neurotically obsessed with "unwholesome" aspects of life, ranging from erotic debauchery to effete snobbery. But if one reflects on both Couperus's life and work, the suspicion insinuates itself that all of this was a deliberate pose to indicate disapproval of the norm. I would subscribe to Richard Gilman's criticism of the term and agree with him that "decadence" meant primarily "the absence or departure from certain norms" (which was especially true in Couperus's case). Those norms, according to Gilman, were the utilitarian nature of the age, a bloodless subscription to material progress, the hegemony of the bourgeois and of mediocrity, the uniformity of the ascendant masses, the pervasive vulgarity of public taste and opinion. Couperus lived in an age that Gilman aptly characterizes as "energetic, to be sure, but the energy went into production, not creation; it was a cold, measured, wholly unlyrical and monochromatic age that gave the imagination no purchase on the fabulous, the vivid, and no space in which to construct dreams. Its health was therefore a type of sickness to the creative person, a sterility for which the cure was thought to be corruption and excess."[7] In light of this, all those elements already mentioned reveal a different dimension; they are not negative but are, instead, laudable criticisms. Art became a rallying cry against fatuity by *insisting* on its impracticality and disdain for progress. Artists were abhorred by the democratic majority, and they countered with a recalcitrant aristocracy. The technology of an age of materialism was opposed by spirituality, and empirical reality was denied its authority by appealing to an unreality or surreality divorced from insensible conventionality.

Such an altered perspective makes us realize that everything Couperus stood for was an act of rebellion, and the aspersions cast at both his character and work become proof of what more charitably could be interpreted as a rather desperate heroism. Notions that were meant to be negative—such as "languor," "debility," "striving toward pleasure of a bizarre, peripheral kind," "extreme refinement," "transgression," "distemper," "veneration of the past"[8]—became weapons of a kind of bravery that, in the end, was futile because the might of vigorous mediocrity will always crush antisocial delicacy. This brief excursion is even more to the point when one knows that one of the declarations of the shortlived journal of the movement, Le Décadent, was that "man is growing more refined, more feminine, more divine"[9] as if to register a protest to the bravado of an age of stolid masculinity. This can be extended to include the hostility between East and West, when artists like Couperus would find all the exotic delinquencies in the Orient and all the repressive might of paternalism solidly ensconced in the Occident.[10]

The exoticist, according to Praz, "transports himself in imagination outside the actualities of time and space" in order to make concrete "an actual former existence in the atmosphere he loves." The exoticist affirms the sensual world investing "remote periods and distant countries with the vibration of his own senses and [naturalizing] them in his imagination." He does so by means of "a sensual and artistic externalization." But the paradox is that such an author, "in exile from his own present and actual self,"[11] achieves that distinctly subjective world by means of objectivity, a distancing that allows a greater indulgence. This also represents the strength of the creative artist, Keats's "negative capability," a cessation of the ego that enables one to know and fashion psyches entirely different from one's own. In his early novel Metamorphosis Couperus had his alter ego, the writer Hugo Aylva, say: "I can give a great deal of myself in my metamorphosis; I can split up into parts which ensoul themselves into wholes, but I don't give of myself entirely" (3:220). Such transformations are the created characters, and Couperus's success as a novelist is that he can partake of any number of characters, understand them, know how their psyches react to reality, and at the same time maintain a distance to ensure them a life of their own.

This gift endowed Couperus with the insight of a psychotherapist. For instance, in the four volumes of The Books of the Small Souls, which chronicle the demise of the Indies-Dutch family of the Van

Lowes, his sympathetic understanding of the "small souls" of ordinary people in this world is masterful. The Van Lowe family was modeled on his own. These are people who, caught between the Indies and Holland, find themselves more susceptible to moral decline.[12] But Couperus's perspective is always tolerant and benevolent, and it would seem that he experienced his own family not so much as an influence but rather as an atmosphere. Like a good therapist, Couperus does not judge, hence his characters are not intellectual strawmen but facsimiles of reality enlivened by "the strength of his imaginative vision." *The Books of the Small Souls* made him famous in England and America. Katherine Mansfield stated without reserve that "we do not know anything in English literature with which to compare this delicate and profound study of a passionately united and yet almost equally passionately divided family." The reason for this achievement, she felt, was that Couperus's characters "are seen ever, and always in relation to life—not to a part of life, not to a set of society, but to the bounding horizon, life."[13] But was Couperus also able to train this searchlight on his own character? The many autobiographical statements from the final years of his life would seem to promise that objectivity, but despite the many confessions, Couperus remained something of an enigma because, though his declarations seem honest enough, they also veil what was the core of his being.

A fop, a dandy, vainglorious about his insistence on elegance, Couperus was a most unlikely Dutchman. The emphasis here is on the *deliberate* nature of his affectations. The effeminate delicacy of his "act" might well have been an intentional flouting of the father's male world; it had a paradoxical success because, despite his "unmanly" tastes and behavior, Couperus was lionized by women.[14] He kept the act going most of his life—perhaps the role became finally second nature to him—because by playing himself against the hostile society he disliked, he could expend a minimum of effort to obtain a maximum of effect. Decadent aestheticism became a way of life, and the young Couperus was described as living a "sofa existence" in his "coquettish study" that had the "oriental temperature" of a hothouse.[15] And like a delicate hothouse plant that would wilt and die if exposed to the cold reality that surrounded the artificial life-support system, Couperus would maintain the role of a languid, effete aristocrat, too indolent either to commit action or to propound and defend aggressive opinions. He always wrote in longhand with an heirloom pen made of gold and agate, and he used only purple ink.[16] He chose the paper he wrote on after much deliberation and despised typewriters (8:435). His desk was very neat with a carefully preserved order of letter openers, bibelots, knickknacks, and a portrait of his mother as young girl which he always kept in front of him. All his life Couperus was neat and fastidious, and it would seem that he could create only under carefully controlled conditions. But in reality Couperus was on the move for most of his adult existence, never staying for very long in any one place, and living for long periods of time out of suitcases. In fact, he could write anywhere, which was a fortunate adjustment no doubt due to necessity because he made his living with his pen.[17] He wrote with enviable ease. His manuscripts show hardly any corrections, despite his extraordinary speed and the intricacy of his style.[18] Besides the articles about himself which he wrote when he was older, there is also a fair amount of novelistic material that was derived from his own life; yet Couperus wrote few letters (the ones that survived reveal very little) and there are no notebooks, nor any other form of notation.[19]

Couperus never denied the duality of his nature. He noted that "everything about me is contradictory and a duality" (9:611), and felt that he did not fit anywhere. Before Jung formulated his theory of the coexistence of the anima and the animus in the human psyche, Couperus devoted a great deal of attention to the theme of androgyny or hermaphroditism, a subject also dear to the authors of fin-de-siècle literature.[20] In his first "mythological" novel, *Dionyzos* (1903), Couperus celebrates Dionysus as an androgynous god who "delivers" Hermaphroditos from the loneliness of his bisexuality (4:625–28). It comes as no surprise that, like other "aesthetes" such as Oscar Wilde (1854–1907) or Jean Lorrain (1855–1906), Couperus had homosexual tendencies.

During the first half of Couperus's life, homosexuality was unequivocally condemned as a degenerate perversion.[21] Not until the turn of the century did intellectual and medical opinion begin to argue against the notion that homosexuality was a criminal deviation. A Dutch critic has shown that Couperus read this enfranchising material, that he corresponded with the author of a study on the androgynous element in life, and that he did not try to hide his preferences in his private life. It has also been asserted that Couperus's early novel *Fate* (*Noodlot*, 1891) contains the first allusion to a homosexual relationship in Dutch literature.[22] It is tempting to view Couperus's sexual preferences as an act of rebellion against patriarchal society, but it was not until 1902, the year his father died, that Couperus assigned deviation from the erotic norm a prominent place in his work. Another link to fin-de-siècle literature was his correspondence with Oscar Wilde who had expressed admiration for *Fate* (published under the title of *Footsteps of Fate* in England in

1891). Wilde sent him a copy of *The Picture of Dorian Gray*, which Couperus's wife later translated into Dutch.[23] The exchange of letters took place in 1895, the year of Wilde's notorious trial and conviction for "sexual abnormalities." During the same year Couperus indicated for the first time that he was contemplating writing a novel about the infamous Roman emperor Heliogabalus (?201–222), better known to historians as Elagabalus. This almost proverbial example of late Roman decadence and profligacy was admired by Flaubert, Gautier, Gide, and others, who saw Heliogabalus as part of the "period of antiquity with which these artists of the *fin-de-siècle* liked best to compare their own."[24] Couperus presented an idiosyncratic interpretation of this imperial debaucher and sun priest in his novel entitled *The Mountain of Light*.

Almost a decade earlier Couperus had acquired a wife by marrying his cousin Elisabeth Baud in 1891. Five years younger than he was, she came from a prominent Indies family. Couperus had played with her as a teenager in Batavia and he renewed the acquaintance in The Hague. While Couperus's childhood years in the Indies had not been overly dramatic, Elisabeth Baud's had been sensational, at least according to her husband in 1910. Her father had been an administrator on the first tobacco plantation in Deli, a northern region of the island of Sumatra. She was ten when she joined her parents there and thirteen when she left. The Baud family was among a handful of Europeans in a wild region populated by hostile Bataks who were known to occasionally revolt. People were killed, children tortured, dwellings burned down. The girl was afraid, as one can well imagine, but her father believed in steeling her.

> Because I was very scared of the dark, daddy would sometimes say in the evening: —Little one, I think I've left my cigar case in the bathroom; why don't you go get it for me. . . . And I went, my heart pounding. Through the black garden, on each side the darkening fields, to the sombering river, to the bathhouse. . . . I thought I saw the white *pontianaks* (female ghosts) spooking there above the water and between the black trees, with their bleeding breasts and loose hair. And shaking all the time, I brought daddy's cigar case back which he had forgotten on purpose. [Sometimes I heard] tigers in the night, around the house, howling tragically and furiously, like immense cats. . . . Once . . . when I was looking outside between the slats of the blinds . . . I *saw* a tiger. . . . The animal slunk away from the house, and disappeared in the night . . . and I,

shaking, immediately went to tell daddy.... The next morning daddy was going on a tiger hunt with the foremen and the servants. ... They looked for tracks ... and they came to realize that the spoor had not been made by tigerpaws but by the flat hands of a human being. The tiger had been a spy, in a tiger skin, a Batak spy. And sometimes we found in the morning some bloody hair nailed to the posts of the house.

And yet, as if to underwrite the irreconcilable difference between the tropical experience and ordinary life, she confessed that she preferred those terrifying events she endured those three years. Later, when she came to live in safe, civilized Java, "I thought that life there was pallid, without interest, without emotion, without spies dressed as tigers, without bloody warnings on the doors, without murder, without fire, and I came to long for that house on the spit of land in the river, back there in Deli ..." (7:675–77).

There is little doubt that Couperus's marriage to Elisabeth Baud was a deliberate attempt to compromise with normalcy and to provide himself with a helpmate. This unorthodox union has been characterized as an "emotional arrangement" whereby Couperus assured himself of unstinted maternal love and concern.[25] There certainly was no desire to procreate (Couperus once refused a hotel room in Genoa because it "smelled of children").[26] Couperus was emotionally incapable of loving a woman sexually, and believed that sex degraded love.[27] He clearly presents this belief, for instance, in the mythical fairy tale *Psyche* (1898) or in one of his novelistic masterpieces, *Of Old People The Things That Pass* (1906), to mention two totally different works. In his earlier work Couperus felt that a man could have a profound and lasting friendship with a woman, a relationship that by its very intensity and through the discovery of shared convictions should be able to transcend the materialism of physical love.[28] Be that as it may, Elisabeth Baud devoted her adult life to her cousin, caring for an often difficult person who had a far from robust constitution and a contradictory personality. Less than a year after their marriage, they began the wandering existence that lasted for most of Couperus's life. If they did come back to The Hague once in a while, they stayed with family or in rented lodgings.

A vagabond existence was essential to Couperus because he "could not root in one spot,"[29] and because it allowed him an ample creative perspective. But this cosmopolitanism also reflected a deliberate decision to refuse the narrow provinciality of Dutch literary life, and the oppressive atmosphere of Dutch society in general, which during Couperus's lifetime was deadening indeed.[30] Such an itinerant life was expensive for a man who required certain amenities. Couperus was well aware of that and admitted that traveling was his one extravagance.[31] He could indulge himself because, for his day and age, he was well paid for his writing. The practice then existed of paying an author a fixed sum for an edition of a book, regardless of subsequent sales.[32] This worked to Couperus's advantage because, though his books were never best sellers, he was very productive. This productivity is perhaps somewhat surprising in a man who liked to perpetuate the legend that he was an indolent aesthete. Couperus once summed up his diligence with Plinius's phrase "nulla dies sine linea" or "not a day without one sentence," because "it is pleasant to work if one does it regularly."[33]

With the exception of the novel *Eline Vere*, Couperus's work before 1900, though interesting, cannot measure up to what he produced in the next two decades. But this earlier work sold well, while the masterpieces created between 1900 and his death in 1923 suffered from increasingly diminishing sales.[34] Couperus was forced to find an alternative method of making a living and turned to journalism. These highlights of his career, and of modern Dutch literature, are *The Hidden Force* (*De Stille Kracht*, 1900), the four volumes of *The Books of the Small Souls* (*De boeken der kleine zielen*, 1901–1903), *The Mountain of Light* (*De Berg van Licht*, 1905–1906), *Of Old People The Things That Pass* (*Van oude mensen de dingen die voorbijgaan*, 1906), and *Iskander* (a novel about Alexander the Great, published in 1920). But beginning with the publication of the novels *The Hidden Force* and *Along Lines of Least Resistance* (*Langs Lijnen van Geleidelijkheid*, 1900), Couperus found himself vilified as an "immoral," "perverse," and "effeminate" author whose work was unfit to be published in periodicals because it corrupted the minds and mores of "the wives, sisters, and daughters of decent Dutchmen." Many critics denounced him for writing "pornography" and "improper decadence."[35] What is puzzling from today's point of view, is that this infamous reputation did not increase sales but rather caused Couperus to be defamed by Holland's literary establishment and ignored by the reading public. The result was that between 1906 and 1907, Couperus privately announced that he would no longer write prose works and that he would perhaps stop writing altogether.[36] Publicly however, he typically ascribed the lapse of productivity to his antisocial persona.

> I no longer write novels because I've become so deliciously lazy . . .
> and when I was still writing them I simply couldn't be lazy. Because

a novel . . . is something horrible! That's a labor . . . for Hercules [he was to publish a novel about Hercules in 1913]. That is a job . . . to drive you mad! That is building Babel [he had published a novel about Babel in 1901] . . . with towers and staircases ascending! That is the creation of worlds and the foundation of cities! That is breeding entire families, with grandmas and great-grandpas and children and grandchildren and great-grandchildren, down to I don't know which umpteenth generation [as he had done in *Of Old People The Things That Pass* and *The Books of the Small Souls*]. Writing a novel is . . . being everything: Our Lord as well as a human being at the same time! That is being: architect, painter, doctor, paperhanger, tailor, psychiatrist, linguist, stylist, and much more: an author is everything and everybody, the author of a novel must have known and seen everything, even if it was only in his imagination: he has to know how a city is built or a village, how winter cedes to spring, and how the first love in the heart of his heroine gives way to the second and the third one; he has to know how an omelet is cooked and how a child is born . . . because if he does not know all of this, and much more, he is liable to make the silliest mistakes, on each page, in each sentence. . . . I repeat: can't you understand that becoming aware of my laziness . . . I blessedly resolved . . . not to write novels for a while? . . . and then came the reaction. I assure you that *I* did not choose the craft, but something, stronger than I, did it for me. . . . I am incapable of doing anything else but . . . write. . . . So I began to write again. There were several pens on my desk: there was a lyrical one, an epic and a historical one: there was an allegorical, a symbolic, an idealistic and a naturalistic one, a realistic and an impressionistic pen: I believe that there were even four or five other ones. (7:524–26)

Among the four or five surplus pens, Couperus found a more profitable one—a "whimsical, frivolous" pen—which enabled him to write feuilletons for newspapers from 1909 to his death in 1923. In keeping with his paradoxical life, this journalism made him famous again. The range of this occasional prose is rather impressive: travel sketches, reminiscences, ironic confessions about his mind and soul, short stories, mood descriptions, anecdotes of everyday life, anything or anyone was grist for the mill of this "sweet mania" (8:429). The product is not, of course, of uniform excellence; grinding out what we call "columns" is not cause for persistent inspiration, and Couperus relied on his inimitable style to carry him through periods of flagging energy and motivation. At times the effect was close to self parody, but what is amazing is not that this happened, but that, relatively speaking, it happened so infrequently. And Couperus did not keep to his resolution to forego more ambitious projects. He wrote several long works of fiction, including his final masterpiece, the novel *Iskander*. But his hesitancy proved accurate, for these works did indeed not sell any better than the superior pieces of work he had produced between 1900 and 1906.

Although his later work always remained a succès d'estime in Holland, Couperus was well known and avidly read abroad. His work was particularly successful in England, the United States, and Germany. English-speaking countries preferred Couperus's realistic or psychological fiction, while Germany was more interested in his historical or mythological texts. His worth was particularly appreciated in England and America where his early novel, *Eline Vere*, was published in both London and New York in 1892. *Majesty*, one of Couperus's worst novels, appeared in 1894–1895 and made him famous on both sides of the Atlantic. By 1927, fifteen of his books had been published in English and his work was praised by Katherine Mansfield, Edmund Gosse, John Cowper Powys, William Plomer, and others. But Couperus was considered immoral in England as well, and a careful scrutiny of the translations will reveal that some sly bowdlerizing was perpetrated at the time.[37] Nevertheless, his reputation prospered and Couperus became the most widely translated author of Dutch literature.

When he visited England in 1898 and 1921 Couperus was feted and admired. Writing about the latter trip for a weekly, Couperus admitted that he was moved when his novels, which were barely read in Holland, were "praised with enthusiasm" in London (12:189). During these same summer months of 1921, Couperus met the influential British critic Edmund Gosse (1849–1928) who, in a valedictory article after Couperus's death in 1923, wrote that he found the Dutch author to be "affectionate and simple and at the same time startlingly penetrating. He had the air and some of the stigmata of genius. I learn, with unaffected grief, that he died. . . . The literature of Europe is the poorer by it."[38]

Gosse noted that "nothing about [Couperus] suggested the conventional idea of a Dutchman,"[39] which was most certainly true and which is also true of many of the best colonial writers (e.g., Multatuli, Du Perron, Walraven, van der Tuuk, Dermoût, or Nieuwenhuys). In the lyrical fluidity of his style, in the foreign latitudes of his imagination, or in the manner of his daily existence, Couperus was a cosmopolitan before he was Dutch. "Though a child from Northern shores, I feel that my soul and my sympathies have always been very southern, very Latin. Italy became a second fatherland for me, often sunnier in *every* aspect than my own country, and endowed me with a great love that one normally doesn't feel for a second object. I therefore spent a great deal of time in Italy, even including my summers. Despite the scant foliage of the Italian landscape—no matter how dear foliage is to me—I searched for the mountains, forests, and beaches of what is at times perhaps too sunny an Italy" (9:327). Couperus wrote a great deal about the Mediterranean, and situated some of his finest novels there. He clearly preferred to follow the lure of his imagination into antiquity and called himself a "passatist" (12:193), a noun he derived from the Italian noun *passato* ("the past"), and published novels about Heliogabalus, Hercules, Alexander the Great, Xerxes, the god Dionysus, Roman tourists in ancient Egypt, itinerant actors in first-century Rome, and also wrote many stories about Greek and Roman subjects. As it had done for E. M. Forster, Italy taught Couperus that he could rely entirely on his imagination and the past and that there was no need to scurry after experiences relevant to the present.

And yet, when he went in 1911 to an exposition of Dutch art in Rome, Couperus discovered that he was moved. Walking around the exhibition, he felt "the atmosphere of my country which, strangely enough, I love, even if I don't live there, even if I am seldom there: around me I felt the atmosphere that had wafted round my youth and boyhood; around me I felt the atmosphere of many of my books: the atmosphere of *The Books of the Small Souls* . . . And it is strange how that atmosphere I fled from is full of memory and melancholy, full of the things of the past, of former suffering, and also that lone, pale sunbeam, also from the past" (8:307). This feeling became stronger until, during the First World War, Couperus had to admit that he had succumbed to sickness that was alien to him.

This year, perhaps for the first time, I have felt like a stranger and felt deserted in Italy. It seemed as if the Italy that I loved, no longer loved me. It seemed as if the Florence I had always spoken of in words ever beautiful, the way a young man in love speaks of his first love, it seemed as if she did not return me what I had always given her . . . and I felt: Patriotism. I think it's an ugly word. I think it's a word for a hero who wants to strike a pose. I am not a hero and I do not strike poses and yet, and I don't know why, I cannot find a different word for my emotion. And I won't look for one. I don't care to find another word, more refined, perhaps, for my feelings. I will have to settle for that somewhat heavy, ponderous word. . . . It is quite strange, but these are strange and unprecedented times we are experiencing: we discover ourselves in ourselves. I am a little confused and somewhat surprised to discover myself in this manner. (9:602–3)

But Couperus was not homeward bound yet. He returned to Holland only to leave again. Quotidian life in Holland could not and would not satisfy him. Perhaps one could also ascribe it to the psychological fact that patriotism meant confessing to a love for a kind of patrimony Couperus would rather go without. Five years after his return to The Hague, at the age of fifty-seven, accompanied by the mother who was his wife, Couperus left for Africa, exclaiming with hyperbolic satisfaction that, once again, he was no longer "domiciled" anywhere (12:52). He had been a proper citizen, had worked hard, and had manfully withstood Holland's "unsettled climate where one lights a fire in August only to wear in October a white pair of pants amidst whirling and yellowing leaves" (12:52). He was again on a continent where one could "experience spring in December" (12:70).

Once escaped, Couperus did not stop. Africa was followed by France, England, his last passage to the Indies, and on to China and Japan. In Japan he became seriously ill and was forced to return to Holland. But his fatherland would never graciously concede him his achievements. Admirers and friends tried to raise money to present Couperus with a modest house on the occasion of his sixtieth birthday. This effort proved to be something of an embarrassment but the house was presented to him nevertheless, and Couperus spent the last few months of his life in a rural setting, working as steadily as ever. Less than a month after he turned sixty, Couperus died of what seems to have been blood poisoning.[40] The rancor that many of his compatriots had always felt for this unlikely Dutchman burst forth once again in numerous memorial articles. God was called upon to mete out just punishment for this "pernicious" corrupter, sensualist, voluptuary, and decadent pagan. "His pagan soul visited Rome, bypassed Athens, and hated Jerusalem. He did not kiss a leper, but sniffed at bouquets of flowers."[41]

This "orchid among onions," as one necrologist characterized Couperus, was a man of contradictory impulses. His dissentient life and character resulted in a nonconformist existence, and in retrospect such characteristics seem to have been well-nigh essential for those writers who produced the best colonial literature. Most of them were mavericks who lived perpetually on the borderline that demarcated the separate worlds of the Indies and the Netherlands. Couperus's restlessness, his exilic life, his hankering for the sun in both a real and a symbolic sense, his sensuality, his nostalgia, his rueful admission that Asia would always vanquish the West by yielding, his self-contradiction, even his stated pleasure in being a "passatist," all this makes him kin to that line of colonial originals who had a certain lavishness in their blood.

Couperus's style was lavish too. Following Cicero's example, Greek rhetoricians during the early decades of the Roman Empire distinguished two kinds of prose style: "Asiatic" and "Attic." Their preference was for the latter because it recalled the glory of Greek oratory that was distinguished by its elegant simplicity and healthy vigor. The "Asiatic style" was criticized as being ingenious Mannerism and came to mean, to quote Matthew Arnold, a style that was "barbarously rich and over-loaded," though Cicero had confessed to its sprightly abundance. Ernst Robert Curtius understood these antithetical styles to indicate two major poles of European literary expression: "Asianism is the first form of European Mannerism, Atticism that of European Classicism." In his study of literary Mannerism, G. R. Hocke went beyond Curtius and claimed that the Attic style—concise, realistic, exact—is conservative, and that the Asiatic style—ambiguous, artificial, excessive—is modern. One could even go beyond literary history and argue that the "natural" Attic style is masculine and the "ornamented" Asiatic style feminine, thereby linking them to one of our main sets of opposites.[42]

One will find that this opposition also applies to the style of colonial authors. It seems that for the best of them the tropical material was intense and colorful enough in its own right, and that frugality would display it to the best advantage though, of course, such deliberate sobriety is just as much subject to craft and artifice as any other superior style of prose. At the opposite extreme were writers who felt compelled to match the riot and exuberance of the tropics with a prose that was dramatic and consciously wrought. This is the more dangerous choice, for purple can quickly shade to puce, and ripeness can degenerate to cloying emotionalism. Couperus took the risks inherent in an Asiatic style, and it is a measure of his genius that he could make such a mannered style seem natural by virtue of an almost hypnotic authorial "voice" which insisted that such a style was indeed the only fitting medium for expression.

From the viewpoint of literary history, the genesis for his style may be found in fin-de-siècle literature, with its preference for suggestion, allusion, the evocation of a kind of magic of the ineffable. The dominant mood was wistful, the preferred perspective, both geographically and emotionally, was that of distance. This scope of vision that wanted to keep a distance, grants contour and shape an indistinct quality because it is "distance [that] lends enchantment to the view."[43] Couperus strove for that effect as well. There is a "mutable rhythm" in his prose, an "incessant delicate motion of words [that is] part and parcel of the meaning of words and of the emotions they convey."[44] The modulation of this prose is like an incantation, perhaps due to Couperus's predilection for iteration. As a critic pointed out, repetition is something else than development; repetition situates the reader before something "that we cannot escape, repetition brings us into an irrational world."[45] And if one scrutinizes the present novel, one will find that such repetitions, which are enjoined by dominant themes to form leitmotifs, create an atmosphere of mystery that suggests that there lurks something greater than man, an insinuation of danger. And one can see how form and content mesh in this particular novel: the deliberate refusal to be precise, the preference for the fluid over the static and for evocation over discursive meaning, is meant to bemuse the reader because the "hidden force" cannot be dissected into a rational aggregate.

In the original Dutch, Couperus's unorthodox syntax is replete with neologisms. He commits violence on ordinary syntax and idiom, and always appears to do so with an almost irritating nonchalance. Couperus played his linguistic instrument with a flourish and grace that is rare in Dutch literature but, paradoxically, not so rare in colonial literature. Couperus was saved from mere prolixity by his genius for narration and characterization. His was an empathic imagination that could muffle its author's considerable vanity to allow his characters to live and breathe on their own without sanction. Such negative capability is essential for a superior novelist, but it comes as a surprise from a writer who had such obvious delight in his virtuosity, elegance, and smartness.

Couperus's use of the Dutch language has been described as "Gallic," "European," or "Mediterranean," and even his most vociferous detractors have never accused him of writing in a manner that was typically Dutch.[46] And yet, despite being a cosmopolitan wanderer for most of his life, Couperus never seriously considered writing in anything but Dutch. Other languages left their imprint: his syntax is more Romance than Germanic, his Dutch is marred by a considerable number of Germanisms, and he adopted a fair number of English words and phrases. But Couperus remained faithful to his native language. "At times I've discovered a feeling of irritation in myself . . . because I was a Dutchman and wrote in Dutch. . . . Yet I've never considered naturalization . . . and do not write in French, although many advised me to. No, I've been faithful to my Dutch violin. Besides, I couldn't have played the French piano the way I play my violin. One can never master two instruments . . ." (8:384). Couperus was not insensitive to this particular duality which, though he could never escape it, he turned to advantage as part of his general structure of antitheses.

It is strange to me, this language which, when abroad, I only speak with my wife, to hear myself use a language that is spoken all around me [here in Holland], and which I sometimes do not recognize. The language, which is my instrument, my "violin," I hear all around me, and sometimes the fear arises . . . that I have lingered too long outside the circle of the national language-music. . . . One cannot always praise her as music, and yet the entire symphony is still something wonderful to me because from *all* the mouths resound those same sounds which I held to be restricted to intimate matters or the music of prose. Now I am again where I belong and yet I feel unfamiliar. Ordinary language is so peculiar to me that I don't always understand it readily and that, therefore, becomes twice as interesting for me. Now I hear my own language spoken all around me as if I were a hermit who had returned to the busy market of the town he had once left behind. Over there that language belonged to *me*, here it is public property. (9:611)

Besides this estrangement of language—a feeling shared by all those authors who were either born or raised in the Indies and were then sent to Holland to mature intellectually—there is one final aspect of Couperus's work that is also peculiarly "colonial." I have noted elsewhere that the prose style of colonial writers was profoundly influenced by and modeled after the spoken word. Storytelling was an integral part of daily life in the Indies, indulged in by both servants and masters. The rhythm of the prose of such writers as Dermoût, Du Perron, or Nieuwenhuys betrays its oral inception. Even such fullblooded Dutchmen (*totoks*) as Friedericy and Alberts delighted in native storytellers, and learned a great deal from them. Because of its artificiality and eccentricity, Couperus's mode of writing does not seem conducive to oral presentation, and yet, paradoxically, the opposite is true. One critic noted that Couperus "wrote in the tempo of speech" and that even his infamous periods to indicate breaks in his sentences "had the function of fermatas in music."[47] His work turned out to be remarkably suited for public declamation and, always the consummate actor, Couperus took full advantage of it. The readings he gave during the last decade of his life became carefully orchestrated "events" that exploited the full effect of his reputed dandyism and aesthetic decadence. He performed under subdued lights against a background of velvet and silk, with fresh flowers always nearby. Dressed in formal evening wear, he would lean upon a marble pillar. The reading was theatrical on purpose, and his somewhat bizarre performances were intended to dumbfound the bourgeois. Couperus seems to have had a high voice, which he used with dramatic flourish, and he accompanied his words with expressive gestures of his bejeweled fingers and his elegantly attired body. This use of body language to dramatize his texts reminded one writer of Chinese storytellers who knew the art of "indicating entire situations with one gesture, even describing entire landscapes with it, not to mention an emotion, a sensation, or an event. I thought at the time that this would be impossible to find in Europe, because there no one really knows what a gesture is. But Louis Couperus does."[48]

From the point of view of the average Dutch citizen there would always be something "oriental" about Couperus the man and about his work. And even though Orientalism was a favorite subject of fin-de-siècle literature, Couperus maintained that it was an integral part of his personality, not donned like some literary garment. There was something extravagant about him, something resplendent, a voluptuousness that did not agree with a society that had always been suspicious of intemperance. And yet there remained the undeniable presence of the Indies which, to the average citizen, continued to be a distant mystery that was indecorous, if not insalubrious. It is, therefore, fitting that Couperus's only novel about the Indies was both a masterpiece and considered the first manifestation of his "obscene decadence."

The Hidden Force is based on material that Couperus collected during his second stay in the Indies. The second time he went to that "strange, alluring land of our colonies" (12:230) he was married and a noted author (he turned thirty-six in Java). He stayed for almost a year, from March 1899 to February 1900. The third and last time, Couperus returned once more with his wife, this time as a well-paid traveling correspondent for a Dutch weekly, a popular writer, and a distinguished novelist. Once again, he was away from Holland for almost a year—October 1921 to October 1922—but this time he stayed only four months in the Indies because the trip also included a visit to China and a prolonged stay in Japan.

The contrast between the two adult encounters with the Indies is striking. The first was a pleasant stay with family in Java, and Couperus was at his best as an ingratiating, avuncular guest. He diligently gathered information from colonial officials and wrote the greater part of *The Hidden Force* in Java although he clearly had doubts about the future of the Dutch colonial empire. The last trip in 1921 was far more touristic and poignant. His weekly dispatches, published in book form in 1923 as *Oostwaarts* (and in London in 1924 as *Eastward*), indicated his sadness at and his dislike of the change progressive ideas had worked in the Indies, at the vanished trappings of former colonial glory, and at the "Europeanization" of the country (12:341). Couperus was clearly overcome by fate in the guise of change and he, as if in self-defense, turned into an apologist for colonialism to the point of stating that if he had a son "who was healthy and had young muscles and who wanted to become a novelist" he would dissuade him and advise him instead to become "an assistant somewhere on a plantation in Deli and leave [the] novels unwritten . . . there's a great future in palm oil too" (12:263). In fact, he confesses that if he hadn't become a writer he would most "certainly have become a bureaucrat in the East Indies" (12:263), an admission that is entirely at odds with his repeated dislike for the "gold braid" of the civil service. There is little doubt that in 1921, two years before his death, Couperus was weary of life and society, and that on this last journey to the Indies he reserved his greatest affection for oxen (12:290, 451).

But back in 1899 his mood had been entirely different. Couperus and his wife spent the greater part of their Javanese sojourn with his younger sister Trude Valette, whose husband was the resident of Tegal. When the latter was suddenly transferred to the more important post in Pasuruan in east Java, the Couperuses followed him. The town Labuwangi in *The Hidden Force* is a fairly accurate re-creation of Pasuruan. Resident Van Oudijck's more admirable character traits were modeled after Valette, who was an esteemed official; Trude engendered the greater part of Eva Eldersma; Léonie was based on his wife's grandmother; and even the Léonie-Addy-Doddy triangle seems to have been inspired by a past incident from the paternal side of Couperus's family.

Valette taught his brother-in-law a great deal about the life and responsibilities of a high colonial official (12:230), but, as Couperus repeatedly emphasized, the supernatural element of the book had nothing to do with Valette. It has been suggested that the governor-general who was then in power—Van der Wijck, who was related to Couperus's wife—gave him access to an official document that dealt with the same kind of events described in the novel, which were alleged to have taken place in 1831 in the house of Assistant Resident Van Kessinger in a town called Sumedang. The report described a rain of stones that fell *inside* the house for sixteen days and had been witnessed by a well-known general of the colonial army, A. V. Michiels, who was not known for his gullibility. A report of what had happened was submitted to an interim governor-general, J. C. Baud. In a book published in Java in 1926, a certain Dr. Baudisch reviewed a number of similar occurrences that took place in Europe and concluded that what happened in Labuwangi were poltergeist phenomena.[49] This pertains to the stone throwing, *sirih* spitting, the hammering on the ceiling, the soiling of Van Oudijck's bed, the glass shattering in his hand, and his whiskey's turning yellow. The sobbing souls of little children in the *waringin* tree and the appearances of the white *hadji* are of a different nature.

Couperus had been criticized for not being entirely accurate about the supernatural events in his novel and it was said that he, like many other Dutch colonials, had no sympathetic understanding of the world of the Javanese. I cannot entirely agree with this assessment. First, such poltergeist phenomena as described in the novel did take place from time to time, and some had been witnessed by sober and incredulous Europeans. Second, magic and mysticism were part and parcel of everyday life in Java. This is still true today.[50] That in Indonesia black magic (*klenik*) and mysticism (*kebatinan*) are not entirely distinct can be ascertained from Sukarno's injunction in 1958 that practitioners of *kebatinan* should be careful not to let it turn into black magic.[51] Similarly, the practice of *tapa* or asceticism can endow the practitioner with the powers of black magic, but it can also lead to the "revelation of the mystery of existence." No matter who or what one consults, there is a general consensus that in Java, past and present, "the relationship between nature and supernature is so intimate that it is impossible to draw a line; both participate in the oneness of existence, and ordinary objects may contain the signs and powers of the all-encompassing cosmic process. . . . Nature and supernature mutually influence each other, and causality is implied in their co-ordination. When co-ordination happens or is brought about, events and conditions have to follow. This thinking is valid both for pure mysticism and for magic; moreover, it is valid for one's personal life, for the condition of society, and the perception of history."[52] Mind and matter are far more readily conceived as adversaries in occidental thought and when Western thinking does entertain itself with irrational forces, it is, more often than not, a momentary diversion with droll toys.

This is hardly the case for the Javanese for whom external reality and the inner spiritual world are suffused with the power of what Yeats

called "the supreme Enchanter."[53] Couperus suggests this opposition
when he presents the European dabblers unable to do more than table-
turning to relieve their boredom, while Java's "hidden force" over-
whelms rationality and the phenomenal world.

Couperus was always susceptible to the influence of irrational forces.
Two decades after writing the present novel he confessed:

> Yes, I believe in the evil power of *datura* flowers; I believe that there
> are *elmus*;[54] I believe that benevolent and hostile forces float
> around us, right through our ordinary, everyday existence; I be-
> lieve that the Oriental, no matter where he comes from, can com-
> mand more power over these forces than the Westerner who is ab-
> sorbed by his sobriety, business, and making money. Sometimes,
> when I look deeply into the eyes of a Javanese or Malay, one instant
> longer than I normally would, then I not only believe but I *know*
> that, if he is friendly disposed to me and despite racial differences,
> he can cause something favorable, or, if he hates me, something un-
> favorable to happen to me. And I feel this so strongly that I am
> amazed when I hear the jovially gainsaying horselaugh of him who
> thinks that he has a lease on wisdom and, naive Westerner that he
> is, wants to explain the entire antique soul of the East that is suf-
> fused with mystery by means of a positivistic cavil. (12:470–1)

That the supernatural was a common manifestation of life in the
Indies was already demonstrated in Couperus's time by H. A. Van Hien
in his study of *The Javanese Spirit World and the Relationship that
exists between the Spirits and the World of the Senses.*[55] This was published in four volumes between 1896 and 1913 and is, to my knowledge, the only work of its kind in Dutch. It would seem likely that Couperus knew of this unique examination of Javanese spiritism, explained
by Van Hien with sympathetic understanding. In the first volume, published in 1896, Van Hien describes three (among eighty-five) negative
spirits whose actions bear some resemblance to what happens in the
novel. For instance, the *gendruwa* or *gandarwa* is described as a garden
or forest spirit that manifests itself by "throwing stones and other objects on the roofs of houses, by spitting at or besmirching a person,
animal, or other objects, with red *sirih* juice, by knocking on doors and
windows, or shaking them."[56] This would concur with the poltergeist
phenomena mentioned before. In the fourth volume, published in
1913, Van Hien discusses a malevolent force called *djihin*, which he
translates as "a devilish power, a silent or secret force," using Couperus's phrase here, "*stille kracht*," which is the Dutch title of *The Hidden*

Force and which, to my knowledge, is original with Couperus. Van Hien explains that there are "formulas" a Javanese can use to incite this *djihin* which "have the power to plague the inhabitants of the designated house with incessant throwing of stones, spitting *suru*, throwing filth, knocking on doors and windows. . . . And what person has not heard of such mysterious stone-throwing and *suru*-spitting, which is often mentioned in newspapers, that presents so many problems to the police, and which at first was attributed to malevolence but which in the final analysis had to be ascribed to a mysterious force. There is not a single Javanese who doesn't know how those mysterious vexations are evoked, but he will rarely speak of it because he's afraid to incite the displeasure of the spirits and he thinks it best to play dumb when confronted by Europeans."[57]

Di djihin (the invocation of *djihin*) could be said to be the source of the supernatural events in the residency. This is not to be confused with the Javanese version of sorcery (*guna-guna*), which Couperus never refers to.[58] Given Couperus's predilection for such irrational powers, it seems likely that he would have wanted to keep the nature of the hidden force undefined, inexact, and suggestive. But the novelist saw that he needed concrete instances for his tale, and so he included them for narrative and dramatic reasons, all the time careful not to reveal their provenance. In other words, Couperus used paranormal events that were plausible within the context of his narration and from the point of view of a Dutchman. Perhaps this seems obvious, but it constitutes the basis of much of the criticism.[59] Couperus does not display this spiritism from the viewpoint of the Javanese—an impossible task that would have been prone to distortion and misunderstanding. He wisely refrained from this, and presented incidents of occultism in the novel as particular occurrences experienced by Europeans, or as topics of gossip and rumor. To be sure, there are intimations that the regent is involved, but nowhere is that firmly established. If it were, it would have destroyed the unique atmosphere and power of the novel, would have reduced it to a confrontation between a skeptic and a magician, would have cheapened the awe that the "hidden force" should elicit, and would have trivialized Van Oudijck's tragedy. And tragedy depends on a feeling of inevitability to demonstrate the uncertainty of our lives and of our world. In *The Hidden Force* this is represented in psychological terms by the inevitable penalty for denying the power of the libido, in symbolic terms by the fated triumph of Asia over Europe, and in metaphysical terms by the inescapable juggernaut of fate.

Fate is the central force of Couperus's work. No matter how rich his imagination, his occasional detours into caressing fantasy, his irony, or fits of ecstasy, Couperus remained convinced of the immutability of the law of mankind's impotence in an indifferent universe. Although he presented it in many different ways, Couperus seldom gave this law a precise label (except in an early and indifferent novel entitled *Noodlot* which means "fate" in Dutch). In a mythic allegory entitled *The Sons of the Sun* (*De Zonen der Zon*, 1903) which remained a personal favorite with Couperus, it is represented by a turning wheel; in a similar text called *Jahve* (1903) it is "Secret"; in one of his masterpieces, *Of Old People The Things That Pass* it is simply "The Thing"; in the present novel it is a "hidden force"; in *Iskander* it is "Asia"; in *The Books of the Small Souls* one of its manifestations is the same somber force of heredity that also ruled naturalism. It can even be subsumed as "monotony" (9:648–652).

Not surprisingly, Couperus often associated fate with fear and the night. He distinguished being afraid ("*bang zijn*") from fear ("*Angst*"): "when one is afraid, one is afraid of something or someone. . . . But when one knows Fear, that Fear is felt as a mystery . . . like a mysterious threat of what will be or happen . . ." (8:377). Night, which "has always given me a certain vague fear," is fear's preferred time, though Couperus also felt a reverence for night because there was "something holy" about that time. Despite its demonic potentiality, night can also bring consolation, offered by its "solicitous maternal hands." In other words, the night is woman (7:696–97). In *The Hidden Force*, the night is described as soft, pliant, lax and velvety; it "dissolves thinking . . . leaving only a warm sensuous vision" that arouses an "inexorable hankering for love."

The Hidden Force is a nocturnal book; most of its major scenes take place at night. Announced in the opening sentence, the novel's titular deity is the moon, the lunar symbol of the female force of life. The moon is red, foreboding disaster and the exercise of supernatural power. Couperus noted later in *Eastward* that the tropical moon of the Indies was "always something of a magic mirror" for him (12:349). In symbolic terms, the novel presents the struggle between the lunar night and the solar day. One representation of the lunar night is the ubiquitous *hadji*. Except for the final scene, the *hadji* is only seen at night, often by moonlight, and only by women. He is expressly identified as a ghost by Urip, the Javanese maid. Van Hien describes a spirit called *antu-darat* who lives most often at the foot of old trees and who goes out at night "in the shape of and dressed like a *hadji*."[60] The solar day is the province of Western authority, and is represented by the resident's ceremonial *pajong* (or sunshade) that is described as a "furled sun." But in this novel the female lunar world of intuition, imagination, and magic, triumphs over the male solar world of reason, reflection, and objectivity.

Van Oudijck is surrounded by the female force as the symbolic power of Asia and by the instinctual drive for immediate gratification. This is most clearly represented by his second wife, Léonie, his daughter, Doddy, and his son Theo, and by Addy de Luce. One has to keep in mind that in 1900, when this novel was published, the egoistic sexuality of this quartet was shocking, while Léonie was at the time an uncommon character in Dutch literature.[61] Couperus drew such a convincing portrait because she reflects certain aspects of his own personality. Though this "white sultana" with her impervious "milky white Creole languor" was born in Java of European parents, she is more Indies than Dutch.[62] Her complacent sexuality is a form of narcissistic indulgence, fueled by her vanity, and protected by her indifference. Like a tropical Venus, Léonie is beyond the moral ken of society; her indifference is well-nigh superhuman, and she is called invulnerable because "destiny does not weigh on her."

Such an embodiment of pure carnality should not be fecund, and it is noted that Léonie does not have children. Yet one cannot consider her truly evil because, like an animal or a flower, she is sufficient unto herself and never seriously troubled by a superego that would insist on standards and ideals. Hence it is not surprising, either psychologically or symbolically, that Léonie is devoid of intellect. Her passing in society is a momentary epiphany that is swiftly gone. Her tastes are adolescent, the private life of her mind is devoted to advertisements and trivia, and it is fitting that her most representative lovers are young males living a prolonged adolescence. Typically, when Léonie is confronted with a choice between Theo and Addy, she simplifies it by reducing them to physical *types*, thereby ignoring the notion of individuality. To have used more rational methods would have been inconceivable for this embodiment of sensuality. That she is inviolable is demonstrated by the fact that when the "hidden force" comes to exact retribution, Léonie's punishment is a form of superficial pollution that, literally and figuratively, can be washed off.

Ironically, the impressive scene in the *mandi* room is far more charged with sex than any other, because for once Léonie's almost inert sensuality is enlivened by the kinetic energy of terror. Sensuality needs specificity to become sexual, and Léonie's languid sensuality that, though yielding, never gives in, is for the moment shocked into unaccustomed reality, and finds itself obscene. Like a frightened adolescent she runs for safety to her mother, her maid Urip. But her punishment for what are, after all, palpable trespasses, is finally little more than infection with the virus of jealousy, which in the end infects the entire household of the residency. As a result, the indulgence of a love goddess becomes tawdrily human, as if a reflection of her crude imaginings. Her illicit trysts, for example, are no longer enjoyed with regal nonchalance in her boudoir, but in the seedy hut of the pandering Mrs. Van Does. And Léonie now also admits to the fear of old age; aging, with its consequent physical deterioration, pollutes her timelessness.

Addy de Luce would be Léonie's twin if it were not for the saving grace of his Javanese blood. He is even less intelligent than the resident's wife, though he also needs only to be physically present in order to be loved. He has the animal vigor and grace of a tiger (as Eva Eldersma noted about Léonie), but Addy is even more godlike than his older and female complement. His prototype was Dionysus, the god Couperus celebrated in his first mythological tale, published in 1904. Addy de Luce is called a "beautiful, southern god," "a devastating young god," an "unthinking god." This "tempter" (in the original capitalized as "Verleider") has a "Moorish face," and there's "something southern and seductive," "something Spanish" about him. Addy shines with physical perfection due to the "harmonious" blending of a Gallic adventurer (perhaps an echo of Léonie's "Creole" origins?) and a Javanese princess. Brainless, hence unchecked by rational control, Addy is both insatiable and uninhibited—perhaps even more so than Léonie.

The De Luce family is described as being quintessential Indies, which is one reason Doddy adores Addy. Yet even here is a link with Léonie, because the way the De Luces are described would fit her as well, as if she were one of their children. It is a family that shows "a great simplicity of mind . . . together with an unbounded weariness and tedium, a life of no ideas and but few words, the ready, gentle smile making good for both."

Theo Van Oudijck also combines European and Javanese blood, but in no way as harmoniously as Addy. Big and blond, Theo looks like his father, yet in him, too, the blood of the Indies will assail Van Oudijck. Just as lazy and indifferent as his stepmother, his sister, and Addy, Theo Van Oudijck purposely avoids work and duty as if to insult the Protestant ethic of his father. He quickly succumbs to the spell of his rival Addy, and just as rapidly surrenders to Si-Oudijck, his father's alleged illegitimate son. This is not surprising behavior for someone who is described as "a blond native" or, what amounts to the same thing, as a "fat blond *sinjo*," whose Indies blood is prominently featured in his sensual mouth, and who considers himself the son of his Indies mother and not at all his father's child. His sister, Doddy, also looks like her mother and, at seventeen, is sexually mature. Thus literally and figuratively, Van Oudijck is surrounded by an alien climate. Both in his domestic world and the larger arena of society and history, he is as inescapably enmeshed in a net of ruin as Agamemnon was. And in Java the net was also cast by the feminine element. His children, for instance, remain "secretly faithful to their mother," Van Oudijck's first wife. She makes her living from gambling, and gambling is a passion, hence something Van Oudijck abhors. And to be sure, gambling is the vice that destroys the regent of Ngadjiwa who, indirectly, proves to be Van Oudijck's undoing. In this fashion Couperus continues to insinuate unobtrusive connections between the world of woman, passion, and Java.

The distinctive nature of the male and female spheres of influence is kept quite clear. Van Oudijck is repeatedly upheld as a paragon of masculinity, with his attributes of reason, logic, work, duty, and pragmatism. He is described as a robust, virile man, blessed with "fine human qualities," who is "simple and practical" and "temperate," altogether an impressive person because of his "masculine simplicity." But due to these very same virtues, Van Oudijck is also incapable of admitting to complexity, nuances, involution, or paradox. Van Oudijck's willful denial of life's complexity, coupled with his genuine desire to be of service, makes him an attractive embodiment of paternalism. In terms of his domestic tragedy, his paternal arrogance and inflexibility is a tragic flaw reminiscent of King Lear. But the novel extends the conflict to the level of society and history, and as the resident of Labuwangi, Van Oudijck also represents the paternalism of colonialism. Yet Couperus refuses to yield to simplicity and suggests another dimension to Van Oudijck's principles. The resident's desire for the clarity of an ordered existence is outworn and no longer viable, not even in the strict world of Javanese aristocracy. In his sorrowful affection for the dead pangéran, Van Oudijck, like his creator, betrays himself to be a "passatist" who, to his dismay, finds his present reality becoming increasingly confusing and contradictory. That reality belies his faith in life's certitude. The power of what Van Oudijck always considered weakness—with its attendant connotations such as unpredictability, doubt, confoundment, insecurity, indefiniteness—comes to undo him with a ferocious insistence that baffles him. Used like a Homeric epithet, formlessness gathers shape and strength, like an incremental repetition, until it has overwhelmed the protagonist.

One of the novel's symbolic correlatives for what is rationally so difficult to define is the anonymous hate mail that Van Oudijck begins to receive. One of the things that he dislikes so much about it is its vagueness, a characteristic that is also a major element of the "hidden force." The hate mail is said to originate—though that too is kept vague—with Van Oudijck's illegitimate son Si-Oudijck. Knowing of Si-Oudijck's existence, Addy de Luce arranges for Theo to meet his supposed half brother. The scene where they meet combines the domestic and the official paternalism of the novel: the two young men are delighted with the prospect of destroying Van Oudijck both as a father and as a high colonial official.

Si-Oudijck represents the dark or nocturnal side of Van Oudijck's personality, his unconscious. He presumably engendered this depraved offspring in Ngadjiwa when still a minor official, the same place that proves to be the origin of his demise. For it is this region that is presided over by Sunario's younger brother, the one responsible for the fatal confrontation of European colonialism with the "island of mystery called Java." Si-Oudijck lives in a *kampong*, the Malay word for a native village. But for the Dutch colonialists "living in the *kampong*" also meant "going native," in the sense of coming down in life, of surrendering to a dissolute element that was supposedly synonymous with native life. When his fortune is at a low ebb, Van Oudijck gives in and sends money to his supposed bastard, "that miserable thing in the *kampong*" and winds up living in a similar village himself with his "new little family . . . [that is] a typical Indies mess."

The *kampong* also represented sexuality, and one may note that that is where Si-Oudijck was conceived, where Tidjem (Addy's *babu*) lives who gives Addy the use of her hut for his nocturnal assignations, and where Addy has his rendezvous with Léonie. And out of the *kampong* night comes the "venomous libel" which, like Léonie's "vermilion pollution" is "spewed forth from quiet corners," "bespattering and besmirching" the colonial hierarchy. The accusations are mostly of a sexual nature, and are associated with nocturnal forces: they represent a stealthy and "mock battle in the dark." The libel, the *kampong*, and the tropical night combine to suggest the id, from which flows the unconscious energy represented by sexual craving.

Van Oudijck's demise must come from this nocturnal world of passions and sexuality. But this is only possible because he is susceptible to it. In the little *kampong* near Garut in western Java, he admits to Eva that he cannot live without a woman. The revenge of the archetypal world of woman is manifested in Van Oudijck's uncharacteristic surrender to irrational, blind jealousy. He is consumed by this elemental, instinctive force which usurps the dynamism of his masculine paternalism and makes it impossible for him to do his work. This irrational emotion is the translation of the supernatural events into affective energy that is without form, unbridled, and dangerous. The entire residency is infected by this virulent disease of jealousy and hatred. It is primarily directed at Léonie, whose "little azure flowers" have grown into a "demoniacal bloom." The blooming of this nightflower is harmful to Van Oudijck because, having lived in imbalance, Van Oudijck must now suffer an inevitable punishment, the unleashing of "untamed and untameable psychic power."[63] The moral blackmail that was posted in the *kampong* night, directs his mind to the perverted sexuality of his wife, destroys his rational control so that he comes to believe in ghosts and supernatural events, and finally estranges this self-possessed man from his own identity. The climate begins to affect him, his health is undermined, and his skin turns yellow like his "ochred whiskey." Having succumbed to the hidden force, Van Oudijck also falls victim to its generally indistinct, inexact, and obscure modus vivendi. The benighted resident comes to vacillate, hesitate, "to muffle anything that was too sharp with half measures." Now that both body and mind are mollified, Van Oudijck comes to resemble Léonie when he gives in to "the gentle weakening of his muscles and the aimless drowsiness of his thoughts." He has no ambition left, the vertical "hierarchical line of the civil service" declines to the tranquility of horizontal repose; the resident has submerged himself in the "lukewarm indifference" that was formerly associated with Léonie. Like his second wife, who always runs away from trouble, Van Oudijck finally slinks away from Labuwangi and his responsibilities and hides in the heart of Java, a heart that was once said to be inconquerable. There the retrogression of his "ascending line" is completed when he confesses his revulsion at colonialism to Eva Eldersma.

The Eldersmas reflect Van Oudijck's duality. Onno, the husband, is the hypertrophied version of the masculine devotion to work. When the resident has become an emotional vagabond, Onno adds his superior's work to his own, already inhuman, load. But it is without reward. His enslavement to the administrative grind dehumanizes him and he returns to Holland a broken man. Eva represents the ethical side of Van Oudijck. She appears to be the only person who understands that there is more depth to Van Oudijck's character than most people allow. One should also note that Eva, a Dutch woman, would have made the perfect complement for Van Oudijck because she combines in her person the practical and the aesthetic. Eva is not superficial or indifferent like Léonie. She supports her husband and is faithful to him, and she cares for the world and is not trapped in the prison of egoism as Léonie is. In societal terms, her house is the "real" residency and she brings life to Van Oudijck's existence and to provincial Labuwangi.

Because Eva is almost Van Oudijck's alter ego, she foreshadows his fate. Although she shows that the Dutch could do a great deal of good, we see the charitable instinct go awry when she forces her maid Saina to accept her patronizing good will. She is resented for it because the Dutch woman fails to comprehend even the simplest Javanese, and for a moment she resembles the purblind do-gooder who Dickens loved to satirize.

It is also fitting that the hidden force's first assault on Eva's Western enthusiasm is executed by nature. She is the only one who can respond to the majesty of Java's nature and she is vulnerable to attack because of her aesthetic sensitivity. The monsoon rains ruin not only the beauty and grace of the "artistic consolation" of her carefully contrived environment, but they also rot and mildew her soul. Couperus fuses Eva's physical and intellectual demise in the fine image of the warped piano that is out of tune because of the humidity and the insects.

It is also through Eva that Couperus insinuates that the hidden force is not only Java or triumphant Asia but also the power of "the other." In a deliberate parallel with the novel's opening scene, Eva, like Van Oudijck, is standing at the foot of Labuwangi's lighthouse. Staring into the night she becomes aware of her "humiliating littleness, as of atoms," "of small people at the foot of the little lighthouse [while] overhead drift[s] the fathomless immensity of the skies and the eternal stars. And from that immensity drift[s] the unutterable, as if it were the superhumanly divine, wherein all that was small and human sank and melted away." Compared to the power of this ineffable relentlessness, Eva's "line of grace and beauty" and Van Oudijck's "ascending line" are rather pathetic aspirations.

Only one character in *The Hidden Force* exhibits what may be considered the correct response to such fatalism. She is Urip, Léonie's personal maid, whose name means "life" in Javanese. While Theo and Léonie shudder with fear when they hear the souls of little children sobbing in the *waringin* tree, Urip "squatted low, humbly, as though accepting all fate as an inexplicable mystery, . . . patient and resigned under the big and little things of life." But none of the other characters shows a similar acceptance. Even Van Oudijck's adversary, the regent Sunario, is really an instrument of this same inevitability. Sunario is only described from the outside, fashioned into a shape from the collective reactions of the resident and other people. All that Van Oudijck knows about the regent is circumstantial information gleaned from rumors. The regent is like an idol wherein resides the strength of his nation, or like the image of a deity that by virtue of its inscrutable power remains unsullied by the pollution of a foreign and ignoble presence. Couperus's presentation of the paradoxical nature of the Indies is also in the regent. He is called "a saint and a sorcerer" who harbors, despite his physical delicacy, an ominous forcefulness that is akin to the slumbering energy of his volcanic homeland. Even in this implacable Javanese aristocrat who does not allow Van Oudijck any purchase on his character or soul, Couperus has maintained the multiple levels of meaning we have been pursuing. This "enigmatic *wajang* puppet" has a "feminine air" about him and his secret rage is described as being identical to the controlled fury of his mother, the radèn-aju. The only animated feature of this instrument of fate is his eyes. What they convey is a power Couperus liked to associate with Asia: a paradoxical strength of aggressive passivity that can destroy its victim without any overt or cognitive means. Van Oudijck's practical sobriety has no defense against such an elusive and irrational power. His fate is like that of the cat, who should be the superior in the confrontation with the lizard that Van Oudijck's youngest sons stage in the residency's garden. But, despite appearances, Van Oudijck, will also "slink away, withdrawing from [his] enemy's beady, black eyes."

The clash between the regent and the resident has been interpreted as the fulcrum of Van Oudijck's tragedy. Such an interpretation went far to rescue this novel from the critics who wanted to dismiss it as a tale of exotic hocus-pocus. But one remains uneasy. From a psychological viewpoint one could call Van Oudijck's defeat tragic, but only in the general sense of causing sorrow or sadness. The resident's denial of his psyche's anima will have serious consequences, for no man is whole who lives to the exclusion of the woman in him. On a symbolic level, Couperus seems to suggest that the masculine Occident will in the end not succeed when it tries to conquer the muliebral world of the Orient, but I think that Couperus intended to convey something more than this.

Walter Kaufmann once perceptively noted that Hegel proposed a dissenting opinion of what made Greek drama tragic. In Kaufmann's words, Hegel realized "that at the center of the greatest tragedies of Aeschylus and Sophocles we find not a tragic hero but a tragic collision, and that the conflict is not between good and evil but between one-sided positions, each of which embodies some good."[64] This is, I think, what is at the core of *The Hidden Force*. One must remember that Van Oudijck is a decent human being who is brought low by an error of judgment, not by vice or depravity, and whose main objective is to labor for the amelioration of the Indies.

Both Van Oudijck and Sunario have responsibility commensurate with their respective positions. Neither is entirely wrong and both embody some good. Nor is either man diminished by guilt. What I think is the irony of their respective positions is that both want only what they deem best for the populace. The radèn looks forward to the prospect of a Java ruled by the flower of its own people, while the resident envisages a Java ruled by a select elite of the usurping Western nation. To achieve his vision, Van Oudijck believes it is necessary to enforce progressive measures and to improve the welfare of the overseas territory. The Javanese nobleman believes it is necessary to defend the sacred trust bestowed on his lineage to rule his island realm, a trust that is a divine right that does not need alien sanction. Both men would have profited from a mutual comprehension of what would be beneficial for a common good, but both remain blind to the best efforts of their adversary because they are not of the same blood, nor blessed with the equanimity of gods.

The "tragic collision" of the resident and the regent can now also be viewed from the larger perspective of the opposition of East to West, of Asia to Europe. If one remembers that the creative soil that nurtured Couperus's imagination was fertilized by the late nineteenth century, one will discover that the foundation for the larger opposition is the perennial fascination of the northern European for the southern world of the Mediterranean. Like E. M. Forster, Couperus found his personal and artistic salvation in Italy, the country where, to quote Forster, "they say 'yes' . . . and where things happen."[65] If one extrapolates from this celebrated and, according to Thomas Mann, fatal duality, it is not difficult to find parallels in such archetypal pairs as reality and art, the rational and the intuitive, the masculine North and the feminine South, or, indeed, the Occident and the Orient. An additional ramification is to view the first as the realm of the father and the latter as the realm of the mother. The paternal realm—exemplified in Couperus's case by his judicial father—is characterized by order, duty, intellect, consciousness, and the disunion of subject and object (Van Oudijck), while the maternal realm—Couperus's indulgent, loving mother—is typified by license, sensual gratification, intuition, the unconscious, sexuality, and unity (Léonie). Quite apart from the relative merit of each sphere of influence, it seems to me that this constitutes the symbolic core of colonial literature.

Asia represents the realm of the mother, and, as if underwriting Bachofen's theory of mother right, Couperus indicates her supremacy in several works of fiction. In *The Mountain of Light* it is the grandmother Julia Moeza who, as the Magna Mater from the Asian East (Syria in this case) presides as the most potent force over the life of her grandson, the Emperor Heliogabalus. In *Of Old People The Things That Pass* three generations are blighted by a crime committed by the grandmother. As a young woman, Grandmother Ottilie murdered her husband with the help of her lover during a stormy night in Java. Like a generational radiation, that lethal passion and its indomitable agent rules the vast family, particularly dominating the males. In *The Hidden Force*, the De Luce family is ruled by the grandmother, while Van Oudijck's fateful confrontation with the "hidden force" is really enacted between him and Sunario's mother, when the resident behaves to her almost as if a supplicant son.

This also applies to Couperus's final masterpiece, the novel *Iskander*. The title is the Asian name for Alexander the Great and is the eponym of various Islamic dynasties. Similarities with Couperus's colonial novel include the fact that this work, too, is ruled by the lunar and nocturnal world of the great goddess, and that its victorious power is as indistinct as the Javanese one. Couperus adds a third dimension to the symbolism of the feminine principle: the ocean. Alexander wants to vanquish both "India and the Ocean, that land of magic and that world-water" (11:631). This is the ocean of the collective unconscious, the third realm of the great goddess as the lunar Isis, Ishtar, or Aphrodite Anadyomene, and also the ocean of time.

Alexander never reached India. He was overpowered by the same forces he had vanquished. He is defeated by Asia, the feminine principle, and one of her instruments is the eunuch Bagoas—an androgyne like Couperus's favorite god Dionysus—who, like Sunario, wants to revenge Asia not by killing Alexander but by seeing him waste away morally. Like Van Oudijck, Alexander also comes to know his defeat. Standing next to the plundered tomb of Cyrus, Alexander knows why he returned, unnecessarily, to Asia. "Never would his mouth confess that, even though he had conquered Asia, Asia had conquered him and had known how to drip into his body and soul the secret poison of her silent and enduring Revenge, into the body of him who was still so young, barely three and thirty years. But he knew it, and he knew that, like the least of his own soldiers, he was exhausted from this immense greatness and this superhuman victory" (11:653).

The initial reason asserted by Couperus for Alexander's desire to conquer Asia is identical to the one Hegel indicated in his lectures (from the 1830s) on *The Philosophy of History*. "It was Alexander's aim to avenge Greece for all that Asia had inflicted upon it for so many years, and to fight out at last the ancient feud and contest between the East and West." Couperus would also agree with Hegel that "Alexander's expedition to Asia was at the same time a journey of discovery."[66] For Hegel this meant no more than disclosing the oriental world to Europe, while for Couperus it meant a confrontation of the self with "the other," of the individual with time, of the male with the female archetype of existence. Yet Hegel also thought of India as the "land of imaginative aspiration, a Fairy region, an enchanted World" that was possessed of "an Idealism of imagination." He compares the Asian subcontinent to a beautiful woman in a passage that is peculiarly seductive. India, as the "Land of Desire," is equated with Nature. Hegel clearly comprehends the heartland of Asia to be feminine and allows it great power, yet he manages to turn these characteristics—which I can only comprehend as positive—into a negative denunciation.[67]

Before Hegel's time, Asia's seductive lure was already a basic motif in Western antiquity, something that Couperus was well aware of. For instance, Aeschylus's *Agamemnon* decries the effeminate luxury of things Asian, while Euripides' last play, *The Bacchae*, describes the god Dionysus as being distinguished by feminine beauty, to have Asia as his provenance, and the great mother goddess (Rhea or Cybele) as his ally. For Couperus, Dionysus symbolized the liberation from the northern world of the father by insisting on the hegemony of the southern realm of the mother. Dionysus as Lusios, or "the Liberator," prefigured Couperus's liberating indulgence in more "irrational impulses" such as his imagination, his emotional ambivalence, the femininity of his nature, or his "orientalism," which, from the very beginning of his career, Couperus claimed to be uniquely his own and not acquired by literary proxy. Dionysus incorporates all these aspects; he is a hybrid god, both Asian and Hellenic, with hermaphroditic traits. This "Zeus of women"[68] is said to have conquered the Near East and to have overwhelmed Asia as far as, and including, India—a feat that Couperus said Alexander wanted to emulate. Dionysus's mother was the lunar goddess Semele, and his grandmother was the great goddess, the magna mater, Rhea.

Dionysus's dual nature was essential for Couperus's interpretation of the god. In the dozen sonnets prefacing his mythic tale about Dionysus,

Couperus confessed for the first time to his bilateral soul that was both "a child of northern woe" and a participant in a "jubilee of blue Mediterranean skies" (4:541). But he also extended to Dionysus the ability to overcome disunion by incorporating opposites, and Couperus has the god very tenderly rehabilitate the melancholy loneliness of "Hermafroditos," the antique misfit who was both the male offspring of Hermes' "radiant intellect" and the female offspring of Aphrodite's "radiant beauty" (4:625).

These constantly overlapping sets of opposites, which were so important to Couperus's personality and art, are also fundamental to colonial literature, and it is therefore fitting that a writer who experienced duality as keenly as Couperus did would create a classic fiction of the cultural schism between East and West. But was there also a way of overcoming this dilemma? In terms of Couperus's lifelong devotion to his art, that consolation can be found in the act of creativity itself, where he fused narrative insight with lyricism. Yet once again, this, too, can be expanded to include the other pairs of opposites I have been trying to isolate.

The convergence of the two opposing principles in the act of literary creation was symbolized by Baudelaire—misleadingly indicated as the eponym of the "decadent" movement in literature—by the thyrsus: the staff, topped by a pine cone and entwined by vines, that is representative of the cult of Dionysus. In one of his inimitable prose poems ("Le Thyrse"), Baudelaire equates the staff with the masculine will and the embracing vines with the feminine imagination. "The flowers are the promenade of your fantasy around your will; it is the feminine element performing its enchanting pirouettes around the masculine one. Straight line and arabesque line, meaning and expression, the will's rigidity and verbal sinuosity, unity of goal, variation of means. . . ."[69]

This would parallel the division at the core of colonialism and colonial literature. In *The Hidden Force*, Hegel's prose world and Baudelaire's masculine "straight line" correspond to the "ascending line" or the "hierarchical line of the [colonial] civil service" of the European paternal world of administrators. Baudelaire's feminine "arabesque line" and Hegel's poetic India correspond to Eva Eldersma's "line of grace" and "line of beauty." In the light of colonial society Eva's husband, Onno, typifies the prose world of the dull administrative drudge, while Van Helderen, the man she feels attracted to, is more in tune with Eva because he can "work toward a beautiful goal but not . . . for the sake of work and not [in order] to fill the emptiness of [his] life." "Beautiful goals" are, of course, anathema to the colonial hierarchy, and Van Helderen's superior, Resident Van Oudijck, warns Eva to be careful with the likes of Van Helderen because "he puts too much literature into his monthly reports."

But what is a shortcoming to Van Oudijck, is from Couperus's point of view a virtue. Hence it is Van Helderen who explains to Eva that the Indies have a prose as well as a lyrical side. The latter he finds in their people, their past, and in their nature, while the prose is represented by "a gigantic but exhausted colony." It is ironic that Couperus endowed Eva with the conscious awareness that both "lines" should exist side by side, ironic because she is an outsider who will return to Europe as a disillusioned woman. Yet it is she who is aware that she has a practical side that can see through the prosaic absurdities of the European community, and an "exotic side" that is able to perceive "what was really poetic, genuinely Indies, purely Eastern, absolutely Javanese." That essence is represented by both the "noble majesty of nature" and by the elegance, grace, and "aristocratic distinction" of the Javanese.

Addy de Luce is the paradigm of such physical grace, but it is an enigmatic beauty that combines perfection from both sexes. He radiates in the flesh what his name connotes, while one can even wonder if his name also contains a lexical echo of "lusios," the epithet of Dionysus. That Couperus wanted to establish a connection between Addy and Dionysus is clear from the number of positive similes that compare him to a Mediterranean deity. For that matter, his entire family is generally referred to in a positive fashion. Addy inherited his grace and elegance from his Javanese mother, who is treated by Sunario's brother, the regent of Ngadjiwa, with the respect normally granted only to Javanese royalty. Couperus indicates that the De Luce family has managed to preserve the best of Indies society, such as its elaborate customs, its generous hospitality, and the emotional security of an extended family. They are unencumbered by the malaise of European introspection because they lack (from a European viewpoint) a stimulating intellect. But Couperus also notes the lack of greed and the simple bonhomie that makes them the only social unit in the novel that lives in peace and harmony.

The description of life in Patjaram, the family compound of the De Luces, comes close to representing a tropical utopia. For Doddy, for instance, Patjaram is an ideal world where brown is the preferred color of distinction and white, one of derision. Patjaram also represents the abundance of life, and its fecundity should be contrasted with the barren beauty of Doddy's stepmother, Léonie. "For Patjaram was her ideal of what a home should be. The big house, full of sons and daughters and children and animals, who were all subjected to the same kindness and cordiality and boredom, while behind those sons and daughters shone the halo of their Solo heritage." And as if to emphasize Patjaram's distinction, Doddy refers to it as "the ideal residence," something that Van Oudijck's colonial seat of power clearly was not.

Presided over by a benign materfamilias, Patjaram's vital élan should be contrasted with the colonial capital of Batavia, which is described as a city of the dead oppressed by "the white burden of mortality." Its European inhabitants live unaware of the surrounding beauty of tropical nature, and human interaction has been reduced to the disembodied intercourse of telephone conversations. In Batavia, white is the color of death; in Patjaram brown is the color of life and health.

Patjaram's world is the world of the "Indo," the Eurasian. For Couperus it seemed to represent a successful combination of the oriental and the occidental strains precisely because he saw it as a racial consolidation. It must be remembered that, like the Dutch colonials, the noble family of the Adiningrats is also in decline, a deterioration personified by the regent of Ngadjiwa who debases both himself and his ancient class. The grandeur of their lineage seems to have been reduced to an all-consuming hatred for the European usurper, an enmity that leaves no room for either vigor or conciliation. This emotional paralysis is not shared by the De Luce family, though it is linked to the glory of the Adiningrats's past by "the halo of their [mutual] Solo heritage." The link with Europe is their paternal founder, a French aristocrat down on his luck who exploited his culinary skills to ingratiate himself with high Javanese society. One cannot help feeling that Couperus was poking fun at European imperialism by reducing its pretensions to the level of a kitchen. But the De Luce family is clearly meant to have benefited from the two racial adversaries by amalgamating them into a mellow intermedium that softened both stringencies.

That the harmonious blending of "the blood of the Solo princess and that of the French adventurer" should be promulgated with figurative allusions to Mediterranean culture is consistent with our previous discussion of Couperus's symbolism. As was mentioned before, when Couperus looked back on his childhood in the Indies, he could see that he had benefited from its solar ardor and had matured both physically and psychologically. But he also realized that he had found an alien sun in Java, one totally different from the memorial sun of antiquity that could warm the heart and mind of an avowed passatist. "Now that I love Italy I know that, even though the Indies enraptured me because of its sun, even though the Indies returned me to the South wherefrom I had been mysteriously banished, I missed the Latin South, and I know now why then, in the Indies, an oleander was dearer to me than a flamboyant. . . . There was the sun, and there was the South, but a South without emotion and without memory, and yet I was the child of parents living in the Indies" (7:671).

This modulation of the symbolic solar power, this preference for a culturally temperate zone, is present in *The Hidden Force* in Couperus's covert predilection for the Eurasian world of Patjaram. Van Oudijck, however, professes to hate "Indos." This is a tragic irony because all his children belong to that group. Their father's dislike is largely because he considers people of mixed blood to be racially desultory, as indistinct as the "hidden force" itself. He is at ease with clear entities such as Europeans or Javanese, and genuinely wants the best for both in a world that the passatist knows to be reliable and unequivocal. But in the reality of the present he finds a bewildering uncertainty, with the "Indos" indicative of the liberality of change. And it is not surprising that in the domestic parallel, Léonie wants to make love to "both white and brown" while Doddy desires to have *only* brown children with Addy.

Though said to be unable to aspire to intellectual supremacy, Patjaram is a world of physical beauty and grace. For Couperus and his age such a world was something of an Eden to be greatly preferred to a bloodless civilization that was choking on braindust. That graceful physicality is symbolized by Addy's dancing, which is compared to "a dream upon the water. This came to him with his mother's blood, this was a survival of the grace of the *srimpis*, among whom his mother had spent her childhood, and the mingling of what was modern European with what was ancient Javanese, gave him an irresistible charm."[70]

This final instance might be the best example of how a personal psychology infused a symbolic pattern, which in turn imbued a cultural position. Couperus's surreptitious partiality for Eurasian society would have been unpopular in his day. The Eurasians were to become the truly dispossessed people of colonialism, an invisible group that was relegated to the periphery of society.[71] The final irony of *The Hidden Force* is that while hiding from his colonial past in western Java, Van Oudijck does not see that he has been granted a measure of solace by living like the society he tried so hard to deny.

A NOTE ON THIS TRANSLATION

This translation by Alexander Teixeira de Mattos was first published in London in 1922 and in New York in 1924. De Mattos was considered "one of the best translators in the world" and worked diligently to promote Couperus's work in the English-speaking world (12:173–225). Altogether he translated ten of Couperus's novels. I won't deny that it was De Mattos's efforts that established Couperus as an important author in England and the United States, but the exaggerated acclaim is not entirely warranted. The reason his translation was kept is chiefly due to his congruence of *tone* with the original and to a similar, somewhat archaic, diction. But there are many lapses, however, mostly due to his ignorance of English idiom, and to startling mistranslations of Dutch words and phrases. Some examples: "outhouse" for "outbuilding," "bearing-power" for "solidity," "bucolic" for "boorish," "the garden stood clean and empty" for "the garden was flooded" (i.e., "de tuin was blank"). He also consistently translated *kampong* as "compound" and several times *tuan* as "madam." The original translation was, therefore, entirely revised and—though I hope I have not erred—any remaining lapses are my responsibility. De Mattos's surreptitious bowdlerizing has been negated by reinstating the original passages.

E. M. Beekman

The Hidden Force

1

The full moon wore the hue of tragedy that evening. It had risen early, during the last gleams of daylight, like a huge ball as red as blood, and, flaming like a sunset down behind the tamarind trees in the Lange Laan,[1] it was ascending, slowly divesting itself of its tragic complexion, in a pallid sky. A deadly stillness extended over all things like a veil of silence, as though, after the long midday siesta, the peace of the evening was beginning without an intervening period of life. In the windless oppression of the evening air, a muffled silence hung over the town, whose white villas and porticoes lay huddled amid the trees of avenues and gardens; it was as though the listless night were weary of the blazing day of the eastern monsoon. The quiet houses shrank away in deathly silence, amid the foliage of their gardens and the evenly spaced, gleaming rows of their great whitewashed flowerpots. Here and there a lamp was already lit. Suddenly a dog barked and another answered, rending the muffled silence into long, ragged tatters: the dogs' angry throats sounded hoarse, panting, harshly hostile; then they too suddenly ceased and fell silent.

At the end of the Lange Laan, the residency lay far back in its garden. Low and vivid in the darkness of the *waringin* trees,[2] it lifted the zigzag outline of its tiled roofs, one behind the other, into the shadow of the garden behind it, with a primitive line that seemed to date it: a roof over each gallery and verandah, a roof over each room, receding into one long outline of irregular roofs. In front, however, the white pillars of the front verandah arose, with the white pillars of the portico, tall, bright and stately, with wide intervals, with a large, welcoming spaciousness, with an expansive and imposing entrance, as if to a palace. Through the open doors, the central gallery was seen in dim perspective, running through to the back and lit by a single flickering light.

An *oppasser* was lighting the lanterns beside the house. Semicircles of great white posts with roses and chrysanthemums, with palms and caladiums,[3] curved widely in front of the house to right and left. A broad gravel path formed the drive to the white pillared portico; next came a wide, parched lawn surrounded by flowerpots, and, in the middle, on a carved stone pedestal, a monumental vase held a tall latania.[4] The only fresh green was that of the meandering pond, which had the giant leaves of a Victoria Regia floating on it, huddled together like round green trays, with here and there a luminous lotuslike flower between them. A path wound beside the pond, and on a circular space paved with pebbles stood a tall flagstaff. The flag had already been taken down, as it always was at six o'clock of every day. A plain gate separated the grounds from the Lange Laan.

The vast grounds were silent. There were now burning, slowly and laboriously lit by the lamp boy, one lamp in the chandelier on the front verandah and one indoors turned low, like two nightlights in a palace which, with its pillars and its vanishing perspective of roofs, was somehow reminiscent of a child's dream. On the steps of the office sat a few *oppassers* in their dark uniforms, talking in whispers. One of them stood up after a while and walked quietly and leisurely to a bronze bell which hung high at the extreme corner of the grounds, by the *oppassers'* lodge. When he had reached it after about a hundred paces, he sounded seven slow, reverberating strokes. The clapper struck the bell with a brazen, booming note, and each stroke was prolonged by an undulating echo, a deep, thrilling vibration. The dogs began to bark again. The *oppasser*, boyishly slender in his blue cloth jacket with yellow facings and trousers with yellow stripes, retraced, slowly and quietly, the hundred paces back to the other *oppassers*.

The light was now lit in the office and also in the adjoining bedroom, from which it filtered through the venetian blinds. The resident, a tall heavy man in a black jacket and white duck trousers, walked across the room and called to the man outside:

"Oppas!"

The chief *oppasser*, in his cloth uniform jacket with the wide yellow trim along the skirt, approached with bended knees and squatted before his master.

"Call Miss Doddy."

"Miss Doddy is out, *kandjeng*," whispered the man, while with his two hands, the fingers placed together, he sketched the reverential gesture of the *semba*.

"Where has she gone?"

"I did not ask, *kandjeng*," said the man, by way of excuse for not knowing, again with his sketchy *semba*.

The resident reflected for a moment. Then he said:

"My cap. My stick."

The chief *oppasser*, still bending his knees as though reverently shrinking into himself, scuttled across the room and, squatting, presented the undress uniform cap and a walking stick.

The resident went out. The chief *oppasser* hurried after him, with a *tali-api*[5] in his hand, a long, slow-burning wick whose glowing tip he waved from side to side so that the resident might be seen by anyone passing in the dark. The resident walked slowly through the garden to the Lange Laan. Along this avenue of tamarind trees and flamboyants were the villas of the more prominent notables of the town, faintly lit, deathly silent, apparently uninhabited, with the rows of whitewashed flowerpots gleaming in the vague dusk of the evening.

First the resident passed by the secretary's house, then, on the other side, a girls' school, then the notary's house, a hotel, the post office, and the house of the president of the criminal court. At the end of the Lange Laan stood the Catholic church, and, further on, across the bridge, was the railway station. Near the station was a large European *toko*, which was more brilliantly lit than the other buildings. The moon had climbed higher, turning a brighter silver in its ascent, and now shone down upon the white bridge, the white *toko*, the white church, all standing around a square, treeless, open space, in the middle of which was a small monument with a pointed spire, the town clock.

The resident met nobody; now and then, however, an occasional Javanese, like a moving shadow, appeared out of the darkness, and then the *oppasser* waved the glowing point of his *tali-api* with great ostentation behind his master. As a rule, the Javanese understood and made himself small, cowering along the edge of the road and passing with a scuttling gait. Now and again, an ignorant native, just arrived from his *dessa*, did not understand, but went by, looking in terror at the *oppasser*, who just waved his light and, in passing, sent a curse after the fellow behind his master's back because he, the *dessa*-lout, had no manners. When a cart approached, or a *sado*,[6] he waved his little fiery star again and again through the darkness and made signs to the driver, who either stopped and alighted or squatted in his little carriage and, so squatting, drove on along the further side of the road.

The resident went on gloomily, with the smart step of a resolute walker. He had turned off to the right of the little square and was now walking past the Protestant church, straight toward a handsome villa adorned with slender, fairly correct Ionian pillars of plaster and brilliantly lit with paraffin lamps set in chandeliers. This was the Concordia Club.[7] A couple of native servants in white jackets sat on the steps. A European in a white suit, the steward, passed along the verandah. But there was no one sitting at the great gin-and-bitters table, and the wide cane chairs opened their arms in vain expectation.

The steward, on seeing the resident, bowed, and the resident raised his finger to his cap, went past the club, and turned to the left. He walked down a lane, past dark little houses, each in its own little demesne, turned off again and walked along the mouth of the *kali*, which was like a canal. Proa after proa lay moored to the banks; the monotonous humming of Maduran seamen[8] came drearily across the water, from which rose a smell of fish. Passing the harbormaster's office the resident went on to the pier which projected some distance into the sea. At the end was a small lighthouse, like a miniature Eiffel Tower, extending its iron form like a candlestick with its lamp at the top.[9] Here the resident stopped and filled his lungs with the night air. The wind had suddenly freshened, the *grongrong* had risen,[10] blowing in from the water, as it did daily at this hour. But sometimes it suddenly dropped again, unexpectedly, as though its fanning wings had been stricken powerless, and the roughened sea fell again, until its curling, foaming breakers, white in the moonlight, were smooth rollers, slightly phosphorescent in long, pale streaks.

The mournful and monotonous rhythm of a whining song approached from the sea, a sail loomed darkly, like a great night bird, and a fishing proa with a high, curved stem, suggestive of an ancient galley, glided into the channel. A melancholy resignation, an acquiescence in all the small, obscure things of the earth beneath that infinite sky, upon that sea of phosphorescent remoteness, was adrift in the night, conjuring up an oppressive mystery. . . .

The tall sturdy man who stood there with his legs spread, breathing in the loitering, fitful wind, tired from his work, from sitting at his desk, from calculating the *duiten* question—that important matter, the abolition of the *duiten,* for which the governor-general had made him personally responsible[11]—this tall sturdy man, practical, cool headed, decisive (due to the long habit of authority), was perhaps unconscious of the dark mystery that drifted over the native town, over the capital of his district, though he was conscious of a longing for affection. He vaguely yearned for a child's arms around his neck, for shrill little voices about him, longed for a young wife awaiting him with a smile. He did not give definite expression to this sentimentality in his thoughts, it was not his custom to indulge in musings: he was too busy, his days were too full of various interests for him to yield to what he knew to be lapses, the suppressed impulses from his youth. But, though he did not reflect, the mood was not to be repulsed; it was like a pressure on his broad chest, like a morbid tenderness, like a sentimental discomfort in the otherwise highly practical mind of this superior official who loved his work and his district, who had its interests at heart, and in whom the almost independent power of his post harmonized entirely with his authoritative nature, who was accustomed with his strong lungs to breathe an atmosphere of spacious activity and extensive, varied work even as he now stood breathing the spacious wind from the sea.

A longing, a desire, a certain nostalgia filled him more than usual that evening. He felt lonely, not only because of the isolation which nearly always surrounds the head of a native government who is either approached conventionally, with smiling respect, for purposes of conversation, or curtly, with official respect, for purposes of business. He felt lonely, though he was the father of a family. He thought of his big house, he thought of his wife and children. And he felt lonely and supported only by his interest in his work. That was the one thing in his life. It filled all his waking hours. He fell asleep thinking of it, and his first thought in the morning was of some matter pertaining to his district.

At this moment, tired of figures, breathing the wind, he inhaled together with the coolness of the sea its melancholy, the mysterious melancholy of the Indian seas, the haunting melancholy of the seas of Java, the melancholy that rushes in from afar on whispering, mysterious wings. But it was not his nature to yield to mystery. He denied mystery. It was not there: there was only the sea and the cool wind. There were only the fumes from that sea, a blend of fish and flowers and seaweed, fumes that the cool wind was blowing away. There was only the moment of relief, and such mysterious melancholy as he nevertheless, irresistibly, felt stealing that evening through his somewhat slack mood he believed to be connected with his domestic circle: he would have liked to feel that this circle was a little more compact, fitting more closely around the father and husband in him. If there were any melancholy at all, it was that. It did not come from the sea, nor from the distant sky. He refused to yield to any sudden sensation of the marvelous. And he set his feet more firmly, flung out his chest, lifted his solid, martial head, and sniffed the smell of the sea and the wind. . . .

The chief *oppasser,* squatting with the glowing lunt in his hand, peeped attentively at his master, as though thinking: "Strange people, those Hollanders! . . . What is he thinking now? . . . Why is he behaving like this? . . . Just at this time and on this spot. . . . The sea spirits are about now. . . . There are crocodiles under the water and every crocodile is a spirit. . . .[12] Look, they have been sacrificing to them there: *pisang* and rice and *deng-deng*[13] and a hard-boiled egg on a little bamboo raft, down by the foot of the lighthouse. . . . What is the *kandjeng tuan* doing here? . . . It is not good here, it is not good here, *tjelaka, tjelaka!* . . ."

And his watching eyes went up and down the back of his master, who simply stood and gazed into the distance. What was he gazing at? . . .

What did he see blowing up in the wind? . . . How strange, those Hollanders, how strange! . . .

The resident suddenly turned, and walked back, with the startled *oppasser* following him, blowing on the tip of his lunt. The resident walked back by the same road; there was now a member sitting at the club, who greeted him; and a couple of young men in white were strolling in the Lange Laan. The dogs were barking.

When the resident approached the entrance to the residency, he saw in front, near the other entrance, two white figures, a man and a girl, who vanished into the darkness under the *waringins*. He went straight to his office; another *oppasser* came up and took his cap and stick. Then he sat down at his desk. He had time for an hour's work before dinner.

2

Several lights were burning. In fact, the lamps had been lit everywhere, but in the long, broad galleries there was barely light. In the grounds and inside the house there were certainly no fewer than twenty or thirty paraffin lamps burning in chandeliers and lanterns, but they provided no more than a vague, yellow twilight throughout the house. A stream of moonlight floated over the garden, making the flowerpots gleam brightly until they shimmered in the pond, and the *waringins* were like soft velvet against the luminous sky.

The first gong had sounded for dinner. In the front verandah a young man was rocking back and forth in a rocking chair, with his hands behind his head. He was bored. A young girl came along the middle gallery, humming to herself, as though in expectation. The house was furnished in accordance with the conventions of up-country residencies, with commonplace splendor. The marble floor of the verandah was white and glossy as a mirror; tall palms stood in pots between the pillars; groups of rocking chairs stood around marble tables. In the first inner gallery, which ran parallel with the verandah, chairs were lined up against the wall as though in readiness for an eternal reception. The second inner gallery, which ran from front to back, showed at the end, where it opened into a wide gallery again, a huge red satin curtain falling from a gilt cornice. In the white spaces between the doors of the rooms hung either mirrors in gilt frames, their lower edges resting on marble console tables, or lithographs—"paintings" they call them in the Indies—of Van Dyck on horseback, Paul Veronese received by a doge on the steps of a Venetian palace, Shakespeare at the court of Elizabeth, and Tasso at the court of Este; but in the biggest space, in a crowned frame, hung a large etching, a portrait of Queen Wilhelmina in her coronation robes. In the middle of the central gallery was a red satin ottoman topped by a palm. Furthermore, many chairs and tables; everywhere great chandeliers. Everything was very neatly kept and distinguished by a pompous banality, an uncomfortable readiness for the next reception, with not one cozy little nook. In the half light of the paraffin lamps—one lamp was lit in each chandelier—the long, wide, spacious galleries stretched in tedious vacancy.[14]

The second gong sounded. In the back verandah the long table—too long, as though it were always expecting guests—was laid for three. The *spen* and half a dozen boys stood waiting by the servers' tables and the two sideboards. The *spen* began immediately to fill the soup plates, and two of the boys placed the three plates of soup on the table, on the top of the folded napkins which lay on the dinner plates. Then they waited again, while the soup steamed gently. Another boy filled the three tumblers with large lumps of ice.

The girl came in, humming a tune. She could be seventeen and resembled her divorced mother, the resident's first wife, a good-looking *nonna* who was now living in Batavia where she was said to keep a quiet gambling house. The young girl had a pale olive complexion that sometimes displayed a hint of a blush. She had beautiful black hair that curled naturally at the temples and that was fastened in a very heavy coil; her black pupils with the sparkling irises floated in a moist blue-white enclosed by her thick lashes which danced up and down, down and up. Her mouth was small and a little full, and her upper lip was shadowed by a dark line of down. She was not tall and already too fully formed, like a hasty rose that has bloomed too soon. She wore a white piqué skirt and white linen blouse with lace inserts, and round her throat was a bright yellow ribbon that accorded well with her olive pallor which could sometimes suddenly be enlivened with a blush as if with a sudden rush of blood.

The young man came sauntering in from the front verandah. He was like his father, tall, broad, and fair haired, with a thick blond mustache. He was barely twenty-three, but looked five years older. He wore a suit of white Russian linen, but with a shirt collar and tie.

Van Oudijck also came at last: his determined step approached as if he were always busy, as if he were coming just to have some dinner in between his work.

"When does Mamma arrive tomorrow?" asked Theo.

"At half-past eleven," replied Van Oudijck; and turning to his body servant behind him, "Kario, remember that the *njonja besar* is to be fetched at the station at half-past eleven tomorrow."

"Yes, *kandjeng*," murmured Kario.

The fish was served.

"Doddy," asked Van Oudijck, "who was with you at the gate just now?"

"At . . . the gate?" she asked slowly and sweetly.

"Yes."

"At . . . the gate? . . . Nobody. . . . Theo perhaps."

"Were you at the gate with your sister?" asked Van Oudijck.

The boy knitted his thick fair eyebrows.

"Possibly . . . don't know. . . . Don't remember. . . ."

They were silent. They hurried through dinner because sitting at the table bored them. The five or six servants, in white *baadjes* with red linen facings, moved softly on their flat toes, serving quickly and noiselessly. Steak and salad were served, a pudding, followed by fruit.

"Always steak," Theo muttered.

"Yes, that *kokkie!*" laughed Doddy, with her little throaty laugh. "She always serves steak when Mamma not here;[15] doesn't matter to her, when Mamma not here. She has no imagination. It's too much really. . . ."

They had been twenty minutes over their dinner when Van Oudijck went back to his office. Doddy and Theo sauntered toward the front of the house.

"Tedious," Doddy yawned. "Come, we play billiards?"

In the first inner gallery, behind the satin hanging, was a small billiard table.

"Come along then," said Theo.

They played.

"Why am I supposed to have been with you at the gate?"

"Oh . . . tut!" said Doddy.

"Well, why?"

"Papa needn't know."

"Who was with you? Addy?"

"Of course!" said Doddy. "Say, band playing tonight?"

"I think so."

"Come, we go, yes?"

"No, I don't care to."

"Oh, why not?"

"I don't want to."

"Come along now?"

"No."

"With Mamma . . . you would, yes?" said Doddy angrily. "I know very well. With Mamma you go always to the band."

"What do you know . . . you little minx!"

"What do I know?" she laughed. "What do I know? I know what I know."

"Hey!" he said, to tease her, trying roughly for a carambole. "You and Addy, hey!"

"Well . . . and you and Mamma!"

He shrugged his shoulders:

"You're crazy."

"No need to hide from me. Besides, everyone says."

"Let them say."

"It's really too much though!"

"Oh, go to hell!"

He flung his cue down and went to the front of the house. She followed him:

"Theo . . . don't be angry now. Come along to the band."

"No."

"I'll never say it again," she entreated coaxingly.

She was afraid that he would stay angry and then she would have nothing and nobody, then she would die of boredom.

"I promised Addy and I can't go by myself. . . ."

"Well, if you won't make any more of those idiotic remarks. . . ."

"Yes, I promise. Theo dear, yes, come then. . . ."

She was already in the garden.

Van Oudijck appeared on the threshold of his office, which always had the door open, but which was separated from the inner gallery by a large screen.

"Doddy!" he called out.

"Yes, Papa?"

"Will you see that there are flowers in Mamma's room tomorrow?"

His voice was almost embarrassed and he blinked his eyes.

"Very well, Papa. . . . I'll see to it."

"Where are you going?"

"With Theo . . . to the band."

Van Oudijck became red and angry.

"To the band? You should have asked me first!" he exclaimed, in a sudden rage.

Doddy pouted.

"I don't like you to go out, without my knowing where you go. You were also out this afternoon, when I wanted you to come for a walk with me."

"Well, *sudah* then," said Doddy, bursting into tears.

"You can go if you want to," said Van Oudijck, "but I insist on your asking me first."

"No, I don't care about it now," said Doddy, in tears. "*Sudah!* No band."

They could hear the first strains in the distance, coming from the Concordia garden.

Van Oudijck returned to his office. Doddy and Theo flung themselves into two rocking chairs on the verandah and rocked furiously to and fro, skating with the chairs over the smooth marble.

"Come," said Theo, "let's go. Addy expects you."

"No," she pouted. "Don't care. I'll tell Addy tomorrow Papa so unkind. He spoils my pleasure. And . . . I'll put no flowers in Mamma's room."

Theo grinned.

"Say," whispered Doddy, "that Papa . . . eh? So in love, always. He was blushing when he asked me about the flowers."

Theo grinned once more and hummed in unison with the band in the distance.

3

Next morning Theo went in the landau to pick up his stepmother at the station at half-past eleven.

Van Oudijck, who was in the habit of taking the police cases at that hour, had made no suggestion to his son, but, when from his office he saw Theo step into the carriage and drive off, he thought it nice of the boy. He had idolized Theo as a child, had spoilt him as a boy, had often come into conflict with him as a young man, but the old paternal fondness still rose in him, irresistibly. At this moment he loved his son better than Doddy, who had maintained her sulky attitude that morning and had put no flowers in his wife's room, so that he had to order Kario to see to it. He now felt sorry that he had not said a kind word to Theo for several days and he resolved to do so again soon. The boy was fickle: in three years he had worked for at least five different coffee plantations, and now he was once again without a job and was hanging around at home, looking for something else.

Theo had not long to wait at the station before the train arrived. He at once saw Mrs. Van Oudijck and the two little boys, René and Ricus[16] —two little *sinjos*, unlike himself—whom she was bringing back from Batavia for the long holidays, and her maid, Urip.

Theo helped his stepmother down, and the stationmaster offered a respectful greeting to the wife of his resident. She nodded in return, with her queenly smile. Still smiling, a trifle ambiguously, she allowed her stepson to kiss her on the cheek. She was a tall woman, with a fair complexion and fair hair; she had turned thirty and possessed the languid dignity of women born in Java, daughters of European parents on both sides. She had something that attracted attention at once. It was because of her white skin, her creamy complexion, her very light blond hair, her strange gray eyes, which were sometimes narrowed a little and always held an ambiguous expression. It was because of her eternal smile, sometimes very sweet and charming and often insufferable and tiresome. One could never tell at the first sight of her whether she concealed anything behind that glance, whether there was any depth, any soul, or whether it was merely a matter of looking and laughing, both with that slight ambiguity. Soon, however, one noticed an expectant indifference in her smiles, as though there were very little that she cared for, as though it would hardly matter to her should the heavens fall, as though she would watch the event with a smile.

Her gait was leisurely. She wore a pink piqué skirt and bolero, a white satin ribbon round her waist and a white sailor hat with a white satin bow. Her summer traveling costume was very smart compared with that of a couple of other ladies on the platform who were strolling in stiffly starched *bébés* that looked like nightgowns, with tulle hats topped with feathers. Yet though she looked very European, it may have been her leisurely walk, that languid dignity that was the only Indies characteristic that distinguished her from a woman newly arrived from Holland.

Theo had given her his arm and she let him lead her to the carriage, followed by the two dark little brothers. She had been away two months. She had a nod and a smile for the stationmaster; she had a nod for the coachman and the groom; and she took her seat slowly, a languid, white sultana, ever smiling. The three stepsons followed her into the carriage, the maid rode behind in a dogcart. Mrs. Van Oudijck looked out once or twice and thought Labuwangi unchanged. But she said nothing. She slowly drew herself away from the window and leaned back. Her face displayed a certain satisfaction, but especially that radiant, laughing indifference, as though nothing could harm her, as though she were protected by a mysterious force. There was something strong about this woman, something powerful in her sheer indifference: there was something invulnerable about her. She looked as though life would have no hold on her, neither on her complexion nor on her soul. She looked as though she were incapable of suffering, and it seemed as though she smiled and were thus contented because no sickness, no suffering, no poverty, no misery existed for her. An irradiation of glittering egoism encompassed her. And yet she was, for the most part, lovable. She was charming and prepossessing because she was so pretty. This woman, with her sparkling self-satisfaction, was loved, no matter what people might say about her. When she spoke, when she laughed, she was disarming and, even more, engaging. This was despite and, perhaps, precisely because of her unfathomable indifference. She took an interest only in her own body and her own soul: all the rest, all the rest was totally unimportant to her. Unable to give anything of her soul, she had never felt anything save for herself; but she smiled so peacefully and enchantingly that she was always thought lovable, adorable. It was perhaps because of the contour of her cheeks, the strange ambiguity in her glance, her inveterate smile, the elegance of her figure, the tone of her voice, and her knack of always hitting on the right word. If at first one thought her insufferable, she did not notice it and simply made herself absolutely charming. If anyone was jealous, she did not notice it and just praised intuitively, indifferently—for she did not care in the least—something that the other had felt to be a deficiency. With the sweetest expression on her face she could admire a dress that she thought hideous and, because she was so completely indifferent, she betrayed no insincerity afterward and did not gainsay her admiration. Her vital power was her unbounded indifference. She had accustomed herself to do everything that she felt inclined to do, but she smiled as she did it. And, however people might talk behind her back, she remained so correct in her behavior, so bewitching, that they forgave her. She was not loved while she was not seen, but as soon as people saw her she won back all that she had lost. Her husband worshipped her, her stepchildren—she had no children of her own—could not help being fond of her, involuntarily; her servants were all under the influence of her charm. She never grumbled, she said one word and the thing was done. If something went wrong, if something were broken, her smile died away for a moment . . . and that was all. And, if her own moral or physical interests were in danger, she was generally able to avoid the danger and settle things to her advantage, without even allowing her smile to fade. But she had gathered this personal interest so closely about her that she could usually control its circumstances. No destiny seemed to weigh upon this woman. Her indifference was radiant, was absolutely indifferent, devoid of contempt, or envy, or emotion: it was merely indifference. And the tact with which instinctively, without ever giving much thought to it, she guided and ruled her life was so great that, if she were to lose everything she now possessed—her beauty, her position, for instance—she would still be able to remain indifferent, due to her incapacity for suffering.

The carriage drove into the grounds of the residency just as the police cases were beginning. The Javanese magistrate, the chief *djaksa*, was already with Van Oudijck in the office; the *djaksa* and the police-*oppassers* led the procession of the accused: the natives tripped along, holding one another by a corner of their *baadjes*, but the few women among them walked alone. They all squatted down to wait under a *waringin* tree, at a short distance from the steps of the office. An *oppasser*, hearing the clock on the verandah, struck half-past twelve on the great bell by the lodge. The loud stroke reverberated like a brazen voice through the scorching heat of the afternoon. But Van Oudijck had heard the sound of the carriage and let the chief *djaksa* wait: he went to welcome his wife. His face brightened: he kissed her tenderly, effusively, asked how she was. He was glad to see the boys back. And, remembering what he had been thinking about Theo, he found a kind word for his firstborn. Doddy, her full little mouth still sulking, kissed Mamma. Mrs.

Van Oudijck allowed herself to be kissed, resignedly, smilingly; she returned the kisses calmly, without coldness or warmth, just doing what she had to do. Her husband, Theo, and Doddy admired her perceptibly and audibly, said that she was looking well; Doddy asked where Mamma had got that pretty traveling dress. In her room she noticed the flowers and, since she knew that Van Oudijck always saw to these, she gently stroked his arm.

The resident went back to his office where the chief *djaksa* was waiting; the hearing began. Pushed along by a police-*oppasser*, the accused came one by one and squatted on the steps, outside the office door, while the *djaksa* squatted on a mat and the resident sat at his desk. During the first case, Van Oudijck was still listening to his wife's voice in the middle gallery, when the prisoner defended himself with a cry of:

"*Bot'n! Bot'n!*"

The resident knitted his brows and listened attentively. . . .

The voices in the middle gallery ceased. Mrs. Van Oudijck had gone to take off her things and to put on *sarong* and *kabaai* for lunch.[17] She wore the dress gracefully: a Solo *sarong*, a transparent *kabaai*, jeweled pins, white leather slippers with little white bows. She was just ready when Doddy came to her door and said:

"Mamma! Mamma! . . . Mrs. Van Does is here!"

The smile died away for a moment, the soft eyes looked dark.

"I'll come at once, dear. . . ."

But she sat down instead and Urip, the maid, sprinkled some scent on her handkerchief. Mrs. Van Oudijck nestled in her chair and lay musing, still languid from her journey. She found Labuwangi desperately dull after Batavia, where she had spent two months staying with relations and friends, free and unencumbered by obligations. Here, as the wife of the resident, she had certain duties, though she delegated most of them to the secretary's wife. She felt tired, out of sorts, dissatisfied. Despite her complete indifference, she was human enough to have her silent moods when she cursed everything. Then she suddenly wanted to do something mad, then she vaguely longed for Paris. . . . She would never let anyone notice this. She was able to control herself, and she controlled herself now, before making her appearance. Her vague Bacchantic longings melted away in her fatigue. She stretched more lazily, and she mused, with eyes almost closed. A curious fancy—hidden from the world—sometimes infiltrated her almost superhuman indifference. She preferred to live in her bedroom her life of perfumed imagination, especially after her months in Batavia. After one of those months of perversity, she felt a need to let her vagrant, rosy imaginings rise like a curling mist before her half-closed eyes. In her otherwise utterly barren soul there was, as it were, an unreal growth of little azure flowers which she cherished with perhaps the only feeling that she could ever experience. She felt for no living creature, but she felt for those little flowers. It was delicious to dream like this of what she would have liked to be if she were not compelled to be what she was. Her fancies rose in a whirling mist: she saw a white palace, with cupids everywhere. . . .

"Mamma . . . come on! Mrs. Van Does is here, Mrs. Van Does, with two jars. . . ."

It was Doddy at the door. Léonie van Oudijck stood up and went to the back verandah, where the Indies lady was sitting, the wife of the postmaster. She kept cows and sold milk, but she also dealt in different merchandise. She was a stout woman, rather dark skinned, with a prominent stomach; she wore a very simple little *kabaai* with a narrow band of lace round it, and she sat stroking her stomach with her small fat hands. In front of her, on the table, were two small jars, with something glittering in them. What was it, Mrs. Van Oudijck wondered: sugar, crystals? Then she suddenly remembered. . . .

Mrs. Van Does said that she was glad to see her again. Two months away from Labuwangi. Too bad, Mrs. Van Oudijck! And she pointed to the jars. Mrs. Van Oudijck smiled. What was inside them?

With an air of mystery, Mrs. Van Does placed a fat, double-jointed finger on one of the jars and said:

"Inten-inten!"

"Oh, really?" asked Mrs. Van Oudijck.

Doddy, wide eyed, and Theo, greatly amused, stared at the jars.

"Yes . . . you know . . . that lady of whom I spoke to you. . . . She doesn't want her name mentioned. *Kassian*, her husband once a big shot . . . and now . . . yes, so unfortunate; she has nothing left! All gone. Only these two little jars. Had all her jewels taken out and keeps the stones in the jars. All counted. She trusts them to me to sell. Know her through my milk business. Will you look at, Mrs. Van Oudijck, yes? *Lovely* stones! The *residèn* he buy for you, now you back home again. Doddy, give me a bit of black stuff: velvet best. . . ."

Doddy sent the *djait* to fetch a bit of black velvet from a cupboard of odds and ends. A boy brought glasses with tamarind syrup and ice. Mrs. Van Does, holding a little pair of tongs in her double-jointed fingers laid a couple of stones carefully on the velvet.

"Ah!" she cried. "Look how clear they are, Madam. Spl . . . endid!"

Mrs. Van Oudijck looked on. She gave her most charming smile and then said, in her gentle voice:

"That stone is not real, dear lady."

"Not real?" screamed Mrs. Van Does. "Not real?"

Mrs. Van Oudijck looked at the other stones.

"And those others, Madam," and she stooped and said in her sweetest voice, "those others . . . are not real either."

Mrs. Van Does looked at her with delight. Then she said to Doddy and Theo, archly:

"That mamma of yours . . . *pinter!* She sees at once!"

And she laughed loud. They all laughed. Mrs. Van Does replaced the crystals in the jar:

"A joke, yes, Madam? I only wanted to see if you understood. Of course you'll take my word for it. I should never sell. . . . But there . . . look! . . ."

And now solemnly, almost religiously, she opened the other little jar, which contained only a few stones, and placed them lovingly on the black velvet.

"That one would be splendid . . . for a *léontine,*"[18] said Mrs. Van Oudijck, gazing at a very large diamond.

"There, what did I tell you?" said the Indies lady.

And they all gazed at the diamonds, at the real ones, which came out of the "real" jar, and held them up carefully to the light.

Mrs. Van Oudijck saw that they were all real.

"I really have no money, my dear," she said.

"This big one . . . for a *léontine* . . . six hundred guilders. . . . A bargain, I assure you, Madam!"

"Oh, Madam, never!"

"How much then? You'd be doing a good deed if you buy. *Kassian,* her husband once a big shot. Council of the Indies."[19]

"Two hundred."

"*Kassian!* What next? Two hundred guilders!"

"Two hundred and fifty, but no more. I really have no money."

"The *residèn,*" whispered Mrs. Van Does, catching sight of Van Oudijck who, now that the cases were finished, was coming toward the back verandah. "The *residèn* . . . he buy for you!"

Mrs. Van Oudijck smiled and looked at the sparkling drop of light on the black velvet. She liked jewels, she was not altogether indifferent to diamonds. And she looked at her husband.

"Mrs. Van Does is showing us a lot of beautiful things," she said, caressingly.

Van Oudijck felt an inward shock. He was never pleased to see Mrs. Van Does in his house. She always had something to sell: at one time, *batik* bedspreads, at another time, a pair of woven slippers, and a third time, magnificent but very expensive table runners, with gold *batik* flowers on yellow glazed linen. Mrs. Van Does always brought something with her, was always in touch with the wives of former "big shots," whom she helped by selling their things for a very high commission. A morning call from Mrs. Van Does cost him each time at least some money and very often fifty guilders, for his wife quite calmly bought things that she did not need but that she was too indifferent to refuse to buy. He did not see the two jars at once, but he saw the drop of light on the black velvet and he understood that the visit would cost him more than fifty guilders this time, unless he was very firm.

"Little lady!" he exclaimed, in dismay. "It's the end of the month, there's no buying of diamonds today! And jars full too!" he added with a shock when he now saw them glittering on the table, among the glasses of tamarind syrup.

"Oh, that *residèn!*" laughed Mrs. Van Does, as though a resident were bound to be always well off.

Van Oudijck hated that little laugh. His household cost him every month a few hundred guilders more than his salary; he was living beyond his means and in debt.[20] His wife never troubled herself with money matters, reserving for them her most smiling indifference.

She made the diamond sparkle in the sun and it darted a blue ray.

"It's a beauty . . . for two hundred and fifty," said Mrs. Van Oudijck.

"For three hundred then, dear lady. . . ."

"Three hundred?" she asked, dreamily, playing with the jewel.

Whether it cost three hundred or four or five hundred was all one to her. It left her wholly indifferent. But she liked the stone and meant to have it, at whatever price. And therefore she quietly put the stone down and said:

"No, my dear woman, really . . . it's too expensive, and my husband has no money."

She said it so prettily that there was no guessing her intention. She was adorably self-sacrificing as she spoke the words. Van Oudijck felt a second inward shock. He could not refuse his wife anything.

"Madam," he said, "you can leave the stone . . . for three hundred guilders. But for God's sake take your jars away with you!"

Mrs. Van Does looked up delightedly.

"There, what did I tell you? I knew for certain the *residèn* would buy for you! . . ."

Mrs. Van Oudijck looked up in gentle reproach.

"But, Otto!" she said. "How *can* you?"

"Do you like the stone?"

"Yes, it's beautiful. . . . But such a lot of money! For one diamond!"

And she drew her husband's hand toward her and suffered him to kiss her on the forehead, because he had been permitted to buy her a three-hundred-guilder diamond. Doddy and Theo stood winking at each other.

(4

Léonie van Oudijck always enjoyed her siesta after lunch. She only slept for a moment, but she loved to be alone in her cool bedroom till five or half-past five. She read a little, mostly the magazines from the circulating library, but as a rule she did nothing but dream. Her dreams were vague imaginings, which rose before her as in an azure mist during her afternoons of solitude. Nobody knew of them and she kept them very secret, like a secret vice, a sin. She committed herself much more readily—to the world—where her liaisons were concerned. These never lasted long, they counted for little in her life, she never wrote letters, and the favors that she granted afforded the recipient no privileges in the daily intercourse of society. Hers was a silent, correct depravity, both physical and moral. Even her fancies, however poetic in an insipid way, were depraved. Her favorite author was Catulle Mendès:[21] she loved all those little flowers of azure sentimentality, those rosy, affected little cupids with their pinkies in the air and their little legs gracefully hovering around the most vicious themes and motives of perverted passion. In her bedroom hung a few engravings: a young woman lying on a lace-covered bed, being kissed by two frolicking angels; another: a lion with an arrow through its breast at the feet of a smiling maiden; last, a large colored advertisement of some scent or other: a sort of floral nymph with a veil that was being torn from her by playful little perfume cherubs. She found that one particularly splendid, and could not imagine anything else with a greater aesthetic appeal. She knew that the picture was monstrous, but she had never been able to prevail upon herself to take the horrible thing down, though it was looked at askance by everybody, by her friends, her stepchildren, all of whom walked in and out of her room with the Indies casualness that makes no secret of getting dressed. She could stare at it for minutes on end, as though bewitched; she thought it most charming, and her own dreams resembled that print. She also treasured a chocolate box with a keepsake picture on it that showed a type of beauty that she admired, even more than her own: the pink flush on the cheeks, the brown eyes under impossible golden hair, the bosom showing through the lace. But she never disclosed this absurdity, which she vaguely suspected; she never spoke of these prints and boxes because she knew that they were hideous. But she thought them lovely, she thought them delightful, she thought them artistic and poetical. Those were her happiest hours.

Here, in Labuwangi, she dared not do what she did in Batavia, and here, in Labuwangi, people hardly believed what was said in Batavia. Nevertheless, Mrs. Van Does was sure that this resident or that inspector—the one traveling for pleasure, the other on an official tour—when they had stayed for a few days at the residency had found their way in the afternoon, during the siesta, to Léonie's bedroom. But all the same, in Labuwangi such actual occurrences were the rarest of interludes between Mrs. Van Oudijck's rosy afternoon visions.

Still, this afternoon it seemed as though, after dozing a little while and after all the weariness from the journey and the heat had cleared away from her milk-white complexion, as though, now that she was looking at the romping angels of the scent advertisement, her thoughts were no longer dwelling on that rosy, doll-like tenderness, but intent on listening to the sounds outside. . . .

She was wearing nothing but a *sarong*, which she had pulled up under her arms and had tied on her breast. Her beautiful blond hair hung loose. Her pretty little white feet were bare, she had not even put her slippers on. And she looked through the slats of the venetian blind.

Between the flowerpots that, standing on the side steps of the house, masked her windows with great masses of foliage, she could see an annex consisting of four rooms—the spare rooms—one of which was Theo's.

She stood peering for a moment and then opened the blind further. And she saw that the blind of Theo's room also opened a bit. . . .

Then she smiled, she knotted her *sarong* more firmly and lay down on the bed again.

She listened.

In a moment she heard the gravel grating slightly under the pressure of a slipper. Her wooden screen doors were closed though not locked. A hand now opened them cautiously. . . .

She looked round smiling.

"What is it, Theo?" she asked.

He came nearer. He was dressed in pajamas and he sat on the edge of the bed and played with her soft white hands. Suddenly he kissed her fiercely.

At that instant a stone whizzed through the bedroom.

They both started, looked up, and stood for a moment in the middle of the room.

"Who threw that?" she asked tremulously.

"One of the boys, perhaps," he said. "René or Ricus, playing outside."

"They aren't up yet."

"Or something may have fallen from above. . . ."

"But it was thrown. . . ."

"A stone so often gets loose."

"But this is gravel."

She picked up the little stone. He looked cautiously outside.

"It's nothing, Léonie. It really must have fallen out of the gutter . . . and then jumped up again. It's nothing."

"I'm frightened," she murmured.

He laughed almost aloud and asked, "But why?"

They had nothing to fear. The room lay between Léonie's boudoir and two large spare rooms that were reserved exclusively for residents, generals, and other high officials. On the other side of the middle gallery were Van Oudijck's rooms—his office and his bedroom—and Doddy's room and the room of the boys, Ricus and René. Léonie was therefore isolated in her wing, between the spare rooms. It made her brazen. At this hour, the grounds were quite deserted. For that matter, she was not afraid of the servants. Urip was wholly to be trusted and often received handsome presents: *sarongs*, a gold *pending*, a long diamond *kabaai*-pin, which she wore as a jeweled silver plaque on her breast. Because Léonie never grumbled, was generous in advancing wages, and displayed an apparently easy-going temperament—although everything always happened as she had wished—she was not disliked. And no matter how much the servants might know about her, they had not betrayed her yet. It made her all the more brazen. A curtain hung before a passage between the bedroom and boudoir, and it was arranged, once and for all, between Theo and Léonie, that at the least danger he would slip away quietly behind that hanging, go out through the garden door of the boudoir, and pretend to be looking at the roses in the pots on the steps. This would make it appear as though he had just come from his own room and were merely inspecting the roses. The inner doors of the boudoir and bedroom were usually locked, because Léonie declared frankly that she did not like to be interrupted unawares.

She liked Theo, because of his fresh youthfulness. And here in Labu-wangi he was her only vice, not counting a passing inspector and the little pink angels. The two were now like naughty children, they laughed silently, in each other's arms. But they had to be careful. It was past four by this time, and they heard the voices of René and Ricus in the garden. They were taking possession of the grounds for the holidays. They were thirteen and fourteen years old, and they enjoyed the garden. They ran about barefoot, in blue striped shirts and pants, and went to look at the horses and at the pigeons. They teased Doddy's cockatoo, which tripped about on the roof of the outbuildings. They had a tame *badjing.* They hunted *tokkès*[22] which they shot with a *sumpitan*, to the great vexation of the servants, because *tokkès* bring luck. They bought *katjanggoreng* at the gate from a passing Chinaman and then mocked him, imitating his accent:

"*Katja-ang golengan!* . . . *Tjina mampus!*"[23]

They climbed the flamboyant and swung in the branches like monkeys. They flung stones at the cats, they incited the neighbors' dogs until they barked themselves hoarse and bit each other's ears to pieces. They splashed about in the water in the pond, made themselves unpresentable with mud and dirt, and dared to pluck the Victoria Regias, which was strictly forbidden. They tested the solidity of the flat, green Victoria leaves, which looked like trays, and tried to stand on them and tumbled in. Then they took empty bottles, set them in a row, and bowled at them with pebbles. Then, with bamboos, they fished out all sorts of unmentionable things from the ditch beside the house and threw them at each other. Their inventiveness was inexhaustible, and the siesta hour was their hour. They had caught a *tokkè* and a cat and were making them fight each other: the *tokkè* opened its jaws, like those of a small crocodile, and hypnotized the cat, which slunk away, withdrawing from its enemy's beady, black eyes, its back arched and bristling with terror. And after that the boys ate unripe mangoes until they were sick.

Léonie and Theo had watched the fight between the cat and *tokkè* through the blind and saw how the boys were now quietly eating the unripe mangoes on the grass. But it was also the hour when the prisoners, twelve in number, worked in the grounds, under the supervision of a dignified old *mandur,* with a little cane in his hand. They fetched water in tubs and in watering cans made from paraffin tins, sometimes in the actual tins themselves, and watered the plants, the grass, and the gravel. Then they swept the grounds with a loud rustle of *lidi* brooms.

Behind the *mandur*'s back, for they were afraid of him, René and Ricus threw half-eaten mangoes at the prisoners and called them names and made faces and grimaces at them. Doddy appeared after her nap, carrying her cockatoo on her wrist. It cried, "Kaka! Kaka!" and raised its yellow crest with swift movements of its neck.

And now Theo stole behind the curtain into the boudoir and, at a moment when the boys were running and bombarding each other with mangoes and when Doddy was strolling toward the pond with the loitering gait and swinging hips peculiar to the Creole, he appeared from behind the plants, smelled at the roses, and behaved as though he had been walking in the garden before going to take his bath.

5

Van Oudijck was in a more pleasant mood than he had been in for weeks. His house seemed to have recovered after those two months of dull boredom, he liked to see his two rascals romping round the garden, even though they did all sorts of mischief, and above all he was very glad that his wife was back.

They were now sitting in the garden, in undress, drinking tea, at half-past five. It was very strange, but Léonie at once filled the large house with a kind of comfortable coziness, because she liked comfort herself. At other times Van Oudijck would hurriedly swallow a cup of tea which Kario brought him in his bedroom, but today this afternoon tea made a pleasant break in the day. Cane chairs and long deck chairs had been put outside, in front of the house, the tea tray stood on a cane table, there was *pisang goreng,* and Léonie, in a red silk Japanese kimono, with her blond hair hanging loose, lay back in a cane chair and played with Doddy's cockatoo, feeding it pastry. It was immediately different, Van Oudijck thought, his wife so sociable, charming, pretty, telling about their friends in Batavia, the races at Buitenzorg,[24] a ball at the residence of the governor-general, the Italian opera; the boys merry, healthy and jolly, however dirty they might make themselves in playing. He called them over to him and romped with them and asked about the gymnasium—they were both in the second year—and even Doddy and Theo seemed different to him. Doddy was plucking roses from the potted trees, looking delightfully pretty and humming a tune and Theo was talking with Mamma and even with him. A pleased expression played around Van Oudijck's mustache. His face looked young, and he hardly looked his forty-eight years. He had a quick, bright glance, a way of suddenly looking up with an acutely penetrating air. He was rather heavily built, and there was a hint that he would become heavier still, but he had retained a soldierly briskness and he was indefatigable on his inspection tours. He was a first-rate horseman. Tall and solid, content with his house and his family, he wore a pleasant air of robust virility and that jovial expression played around his mustache. Letting himself go, he stretched full-length in his cane chair, drank his cup of tea, and gave words to the thoughts that generally welled up in him at such moments of satisfaction. Yes, it was not a bad life in the Indies, working for the colonial government. At least, it had always been good to him, but then he had been pretty lucky. Promotion these days was a desperate business; he knew any number of assistant residents who were his contemporaries and who had no chance of becoming residents for years to come. And that certainly was a bad situation, to continue so long in a subordinate position, to be compelled at that age to await the orders of a resident. He could never have stood it, at forty-eight! But to be a resident, to give orders on his own initiative, to rule so large and important a district as Labuwangi, with such extensive coffee plantations, with such numerous sugar factories, with so many leased concessions—that was a delight, that was living, that was a life grander and more expansive than any other, a life that could not be compared to anything in Holland. His great responsibility delighted his authoritative nature. His activities were varied: office work and inspection tours; the interests of his work were varied: a man was not bored to death in his office chair; after the office there was the open air, and there was always a change, always something different. He hoped to become in a year and a half resident of the first class, if a first-class residency became vacant: Batavia, Semarang, Surabaja, or one of the Principalities.[25] And yet it would bother him to leave Labuwangi. He was attached to his district, for which he had done so much during the past five years, which in those years had prospered, insofar as prosperity was possible in these times of general depression, with the colonies poor, the population impoverished, the coffee crops worse than ever, and with sugar threatened with a serious crisis in two years' time.[26] The Indies were languishing, and even in industrial east Java inertia and lack of vitality were spreading like a blight; but still he had been able to do much for Labuwangi. During his administration the people had thrived and prospered, the irrigation of the rice fields was excellent, after he had succeeded in tactfully winning over the engineer who at first was in continual conflict with the government. Miles and miles of tramways had been laid down. The secretary, his assistant residents, and his controllers cooperated willingly, though he kept them hard at work. But he had a pleasant way with them, even though the work was hard. He knew how to be jovial and friendly, even though he was the resident. He was glad that all of them, his controllers, his assistant residents, represented the wholesome, cheerful type of official who was pleased with his life, liked his work, although nowadays he would study the *Government Almanack* and the *Colonial List* with a view to his promotion. And it was Van Oudijck's hobby to compare his officials with the judicial functionaries, who did not represent the same buoyant type: there was always a slight jealousy and animosity between the two groups.... Yes, it was a pleasant life, a pleasant sphere of activity, everything was all right. There was nothing

to beat the colonial administration. His only regret was that his relations with the regent were not easier and more agreeable. But it was not
his fault. He had always conscientiously given the regent his due, had
left him in the enjoyment of his full rights, had seen to it that he was duly
respected by the Javanese population and even by the European officials. Oh, how intensely he regretted the death of the old pangéran,
the regent's father, the old regent, a noble enlightened Javanese. Van
Oudijck had always felt sympathy for him, had won him over immediately with his tact. Had he not five years ago, when he arrived in
Labuwangi to take over the administration, invited the pangéran—a
genuine Javanese nobleman—to sit beside him in his own carriage,
rather than have him follow in a second carriage, behind the resident's
carriage, as was usual? And had this civility toward the old prince not
immediately won over all the Javanese heads and officials and flattered
them in their respect and love for their regent, the descendant of one
of the oldest Javanese families, the Adiningrats, who were sultans of
Madura in the Company's time? . . . But Sunario, the son, now the
young regent, he was unable to understand, unable to fathom.[27] This he
confessed silently only to himself—that enigmatic *wajang* puppet, as he
called him—always stiff, keeping his distance from him, the resident, as
though he, the prince, looked down on the Dutch burgher, and who was
completely absorbed in all sorts of superstitious observances and fanatical speculations.[28] He never said this openly, but something in the
regent escaped him. He was unable to incorporate into reality that delicate figure with the fixed coal-black eyes, as he had always been able to
do with the old pangéran. The latter had always been to him, in accordance with his age, a fatherly friend or in accordance with etiquette,
his "younger brother," but always the fellow ruler of his district. But
Sunario seemed to him unreal, not a functionary, not a regent, merely
a fanatical Javanese who always shrouded himself in mystery: such
nonsense, thought Van Oudijck. He laughed at the reputation for holi-
ness which the populace bestowed upon Sunario. He thought him im-
practical, a degenerate Javanese, an unhinged Javanese fop.

But the discord that existed between him and the regent (a difference
in personality, really, because it had never developed into actual fact—
why, he could twist the manikin round his finger!) was the only great
problem that had arisen during all these years. And he would not have
exchanged his life as a resident for any other life whatever. Why, he was
already fretting about what he would do later, after he was retired. He
would prefer to continue as long as possible in the service, as a member

of the Council, as vice president. The object of his unspoken ambition was the throne of Buitenzorg. But nowadays there was that strange mania in Holland for appointing outsiders to the highest posts—men sent straight from Holland, newcomers who knew nothing about the Indies—instead of remaining faithful to the principle of selecting old colonial officials who had made their way up from subcontroller and who knew the whole official hierarchy by heart. . . . Yes, what would he do, when he retired? Live in Nice? With no money? For saving was impossible; his life was comfortable, but expensive; and instead of saving he was running up debts. Well, that didn't matter now, the debts would be paid off in time, but later, later. . . . The future, the existence of a retired official, was anything but an agreeable prospect for him. To vegetate in The Hague, in a small house, with a gin-and-bitters at the Witte or at the Besogne Club—among the old fogies. . . .²⁹ The very idea made him shudder. He better not think about it, he preferred not to think about it at all, perhaps he'd be dead by that time. But now everything was fine: his work, his house, the Indies. There was absolutely nothing to compare with it.

Léonie had listened to him with a smile, she was accustomed to his quiet enthusiasm, his rhapsodizing about his job, or, as she put it, his adoration of the colonial government. She also valued the luxury of being a resident's wife. The comparative isolation she did not mind, she usually was sufficient unto herself. And she answered him with a smile, contented, charming, with her creamy complexion, which looked even fairer under the light coat of *bedak* powder against the red silk of her kimono and which was beautiful amidst the surrounding waves of her blond hair.

That morning she had felt irritated for a moment and Labuwangi, after Batavia, had depressed her with the tedium of a provincial capital. But since then she had acquired a large diamond, since then she had Theo back again. His room was close to hers. And it was sure to be a long time before he would find employment again.

These were her thoughts while her husband was still blissfully reflecting on his pleasant confidences. Her thoughts went no deeper than this, something like remorse would have surprised her very much, had she been capable of feeling it. . . . It began to grow dark slowly, the moon was already rising and shining brightly, and behind the velvety *waringins,* behind the feathery boughs of the coconut palms, which waved gently like tall, majestic sheaves of dark ostrich feathers, the last light of the sun threw a faintly stippled, dull-gold reflection, against which the softness of the *waringins* and the pomp of the palm trees stood out as though etched in black. From the distance came the monotone of the *gamelan*,[30] so mournful, like a crystal-clear piano of glass, with a profound dissonance at intervals. . . .

6

Since Van Oudijck was in a pleasant mood because of his wife and children, he suggested they go for a drive, and the horses were put to the landau. Van Oudijck looked glad and jovial under the broad, gold-laced peak of his cap. Léonie, seated beside him, was wearing a new mauve muslin frock from Batavia, and a hat with mauve poppies. A lady's hat in the provincial districts is a luxury, a colossal elegance, and Doddy, who sat facing her and was not wearing a hat, was secretly vexed and thought that Mamma might just as well have told her she was going to "use" a hat, to use Doddy's idiom. She was now such a contrast to Mamma, she couldn't bear them now, those softly swaying poppies. René was the only one of the boys with them, dressed in a clean white suit. The chief *oppasser* sat beside the coachman, holding against his side the great golden *pajong,* the symbol of authority.[31] It was past six, and already growing dark. At this hour a velvety silence hung over Labuwangi; the tragic mystery of the twilit atmosphere marked the days of the eastern monsoon. Sometimes a dog barked, or a wood pigeon cooed, breaking the unreality of the silence, which was that of a deserted town. But now the rattle of the carriage drove right through the silence, and the horses trampled the silence to shreds. No other carriages were met, and the absence of all signs of human life cast a spell upon the gardens and verandahs. A couple of young men on foot, in white, took off their hats.

The carriage had left the wealthier part of the town and entered the Chinese quarter,[32] where the lights were lit in the little shops. Business was almost finished and the Chinese were resting, in all sorts of limp attitudes, with their legs dangling or crossed, their arms round their heads, their pigtails loose or twisted around their skulls. When the carriage approached, they rose and remained standing, respectfully. The Javanese for the most part—those who were well brought up and knew their manners—squatted down. Along the road was a row of little portable kitchens, lit by small paraffin lamps, the drink vendors, the pastry sellers. The prevailing color in the evening darkness, lit by innumerable little lamps, was dingy and motley. The Chinese shops were crammed with goods, painted with red and gold characters and pasted with red and gold labels with inscriptions; in the background was the domestic altar with the sacred print: the white god seated, with the black god grimacing behind him. But the street widened and became suddenly more impressive: rich Chinese houses loomed up softly, like white villas. The most striking was the gleaming, palatial villa of an immensely wealthy retired opium dealer, who had made his money in the days before the opium monopoly:[33] a gleaming palace of graceful stucco work, with numerous outbuildings. The porticoes of the verandah were in a monumental style of imposing elegance and in many soft shades of gold; in the back of the open house the immense domestic altar was visible, with the print of the gods conspicuously illuminated; the garden was laid out with conventional, winding paths, but was beautifully filled with square pots and tall vases of dark blue and green glazed porcelain, containing dwarf trees—handed down from father to son—and always kept radiantly clean, a careful neatness of detail, eloquent of the prosperous, spick-and-span luxury of a Chinese opium millionaire. But not all the Chinese houses were so ostentatiously open: most of them were hidden behind closed doors in high-walled gardens, tucked away in the secrecy of their domestic life.

But suddenly the houses came to an end and Chinese graves stretched along a broad road: rich graves, each grassy mound with a stone entrance—the door of death—raised in the symbolic form of the female organ—the door of life—and surrounded by an ample lawn (to the great vexation of Van Oudijck, who had calculated how much ground was lost to cultivation by these burial places of the rich Chinese). And the Chinese seemed to triumph in life and death in this mysterious town which was otherwise so silent: the Chinese gave it its actual character of busy traffic, of trade, of making money, of living and dying, because, when the carriage drove into the Arab quarter—a district of houses like any other, but gloomy, lacking in style, with life and prosperity hidden away behind closed doors, with chairs on the verandah, but the master of the house gloomily squatting on the floor, following the carriage with a somber look—this quarter seemed even more mysterious than the fashionable part of Labuwangi and seemed to radiate its unutterable mystery like an atmosphere of Islam that spread over the whole town, as though it were Islam that had poured forth the dusky, fatal melancholy of resignation that filled the shivering noiseless evening.... They did not feel this in their rattling carriage, accustomed as they were to that atmosphere from childhood, and no longer sensitive to the gloomy secret that was like the approach of a dark force which had always breathed upon them, the rulers with their Creole blood, so that they should never suspect it. Perhaps when Van Oudijck now and again read about Pan-Islam[34] in the newspapers, he was dimly conscious in his deepest thoughts of this dark force, this gloomy secret. But at moments like the present—driving with his wife and children, amid the rattling of his carriage and the trampling of his fine Australian horses, the *oppasser* with the furled *pajong,* which glittered like a furled sun, next to the driver— he felt too intensely aware of his individuality, his authoritative, over-bearing nature, to feel anything of the dark secret, to divine anything of the black peril. And he was now in far too pleasant a mood to feel or see anything melancholy. In his optimism he did not see even the decline of this town that he loved; he was not struck, as they drove past, by the immense, porticoed villas, witnesses to the prosperity of former plant-ers, but now deserted, neglected, and standing in yards that had become overgrown, one of them taken over by a lumber company that allowed the foreman to live there and stack his logs in the front garden. The de-serted houses gleamed sadly with their pillared porticoes which, amid the desolate grounds, loomed spectral in the moonlight, like temples of disaster. But they did not see it like that, they enjoyed the rocking of the soft carriage springs, Léonie smiled and dozed, while Doddy, now that they were approaching the Lange Laan again, looked out to see whether she could catch sight of Addy. . . .

7

The secretary, Onno Eldersma, was a busy man. The daily mail brought an average of two hundred letters and documents to the residency office which employed two senior clerks, six juniors, and a number of *djurutulis* and *magangs,* and the resident grumbled whenever the work fell behind. He himself was an energetic worker, and he expected his subordinates to show the same spirit. But sometimes there was an avalanche of documents, claims, and applications. Eldersma was a typical government official, completely wrapped up in his minutes and reports, and Eldersma was always busy. He worked morning, noon, and night. He allowed himself no siesta. He took a hurried lunch at four o'clock and then rested for a little. Fortunately he had a sound, robust, Frisian constitution, but he needed all his blood, all his muscles, all his nerves for his work. It was not mere scribbling, or shuffling papers, it was manual labor with the pen, muscular work, nervous work, and it never ceased. He consumed himself, he spent himself, he was always writing. He had no other ideas left, he was nothing but an official, a civil servant. He had a charming house, a most charming and exceptional wife, a delightful child, but he never saw them, though he lived, vaguely, amid his home surroundings. He just slaved away conscientiously, finishing what he could. Sometimes he would tell the resident that it was impossible for him to do any more, but on this point Van Oudijck was inexorable, pitiless. He himself had been a district secretary, he knew what it meant. It meant work, it meant plodding on like a dray horse. It meant living, eating, sleeping with your pen in your hand. Van Oudijck would show him this or that piece of work that had to be finished, and Eldersma, who had said that he could do no more than he was doing, finished the work and therefore always did do something more than he believed he was capable of. Then his wife, Eva, would say:

"My husband has ceased to be a human being, my husband has ceased to be a man, my husband is an official."

The young wife, very European, had never lived in the Indies before and had never known, until her two years in Labuwangi, that it was possible to work as hard as her husband did, in a place as hot as Labuwangi was during the eastern monsoon. She had resisted at first, had tried to insist on her rights but, when she saw that he had really not a minute to spare, she waived her rights. She had immediately realized that her husband could not share her life, nor could she share his, not because he wasn't a good husband and very fond of his wife, but simply because the mail brought two hundred letters and documents daily. She had realized immediately that there was nothing for her in Labuwangi, that she would have to console herself with her house and, later, with her child. She arranged her house like a temple of art and comfort and racked her brains about the education of her little boy. She was an artistically cultivated woman and came from an artistic environment. Her father was Van Hove, the great landscape painter, her mother was Stella Couberg, the famous concert singer. Eva, brought up in an atmosphere of art and music that she had absorbed since childhood from her picture books and nursery rhymes, had married a colonial civil servant and had accompanied him to Labuwangi. She loved her husband, a robust Frisian and a man of sufficient culture to take an interest in many subjects. And she had gone, happy in her love and filled with illusions about the Indies, about the orientalism of the tropics. She had tried to preserve her illusions, despite the warnings she had received. In Singapore she was struck by the color of the naked Malays, like that of a bronze statue, by the motley orientalism of the Chinese and Arab quarters, and by the poetry of the Japanese teahouses. But soon after, in Batavia, a gray disappointment had fallen like a cold drizzle on her expectation of seeing everything in the Indies as a beautiful fairy tale, a story out of the *Arabian Nights*. The habits of ordinary, everyday existence dampened her refreshing desire to admire, and she suddenly saw everything that was ridiculous even before she discovered anything more that was beautiful. At her hotel, the men in pajamas lounging at full length in the long chairs, their lazy legs on the extended leg rests, their feet—although well taken care of—bare and their toes moving quietly in a genial game of big toe and little toe, even while she was passing. The ladies were in *sarong* and *kabaai*—the only practical morning dress, because it can be easily changed two or three times a day—which is becoming to so few; the way the *sarong* falls straight in the back is particularly angular and ugly, however elegant and expensive the costume. . . . And then how common the houses were with their whitewash and their rows of fragile and ugly flowerpots, or how parched and scorched nature, or how filthy the natives. And all the minor absurdities of the life of the Europeans: the *sinjo* accent, with the constant little exclamations, the provincial conventionality of the officials, for instance, how only members of the Council of the Indies were allowed to wear top hats. And then the strict etiquette: at a reception, the highest functionary is the first to leave and the others follow according to rank. And the little peculiarities of tropical customs, such as the use of Devoe crates or the use of tins filled with petroleum for this or that; the wood for shop windows, for garbage cans and homemade furniture; the tins for gutters and watering cans and all kinds of domestic utensils. . . .

The young and cultured little woman, with her *Arabian Nights* illusions, was unable, amid these first impressions, to distinguish between what was colonial—the practices of a European who acclimatizes himself to a country that is alien to his blood—and what was really poetic, genuinely Indies, purely Eastern, absolutely Javanese. Because of these and other little absurdities she had at once felt disappointed, as everyone with an artistic inclination will feel disappointed in the colonial Indies, which is not at all artistic or poetic, where the roses in their white pots are carefully fertilized with horse droppings packed as high as the rim of the pots with the result that, when there's a breeze, the scent of the roses mingles with the stench of fresh manure. And she became unjust—as does every Hollander, every newcomer to that beautiful country which he would like to see according to a preconceived literary vision, but which impresses him at first with its colonial absurdities. And she forgot that the country itself, originally so absolutely beautiful, was in no way to blame for this absurdity.

She had had a couple of years of it and had been astonished, occasionally alarmed, then again shocked, had laughed sometimes and then again been annoyed and, at last, with the reasonableness of her nature and the practical side of her artistic soul, had grown accustomed to it all. She had grown accustomed to the toes playing their game, to the manure around the roses; she had grown accustomed to her husband, who was no longer a human being, no longer a man, but an official. She had suffered a great deal, she had written despairing letters, she had been sick with longing for the home of her parents, she had been on the verge of leaving, but she had not gone because she didn't want to leave her husband in his loneliness, and she had accustomed herself to things and made the best of them. She had not only the soul of an artist—she played the piano exceptionally well—but also the heart of a plucky woman. She had kept on loving her husband and felt that, after all, she provided him with a pleasant home. She gave serious attention to the education of her child. And, once she had grown accustomed to things, she became less unjust and suddenly saw much of what was beautiful in the Indies, admired the stately grace of a coconut palm, the exquisite, paradisiacal flavor of the tropical fruits, the glory of the blossoming trees; and, in the inland districts, she had realized the noble majesty of nature, the harmony of the undulating hills, the faerie forests of gigantic ferns, the menacing ravines of the craters, the shimmering terraces of the flooded *sawahs* with the tender green of the young paddy. And the character of the Javanese had been a relevation to her: his elegance, his grace, his salutation, and his dance, his aristocratic distinction, so often evidently handed down directly from a noble race, from an age-old chivalry, now modernized into a diplomatic suppleness, worshipping authority by nature and inevitably resigned under the yoke of the rulers whose gold braid arouses his innate respect.

In her father's house, Eva had always felt the cult of the artistic and the beautiful around her, even to the point of decadence; those around her had always directed her attention, in an environment of perfectly beautiful things, in beautiful words, in music, to life's line of grace, and perhaps too exclusively to that alone. And she was now too well trained in that school of beauty to persist in her disappointment and to see only the whitewash and the tar of the houses, the petty airs of the officials, the Devoe crates and the horse manure. Her literary mind now saw the palatial character of the houses, the typical character of that official pride (which could hardly be different from what it was) and she saw all these details more accurately, obtaining a broader insight into the entire world of the Indies, until revelation followed upon revelation. Only she continued to feel something strange, something she could not analyse, a certain mystery and dark secrecy, which she felt creeping softly over the land at night. But she thought that it was no more than a mood produced by the darkness and the very dense foliage, that it was like the very quiet music of stringed instruments of a kind quite strange to her, a distant murmur of harps in a minor key, a vague voice of warning no more than a whispering in the night that evoked poetic imaginings.

In Labuwangi, the small provincial capital, she often astonished the local gentry because she was somewhat excitable, because she was enthusiastic, spontaneous, glad to be alive—even in the Indies—glad of the beauty of life, because she had a healthy nature, softly tempered and shaded into a charming pose of caring for nothing but the beautiful: beautiful lines, beautiful colors, artistic ideas. Those who knew her, either disliked her or were very fond of her, but few felt indifferent to her. She had gained a reputation for unusualness: her house was unusual, her clothes unusual, the education of her child unusual; her ideas were unusual and the only ordinary thing about her was her Frisian husband, who was almost too ordinary in that environment, which might have been cut out of an art magazine. She was fond of society and gathered around her as much of the European element as possible, though, indeed, it was seldom artistic; but she imparted a pleasant tone to it, something that reminded everybody of Holland. This little clique, this group admired her and instinctively adopted the tone that she set. Be-

cause of her greater culture, she ruled over it, though she was not a des-
pot by nature. But not everybody approved of all this; others called her
eccentric. The clique, however, that group remained faithful to her, for
she awakened them, in the soft languor of Indies life, to the existence of
music, ideas, and joie de vivre. She had drawn into her circle the doctor
and his wife, the chief engineer and his wife, the *controleur-kota*[35] and
his wife, and sometimes a couple of outside controllers, or a few young
fellows from the sugar factories. In this manner she surrounded herself
with a merry little band of adherents. She ruled over them, organized
amateur theatricals for them, picnicked with them, and charmed them
with her house and her frocks and the epicurean and artistic flavor of
her life. They forgave her everything that they did not understand—her
aesthetic principles, her enthusiasm for Wagner—because she gave
them merriment and a little joie de vivre and a sociable feeling in the
deadliness of their colonial existence. For this they were fervently grateful to her. And thus it had come about that her house became the real
center of social life in Labuwangi, whereas the residency, across the
street, withdrew with dignified reserve into the shadow of its *waringin*
trees. Léonie van Oudijck was not jealous of this. She loved her repose
and was only too glad to leave everything to Eva Eldersma. And so Léonie did not involve herself with anything—neither entertainments and
musical societies, nor dramatic societies and charities—and delegated
to Eva all the social duties that as a rule a resident's wife feels bound to
take upon herself. Léonie had her monthly receptions, at which she
spoke to everybody and smiled upon everybody, and gave her annual
ball on New Year's Day. With this the social life of the residency began
and ended. Apart from this she lived there in her egoism, in the comfort
with which she had selfishly surrounded herself, in her rosy dreams of
cherubs and in such love as she was able to gather. She sometimes felt a
need to go to Batavia and left to spend a month or two there. And so she,
as the resident's wife, led her own life, while Eva did everything, Eva set
the tone. It sometimes gave rise to a little jealousy, for instance, between
her and the wife of the inspector of finances, who considered that the
first place after Mrs. Van Oudijck belonged to her and not to the secretary's wife. This would occasion a good deal of bickering over official
etiquette, and stories and rumors would make the rounds, were elabo-
rated, exaggerated, until they reached the remotest sugar factory in the
district. But Eva took no notice of all this gossip and preferred to devote
herself to providing a little sociability in Labuwangi. And, to keep
things going properly, she and her little circle ruled the roost. She had
been elected president of the Thalia Dramatic Society and she accepted,

but on condition that the rules should be abolished. She was willing to be queen, but without a constitution. Everybody said that this would never do, there had always been rules. But Eva replied that, if there were to be rules, she must refuse to be president. And they gave way: the constitution of the Thalia was abolished and Eva held absolute sway, chose the plays and distributed the parts. It was the golden age of the society: directed by her, the members acted so well that people came from Surabaja to attend the performances at the Concordia. The plays were of a quality that had never been seen before at the Concordia.

And the result was that people either loved her or did not like her at all. But she persisted and provided a little European civilization, so that they might not grow too "musty" at Labuwangi. And people resorted to all kinds of tricks to get invited to her little dinners, which were famous and notorious. For she stipulated that her male guests should come in formal clothes and not in their Singapore jackets, without shirts. She introduced tails and white ties and she was inexorable. The women customarily wore decolleté gowns, for the sake of coolness, and thought it delightful. But the poor men objected, gasping for air at first, and felt constricted in their stiff collars. The doctor declared that it was unhealthy, and the old timers protested that it was madness and contrary to all the good old Indies customs.

But after they had gasped for a while in their dress coats and stiff collars, they all found Mrs. Eldersma's dinners charming, precisely because they were so European.

8

Eva was at home to her friends once every two weeks. "You see, resident, it's not a reception," she always said, defensively, to Van Oudijck. "I know that no one's allowed to 'receive' in the provinces, except for the resident and his wife. It's really not a reception, resident. I wouldn't dare to call it that. I'm just at home to everybody once every two weeks, and I'm glad if our friends care to come. . . . It's all right, isn't it, resident, as long as it's not a 'reception'?"

Van Oudijck would laugh merrily, which made his military mustache tremble, and ask if the little lady were pulling his leg. She could do anything she wanted, as long as she continued to provide a little gaiety, a little acting, a little music, a little sociability. Because that had become her duty: to provide a touch of class in Labuwangi.

There was nothing colonial about her at-home days. For instance, at the resident's, the receptions were regulated according to the old Indies practice: all the ladies sat in a row of chairs along the walls, and Mrs. Van Oudijck would walk past them and talk to each of them for a moment, standing, while they remained seated; the resident chatted to the men in another gallery. The men and women were kept apart. Bitters, port, and iced water were served.

At Eva's, people strolled about, walked through the galleries, sat down anywhere they pleased, and everybody talked to everybody. There was not the same ceremony as at the resident's, but here one could find the chic of a French drawing room, with an artistic touch to it. And it had become a custom for the ladies to dress more for Eva's days than for the resident's receptions: at Eva's they wore hats, a symbol of extreme elegance in the Indies. Fortunately, Léonie did not care; it left her totally indifferent.

Léonie was now sitting in the middle gallery, on a couch, and remained sitting with the radèn-aju, the wife of the regent. She thought that old custom pleasant: everybody came up to her, whereas at her own receptions she had to do so much walking, past the row of ladies along the wall. Now she took her ease, remained sitting, smiling to those who came to pay her their respects. But, apart from this, there was a restless movement of guests. Eva was everywhere.

"Do you think it's pretty here?" Mrs. Van der Does asked Léonie, with a glance at the middle gallery.

And her eyes wandered in surprise over the dull arabesques, painted with lime on the pale gray walls, like frescoes; over the *djati* wainscoting, carved by skillful Chinese cabinetmakers after a drawing in *The Studio;*[36] over the bronze Japanese vases on their *djati* pedestals, in which branches of bamboo and bouquets of gigantic flowers cast their shadows right up to the ceiling.

"Odd . . . but very pretty! Unusual," murmured Léonie to whom Eva's taste was always a conundrum.

Withdrawn into herself as if in a temple of egoism, she did not mind what others did or felt, nor how they arranged their houses. But she could not have lived here. She liked her own lithographs—Veronese and Shakespeare and Tasso: she thought them distinguished—liked them better than the handsome sepia photographs after Italian masters that Eva had standing here and there on easels. Above all, she loved her chocolate box and the scent advertisement with the little angels.

"Do you like that dress?" Mrs. Van der Does asked next.

"Yes, I do," said Léonie, smiling pleasantly. "Eva's very clever: she painted those blue irises herself, on Chinese silk. . . ."

She never said anything but kind, smiling things. She never spoke evil; it left her indifferent. And she now turned to the radèn-aju and thanked her in kindly, drawling sentences for some fruit that the latter had sent her. The regent came to speak to her and she asked after his two little sons. She talked in Dutch, while the regent and the radèn-aju both answered in Malay. The regent of Labuwangi, Radèn Adipati Surio Sunario, was still young, just turned thirty. He had a refined Javanese face like a conceited *wajang* puppet, a little mustache, with the points carefully twisted, and, above all, a staring gaze that struck the beholder. It was a gaze that stared as though in a continuous trance, a gaze that seemed to pierce the visible reality and to see right through it, a gaze that issued from the eyes like coals, sometimes dull and weary, sometimes flashing like sparks of ecstasy and fanaticism. Among the population—which was almost slavishly attached to its regent and his family—he enjoyed a reputation for sanctity and mystery, though no one ever knew the truth of the matter. Here, in Eva's gallery, he merely produced the impression of a puppetlike figure, of a distinguished Indies prince, save that his trancelike eyes occasioned surprise. The *sarong*, drawn smoothly around his hips, hung low in front in a bundle of flat, regular pleats, which fluttered open; he wore a white starched shirt with diamond studs and a little blue tie; over this was a blue uniform jacket, with gold uniform buttons, with the royal W and the crown;[37] his bare feet were encased in black patent leather pumps with points turned up at the toes; the kerchief carefully wound about his head in narrow folds imparted a feminine air to his refined features, but the black eyes, now and then weary, constantly flashed that trancelike stare. The golden kris was stuck in his blue and gold waistband behind him at the small of his back; a large jewel glittered on his small and slender hand, and a cigarette case of braided gold wire peeped from the pocket of his jacket. He did not say much—sometimes he looked as though he were asleep; then his strange eyes would flash up again—and his replies to what Léonie said consisted almost exclusively of a curt, clipped: "*Saja.* . . ." He uttered the two syllables with a hard, sibilant accent of politeness, putting equal stress upon each. He accompanied his little word of civility with a short, automatic nod of the head. The radèn-aju, who was seated beside Léonie, answered in the same way. But she always followed it up with a shy little laugh. She was very young, perhaps barely eighteen. She was a Solo princess, and Van Oudijck could not stand her, because she introduced Solo manners and Solo expressions into Labuwangi, in her conceited arrogance, as though nothing could be so distinguished and so purely aristocratic as what was done and said at the court of Solo.[38] She employed court phrases which the Labuwangi population did not understand; she had forced the regent to engage a Solo coachman, with the Solo state livery, including the wig and the false beard and mustache, at which the people stared in amazement. Her yellow complexion was made to appear even paler by a light layer of *bedak,* applied moist; her eyebrows were slightly arched with a streak of black; jeweled hairpins were stuck in her glossy *kondé* that had a *kenanga* flower in its center. Over a *kain pandjang* which, according to the custom of the Solo court, had a long trail in front, she wore a *kabaai* of red brocade, relieved with gold braid and fastened with three large gems. Two fabulous stones, in heavy silver settings, dragged her ears down. She wore light-colored mesh stockings and gold *sonket* slippers.[39] Her little thin fingers were stiff with rings, as though set in diamonds, and she held a white marabou fan in her hand.

"*Saja* . . . *saja,*" she answered civilly, with her shy little laugh.

Léonie was silent for a moment, tired of carrying on the conversation by herself. After she had spoken to the regent and the radèn-aju about their sons, she did not have much more to say. Van Oudijck, after Eva had shown him around the galleries—for there was always something new to admire—joined his wife. The regent rose to his feet.

"And, Regent," asked the resident, in Dutch, "how is the radèn-aju pangéran?"

He was inquiring after Sunario's mother, the old regent's widow.

"Very well . . . thank you," murmured the regent, in Malay. "But Mamma didn't come with us . . . so old . . . easily tired."

"I want to speak to you, Regent."

The regent followed Van Oudijck on to the front verandah, which was empty.

"I am sorry to have to tell you that I have just had another bad report about your brother, the regent of Ngadjiwa. . . . I am informed that he has lately been gambling again and has lost large sums of money. Do you know anything about it?"

The regent shut himself up, as it were, in his puppetlike stiffness and kept silent. Only his eyes stared, as if he saw distant things, through Van Oudijck.

"Do you know anything about it, Regent?"

"*Tida*. . . ."

"I request you, as head of the family, to look into it and to watch your brother. He gambles, he drinks, he does your name no credit, Regent. If the old pangéran could have guessed that his second son would fall this low, it would have pained him greatly. He held his name high. He was one of the wisest and noblest regents that the government ever had in Java, and you know how greatly the government valued the pangéran. Even in the Company's days, Holland owed much to your house, which was always loyal to her. But times seem to be changing. . . . It is very regrettable, Regent, that an old Javanese family with such lofty traditions as yours should be unable to remain faithful to those traditions. . . ."

Radèn Adipati Surio Sunario turned olive pale. His hypnotic eyes pierced the resident, but he saw that the latter also was boiling with anger. And he dimmed the strange glitter of his gaze into a drowsy weariness.

"I thought, Resident, that you had always felt an affection for my house," he murmured, almost plaintively.

"And you thought right, Regent. I loved the pangéran. I have always admired your house and have always tried to uphold it. I want to uphold it still, together with yourself, Regent, hoping that you see not only, as your reputation suggests, the things of the next world, but also the realities about you. But it is your brother, Regent, whom I do *not* love and cannot possibly esteem. I have been told —and I can trust the words of those who told me—that the regent of Ngadjiwa has not only been gambling . . . but also that he has failed this month to pay the heads at Ngadjiwa their salaries. . . ."

They looked at each other fixedly, and Van Oudijck's firm and steady glance met the regent's hypnotic gaze.

"The persons who act as your informants may be mistaken. . . ."

"I am assuming that they would not bring me such reports without

the most incontestable certainty. . . . Regent, this is a very delicate matter. I repeat, you are the head of your family. Inquire of your younger
brother to what extent he has misapplied the money of the government
and make it all good as soon as possible. I am purposely leaving the matter up to you. I will not speak to your brother about it, in order to spare
a member of your family as long as I can. It is for you to admonish your
brother, to call his attention to what in my eyes is a crime, but one which
you, from your prestige as head of the family, are still able to undo. For-
bid him to gamble and order him to master his passion. Otherwise I
foresee very grievous things and I shall have to propose your brother's
dismissal. You yourself know how I should dislike to do that. For the regent of Ngadjiwa is the second son of the old pangéran, whom I held in
high esteem, even as I should always wish to spare your mother, the
radèn-aju pangéran, any sorrow."

"I thank you," murmured Sunario.

"Reflect seriously upon what I am saying to you, Regent. If you cannot make your brother listen to reason, if the salaries of the heads are
not paid at the earliest possible date, then . . . then I shall have to act.
And, if my warning is of no avail, then it means your brother's fall. You
yourself know, the dismissal of a regent is such a very exceptional thing
that it would bring disgrace upon your family. Assist me in saving the
house of the Adiningrats from such a fate."

"I promise," murmured the regent.

"Give me your hand, Regent."

Van Oudijck pressed the thin fingers of the Javanese.

"Can I trust you?" he asked.

"In life, in death."

"Then let us go inside. And tell me as soon as possible what you have
discovered."

The regent bowed. An olive pallor betrayed the silent, secret rage that
was working inside him like the fire of a volcano. His eyes, behind Van
Oudijck's back, darted with a mysterious hatred at the Hollander, the
lowly Hollander, the base commoner, the infidel Christian, who had no
business to feel anything, with that unclean soul of his, concerning *him*,
his house, his father, his mother, or their supremely sacred aristocracy
and nobility . . . even though they had always bowed beneath the yoke
of those who were stronger than they. . . .

9

"I have counted on your staying for dinner," said Eva.

"Of course," replied Van Helderen, the controller, and his wife.

The reception—not a reception, as Eva always defended herself—was nearly over. The Van Oudijcks had been the first to go, the regent followed. The Eldersmas were left with their little band of intimates: Dr. Rantzow and Doorn de Bruijn, the senior engineer, with their wives, and the Van Helderens. They sat down on the front verandah with a certain sense of relief and rocked comfortably to and fro. Whiskies and soda, glasses of lemonade, with great lumps of ice in them, were handed round.

"Always chock full, reception at Eva's," said Mrs. Van Helderen. "Fuller than other day at resident's. . . ."

Ida van Helderen was a typical little white *nonna*. She always tried to behave in a very European fashion, to speak Dutch well, and even pretended to speak bad Malay and to care for neither *rijsttafel* nor *rudjak*.[40] She was short and plump, very white, with big, black, astonished eyes. She was full of little mysterious whims and hatreds and affections; all her actions were the result of mysterious little impulses. Sometimes she hated Eva, sometimes she doted on her. She was absolutely unreliable, her every action, every movement, every word might be a surprise. She was always in love, tragically. She took all her little affairs very dramatically, on a very large and serious scale, with not the least sense of proportion, and then unburdened herself to Eva, who laughed and comforted her.

Her husband, the controller, had never been in Holland. He had been educated entirely in Batavia, in the William III College, and its colonial department.[41] It was very strange that this Creole, apparently quite European, tall, fair, and pale, with his fair mustache, his blue eyes expressing animation and interest and his manners which displayed a finer courtesy than could be found in the smartest circles of Europe, did not have anything that was typically Indies in his thought, speech, or dress. He would speak of Paris and Vienna as though he had spent years in both capitals, whereas he had never been away from Java. He loved music, though he found it difficult to appreciate Wagner, whom Eva was so fond of playing, and his great illusion was that he must really go to Europe on leave next year, to see the Paris Exhibition. There was a wonderful distinction and innate style about young Van Helderen, as though he were not the offspring of European parents who had always lived in the Indies, as though he were a foreigner from an unknown country, of a nationality that you could not place immediately. His accent barely betrayed a certain softness, resulting from the climate, and he spoke Dutch so correctly that it would have sounded almost stiff if compared to the slovenly slang of the mother country; and he spoke French, English, and German with greater facility than most Dutchmen. Perhaps he owed to a French mother that exotic politeness and courtesy, innate, pleasant, and natural. In his wife, who was also of French extraction, springing from a Creole family in Réunion,[42] this exoticism had become a mysterious mixture that had never developed beyond a kind of childishness and a jumble of petty emotions and petty passions, while she tried to read tragedy into her life with those great, somber eyes, even if she did no more than just dip into it as into a badly written magazine story.

At the moment, she imagined herself to be in love with the senior engineer, the oldest of the little band, a man already turning gray, with a black beard, and, in her tragic fashion, she pictured scenes with Mrs. Doorn de Bruijn, a stout, placid, melancholy woman. Dr. Rantzow and his wife were German; he, fat, blond, vulgar, with a potbelly; she, with a serene German face, pleasant and matronly, talking Dutch vivaciously with a German accent.

This was the little clique over which Eva Eldersma reigned. In addition to Frans van Helderen, the controller, it consisted of quite ordinary Indies and European elements, people without artistic sense, as Eva said, but she had no other choice in Labuwangi, and therefore amused herself with Ida's little *nonna* tragedies and made the most of the others. Onno, her husband, tired as usual from his work, did not join much in the conversation, but sat and listened.

"How long was Mrs. Van Oudijck in Batavia?" asked Ida.

"Two months," said the doctor's wife. "A very long visit, this time."

"I hear," said Mrs. Doorn de Bruijn, placid, melancholy, and quietly venomous, "that this time one member of Council, one head of a department, and three young businessmen kept Mrs. Van Oudijck amused in Batavia."

"And I can assure you people," said the doctor, "that, if Mrs. Van Oudijck did not go to Batavia regularly, she would miss a beneficial cure, even though she does it on her own and not . . . by my prescription."

"Let's not speak evil!" Eva interrupted, almost entreatingly. "Mrs. Van Oudijck is beautiful—with a tranquil Junoesque beauty and the eyes of Venus—and I can forgive beautiful people everything. And you, Doctor," threatening him with her finger, "mustn't betray professional secrets. The doctors in the Indies, you know, are often far too outspoken about their patients' secrets. When I'm ill, it's never anything but a headache. Will you make a careful note of that, Doctor?"

"The resident seems preoccupied," said Doorn de Bruijn.

"Could he know . . . about his wife?" asked Ida somberly, her great eyes filled with black velvet tragedy.

"The resident is often like that," said Frans van Helderen. "He has his moods. Sometimes he's pleasant, cheerful, jovial, as he was recently, on tour. Then again he has his gloomy days, working and working and grumbling that nobody does any work except himself."

"My poor, unappreciated Onno!" sighed Eva.

"I believe he's overworking himself," said Van Helderen. "Labuwangi is a tremendously busy district. And the resident takes things too much to heart, both in his own house and outside, both his relations with his son and his relations with the regent."

"I would sack the regent," said the doctor.

"But, Doctor," said Van Helderen, "you know enough about our conditions in Java to know that things can't be done that way. The regent and his family are closely identified with Labuwangi and too highly considered by the population. . . ."

"Yes, I know the Dutch policy. The English in British India deal with their Indian princes in a more arbitrary and high-handed fashion. The Dutch treat them much too gently."

"The question might arise which of the two policies is the better in the long run," said Van Helderen, drily, because he hated to hear a foreigner disparage anything about a Dutch colony. "Fortunately, we know nothing here of the continual poverty and famine that prevail in British India."

"I saw the resident speaking very seriously to the regent," said Doorn de Bruijn.

"The resident is too susceptible," said Van Helderen. "He allows himself to get depressed about the gradual decline of that old Javanese family, which is doomed to be ruined and which he would like to uphold. The resident, cool and practical though he is, is a bit of a romantic in this, though he might refuse to admit it. But he remembers the Adiningrats' glorious past, he remembers that last fine figure, the noble old pangéran, and he compares him with his sons, the one a fanatic, the other a gambler. . . ."

"I think our regent—not the Ngadjiwa one: he's a coolie—delightful!" said Eva. "He's a living *wajang*-puppet. Except his eyes: they frighten me. What terrible eyes! Sometimes they're asleep and sometimes they're like a maniac's. But he is so refined, so distinguished! And the radèn-aju too is an exquisite little doll: '*Saja...saja!*' She says nothing, but she looks very decorative. I'm always glad when they adorn my at-home day and I miss them when they're not there. And the old radèn-aju pangéran, gray-haired, dignified, a queen. ..."

"A passionate gambler," said Eldersma.

"They gamble away all they possess," said Van Helderen, "she and the regent of Ngadjiwa. They're no longer rich. The old pangéran used to have splendid insignia of rank for state occasions, magnificent lances, a jeweled *sirih* box, spittoons—useful objects, those!—of priceless value.[43] The old radèn-aju has gambled them all away. I doubt if she has anything left but her pension: two hundred and forty guilders, I believe. And how our regent manages to keep all his cousins, male and female, in the *kabupatèn*, according to the Javanese custom, is beyond me."[44]

"What's that custom?" asked the doctor.

"Every regent collects his whole family around him like parasites, clothes them, feeds them, provides them with pocket money . . . and the natives think it dignified and smart."

"Sad . . . that ruined greatness!" said Ida, gloomily.

A boy came to announce dinner and they went to the back verandah and sat down at the table.

"And what do you have in store for us, Madam?" asked the senior engineer. "What are the plans? Labuwangi has been very quiet lately."

"It's really terrible," said Eva. "If I didn't have all of you, it would be terrible. If I weren't always planning something and coming up with new ideas, it would be terrible, living here in Labuwangi. My husband doesn't feel it, he works, as all you men do. What else is there to do in the Indies but work, regardless of the heat? But for us women! What a life, if we didn't find out happiness purely in ourselves, in our home, in our friends . . . when we have the good fortune to possess those friends! Nothing from outside. Not a picture, not a statue to look at, no music to listen to. Don't be cross, Van Helderen. You play the cello charmingly, but nobody in the Indies can keep up to date. The Italian Opera plays *Trovatore*. The amateur companies—and they're really first-rate in Batavia—play . . . *Trovatore*. And you, Van Helderen . . . don't object. I saw you in ecstasy when the Italian company from Surabaja was here lately, at the club, and played . . . *Trovatore*. You were enchanted."

"There were some beautiful voices among them."

"But twenty years ago, so they tell me, people here were also enchanted with . . . *Trovatore*. Oh, it's terrible! Sometimes, suddenly, it oppresses me. Sometimes I feel suddenly that I have not grown used to the Indies and that I never shall, and I begin to long for Europe, for real life!"

"But Eva," Eldersma began, in alarm, dreading that she would really go home one day, leaving him alone in what would then be his utterly joyless work in Labuwangi, "sometimes you do appreciate the Indies, your house, the pleasant, spacious life. . . ."

"Materially. . . ."

"And don't you appreciate your own work, I mean the many things which you are able to do here?"

"What? Arranging parties? Arranging theatricals?"

"You're the real resident," gushed Ida.

"Thank goodness, we're coming back to Mrs. Van Oudijck," said Mrs. Doorn de Bruijn, teasingly.

"And to professional secrecy," said Dr. Rantzow.

"No," sighed Eva. "We want something new. Dances, parties, picnics, trips into the mountains . . . we've exhausted all that. I know nothing more. The tropical sadness is coming over me. I'm in one of my low moods. Those brown faces of my boys around me suddenly strike me as uncanny. The Indies frighten me at times. Do any of you ever feel that? A vague dread, a mystery in the air, something menacing. . . . I don't know what it is. The evenings are sometimes so full of mystery and there is something mysterious in the character of the native, who is remote from us, who differs so much from us. . . ."

"Artistic feelings," mocked Van Helderen. "No, I don't feel like that. The Indies are my country."

"You're true to type!" said Eva, teasing him in return. "What makes you what you are, so curiously European? I can't call it Dutch."

"My mother was a French woman."

"But, after all, you're a *njo*, born here, brought up here. . . . And you have nothing of a *njo* about you. I think it's wonderful to have met you. I like you as a change. . . . Help me, can't you? Suggest something new. Not a dance and not a trip in the mountains. I want something new. Else I shall get a craving for my father's paintings, for my mother's singing, for our beautiful, artistic house in The Hague. If I don't have something new, I shall die. I'm not like your wife, Van Helderen, always in love."

"Eva!" Ida entreated.

"Tragically in love, with her beautiful, somber eyes. Always, first with her husband and then with somebody else. I am never in love. Not even with my husband any longer. He is with me, though. But I have not an amorous nature. There's a great deal of lovemaking in the Indies, isn't there, Doctor? . . . Well, we've ruled out dances, excursions in the mountains, and lovemaking. What then, in Heaven's name, what then?"

"I know of something," said Mrs. Doorn de Bruijn, and a sudden anxiety replaced her placid melancholy.

She glanced at Mrs. Rantzow, and the German woman grasped her meaning.

"What is it?" asked the others, eagerly.

"Table-turning," whispered the two ladies.

There was general laughter.

"Oh dear!" sighed Eva, disappointed. "A trick, a joke, an evening's amusement. No, I want something that will fill my life for at least a month."

"Table-turning," repeated Mrs. Rantzow.

"Listen to me," said Mrs. Doorn de Bruijn. "The other day, for a joke, we tried making a teapoy turn.[45] We all promised not to cheat. The table . . . moved, spelled out words, tapping them out by the alphabet."

"But was there no cheating?" asked the doctor, Eldersma, and Van Helderen.

"You'll have to trust us," declared the two ladies, in self-defense.

"All right," said Eva. "We've finished dinner. Let's have some table-turning."

"We must all promise not to cheat," said Mrs. Rantzow. "I can see that my husband will be . . . antipathetic. But Ida . . . is a great medium."

They rose.

"Must we have the lights out?" asked Eva.

"No," said Mrs. Doorn de Bruijn.

"An ordinary teapoy?"

"A wooden teapoy."

"The eight of us?"

"No, we must begin by choosing. For instance, yourself, Eva, Ida, Van Helderen, and Mrs. Rantzow. The doctor is not sympathetic, neither is Eldersma. De Bruijn and I will relieve you."

"Off we go, then!" said Eva. "A new diversion for Labuwangi society. And no cheating. . . ."

"We must give one another our word of honor, as friends, not to cheat."

"Done," they all said.

The doctor snickered. Eldersma shrugged his shoulders. A boy brought a teapoy. They sat round the little wooden table and placed their fingers on it lightly, looking at one another expectantly and suspiciously. Mrs. Rantzow was solemn, Eva amused, Ida somber, Van Helderen smilingly indifferent. Suddenly a strained expression appeared on Ida's beautiful *nonna* face.

The table quivered. . . .

They exchanged frightened glances, the doctor snickered.

Then, slowly, the table lifted one of its three legs and carefully put it back down again.

"Did anybody move?" asked Eva.

They all shook their heads. Ida had turned pale.

"I feel a trembling in my fingers," she murmured.

The table once more lifted a leg, described an angry, grating semicircle over the marble floor and put its leg down with a violent bang.

They looked at one another in surprise. Ida sat as though bereft of life, staring, with fingers outspread, ecstatic.

And the table tilted a leg for the third time.

It was certainly very curious. Eva suspected for a moment that Mrs. Rantzow was lifting the table, but, when she questioned her with a glance, the German doctor's wife shook her head and Eva saw that she was not lying. They once more promised absolute honesty. And, when they were now certain of one another, in full confidence, it was most curious how the table continued to describe angry, grating semicircles, raising a leg and tapping on the marble floor.

"Is there a spirit present, revealing itself?" asked Mrs. Rantzow, with a glance at the leg of the table.

The table tapped once: "Yes." But, when the spirit was asked to spell its name, to tap out the letters of its name with the alphabet, all that came was "Z X R S A."

The manifestation was incomprehensible.

Suddenly, however, the table began spelling hurriedly, as if it were pursued. The taps were counted and spelled:

"Le . . . onie Ou . . . dijck. . . ."

"What about Mrs. Van Oudijck?"

A coarse word followed.

The ladies started, except Ida, who sat as if in a trance.

"The table has spoken. What did it say? What is Mrs. Van Oudijck?" cried the voices, all speaking at once.

"It's incredible!" murmured Eva. "Are we all playing fair?"

They all protested their honesty.

"Let us really be honest, else there's no fun in it. . . . I wish I could be certain."

They all wished that: Mrs. Rantzow, Ida, Van Helderen, Eva. The others looked on eagerly, believing, but the doctor did not believe and sat there snickering.

Again the table grated angrily and tapped, and the leg repeated:

"A . . ."

And the leg repeated the coarse word.

"Why?" asked Mrs. Rantzow.

The table began to tap.

"Write it down, Onno!" said Eva to her husband.

Eldersma fetched a pencil and paper and wrote it down.

Three names followed: one of a member of the Council of the Indies, one of a departmental head, one of a young businessman.

"When people aren't backbiting in the Indies, the tables begin to backbite!" said Eva.

"The spirits," murmured Ida.

"These are generally mocking spirits," said Mrs. Rantzow, didactically.

But the table went on tapping.

"Take it down, Onno!" said Eva.

Eldersma wrote it down.

"A-d-d-y!" the leg tapped out.

"No!" the voices all cried together, in vehement denial. "This time the table's mistaken! . . . At least, young De Luce has never yet been mentioned in connection with Mrs. Van Oudijck."

"T-h-e-o!" said the table, correcting itself.

"Her stepson! It's terrible! That's different! Everybody knows it!" cried the voices in assent.

"But we know that!" said Mrs. Rantzow, with a glance at the leg of the table. "Come, tell us something we don't know. Come on, table! Come on, spirit! Please! . . ."

She addressed the table leg sweetly, trying to coax it. Everybody laughed. The table grated.

"Be serious!" Mrs. Doorn de Bruijn warned.

The table bumped against Ida's lap.

"*Adu!*" cried the pretty *nonna*, waking out of her trance. "Right against my stomach!"

They laughed and laughed. The table turned round fiercely and they rose from their chairs, with their hands on the table, and accompanied its angry, waltzing movements.

"Next . . . year," the table rapped out.

Eldersma wrote it down.

"Frightful . . . war. . . ."

"Between whom? . . ."

"Europe . . . and . . . China."[46]

"It sounds like a fairy tale!" grinned the doctor.

"La . . . bu . . . wangi," tapped the table.

"What about it?" they asked.

"Is . . . a . . . hole. . . ."

"Say something serious, table, do!" Mrs. Rantzow implored pleasantly, in her best German-matron manner.

"Dan . . . ger," tapped the table.

"Where?"

"Threat . . . ens," the table continued, "La . . . bu . . . wangi."

"Danger threatens Labuwangi?"

"Yes!" the table tapped once, angrily.

"What danger?"

"Rebellion. . . ."

"Rebellion? Who's going to rebel?"

"In . . . two months . . . Sunario."

They became thoughtful.

But the table, suddenly, unexpectedly, banged against Ida's lap again.

"*Adu! Adu!*" she cried.

The table refused to go on.

"Tired . . ." it tapped out.

They continued to hold their hands on it.

"Stop it . . ." tapped the table.

The doctor, snickering, put his short, broad hand on it, as though to compel it.

"Go to hell!" cried the table, grating and turning. "Creep!"

And worse words followed, aimed at the doctor, as if said by a bum: obscene words, senseless and incoherent.

"Who's suggesting those words?" asked Eva, indignantly.

Obviously, no one was suggesting them—neither the three ladies nor Van Helderen, who was always very punctilious and who was manifestly indignant at the mocking spirit's coarseness.

"It really is a spirit," said Ida, looking very pale.

"I'm going to stop," said Eva, nervously, lifting her fingers. "I don't understand this nonsense. It's quite amusing, but the table's not accustomed to polite society."

"We've got a new resource for Labuwangi!" said Eldersma. "No more picnics, no dances . . . but table-turning!"

"We must practice!" said Mrs. Doorn de Bruijn.

Eva shrugged her shoulders.

"It's inexplicable," she said. "I believe that nobody was cheating. It's not the sort of thing Van Helderen would do, to suggest words like those."

"Madam!" said Van Helderen, defending himself.

"We must do it again," said Ida. "Look there's a *hadji* leaving the grounds."

She pointed to the garden.

"A *hadji*?" asked Eva.

She looked toward the garden. There was nothing.

"Oh no, it's not!" said Ida. "I thought it was a *hadji*. It's nothing, only the moonlight."

It was late. They said goodnight, laughing gaily, wondering, but finding no explanation.

"I do hope this hasn't made you ladies nervous?" said the doctor.

No, considering all things, they were not nervous. They were more amused, even though they did not understand.

It was two o'clock when they went home. The moonlight was streaming down on the town, which lay deathly silent, slumbering in the velvet shadows of the gardens.

10

Next day, when Eldersma had gone to the office and Eva was being domestic in *sarong* and *kabaii*, she saw Frans van Helderen coming through the garden.

"May I?" he called out.

"Certainly," she called back. "Come in. But I'm on my way to the *gudang.*"

And she held up her key basket.

"I'm due at the resident's in half an hour, but I'm too early . . . so I came by."

She smiled.

"But I'm busy, you know!" she said. "Come along to the *gudang.*"

He followed her: he was wearing a black lustre jacket, because he had to go to the resident.

"How's Ida?" asked Eva. "Did she sleep well after the séance last night?"

"So-so," said Frans van Helderen. "I don't think she ought to do it any more. She kept waking up frightened, embraced me, and begged me to forgive her, I don't know what for."

"It didn't upset me at all," said Eva, "although I don't understand it in the least."

She opened the *gudang*, called the *kokkie*, and gave the woman her orders. The *kokkie* was *latta*, and Eva loved to tease the old woman.[47]

"La . . . la-illa-lala!" she cried.

And the *kokkie* jumped, repeated the cry, and recovered herself the next moment, begging for forgiveness.

"*Buang, kokkie, buang!*" cried Eva.

And the *kokkie*, acting on the suggestion, flung down a tray of *rambutans* and *mangistans*, and, at once recovering, stooped and picked up the scattered fruits from the floor, imploring to be forgiven and shaking her head and clicking her tongue.[48]

"Come, we'd better go!" said Eva to Frans, "or she'll be breaking my eggs in a minute. *Ajo, kokkie, kluar!*"

"*Ajo, kluar!*" repeated the *latta* cook. "*Alla, njonja, minta ampon, njonja, alla sudah, njonja!*"[49]

"Come and sit down for a while," said Eva.

He followed her.

"You're so cheerful," he said.

"Aren't you?"

"No, I've been feeling sad lately."

"I too. I told you so yesterday. It's something in the Labuwangi air. There's no telling what this table-turning has in store for us."

They sat down on the back verandah. He sighed.

"What's the matter?" she asked.

"I can't help it," he said. "I like you, I love you."

She was silent for a moment.

"Again?" she said, reproachfully.

He did not answer.

"I told you, mine is not a passionate nature. I am cold. I love my husband and my child. Let's be friends, Van Helderen."

"I'm fighting it, but it's no use."

"I'm fond of Ida, I don't want to make her unhappy for anything in the world."

"I don't think I ever loved her."

"Van Helderen. . . ."

"If I did, it was only for her pretty face. But, white though Ida may be, she's a *nonna*. With her whimsies and her childish little tragedies. I didn't see it so much at first, but I do now. I've met European women before you, but you were a revelation to me, a revelation of all the charm and artistic grace that a woman can possess. . . . And the exotic side in you appeals to my own exotic nature."

"I value your friendship highly. Let's leave it at that."

"It's crazy, but sometimes I dream . . . that we're traveling in Europe together, that we're in Italy or Paris. Sometimes I see us sitting together by a fire, in a room of our own, you talking about art, I about the modern, social developments of our time. But, after that, I see us more intimately."

"Van Helderen. . . ."

"It doesn't matter if you warn me anymore. I love you, Eva, Eva. . . ."

"I don't think that there's another country where there's so much love going on as in the Indies. It must be the heat. . . ."

"Don't destroy me with your sarcasm. No other woman ever appealed so much to my entire body and soul as you do, Eva. . . ."

She shrugged her shoulders.

"Don't be angry, Van Helderen, but I can't stand those commonplaces. Let's be sensible. I have a charming husband, you have a sweet wife. We're all good friends together."

"You're so cold."

"I don't want to spoil the happiness of our friendship."

"Friendship!"

"Friendship is what I said. There is nothing I value so highly, except my domestic happiness. I couldn't live without friends. I am happy with my husband and my child, but I also need friends."

"So that they can admire you, so that you can rule over them," he said, angrily.

She looked at him.

"Perhaps," she said, coolly. "Perhaps I need to be admired and to rule over others. We all have our weaknesses."

"I have mine," he said, bitterly.

"Come," she said, in a kinder tone, "let's remain friends."

"I am terribly unhappy," he said, in a dull voice. "I feel as if I had missed everything in life. I have never been out of Java and I feel there's something lacking in me because I have never seen ice and snow. Snow. . . . I think of it as a sort of mysterious, unknown purity, which I long for, but which I never seem to meet. When shall I see Europe? When will I stop raving about *Il Trovatore* and manage to get to Bayreuth? When will I get to you, Eva? I keep on reaching for things as if with antennae, like a wingless insect. . . . What kind of life do I have? With Ida, with three children who will look like their mother, I shall remain a controller for years and then—perhaps—be promoted to assistant resident . . . and that'll be it. And then at last they'll let me go—or I'll ask for it—and go live in Sukabumi, to vegetate on a small pension.[50] Everything in me is longing for idleness. . . ."

"But you like your work, you're a first-rate official. Eldersma always says that in the Indies a man who doesn't work and who doesn't love his work is lost."

"Your nature is not made for love and mine is not made for work, nothing but work. I can work toward a beautiful goal, but I can't work . . . just for the sake of work and to fill the emptiness of my life."

"Your goal is the Indies. . . ."

"A fine phrase," he said. "It may be so for a man like the resident, who has succeeded in his career and who never has to study the *Colonial List* and figure on the illness of this man or the death of that man . . . so that he'll be promoted. It's all right for a man like Van Oudijck, who, in his idealistic honesty thinks that his aim is the Indies, not because of Holland, but because of the Indies themselves, because of the native whom he, the official, protects against the tyranny of the landlords and planters. I am more cynical by nature. . . ."

"But don't be so lukewarm about the Indies. It's not merely a fine phrase, I feel like that myself. The Indies are our whole greatness, the greatness of us Hollanders. Listen to foreigners speaking about the Indies, they are all enchanted with their glory, with our methods of colonization. . . . Don't have anything to do with that miserable Dutch spirit of our people at home, who know nothing about the Indies, who always sneer at them, who are so petty and stiff and bourgeois and narrowminded. . . ."⁵¹

"I didn't know that you were so enthusiastic about the Indies. Only yesterday you felt afraid here and I was defending my country. . . ."

"Oh, it makes me shudder, the mystery in the evenings, when something seems to threaten, but I don't know what. I'm afraid of the future, there's some danger ahead of us. . . . I feel that I, personally, am still very remote from the Indies, though I don't want to be. I miss the art that I grew up with, and I miss it in our lives here, the line of beauty which both my parents always exposed me to. . . . But I am not unjust. And I think that, as our colony, the Indies are great, I think that we, in our colony, are great. . . ."

"Formerly, perhaps, but now everything is going wrong, nowadays, we are no longer great. You have an artistic nature, and you are always looking for the artistic in the Indies, though you seldom find it. And then your mind is confronted with that greatness, that glory. That's the poetry of it, but the prose is a gigantic but exhausted colony, still governed from Holland with one idea: to make a profit. The reality is not the Indies under a great ruler, but the Indies under a petty, mean bloodsucker; the country sucked dry, and the real population—not the Hollander, who spends his colonial money in The Hague, but the population, the native population, attached to the native soil—oppressed by the disdain of its overlord, who once improved it with his own blood, is now threatening to revolt against this oppression and disdain. . . . You, as an artist, feel the danger approaching, vaguely, like a cloud in the sky, in the tropical night; I see the danger as something very real, something arising—for Holland—if not from America and Japan, then from the soil of this country itself."⁵²

She smiled.

"I like you when you talk like that," she said. "I might end up agreeing with you."

"If I could achieve *that* by talking!" he laughed, bitterly, and got up. "My half hour is over: the resident is expecting me and he doesn't like waiting. Good-bye, and forgive me."

"Tell me," she said, "am I a flirt?"

"No," he replied. "You are what you are. And I can't help it: I love you. . . . I'm always stretching out my poor antennae. That is my fate. . . ."

"I shall help you to forget me," said she, with affectionate conviction. He laughed a little, bowed, and went away. She saw him cross the road to the grounds of the resident's house, where an *oppasser* met him.

"When all is said and done, life is one long self-deception, a wandering amid illusions," she thought sadly and despondently. "A great aim, a universal aim . . . or even a modest aim for one's self, for one's own body and soul. . . . O God, how paltry everything is! And how we wander around without knowing anything. And each of us seeks his own small aim, his illusion. The only happy people are exceptions like Léonie van Oudijck, who lives no different from a beautiful flower, or a beautiful animal."

Her child came toddling up to her, a pretty, blond, plump little boy.

"My little darling," she thought, "what's going to happen to you? What will be your share? Perhaps nothing new, perhaps a repetition of what has so often been before. Life is a novel which is always being repeated. . . . Oh, when we feel like this, how oppressive the Indies can be."

She kissed her boy, and her tears fell into his fair curls.

"Van Oudijck has his residency, I have my little circle of . . . admirers and subjects, Frans has his love . . . for me. . . . We all have our playthings, just like my little Onno playing with his little horse. How small we are, how small! . . . All our lives, we make believe, imagine all sorts of things, think to give direction to our poor, aimless little lives. Oh, why am I like this, my little darling? And what's in store for you?"

11

The Patjaram sugar factory was fourteen miles from Labuwangi and twelve from Ngadjiwa and belonged to the half-Indo, half-Solo family of De Luce, a family who had once been millionaires, but who were no longer so well off, owing to the recent sugar crisis, though they still supported a numerous household. This family always kept together—the old mother and grandmother, a Solo princess; the eldest son, who was the manager; three married daughters and their husbands, clerks in the factory, all living in its shadow; three younger sons employed in the factory; the countless grandchildren who played round and about the factory; the great-grandchildren springing up round and about the factory—this family maintained the old Indies traditions which, at one time universal, are now becoming rarer thanks to the more frequent contact with Europeans. The mother and grand-mother was the daughter of a Solo prince, and had married a young and enterprising bohemian adventurer, Ferdinand de Luce,[53] a member of a French titled family in Mauritius, who, after wandering about for many years in search of his place in the sun, had sailed to the Indies as a ship's steward and, after all sorts of vicissitudes, had found himself stranded in Solo, where he had achieved fame through a dish prepared with tomatoes and another consisting of stuffed *lomboks*. Thanks to these recipes, Ferdinand de Luce won the favor of the Solo prince whose daughter he later married, and even gained the confidence of the old susuhunan. After his marriage he became a landowner and, according to Solo *adat*,[54] a vassal of the susuhunan whom he supplied daily with rice and fruits for the household of the *dalem*. Then he got into sugar, divining the millions which a lucky fate held in store for him. He had died before the crisis, laden with wealth and honors.

The old grandmother, in whom there was not a trace left of the young princess whom Ferdinand de Luce had wedded to promote his fortunes, was always approached by the servants and the Javanese staff with cringing reverence, and everybody accorded her the title of radèn-aju pangéran. She did not speak a word of Dutch. Wrinkled like a shriveled fruit, with clouded eyes and a withered, *sirih*-stained mouth, she was peacefully living her last years, always dressed in a dark silk *kabaai*, with the neck and the light sleeves fastened with precious stones. Before her yellowed gaze there hovered the vision of her former *dalem* grandeur, which she had abandoned for love of that French nobleman-cook who had pandered to her father's taste with his dainty recipes; in her ears buzzed the constant murmur of the centrifugal separators, like the screws of steamers, throughout the milling season, lasting for months on end; around her were her children, grandchildren, and great-grand-children: the sons and daughters addressed as radèn and radèn-adjeng by the servants; all of them still surrounded by the pale halo of their Solo descent. The eldest daughter was married to a full-blooded, blond Dutchman, the son who came after her married an Armenian girl, the two other girls were married to Indos, both brown, and their brown children—who were also married and also had children—mingled with the blond family of the eldest daughter, but the pride of the whole fam-ily was the youngest son and brother, Adrian, or Addy, who courted Doddy van Oudijck and who was constantly in Labuwangi, the busy milling season notwithstanding.

In this family, traditions were still maintained that were now quite obsolete, traditions people remembered from Indies families of long ago. Here you still saw, in the grounds, on the back verandah, the num-berless *babus,* one rubbing *bedak* into a fine powder, another preparing *dupa,* another pounding *sambal,* all with dreamy eyes, all with slender, nimbly moving fingers. Here the habit still prevailed of an endless array of dishes at the *rijsttafel,* with a long row of servants, one after the other, solemnly handing round one more vegetable, one more *lodèh,* one more dish of chicken, while, squatting behind the ladies, the *babus* pounded *sambal* in an earthenware mortar, according to the several tastes and requirements of the sated palates. Here it was still the custom, when the family attended the races at Ngadjiwa, for each of the ladies to appear followed by a *babu,* moving slowly, lithely, solemnly, one *babu* carry-ing a *bedak* pot, another a *bonbonnière* filled with peppermints, or a pair of binoculars, or a fan, or a scent bottle—the whole resembling a ceremonial procession bearing the insignia of state. Here, too, you still found the old-fashioned hospitality: the row of spare rooms ready for anyone who cared to knock; here everybody could stay as long as they pleased and no one was ever asked the object of his journey or the date of departure. A great simplicity of mind, an all-embracing, spontane-ous, innate cordiality provided, together with an unbounded weariness and tedium, a life of no ideas and but few words, the ready, gentle smile making good the lack of both. Material life was full and sated, a life of cool drinks and *kwee kwees* and *rudjak* handed round all day, three *babus* being specially appointed to make *rudjak* and *kwee kwees.* Any number of animals were scattered over the estate: there was a cage full of monkeys, a few parrots, dogs, cats, some tame squirrels, and a *kantjil,* an exquisite little deer which ran about loose. The house, built onto the factory, groaning during the milling season with the sound of machinery—the noise like the screw of a steamer—was spacious and furnished with the old, old-fashioned furniture: the low wooden bedsteads with four carved bedposts hung with mosquito nets, the tables with heavy legs, the rocking chairs with peculiarly round backs, all things that are now no longer obtainable, everything without the slightest touch of modernity, except—and only during the milling season—the electric light on the front verandah! The occupants were always in indoor dress: the men in white or blue-and-white, the ladies in *sarong* and *kabaai,* toying with a monkey or parrot or *kantjil,* with utter simplicity, with ever the same pleasant jest, drawling and slow, and the same gentle little laugh. The passions, which were certainly there, slumbered, in that gentle smile. Then—when the milling season was over, when all the bustle was over, when the files of sugar carts, drawn by the superb *sappis* with glossy brown hides, had brought an ever increasing amount of sugar cane over the *ampas*-covered road, which was cut to pieces by the broad cart ruts, when the *bibit* had been bought for next year and the machines were stopped—at that time came the sudden relaxation after the incessant labor, the long, long holiday, the many months' rest, the craving for festivity and enjoyment. There was the big dinner given by the lady of the house, followed by a ball and *tableaux-vivants;*[55] the whole house full of visitors, both known and unknown, who stayed on and on; the old, wrinkled grandmamma, the lady of the house, the radèn-aju, Mrs. De Luce, whatever you liked to call her, amiable with her clouded eyes and her *sirih* mouth, amiable to one and all, with always an *anak mas,* a "golden child" (a poor little adopted princess) at her heels, carrying a gold *sirih* box behind the great princess from Solo.[56] The child was a little eight-year-old girl, her hair in front cut into a fringe, her forehead whitened with moist *bedak,* her already rounded little breasts confined under the little pink silk *kabaai,* with the miniature gold *sarong* round the slender hips, a doll, a toy for the radèn-aju, for Mrs. De Luce, for the dowager De Luce. And for the *kampongs* there were the popular rejoicings, a time-honored lavishness, which all Patjaram shared, according to the secular tradition which was always observed, despite crisis or unrest.

Both the milling season and the rejoicings were now over. There was comparative peace indoors, and a languorous Indies calm had set in. But Mrs. Van Oudijck, Theo, and Doddy had come over for the festivities and were staying on a few days longer. A great circle of people sat round the marble table covered with glasses of syrup, lemonade, and whiskey and soda; they did not speak much, but rocked contentedly, exchanging an occasional word. Mrs. De Luce and Mrs. Van Oudijck spoke Malay, but did not say much. A gentle, good-humored boredom drifted down on all those rocking people. It was strange to see the different types: the pretty, milk-white Léonie beside the yellow, wrinkled radèn-aju dowager; Theo, pale and blond as a Dutchman, with his full, sensual lips, which he had inherited from his *nonna* mother; Doddy, already looking like a ripe rose, with the sparkling irises and black pupils in her dark eyes; the manager's son, Achille de Luce, brown, tall, and stout, whose thoughts were only concerned with his machinery and his *bibit;* the second son, Roger, brown, short, and thin, the bookkeeper, who was only thinking about the year's profits, with his little Armenian wife; the eldest daughter, old already—brown, stupid, ugly—with her full-blooded Dutch husband, who looked like a peasant; the other sons and daughters, in every shade of brown and not easily distinguished one from the other; around them the children, the grandchildren, the little, golden adopted children, the *babus,* the parrots, and the *kantjil.* And over all these people, children, and animals, as though shaken down upon them, was a kindly solidarity, while they also shared a common pride in their Solo ancestors, crowning their heads with the pale halo of Javanese aristocracy, and the Armenian daughter-in-law and the boorish Dutch son-in-law were perhaps the proudest of this heritage.

The liveliest of all these elements, which had commingled, as it were, through long communal life under the patriarchal roofs, was the youngest son, Adrien de Luce, Addy, in whom the blood of the Solo princess and that of the French adventurer had blended harmoniously. It had not given him any brains, but it had given him the physical beauty of a young *sinjo,* with something of the Moor about it, something southern and seductive, something Spanish, as though in this last child the two alien racial elements had for the first time mingled harmoniously, for the first time been wedded in absolute mutual knowledge, as though in him, this last child after so many children, adventurer and princess had for the first time met in harmony. Addy did not seem to possess a modicum of intellect or imagination, and was incapable of uniting two ideas into one composite thought. He merely felt, with that vague good nature that had settled on the entire family. For the rest, he was like a beautiful animal, degenerate in soul and brain, but degenerated to nothing, to one great nothing, to one great emptiness, while his body had become like a renewal of race, full of strength and beauty, while his marrow, his blood, his flesh, and his muscles had become one harmony of physical seductiveness, so perfectly and stupidly beautiful, that its harmony had for a woman an immediate appeal. The boy had only to appear, like a beautiful, southern god, and all the women would look at him and take him down into the depths of their imagination, only to recall him mentally again and again. The boy had but to go to a ball in Ngadjiwa for all the girls to fall in love with him. He plucked love where he found it, and it was particularly plentiful in the Patjaram *kampongs*. And everything feminine was in love with him, from his mother down to his little nieces. Doddy van Oudijck was crazy about him. From the day she was seven she had been in love hundreds of times, with anybody who passed before her flashing eyes, but never as much in love as with Addy. Her love shone so strongly from her whole being that it was like a flame that everybody noticed and smiled at. The milling feast had been to her one long delight . . . when she danced with him, and one long torture . . . when he danced with others. He had not asked her to marry him, but she thought of asking *him* and was prepared to die if he refused. She knew that the resident, her father, would object. He did not like those De Luces, that Solo-French crew, as he called them, but, if Addy was willing, her father would consent rather than see her die. To this child of love that lovable boy was the world, the universe, was life itself. He courted her, he kissed her on the lips, but this was no more than he did to others, unthinkingly; he kissed other girls as well. And, if he could, he went further, like a devastating young god, an unthinking god. But he was still a little awed by the resident's daughter. He had neither courage nor effrontery, his passions were not markedly selective, he looked on a woman as a woman and was so much sated with conquest that obstacles did not stimulate him. His garden was full of flowers which all lifted themselves up to him; he stretched out his hand, almost without looking, he merely plucked.

As they sat rocking around the table, they saw him come through the garden, and the eyes of all the women were drawn to him as to a young tempter, stepping out of the sunshine, and surrounded him as with a halo. The radèn-aju dowager smiled and gazed at him, enamored of her youngest son, her favorite. Squatting on the floor behind her, the little golden adopted child stared with wide-open eyes, the sisters looked, the little nieces looked, Doddy turned pale, and Léonie van Oudijck's milky complexion became tinged with a rosy shade which mingled with the glamour of her smile. She automatically glanced at Theo, and their eyes met. And these souls of sheer love, love of the eyes, of the lips, love of the glowing flesh, understood each other, and Theo's jealousy burnt so fiercely that her rosy shade died away and she became pale and fearful, with a sudden, unreasoning fear which shuddered through her usual indifference, while the tempter, in his halo of sunshine, came nearer and nearer. . . .

12

Mrs. Van Oudijck had promised to stay in Patjaram a few days longer, and she rather disliked the prospect because she did not feel quite at home in these old-fashioned surroundings. But when Addy appeared she thought better of it. In the deepest secrecy of her heart this woman worshipped her sensuality as if in the temple of her egoism, and the milky white Creole offered up the most intimate dreams of her rosy imagination and unquenchable longing. In this cult she had achieved, as it were, an art, a knowledge, a science, that of deciding for herself at a glance what it was that attracted her in the man who approached her, in the man who passed by her. In one it was his bearing or his voice, in another it was the way his hand rested on his knee. But whatever it was, she saw it directly, at a glance, she knew it instantly, she had judged the passerby in an indivisible second, and she knew at once whom she rejected—and they were the majority—and whom she approved—and they were many. And those whom she rejected in that indivisible moment of her supreme judgment, with that single glance, in that single instant, didn't need to entertain any hope. She, the priestess, did not admit them to the temple. To the others, the temple was open, but only behind the curtain of her rectitude. However shameless, she was always correct, her love was always secret; to the world, she was nothing but the charming, smiling wife of the resident, a little indolent in her ways, but winning everybody with her smile. When people did not see her, they spoke ill of her, but when they saw her, she conquered them immediately. Among those with whom she shared the secret of her love there was a kind of freemasonry, a mystery of worship; when two of them met, they would scarcely whisper a word or two about a similar recollection. And Léonie could sit there smiling, milky white, tranquil in the great circle around a marble table, with at least two or three men who knew the secret. It did not disturb her tranquillity nor mar her smile. She smiled to the point of boredom. Her glance would barely glide from one to the other, while she judged them once again, with her infallible judgment. Scarcely would the memories of past hours rise hazily within her, scarcely would she think of the assignation for the following day. The secret lay wholly in the mystery of the meeting and indeed was never uttered before the profane world. If a foot in the circle sought to touch her foot, she drew hers away. She never flirted, she was sometimes even a little boring, stiff, correct, smiling. In the freemasonry between her and the initiated, she unveiled the mystery, but before the world, in the circles about the marble tables, she vouchsafed not a glance, not a pressure of the hand or knee, nor did her dress ever incline to a trouser leg.

She had been bored during those days in Patjaram. She had accepted the invitation to the milling feast only because she had refused it in past years. But now that she saw Addy approaching she was bored no longer. Of course she had known him for years, and she had seen him grow from a child into a boy, into a man, and she had even kissed him as a boy. She had long ago judged him, the tempter. But now, as he approached with his halo of sunshine, she judged him once more: his comely, slender sensuality and the glow of his tempter's eyes in the shadowy brown of his young Moorish face, the curve of his lips meant only for kissing, with the young down of his mustache; the feline strength and litheness of his Don Juan limbs: it all dazzled her, made her blink her eyes. While he greeted his mother's visitors and sat down, casting a gaiety of words around that circle of languid conversation and drowsy thoughts—as though he were casting a handful of his sunshine, of the gold dust of his temptation over them all, over all those women, mother and sisters and nieces and Doddy and Léonie—Léonie looked at him, as they all looked at him, and her eyes slipped down to his hands. She could have kissed those hands, she suddenly became smitten with the shape of the fingers, with the brown, tiger strength of the palms: she suddenly became smitten with the wild young animal vigor which breathed like a fragrance of manhood from his boyish frame. She felt her blood throbbing, almost uncontrollably, despite her great art of remaining cool and correct in the circles around the marble tables. She was no longer bored. She had an object to fill the days that were coming. Only . . . her blood throbbed so violently that Theo had noticed her blush and the quivering of her eyelids. Enamored of her as he was, his eyes had penetrated her soul. And, when they rose to go to lunch on the back verandah, where the *babus* had already squatted to crush everybody's different *ulek* with pestles and mortars, he whispered two words between his teeth:

"Take care!"

She started; she felt that he was threatening her. This had never happened before; all who had shared in the mystery had always respected her. She started so violently, she was so indignant at this wrenching away of the temple curtain—on a verandah full of people—that her tranquil indifference seethed with anger and she was roused to rebellion despite her ever serene self-mastery. But she looked at him and she saw him, broad and tall and blond, a young version of her husband, his Indies blood showing only in his sensual mouth. And she did not want to lose him; she wanted to keep his type beside the type of the Moorish tempter. She wanted them both; she wanted to taste the difference between their male charms, the difference between the white-skinned Dutch type, which had only slightly been influenced by the Indies, and Addy's wild, animal type. Her soul quivered, her blood thrilled, while the endless array of dishes were solemnly handed round. She was in such a state as she had never experienced before. The awakening from her placid indifference was like a rebirth, like an unknown emotion. She was surprised to be thirty and to feel this for the first time. A feverish depravity blossomed up within her, as though bursting into intoxicating red flowers. She looked at Doddy, sitting beside Addy: the poor child, glowing with love, was hardly able to eat. . . . Oh, the tempter, who had only to appear! . . . And Léonie, in that fever of depravity, rejoiced at being the rival of a stepdaughter so many years younger than she was. She would look after her, she would even warn Van Oudijck. Would it ever come to a wedding? What did she care: what harm could marriage do to her, Léonie? Oh, the tempter! Never had she dreamt of him thus, the supreme lover, in her rosy hours of siesta! This was no charm of little cherubs; this was the strong scent of tiger enchantment: the golden glitter of his eyes, the sinewy litheness of his stealthy claw. . . . And she smiled at Theo, with just one glance of self-surrender, a very exceptional thing in this circle of people eating rice. As a rule, she never surrendered herself in public. Now she surrendered herself for a moment, because she was pleased by his jealousy. She was madly in love with him. She thought it delightful that he should look pale and angry with jealousy. And round about her the afternoon was one blaze of sunlight and the *sambal* stung her dry palate. Faint beads of perspiration stood on her forehead and pearled down her breasts under the lace of her *kabaai*. And she would have liked to have held them both, Theo and Addy, in one embrace, in one commingling of different passions, pressing them both to her amorous body. . . .

13

The night was like a veil of softest velvet wafting slowly from the heavens. The moon, in its first quarter, displayed a very narrow, horizontal sickle, like a Turkish crescent, between whose points the unlit portion of the disk was faintly traced against the sky. A long avenue of *tjemara* trees stretched in front of the house, their trunks straight, their leafage like tattered plush or raveled velvet, showing like balls of cotton against the clouds, which, drifting low, announced the approaching rainy monsoon fully a month in advance. Wood pigeons cooed at times and a *tokkè* was calling, first with two rattling, preliminary notes, as though tuning up, then with his call of *"Tokkè! Tokkè!"* four or five times repeated, first loudly, then submissively and more faintly.

A *gardu*, in his hut in front of the house on the main road, where the sleeping *pasar* now showed its empty stalls, struck eleven wooden blows on his *tong-tong* and, when a last, belated cart drove past, he cried in a hoarse voice: *"Werr-da?"*

The night was like softest velvet wafting slowly down from the heavens, like a whirling mystery, like an oppressive menace of the future. But, in that mystery, under the rent black cotton, the tattered plush of the *tjemaras,* there was an inexorable hankering for love, in the windless night, like a whisper that this hour should not be wasted. True, the *tokkè* was heckling like a mocking imp with a dry kind of humor; and the *gardu,* with his *"Werda!"* was startling, but the wood pigeons cooed softly and the whole night was like a down of softest velvet, like a great alcove curtained by the plush of the *tjemaras,* while the distant, sultry rain clouds, hanging all that month from the horizon, ringed the skies with an oppressive magic. Mystery and enchantment hovered in the down night, wafting down in the twilit alcove, and dissolved thinking, if not the very soul, leaving only a warm sensuous vision. . . .

The *tokkè* fell silent, the *gardu* fell asleep, the downy night reigned like an enchantress crowned with the sickle of the moon. They came walking slowly, two youthful figures, their arms around each other's waists, lips seeking lips under the tyranny of the enchantment. They were as shadows under the tattered velvet of the *tjemaras,* and softly, in their white garments, they disclosed themselves like the eternal pair of lovers who are forever and everywhere repeating themselves. And especially here the lovers were inevitable in the enchanted night, one with the night, conjured up by the reigning enchantress, here they were inevitable, unfolding like a twin flower of predestined love, in the velvet mystery of the compelling heavens.

And the tempter seemed to be the son of that night, the son of that inexorable queen of the night, bearing with him the tender girl. In her ears the night seemed to sing with his voice, and her small soul melted her tender weakness to the brim, under the magic powers. She walked in contact with his side, feeling the warmth of his body penetrate her yearning maidenhood, and she lifted her brimming gaze to him, with the languid light of her sparkling pupils glittering like a diamond in her irises. He, drunk with the power of the night, the enchantress, who was like his mother, thought first of leading her still further, no longer thinking of reality, no longer feeling any awe of her, no longer afraid of anyone—thought to lead her on, past the slumbering *gardu*, across the main road, into the *kampong*, which lay hidden between the stately plumes of the coconut palms that would form a canopy for their love— to lead her to a hideout, a house that he knew, a bamboo hut they would open for him, when suddenly she stopped, startled. And she gripped his arm and pressed herself still more tightly against him and implored him to go no further. She was frightened.

"Why not?" he asked gently, in his soft voice, which was as deep and velvety as the night. "Why not tonight, tonight at last? There is no danger."

But she shuddered and shook and entreated:

"Addy, Addy, no . . . no . . . I don't dare go any further. . . . I'm frightened that the *gardu* will see us . . . and then . . . there's a *hadji* walking over there . . . in a white turban. . . ."

He looked down the road. On the other side waited the *kampong* under the canopy of the palms, with the bamboo hut that would be opened to him. . . .

"A *hadji*? . . . Where, Doddy? I don't see anybody. . . ."

"He crossed the road, he looked back at us, he saw us. I saw his eyes gleaming, and he went into the *kampong*, behind those trees."

"Darling, I saw nothing, there's no one there."

"Yes, there is! Yes, there is! Addy, I don't dare, let's go back!"

His handsome Moorish face darkened; he already saw the door of the little hut opened by the old woman he knew, who worshipped him as every woman worshipped him from his mother down to his little nieces.

And he again tried to persuade her, but she refused, stood still, would not budge. Then they turned back and the clouds were sultrier, low on the horizon, and the nightdown was thicker, like warm snow, and the tattered *tjemaras* were fuller and blacker than before. The house loomed up before them, sunk in sleep, with not a light showing. And he entreated her, he implored her not to leave him that night, saying that he would die, that night, without her.... Already she was yielding, promising, with her arms around his neck ... when again she was frightened and again cried:

"Addy! Addy!... There it is again!... That white figure!...."

"You appear to see *hadjis* everywhere!" he said mockingly.

"Look for yourself then ... over there!"

He looked and now he did see a white figure approaching them on the front verandah. But it was a woman.

"Mamma!" cried Doddy.

It was indeed Léonie, slowly coming toward them.

"Doddy," she said gently, "I have been hunting all over for you. I was so frightened, I didn't know where you were. Why do you go out walking so late? Addy," she continued gently, in kind, motherly tones, as though addressing two children, "how *can* you behave like this and be out with Doddy so late? You really mustn't do it again. I mean it! I know that there's nothing in it, but suppose somebody saw you! You must promise me *never* to do it again! You'll promise, won't you?"

She begged this prettily, in tones of engaging reproach, as though to show that she quite understood him, quite realized that they were yearning for each other in that velvet night of enchantment, forgiving them already with her choice of words. She looked like an angel, with her round, white face amidst loose, waving, blond hair, in the white silk kimono that hung round her in pliant folds. And she drew Doddy to her and kissed the girl and wiped away Doddy's tears. And then, gently, she pushed Doddy away, to her room in the annex, where she slept safely between so many other rooms full of the daughters and grandchildren of old Mrs. De Luce. And while Doddy, crying softly, went to the loneliness of her room, Léonie continued to speak words of gentle reproach to Addy, warning him, prettily now, as a sister might do, while he, brown and handsome, with his Moorish look, stood before her with shy bravado. They were in the dusk of the dark front verandah, and the night outside exhaled its inexorable breath of luxuriance, love, and velvet mystery. And she reproached him and warned him and said that Doddy was a child and that he should not take advantage of her. He shrugged his shoulders, defended himself, with his bravado, and his words fell upon her like gold dust, while his eyes glittered like a tiger's. While she argued that he really must spare Doddy in the future, she seized his hand —that hand she was in love with, his fingers, his palm, which she could have kissed that morning in her confusion—and she pressed it and almost cried and implored him to have mercy on Doddy. . . . He suddenly realized it; he looked at her with the lightning of his wild-animal glance, and he thought her beautiful, thought her a woman, white as milk, and he knew her for a priestess full of secret knowledge. And he too spoke about Doddy, coming closer to Léonie, touching her, pressing her hands between his two hands, giving her to understand that he understood. And, still pretending to weep and entreat and implore, she led him on and opened the door of her room. He saw a faint light and her maid Urip, who disappeared through the outer door and lay down to sleep there like a faithful dog, on a little mat. Then she gave him a laugh of welcome, and he, the tempter, was amazed at the glow of that laugh and this white, blond temptress, who flung her silken kimono to the ground and stood before him like a nude statue, spreading out her arms.

Outside, Urip listened for a moment. And she was about to lie down to sleep, smiling, dreaming of the lovely *sarongs* which the *kandjeng* would give her tomorrow, when she was startled as she saw walking over the grounds and disappearing in the night a *hadji* in a white turban. . . .

14

That day, the regent of Ngadjiwa, Sunario's younger brother, was to pay a visit in Patjaram, because Mrs. Van Oudijck was leaving on the following day. They were waiting for him on the front verandah, rocking in their chairs around the marble table, when his carriage came rattling down the long avenue of *tjemaras*. They all stood up. And now it appeared more plainly than ever how highly respected the old radèn-aju, the dowager, was and how closely related to the susuhunan himself, because the regent alighted and, without taking another step, squatted on the lowest step of the verandah, and salaamed respectfully, while behind his back a retainer, holding the closed gold-and-white *pajong* like a furled sun, made himself still smaller and shrank together as if to annihilate himself. And the old woman, the Solo princess, who saw the *dalem* shining before her eyes again, went up to him and welcomed the regent with all the courtesy inherent in the Javanese spoken at court—the language spoken among princely equals—till the regent rose, and, following her, approached the family circle. And the manner in which he then for the first time bowed to the wife of his resident, however polite, was almost condescending, compared with his obsequiousness of a moment ago. . . . He sat down between Mrs. De Luce and Mrs. Van Oudijck and began a leisurely conversation. The regent of Ngadjiwa was a different type from his brother Sunario, taller, coarser, without the other's look of a *wajang* puppet. Though younger, he looked the older of the two, his features hardened by passion, his eyes burned-out from passion: passion for women, for wine, for opium; the passion, above all, for gambling. And a silent thought seemed to flash up in that listless, slow conversation, with few words and no ideas, ever and again interrupted by the courtly *"Saja, saja,"* behind which they all concealed their secret longing. . . . They spoke Malay because Mrs. Van Oudijck did not dare speak Javanese, that refined, difficult language, full of shades of etiquette, which hardly a single Hollander would venture to use with Javanese persons of rank.[57] They spoke little, they rocked gently; a vague, courteous smile showed that all were taking part in the conversation, though only Mrs. De Luce and the regent exchanged an occasional word. . . . Until at last the De Luces—the old mother, her son Roger, her brown daughters-in-law—were no longer able to restrain themselves, not even in Mrs. Van Oudijck's presence, and laughed shyly while drinks and cake were handed round; until, notwithstanding their courtesy, they rapidly consulted one another, over

Léonie's head, in a few words of Javanese; until the old mother, no longer mistress of herself, at last asked her whether she would mind if they had a little game of cards. And they all looked at her, the wife of the resident, the wife of the high official who, they knew, hated the gambling which was their ruin, which was destroying the grandeur of the Javanese families whom he wished to uphold in spite of themselves. But she was too indifferent to think of preventing them for her husband's sake with a single word of tactful jest; she, the slave of her own passion, allowed them to be the slaves of theirs, in the luxury of their enslavement. She just smiled and readily permitted the players to withdraw to the wide, square inner gallery, the ladies, eagerly counting the money in their handkerchiefs, alternating with the men, until they sat down close together and, with their eyes on the cards or spying into one another's eyes, gambled and gambled endlessly, winning, losing, paying or receiving, opening and closing the handkerchiefs containing the money, with not a word, not a sound but the faint rustle of the cards in the shadows of the inner room. Were they playing *slikur* or *stoteren*?[58] Léonie did not know, did not care, indifferent to that passion and glad that Addy had remained beside her and that Theo was glaring at him jealously. Did he know, did he suspect anything? Would Urip always hold her tongue? She enjoyed the emotion, and she wanted them both, she wanted both white and brown; and the fact that Doddy was sitting on the other side of Addy and almost swooning as she rocked to and fro afforded her an acute and wicked delight. What else was there in life but to yield to one's luxurious cravings? She had no ambition, was indifferent to her exalted station; she, the first woman in the residency, who delegated all her duties to Eva Eldersma, who was quite unmoved when hundreds of people at the receptions in Labuwangi, Ngadjiwa, and elsewhere greeted her with a ceremony not far short of royal honors, who silently, in her rosy, perverse daydreams, with a novel by Catulle Mendès in her hands, laughed at that exaggeration of the provinces, where the wife of a resident can be a queen. She had no other ambition than to be loved by the men whom she selected, no other emotional life than the worship of her body, like an Aphrodite who choses to be her own priestess. What did she care if they played cards in there, if the regent of Ngadjiwa ruined himself completely! On the contrary, she thought it interesting to watch how the ruination etched itself in his face, and she would make sure that she'd be even more carefully groomed, to let Urip massage her face and limbs, to make Urip prepare even more of the white liquid *bedak*, the wonder cream, the magic salve of which Urip knew the secret and which kept her flesh firm and unwrinkled and white as a *mangistan*. She thought it exciting to see the regent of Ngadjiwa burning away like a candle, foolishly, brutalized by women, wine, opium, and cards, perhaps most of all by cards, by the dazed staring at cards, gambling, calculating chances that defied calculation, superstitiously calculating, reckoning by the science of the *petangans* the day and the hour when he should play in order to win, the number of the players, the amount of his stake. . . .[59] Now and then she furtively looked at the faces of the players, in the inner gallery darkened by dimness and the lust of gain, and reflected on what Van Oudijck would say, how angry he would be if she told him about it. . . . What did it matter to him if the regent's family ruined itself? What did his policy matter to her, what did the whole Dutch policy matter, which wants to secure the position of the Javanese nobility, through whom it governs the population? What did it matter to her that Van Oudijck, thinking of the noble old pangéran, felt grieved at his children's visible decline? None of it mattered to her; what mattered was only herself and Addy and Theo. She must really tell her stepson, her blond lover, that afternoon, not to be so jealous. It was becoming obvious, she was sure that Doddy noticed it. . . . Didn't she save the poor child yesterday? But how long would that yearning last? Hadn't she better warn Van Oudijck, like a kind, solicitous mother? . . . Her thoughts wandered languidly. It was a sultry morning, during those last, scorching days of the eastern monsoon, which covers the limbs with trickling moisture. Then her body quivered. And, leaving Doddy with Addy, she carried Theo off and reproached him for looking so savage with impotent jealousy. She pretended to be a little angry and asked him what he wanted.

They had gone to the side of the house, to the long side verandah, where there were monkeys in a cage, surrounded by the skins from the bananas which the animals had eaten, fed to them by the children.

The luncheon gong had already been struck twice, and the *babus* were already squatting on the back verandah, preparing the various *sambals*. But the people around the card table seemed to hear nothing. The whispering voices became louder and shriller, and both Léonie and Theo, both Addy and Doddy sat up and listened. A dispute seemed suddenly to burst forth between Roger and the regent, notwithstanding Mrs. De Luce's attempts to hush it. They spoke Javanese, but without the courtesy. They called each other cheats like two coolies, constantly interrupted by the soothing efforts of old Mrs. De Luce, aided by her daughters and daughters-in-law. But the chairs were roughly thrust back, a glass was broken, and Roger seemed to throw his cards down in anger. All the women in the inner room joined in the soothing, with high voices, with stifled voices, in whispers, with little exclamations, with little cries of apology and indignation. The innumerable servants were listening in every corner of the house. Then the dispute abated, but long explanatory arguments still continued between the regent and Roger; the women tried to hush them down—"Ssh!... Ssh!"—embarrassed because of the resident's wife, looking out to see where she might be. And at last all was quiet and they sat down silently, hoping that not too much of the dispute had reached her ears. Until at length, very late—it was almost three o'clock—old Mrs. De Luce, with the gambling passion still flickering in her dim eyes, summoning all her distinction and princely prestige, went to the verandah and, as though nothing had happened, asked Mrs. Van Oudijck if she would not come in to lunch.

15

Yes, Theo knew. He had spoken to Urip after lunch, and although the maid had at first tried to deny everything, afraid of losing the *sarongs,* she had been unable to continue lying and had contented herself with feeble little protests of no . . . no. . . . And, still early that same afternoon, raging with jealousy, he sought out Addy. But Theo was calmed by the indifferent composure of the handsome youth, with his Moorish face, already so fully sated with his conquests that he never felt any jealousy. Theo was calmed by the complete absence of thought in this tempter, with his instant forgetfulness after an hour of love, a forgetfulness so harmonious that he looked up with eyes of naive surprise when Theo, red and boiling with fury, burst into his room and, standing before his bed—where he was lying quite naked, as was his habit during his siesta, with the magnificence of a bronze statue, sublime as an ancient sculpture—declared that he would strike him across the face. And Addy's surprise was so artless, his indifference so harmonious, he seemed to have so utterly forgotten his hour of love of the night before, he laughed so serenely at the idea of fighting about a woman, that Theo quieted down and came and sat on the edge of his bed. And then Addy, who was a couple of years younger but possessed incomparable experience, told him that he really mustn't do this again, get so angry about a woman, a mistress who gave herself to another. And Addy patted him on the shoulder with almost fatherly compassion, and now, since they understood each other, they went on confidentially chatting and questioned each other.

They exchanged further confidences, about women, about girls. Theo asked if Addy was going to marry Doddy. But Addy said that he wasn't thinking of marrying and that the resident wouldn't be willing either, because he didn't care for Addy's family and thought them too Indies. Then with a few words he betrayed his pride in his Solo heritage and his pride in the halo that shone dimly behind the heads of all the De Luces. And Addy asked if Theo knew that he had a young brother running around in the *kampong.* Theo knew nothing about it. But Addy assured him that it was so: a young son of Papa's, mark you, from the time when the old man was still controller at Ngadjiwa; a fellow of their own age, completely a *sinjo;* the mother was dead. Perhaps the old man himself didn't know that he still had a child in the *kampong,* but it was true, everybody knew it: the regent knew, the *patih* knew, the *wedono* knew, and the lowliest coolie knew. There was no actual proof, but something that was known the whole world over was as true as that the world itself existed. What did the fellow do? Nothing, except curse and swear, declaring that he was a son of the kandjeng tuan residèn, who allowed him to rot in the *kampong*. What did he live from? From nothing, from what he got by shameless begging, from what people gave him and then . . . from all sorts of things: by going round the districts, through all the *dessas*, and asking if there were any complaints and then drawing up little petitions; by encouraging people to go to Mecca and letting him book their passages with very cheap small steamship companies of which he was the unofficial agent. He would go to the furthest *dessa* and display colored posters representing a steamer full of Mecca pilgrims and the *Kaaba* and the Sacred Tomb of Mohammed.[60] He would mess around like this, sometimes mixed up in fights, once in a *ketju,* sometimes dressed in a *sarong,* sometimes in an old striped calico suit. And he slept anywhere. And, when Theo showed surprise and said that he had never heard of this half brother of his and expressed curiosity, Addy suggested that they should go and look him up, if they could find him in the *kampong*.

It was already dusk under the massive trees; the bananas lifted the cool green paddles of their leaves and, under the stately canopy of the coconut palms the little bamboo houses hid, poetically oriental, idyllic with their *atap* roofs, their doors often already closed or, if open, framing the small black interior with the vague outline of a *baleh-baleh* on which squatted a dark figure. The hairless, mangy dogs barked, the children, naked, with bells dangling from their stomachs, ran indoors and stared out of the houses, the women kept quiet, recognizing the tempter and vaguely laughing, blinking their eyes as he passed in his glory. And Addy pointed to the little house where his old *babu* lived, Tidjem, the woman who helped him, who always opened her door to him when he wanted the use of her hut, who worshipped him the way his mother did and his sisters and his little nieces. He showed Theo the house and thought of his walk with Doddy last night under the *tjemaras.* Tidjem the *babu* saw him and ran up to him delightedly. She squatted down beside him, she pressed his leg against her withered breast, she rubbed her forehead against his knee, she kissed his white shoe, she gazed at him in rapture, her beautiful prince, her radèn, whom she had rocked as a little chubby boy in her already infatuated arms. He tapped her on the shoulder and gave her some money and asked if she knew where Si-Oudijck[61] was, because his brother wished to see him.

Tidjem stood up and beckoned to him to follow; it was quite a walk. They left the *kampong* and came out on an open road with rails along it, whereon the *krandjangs* of sugar were transported to the proas which lay moored at a landing in the Brantas River.[62] The sun was going down in a fan-shaped glory of orange sheaves, and the distant rows of trees that outlined the *bibit* fields were like dark soft velvet against this arrogant glow. These fields were not yet planted, and their somber, earth-colored expanse lay there unploughed. From the factory came a few men and women, on their way home. Beside the river, by the landing, a small *pasar* of portable kitchens had been set up under a sacred *waringin* tree with extensive roots, its five trunks merging into one another. Tidjem called the ferryman and he ferried them across, across the orange Brantas, in the sun's last yellow rays spread out fanwise like a peacock's tail. When they were on the other side, night descended on everything, like the hasty fall of a gauze curtain, and the clouds, which all through November had threatened on the low horizons, hung oppressively in the sultry air. They entered another *kampong*, lit here and there by a paraffin light that had been put on the ground, in a tall lamp glass, without a globe. At last they came to a little house, built partly of bamboo, partly of old packing cases, and roofed partly with tiles, partly with *atap*. Tidjem pointed at it and, once more squatting on the ground and embracing and kissing Addy's knee, asked permission to leave. Addy knocked at the door; a grumbling and stumbling within was the only answer, but, when Addy called out, the door was kicked open and the two young men stepped into the one room of which the hut consisted: half bamboo, half boards from crates, a *baleh-baleh* with a couple of dirty pillows in a corner, with a limp chintz curtain dangling in front of it, a rickety table with a chair or two; on the table, a paraffin lamp without a globe and a litter of odds and ends stacked on a crate in a corner. Everything was permeated with the acrid odor of opium.

Si-Oudijck was sitting at the table with an Arab, while a Javanese woman squatted on the *baleh-baleh*, preparing herself some *sirih*. A few sheets of paper lay on the table between the Arab and the *sinjo*. The latter, evidently annoyed by the unexpected visit, hurriedly crumpled the papers together. But he recovered his composure and, assuming a jovial air, cried:

"Hullo, Adipati! Susuhunan! Sultan of Patjaram! Sugarlord! How are you, you handsome lug, woman chaser?"

His jovial torrent of greetings continued while he scrambled the papers together and made a sign to the Arab, who disappeared through the other door, at the back.

"And who's that with you, Radèn Mas Adrianus . . . ?"

"Your brother," said Addy.

Si-Oudijck looked up suddenly:

"Oh, is it really?" said he, speaking broken Dutch, Javanese, and Malay in the same breath. "I can see it is: my legitimate one. And what does the fellow want?"

"He's come to see what you're like."

The two brothers looked at each other: Theo curious, glad to have made this discovery as a weapon against the old man, if the weapon ever became necessary; the other, Si-Oudijck, secretly restraining, behind his brown, crafty, leering face, all his jealousy, bitterness, and hatred.

"Is this where you live?" asked Theo, for the sake of saying something.

"No, I'm just staying with her for the time being," replied Si-Oudijck, with a jerk of his head toward the woman.

"Has your mother been dead long?"

"Yes. Yours is still alive, isn't she? She lives in Batavia. I know her. Do you ever see her?"

"No."

"H'm. . . . Do you prefer your stepmother?"

"Pretty much," said Theo, drily. And, changing the subject, "I don't believe the old man knows that you exist."

"Yes, he does."

"I doubt it. Have you ever spoken to him?"

"Yes, formerly. Years ago."

"Well?"

"No use. He says I'm not his son."

"It must be difficult to prove."

"Legally, yes. But it's a fact and everybody knows it. It's known all over Ngadjiwa."

"Do you have any kind of evidence?"

"Only the oath which my mother took when she was dying, before witnesses."

"Come, tell me things," said Theo. "Take a walk with us, it's stuffy in here."

They left the hut and sauntered back through the *kampongs*, while Si-Oudijck told his story. They strolled along the Brantas, which wound vaguely in the evening dusk under a sky powdered with stars.

It did Theo good to hear about all this, about that housekeeper of his father's, in the days of his controllership, rejected for an infidelity of which she was guiltless. The child born later and never recognized, never supported; the boy wandering from *kampong* to *kampong*, romantically proud of his inhuman father, whom he watched from a distance, keeping a jealous eye on him when the father became assistant resident and resident, married, divorced his wife, and married again; slowly learning to read and write from a *magang* of his acquaintance. It did the legitimate son good to hear all this, because in his innermost self, blond and fair-skinned though he might be, he was more the son of his mother, the *nonna*, than of his father. In his innermost self he hated his father, not for this or that reason, but from a secret antipathy in his blood, because, despite the appearance and behavior of a blond and fair-skinned European, he felt a secret kinship with this illegitimate brother, felt a vague sympathy for him. Were they not both sons of the selfsame motherland, for which their father felt nothing except as a result of his acquired development, the artificially, humanely cultivated love of the ruler for the territory that he governs. Theo had felt like that from his early childhood, far removed from his father, and later that antipathy had grown into a slumbering hatred. It gave him pleasure to hear demolished that impeccability of his father, a magnanimous man, a functionary of the highest integrity, who loved his domestic circle, who loved his residency, who loved the Javanese, who was anxious to uphold the regent's family, not only because his official instructions prescribed that the Javanese nobility should be respected, but because his own heart told him as much, when he thought of the noble old pangéran. . . . Theo knew that his father was all this, blameless, high-minded, upright, magnanimous; and it did him good, here, in the mysterious evening beside the Brantas, to hear that blamelessness, that highminded, upright magnanimity torn to ribbons. It did him good to meet an outcast who in one moment defiled that towering paternal figure with mud, dragging him from his pedestal, bringing him down to the level of everybody else, sinful, wicked, heartless, ungenerous. It filled him with a wicked joy similar to the one he felt at possessing his father's wife, whom his father adored. What to do with this dark secret he did not yet know, but he clutched at it as a weapon; he was sharpening it there, that very evening, while he listened to the end of what that ranting and raving furtive-eyed half-caste had to say. And Theo hid his secret, hid his weapon deep down within himself.

Grievances rose in his mind, and he too now, the legitimate son, abused his father, declared that the resident did no more to help his own lawful son to get ahead than he would do for any of his clerks; told him how he had once recommended him to the manager of an impossible business, a rice plantation, where he had been unable to stay longer than a single month, and how afterwards his father had left him to his fate, thwarting him when he went hunting after concessions, even in other residencies, even in Borneo, until he was now forced to hang around the house, unable to find a job, thanks to his father, and merely tolerated in that house where he disliked everything.

"Except your stepmother!" Si-Oudijck interrupted calmly.

But Theo went on, growing confidential in his turn and telling his brother that it would be no great advantage for him even if he were acknowledged and legitimatized. And in this way they both became excited, glad to have met each other, to have grown intimate in this brief hour. And beside them walked Addy, surprised at that quick mutual attraction, but otherwise devoid of thought. They had crossed a bridge and by a circuitous route had come out behind the factory buildings of Patjaram. Here Si-Oudijck said goodnight and shook hands with Theo, who slipped some money into his palm. It was accepted greedily, with a flicker of the furtive glance but without a word of thanks. And Addy and Theo went on past the silent factory, to the house. The family were strolling, outside, in the garden and in the *tjemara* avenue. And as the two young men approached, the golden, eight-year-old child came running toward them, the old grandmother's little foster princess, with her fringe of hair and her whitened forehead, in her rich, little doll dress. She came running up to them and suddenly stopped in front of Addy and looked up at him. Addy asked her what she wanted, but the child did not answer and only looked up at him and then, putting out her little hand, stroked his hand. It was all so clearly the result of an irresistible magnetism in the shy child, this running up, stopping, looking up and stroking, that Addy laughed aloud and stooped and kissed her lightly. The child skipped back contentedly. And Theo, still excited by that evening, first by his conversation with Urip, then by his confession to Addy, his meeting with his half brother, his own confidences about his father, was so greatly irritated by this trivial behavior of Addy and the child that he exclaimed, almost angrily:

"Oh, you . . . you'll never be anything but a skirt chaser! . . ."

16

Life had generally been good to Van Oudijck. Born of a simple Dutch family with no money, he had found his youth a tough but never cruel school of precocious earnestness, of hard work from the very beginning, of immediate looking forward to the future, to a career, to the honorable position that he hoped to obtain as quickly as possible. His years of oriental study at Delft[63] had been just gay enough to enable him later to believe that he had once been young, and, because he had taken part in a masquerade, he even thought that he had spent quite a dissolute life, with much squandering of money and riotous living. His character was fashioned from quiet Dutch respectability and an earnest outlook on life, an outlook that generally was rather gloomy and boring, though intelligent and practical. He was accustomed to envisioning his honorable position in society, and his ambition had developed rhythmically and steadily into a temperate thirst for position, but only along the lines that his eyes were always wont to follow: the hierarchical line of the civil service. Things had always gone well with him. Displaying great capacity, he had been greatly valued, and he had become an assistant resident earlier than most, and a resident while still young. His ambition was now really satisfied because his authoritative office was in complete harmony with his nature, whose love of rule had progressed with its ambition. He was now really content and, though his eyes looked still further ahead and saw glimmering before them a seat on the Council of the Indies and even the throne in Buitenzorg, he had days when, serious and contented, he declared that to become a resident of the first class—except for the higher pension—had little in its favor, except at Samarang and Surabaja, but that the "Principalities" were absolutely a burden and Batavia occupied such a peculiar and almost derogatory position, crawling with high officials, members of the Council, and directors. And, though he kept his eyes trained on the further goal, his practical and temperate nature would have been quite satisfied if anyone could have prophesied that he would die as resident of Labuwangi. He loved his district and loved the Indies. He never yearned for Holland, nor for the pageant of European civilization, even though he himself had remained very Dutch and above all hated anything that was half-caste. This was the inconsistency in his character, for he had married his first wife, a *nonna*, purely out of love and, as for his children, in whom the Indies blood was eloquent—outwardly in Doddy, inwardly in Theo, while René and Ricus were completely little *sinjos*—he loved them with an intense feeling of paternity, with all the tenderness and sentiment that slumbered in the depths of his nature: a need to give much and receive much in the circle of his domestic life. Gradually this need had extended to the circle of his district: he took a paternal pride in his assistant residents and controllers, among whom he was popular and beloved. During the six years he had been resident of Labuwangi, he had only once been unable to get on with a controller. The man was a half-caste and he had had him transferred, had him sacked, as he put it. And he was proud that, despite his strict discipline, despite his stern insistence on work, he was loved by his officials. He was all the more grieved, however, by the constant secret enmity of the regent, his "younger brother," to use the Javanese title, in whom indeed he would gladly have found a younger brother to govern his native population under himself, the elder brother. It grieved him that things had happened this way, and he would think of other regents, not only of this one's father, the noble pangéran, but of others he had known: the regent of D——, a cultivated man who spoke and wrote Dutch fluently, contributing lucid Dutch articles to newspapers and magazines; the regent of S——, a trifle frivolous and vain but very rich and very benevolent, who was a dandy in European society and polite to the ladies. Why should it have turned out this way in Labuwangi, with this silent, spiteful, secretive fanatical *wajang* puppet, with his reputation as a saint and sorcerer, stupidly idolized by the people in whose welfare he took no interest and who adored him only for the glamour of his ancient name, a man in whom he always felt an antagonism, never uttered in words but yet so plainly palpable under his icy correctness. And then also in Ngadjiwa the brother, the cardplayer, the gambler: Why should just he be so unlucky in his regents?

Van Oudijck was in a gloomy mood. He was accustomed to receiving, regularly, anonymous letters, venomous libels spewed forth from quiet corners, bespattering at one time an assistant resident, at another a controller, besmirching now the native headman, and now his own family. Sometimes they took the form of a friendly warning, sometimes displaying a malicious delight in wounding, anxious to open his eyes to the shortcomings of his officials and to his wife's misconduct. He was completely used to this and never counted the letters, reading them hastily or hardly at all and carelessly destroying them. Accustomed as he was to judging for himself, the spiteful warnings made no impression on him, though they reared their heads like hissing snakes among the letters which the mail brought him daily. And where his wife was concerned he was so blind, he had always been so much in the habit of picturing Léonie in the tranquillity of her smiling indifference and in the domestic sociability which she most certainly attracted around her—in the hollow void of the residency, whose chairs and ottomans seemed always arranged for a reception—that he could never believe even the most trivial slander.

He never mentioned them to her. He liked his wife, he was in love with her, and, since he always saw her almost silent in society, since she never flirted, he never glanced into the depth of corruption that was her soul. At home he was completely blind. At home he displayed that utter blindness that can often be found in men who are very capable and efficient in their business or profession, who are accustomed to scan with sharp eyes the wide perspective of their official duties but who are nearsighted at home. Such men are used to analyzing things en masse, but not the details of a soul; their knowledge of mankind is based on principles and they divide mankind into types, as in an old-fashioned play; they can immediately plumb capabilities of their subordinates, but are utterly incapable of realizing the intricate complex, like a tangled arabesque, of the psychic involution of those who form their own household, and are always gazing over their heads, failing to grasp the inner meaning of their speech and taking no interest in the kaleidoscopic emotions of hatred and jealousy and life and love that shine with prismatic hues right before their eyes. He loved his wife and he loved his children because the feeling and the fact of paternity were necessities of his being, but he knew neither his wife nor his children. He knew nothing about Léonie, and he had never realized that Theo and Doddy had remained secretly faithful to their mother, so far away, in Batavia, ruined by her unspeakable mode of life, and that they felt no love for him. He thought that they did give him their love, and as for him . . . when he thought of them, a slumbering affection awoke in him.

He received the anonymous letters daily. They had never made an impression on him, yet he no longer destroyed them but read them attentively and put them aside in a secret drawer. He could not have said why. They contained accusations against his wife, they contained imputations against his daughter. They sought to intimidate him by threatening that he might be stabbed in the dark. They warned him that his spies were utterly untrustworthy. They told him that his divorced wife was suffering from poverty and hated him, they told him he had a son whom he had left unprovided for. It was like a silent digging in the secret darkness of his life and his career. It depressed him in spite of himself. It was all very vague, and he had nothing with which to reproach himself. In his own eyes and the world's he was a good official, a good husband,

and a good father; he was a good man. That he should be blamed for having judged too unjustly and unfairly here, for having acted cruelly there, for having divorced his first wife, for having a son running wild in the *kampong*, that filth was thrown at Léonie and Doddy—it all depressed him nowadays. For it was incomprehensible that people should do this. To this man, with his practical good sense, the vagueness was the most irritating aspect of it. He would not fear an open fight, but this mock battle in the dark upset his nerves and his health. He could not conceive why it was happening. There was nothing to tell him. He could not conjure up the face of an enemy. And the letters came day after day, and every day hostility lurked in the shadows around him. It was too mystical for his nature not to make him bitter, depressed, and sad. Then there appeared in the lesser papers utterances of a mean and hostile press, vague accusations or palpable falsehoods. Hatred was seething all around him. He could not fathom the reason of it; he became ill from brooding over it. And he discussed it with nobody and hid his suffering deep down within himself.

He did not understand it. He could not imagine why it was, why it should be so. There was no logic in it. Logically, he should be loved, not hated, however strict and authoritarian he might be considered. Indeed, did he not often temper his strictness with the jovial laugh under his thick mustache, with a friendly, genial warning and exhortation? Was he not a pleasant resident when on tour, one who regarded such a tour with his officials as a relaxation, as a delightful trip on horseback through the coffee plantations, stopping at the coffee *gudangs;* as a pleasant excursion, which relaxed one's muscles after all those weeks of office work; the big staff of district heads following on their little horses, riding their skittish animals like nimble monkeys, with flags in their hands, with the *gamelan* tinkling out its blithe crystal notes of welcome wherever he went, with the carefully prepared dinner in the *pasangrahan* in the evening and cardplaying till late at night? Had not his officials, in unguarded moments, told him that he was a regular sport, an indefatigable rider, jovial at meals, and so young that he would actually take the scarf from the *tandak* girl and *tandak* with her for a moment, very cleverly performing the lissome ritual movements of the hands and feet and hips, instead of buying himself off with some money and leaving her to dance with the *wedono?* Never did he feel so happy as on tour. And now that he was gloomy and depressed, dissatisfied, not knowing what hidden forces were opposing him in the dark—straight, honest man that he was, a man of simple principles, a serious worker—he thought that he would go on tour very soon and rid himself of the gloom that was oppressing him. He would ask Theo to go with him, so he would have a change for a few days.

He was fond of his boy, even though he considered him stupid, thoughtless, reckless, lacking in perseverance, never satisfied with his superiors, tactlessly opposing his manager, until he had once more made himself impossible on a coffee plantation or in a sugar factory where he happened to be employed. He considered that Theo ought to make his own way as he, Van Oudijck, had done before him, instead of relying entirely on his father's position as resident. He did not like nepotism. He would never favor his son above anyone else who had the same rights. He had often told some nephews, eager to obtain concessions in Labuwangi, that he would rather have no relations in his district and that they must expect nothing from him except absolute impartiality. That was how he had got on, and that was how he expected them to get on, Theo included. And yet he watched Theo silently, with all the love of a father, with an almost sentimental tenderness. He regretted silently but profoundly that Theo was not more persevering and did not pay more attention to his future, to his career, to an honorable position in society, be it based on money or esteem. The boy merely lived from day to day, without a thought of tomorrow. . . . Perhaps he was a little cold to Theo, outwardly; well, he would have a confidential talk with him some day, would advise him. At any rate, he was now going to ask Theo to go on tour with him.

And the thought of riding for five or six days in the pure air of the mountains, through the coffee plantations, inspecting the irrigation works, doing what most of all attracted him in his official duties, the thought of this relieved his soul, brightened his outlook, till he ceased to think about the letters. He was a man for the plain and simple life: he found life natural, not complex and involved. His life had followed a perceptible ascent, open and gradual, looking out toward a glittering summit of ambition, and the things that teemed and swarmed in the shadows and the darkness, the things that bubbled up from the abyss, these he had never been able or anxious to see. He was blind to the life that works under life. He did not believe in it, anymore than mountain people who have lived long on a quiet volcano believe in the inner fire that persists in its mysterious depths and escapes only in the form of hot steam and the smell of sulphur. He believed neither in the force above things nor in the force of things themselves. He did not believe in silent fate nor in quiet inevitability. He believed only in what he saw with his own eyes: the harvest, the roads, districts, and *dessas,* and in the welfare of his province; he believed only in his career, which he saw before him like an ascending path. And in the unclouded clarity of his simple, masculine nature, in the universally perceptible obviousness of his upright love of authority, in his legitimate ambition and his practical sense of duty there was only one weak point: his affection, his deep, almost effeminate, sentimental affection for the members of his domestic circle —into whose soul he could not see, being blind—seeing them only in the light of his fixed principle, seeing his wife and children as they *ought* to be.

Experience had taught him nothing. For he had loved his first wife as much as he now loved Léonie. . . . He loved his wife because she was his wife, because she belonged to him, because she was the principal person in his circle. He loved the circle as such and not as so many individuals who formed its links. Experience had taught him nothing. His thoughts were not in accordance with the changing hues of his life; he thought according to his own ideas and principles. They had made him a man, powerful, and also a good official. They had also allowed him to become what he considered to be a good man. But, because he possessed so much affection, unconscious, unanalyzed, and merely deeply felt, and because he did not believe in the hidden force, in the life within life, in the force that teemed and swarmed like volcanic fires under the mountains of majesty, like troubles under a throne, because he did not believe in the mysticism of tangible things, life sometimes found him weak and unprepared when—serene as the gods and more powerful than men—it deviated from what *he* regarded as logical.

17

The mysticism of concrete things on that island of mystery called Java. . . . Outwardly, a docile colony with a subject race, which was no match for the rude trader who, in the golden age of his republic, with the young strength of a youthful people, greedy and eager for gain, plump and phlegmatic, planted his foot and his flag on the crumbling empires, on the thrones that tottered as though the earth had been in seismic labor. But, down in its soul, it had never been conquered, though smiling in proud contemptuous resignation and bowing submissively beneath its fate. Deep in its soul, despite a cringing reverence, it lived in freedom its own mysterious life, hidden from Western eyes, however these might seek to fathom the secret—as though with a philosophic intention of maintaining before all a proud and smiling tranquillity, pliantly yielding and to all appearances courteously approaching—but deep within itself divinely certain of its own views and so far removed from all its rulers' ideals of civilization that no fraternization between master and servant will ever take place, because the difference that ferments in soul and blood remains insuperable. And the European, proud in his might, in his strength, in his civilization and his humanity, rules arrogantly, blindly, selfishly, egoistically, amidst all the intricate machinery of his authority, which he slips into gear with the certainty of clockwork, controlling its every movement, till to the foreigner, the outside observer, this lording it over tangible things, this colonizing of territory alien in race and mentality, appears a masterpiece, a world created.

But under all this show the hidden force lurks, slumbering now and unwilling to fight. Under all this appearance of tangible things the essence of that silent mysticism threatens, like a smouldering fire underground, like hatred and mystery in the heart. Under all this peace of grandeur the danger threatens and the future rumbles like subterranean thunder in the volcanoes, inaudible to human ears. And it is as though the subject race knows it and leaves matters to the latent force of things and awaits the divine moment that is to come, if there be any truth in the calculations of the mystics. It reads the overlord with a single penetrating glance, it sees in him the illusion of civilization and humanity, and it knows that they are nonexistent. While it gives him the title of lord and the *hormat* due to the master, it is profoundly aware of his democratic, commercial nature and despises him for it in silence and judges him with a smile which its brother understands. Never does it offend against the form of slavish servility and, with the *semba,* it acts as though it were inferior, but it is silently aware that it is superior. It is conscious of the hidden, unuttered force; it feels the mystery borne upon the surging winds of the mountains, in the silence of the secret, sultry nights, and the subjected man foresees events that are as yet remote. What is, will not always be: the present is disappearing. Dumbly he hopes that God will lift up those who are oppressed, sometime, sometime in the distant advent of the dawning future. But he feels and hopes and knows it in the innermost depths of his soul, which he never unlocks for his ruler, which he would not even be able to unlock, which always remains an indecipherable book, in the unknown, untranslatable tongue in which the words may be the same but the shades of meaning expressed by them are different and in which the manifold hues of the two ideals show different spectra: spectra in which the colors differ as though radiated by two separate suns, rays from two separate worlds. And never is there the harmony that understands; never does that love blossom forth which is conscious of unity, and between the two there will always be the gap, the chasm, the abyss, the distance, the width whence looms the mystery wherefrom, as from a cloud, the hidden force will one day flash forth. . . .

So it was that Van Oudijck did not feel the mysticism of tangible things.

And the godlike, serene life left him weak and unprepared.

18

Ngadjiwa was a livelier place than Labuwangi. There was a garrison; managers and employers often came down from the coffee plantations in the interior for a few days' amusement; there were races twice a year, accompanied by festivities which filled a whole month: the reception of the resident, a horse raffle, a parade of floats decorated with flowers, and an opera, two or three balls, divided by the revelers as the fancy-dress ball, the ceremonial ball, and the *soirée dansante;* it was a time of early rising and late retiring, of losing hundreds of guilders either at cards or at the track.... The longing for pleasure and a sheer joy of life were freely indulged in those days; coffee planters and employees of the sugar factories looked forward to it for months, and people saved for it during half the year. The two hotels were filled with guests from all directions, and every household entertained its own visitors. People betted furiously, while champagne flowed in torrents, and everybody, including the ladies, knew the race horses as if they were their own property. People felt quite at home at the dances; everybody knew everybody else, as if they were family parties. Waltzes and Washington Posts and *grazianas* were danced with the languorous grace of the Indo dancers, to a swooning measure, the trains gently floating, a smile of quiet rapture on the parted lips, with that dreamy voluptuousness which the Indies settlers express so charmingly in their dances, especially those who have Javanese blood in their veins. With them dancing is not a rough diversion, all bumping against one another with rude leaps and loud laughter, not the wild whirl of dancers in Holland, but represents, especially to the Indos, nothing but courtesy and grace: a serene blossoming of the poetry of motion, a gracefully designed curve of precise steps to a pure measure, an almost eighteenth-century harmony of youthful nobility, waving and trailing and swaying in the dance, despite the primitive boom-booming of the local musicians. This was how Addy de Luce danced, with the eyes of every woman and girl fixed upon him, following him, imploring him with their glances to take them with him into that waving and undulating motion, which was like a dream upon the water. ... This came to him with his mother's blood; this was a survival of the grace of the *srimpis*[64] among whom his mother had spent her childhood, and the mingling of what was modern European with what was ancient Javanese gave him an irresistible charm.

And now, at the last ball, the *soirée dansante,* he was dancing like this with Doddy and, after her, with Léonie. It was late at night, or rather

early in the morning: the day was dawning outside. Fatigue hung over
the ballroom, and Van Oudijck at last intimated to the assistant resident, Vermalen, with whom he and his family were staying, that he was
ready to go home. At that moment he was on the front verandah of the
club, talking to Vermalen, when the *patih* suddenly ran up to him from
the shadow of the garden and, suffering from obvious excitement,
squatted, salaamed, and said:

"*Kandjeng! Kandjeng!* Please advice me, tell me what to do! The
regent is drunk, he is walking along the street and forgetting all his
dignity."

The revelers were going home. The carriages drove up, the owners
stepped in, the carriages drove away. On the road outside the club the
resident saw a Javanese: his torso was bare, he had lost his headdress,
and his long, black hair fell freely, while he talked very loudly, with violent gestures. Groups gathered in the dusky shadows, looking on from a
distance.

Van Oudijck recognized the regent of Ngadjiwa. Already at the ball
the regent had behaved without self-control, after he had lost heavily at
cards and had mixed all sorts of wines.

"Didn't the regent go home already?" asked Van Oudijck.

"Yes, *kandjeng!*" replied the *patih*, plaintively. "I took the regent
home as soon as I saw that he was no longer able to control himself. He
flung himself on his bed, I thought he was sound asleep. But look, he
woke and got up, he left the *kabupatèn* and came back here. See how
he's behaving! He's drunk, he's drunk and he forgets who he is and who
his fathers were!"

Van Oudijck went outside with Vermalen. He walked up to the regent, who was making violent gestures and delivering an unintelligible
speech in a loud voice.

"Regent!" said the resident. "Don't you know where and who you
are?"

The regent did not recognize him. He ranted at Van Oudijck, he
called down all the curses of heaven upon his head.

"Regent!" said the assistant resident. "Don't you know who's speaking to you and to whom you're speaking?"

The regent swore at Vermalen. His bloodshot eyes flashed with
drunken fury and madness. Assisted by the *patih*, Van Oudijck and
Vermalen tried to help him into a carriage, but he refused. Splendid and
sublime in his decline, he gloried in the madness of his tragedy; he stood
as though some explosive force had made him beside himself, half
naked, with loose hair and great gestures of his crazy arms. He was no

longer coarse and bestial but had become tragic, heroic, fighting against his fate, on the edge of the abyss. . . . The excess of his drunkenness seemed with a strange force to raise him out of his slow bestialization and, befuddled as he was, he drew himself up, towering high, dramatically, over the Europeans.

Van Oudijck looked at him with amazement. The regent was now coming to blows with the *patih,* who addressed him in beseeching tones. On the road a crowd collected, silent and dismayed. The last guests were leaving the club, where the lights were growing dim. Among them were Léonie van Oudijck, Doddy, and Addy de Luce. All three still showed in their eyes the weary voluptuousness of the last waltz.

"Addy," said the resident, "you're an intimate friend of the regent's. Just see if he knows you."

The young man spoke to the tipsy madman, in subdued Javanese. At first the regent went on swearing with his wide, raving gestures, but then it seemed that the softness of the language held a familiar memory for him. He gave Addy a long look. His gestures subsided, his drunken glory evaporated. It was as though his blood suddenly understood that of the young man, as though their souls recognized each other. The regent nodded dolefully and began a long lament, with his arms raised on high. Addy tried to help him into a carriage, but the regent resisted and refused. Then Addy took his arm with gentle force and slowly walked away with him. The regent, still lamenting, with tragic gestures of despair, suffered himself to be led. The *patih* followed with one or two underlings, who had run after the regent out of the *kabupatèn,* helplessly. The procession vanished in the darkness.

Léonie, smiling wearily, stepped into the assistant resident's carriage. She remembered the quarrel during the gambling in Patjaram; she took pleasure in observing the gradual deterioration, a visible degradation from a passion controlled by neither tact nor moderation. And, where she was concerned, she felt stronger than ever, because she enjoyed her passions and controlled them and made them the slaves of her enjoyment. . . . She despised the regent and it gave her a romantic satisfaction, an artistic pleasure, to watch the successive phases of that decline. In the carriage she glanced at her husband, who sat in gloomy silence. And his gloom delighted her, because she thought him sentimental, with his championing of the Javanese nobility, the result of sentimental guidelines that Van Oudijck took even more sentimentally. And she delighted in his sorrow. From her husband she glanced at Doddy, detecting in the dance-weary eyes of her stepdaughter a jealousy due to that last, that very last waltz she had danced with Addy. And she rejoiced in that jealousy. She felt happy, because sorrow had no hold upon her, anymore than passion. She played with the things of life and they slid from her and left her as unperturbed and calmly smiling and unwrinkled and creamy white as before.

Van Oudijck did not go to bed. With his head aflame, with a fury of mortification in his heart, he immediately took a bath, put on pajamas, and had coffee served on the verandah outside his room. It was six o'clock; the air was steeped in a delightful coolness of morning freshness. But he suffered from so fierce an anger that his temples throbbed, his heart thumped in his chest, his every nerve quivered. That scene at daybreak kept on flickering before his eyes. What angered him above all was the impossibility of it, the illogicality, the unthinkableness of it. That a Javanese of high birth, forgetful of all the noble traditions in his blood, should have been able to behave as the regent of Ngadjiwa had behaved just now would never have seemed possible to him. He would never have believed it, if he had not seen it with his own eyes. To this man of predetermined logic, the fact was simply monstrous, like a nightmare. Extremely susceptible to surprise, which he did not consider logical, he was angry with reality. He wondered if he had been dreaming, if he had been drunk himself. That the scandal should have occurred made him furious. But, since this was the way things were, he would recommend the regent for dismissal. There was no alternative.

He dressed, spoke to Vermalen, and went to the *kabupatèn* with him. They both forced their way in to see the regent, notwithstanding the hesitation of the retainers, notwithstanding the breach of etiquette. They did not see his wife, the radèn-aju. But they found the regent in his bedroom. He was lying on his bed, with his eyes open, recovering gloomily, not yet sufficiently restored to life fully to realize the strangeness of this visit, of the presence of the resident and assistant resident by his bedside. He recognized them nevertheless, but did not speak. While the two of them tried to bring home to him the gross impropriety of his behavior, he stared shamelessly in their faces and persisted in his silence. It was so strange that the two officials looked at each other to ask whether the regent was not mad, whether he was really responsible. He had not spoken a single word, and continued to be silent. Though Van Oudijck threatened him with dismissal, he did not say a word, staring shamelessly into the resident's eyes. He did not move his lips, maintaining absolute silence. At the most, an ironical smile formed about his lips. The officials, really thinking that the regent was mad, shrugged their shoulders and left the room.

In the gallery they met the radèn-aju, a small woman, downtrodden like a whipped dog, a beaten slave. She approached, weeping; she begged, she implored forgiveness. Van Oudijck told her that the regent refused to speak, despite his threats, that he was silent with an inexplicable but obviously deliberate silence. Then the radèn-aju whispered that the regent had consulted a *dukun*, who had given him a *djimat* and assured him that, if he only persisted in maintaining complete silence, his enemies could obtain no hold upon him.[65] Terrified, she begged for help, for forgiveness, gathering her children round her as she spoke. After sending for the *patih* and enjoining him to keep a strict watch on the regent, the two officials went away.

Although Van Oudijck had often encountered the superstition of the Javanese, it always enraged him because it opposed what he called the laws of nature and life. After all, nothing but his superstition could induce a Javanese to depart from the correct path of his innate courtliness. Whatever they might now wish to put before him, the regent would remain silent, would persist in the absolute silence prescribed by the *dukun*. In this way he considered himself protected against those whom he regarded as his enemies. And this preconceived notion of hostility in one whom he would so gladly have regarded as his younger brother and fellow ruler was what disturbed Van Oudijck most of all.

He returned to Labuwangi with Léonie and Doddy. Once at home, he felt for a moment the pleasure of being back in his own house again, an enjoyment of domesticity that always soothed him: the material pleasure of seeing his own bed again, his own desk and chair, of drinking his own coffee, made the way he liked it. These minor amenities put him in a good humor for a little while, but his bitterness returned again when he saw, under a pile of letters on his desk, the disguised handwritings of a couple of furtive correspondents. Automatically he opened these first and felt sick when he read Léonie's name coupled with Theo's. Nothing was sacred to those swine. They concocted the most monstrous, the most unnatural libels, the most loathsome imputations, even as low as incest. All the filth flung at his wife and son only increased his love for them, placed them on an inviolable summit, and made him cherish them with a deeper and more fervent affection. But his bitterness, once stirred up, brought back his displeasure. Its cause was that he had to propose the regent of Ngadjiwa's dismissal and he did not enjoy the prospect. But this one necessity embittered his whole being, upset his nerves, and made him ill. If he could not follow the path that he had determined upon, if life strayed from the possibilities which he, Van Oudijck, had a priori fixed, this reluctance, this rebellion upset his nerves and made him ill.

He had once and for all resolved, after the death of the old pangéran, to raise up the declining race of the Adiningrats, both from his affectionate memory of that excellent Javanese prince, the imperatives of his office, and because of a sense of lofty humanity and hidden poetry in himself. And he had never been able to do so. He had immediately been thwarted—unconsciously, by force of circumstances—by the old radèn-aju pangéran, who gambled away everything, who was ruining herself and her kin. He had exhorted her as a friend. She had not been deaf to his advice, but her passion had proved too strong for her. Van Oudijck had, even before the father's death, judged her son, Sunario, the regent of Labuwangi, unfit for the actual position of regent. The fellow was petty and insignificant, insufferably proud of his descent, never in touch with the reality of life, devoid of any talent for ruling or any consideration for his inferiors, a great fanatic, always occupied with *dukuns*, with sacred calculations, or *petangans*, always reticent and living in a dream of obscure mysticism and blind to what would spell welfare and justice for his Javanese subjects. And the population adored him nevertheless, both because of his noble birth and because he was reputed to possess sanctity and a far-reaching power, a divine magic. Silently, secretly, the women of the *kabupatèn* sold bottles of the water that had flowed over his body in the bath, as a healing remedy for various diseases. That was the elder brother, and the younger had quite forgotten himself on the previous night, frenzied by cards and drink. In these two sons the once so brilliant race was tottering to its ruin. Their children were young; a few cousins were *patihs* in Labuwangi and the adjoining residencies, but their veins contained not a drop of the noble blood. No, Van Oudijck had never been able to do what he wanted to. The very people whose interests he defended were opposing his efforts. Their day was over. But why this must be, he could not understand, and it upset him and embittered him.

And he had pictured to himself a very different line, a beautiful ascending line—as he saw his own life before him—whereas with them the line of life wound tortuously downward. And he did not understand what it was that was stronger than he, even if he put his mind to it. Had it not always happened in his life and his career that the things he wanted the most had come to pass with the logic that he himself day after day had attributed to the things that were about to happen? His ambition had now established the logic of the ascending line, for his ambition had established as its aim the revival of this Javanese family. . . .

Would he fail? Fail in striving for an aim that he had set himself as an official: he would never forgive himself! Until now he had always succeeded in achieving what he had willed. But what he now wanted to achieve was, unknown to himself, not only an official aim, a part of his work, but a goal that originated in his humanity, sprang from the noblest part of himself. What he now wanted to achieve was an ideal, the ideal of the European in the East and of the European who sees the East as he wishes to see it, and sees it only that way.

And that there were forces that gathered into one force, which threatened him, mocked his proposals, laughed at his ideals, and which were all the stronger because they were more deeply hidden—this he would never admit. It was not in his nature to acknowledge them, and even the clearest revelation of them would be a riddle to his soul and would remain a myth.

19

Van Oudijck had been to the office that day when Léonie met him the moment he returned.

"The radèn-aju pangéran is here," she said. "She has been here an hour, Otto. She wants to speak to you very badly. She has been waiting for you."

"Léonie," he said, "I want you to look through these letters. I often get this sort of thing and I've never mentioned them to you. But perhaps it's better that you should not be left in ignorance. Perhaps it's better for you to know. But please don't take them to heart. I needn't assure you that I don't for one moment believe a word of all this filth. So don't get upset about it and give them back to me personally. Don't leave them lying around. . . . And send the radèn-aju pangéran to my office. . . .

Léonie, with the letters in her hand, went to the verandah in the back and returned with the princess, a distinguished, gray-haired woman, with a proud, royal bearing in her still slender figure. Her eyes were a somber black; her mouth, which seemed wider because of the *sirih* juice and which grinned with filed, black, lacquered teeth, was like a grimacing mask and spoilt the proud nobility of her expression. She wore a black satin *kabaja* fastened with jeweled buttons. It was above all her gray hair and her somber eyes that gave her a peculiar mixture of venerable dignity and smouldering passion. Tragedy hung over her old age. She herself felt that fate was pressing tragically upon her and hers, and she placed her only hope in the far-reaching, divinely appointed power of her first-born, Sunario, the regent of Labuwangi.

While the old princess preceded Van Oudijck into the office, Léonie examined the letters, in the middle gallery. They were lampoons couched in foul language, about her and Addy and Theo. Always wrapped in the selfish dream of her own life, she was never too much concerned with what people thought or said about her, especially since she knew that she could immediately win everyone over again with her personality, and with her smile. She possessed a tranquil charm which was irresistible. She herself never spoke ill of others, out of indifference: she made amiable excuses for everything and everybody; and she was loved . . . when people saw her. But she considered these dirty letters, spat out from some dark corner, tiresome and unpleasant, even though Van Oudijck did not believe them. Suppose that, one day, he began to believe things? She must be prepared for it. She must above all retain for that possible day her most charming tranquillity, all her invulnerability and inviolability. Who could have sent the letters? Who hated her so much, who could be interested in writing like this to her husband? How strange that it was known . . . Addy? Theo? How did they know? Was it Urip? No, not Urip. . . . But who then? And was everything known? She had always thought that what happened in secret alcoves would never be known to the world. She had even believed—naïvely—that the men never discussed her with one another, that they discussed other women, but not her. Her mind harbored such simple illusions, despite all her experience, a naïveté that harmonized with the partly perverse, partly childish poetry of her rose-tinted imagination. Could she then never keep hidden the secrets of her mystery, the secrets of reality? It annoyed her for a moment, that reality, which was being revealed despite her superficial correctness. . . . Thoughts and dreams always remained secret. It was the real actions that were so troublesome. For an instant she thought of being more careful in the future, of refraining. But then she saw Theo and Addy, her fair love and her dark love, and she felt that she was too weak for that. She knew that in this she could not conquer her passions, though she controlled them. Would they end by proving her destruction, notwithstanding all her tact? But she laughed at the thought: she had a firm faith in her invulnerability. Life always slid from her shoulders.

Still, she wanted to prepare herself for what might happen. She had no higher ideal in life than to be free from pain, free from grief, free from poverty, and to make her passions the slaves of her enjoyment, so that she might possess this enjoyment as long as possible, lead this life as long as possible. She reflected what she should say and do if Van Oudijck suddenly questioned her, suspicious because of these anonymous letters. She reflected whether she had better break with Theo. Addy was enough for her. And she lost herself in her preparations, as if they were the vague combinations of a play about to be enacted. Then she suddenly heard from the office the radèn-aju pangéran's voice, very loud as compared to her husband's calmer tone. She listened, inquisitively foreseeing a tragedy, and was quietly relieved that this tragedy too would not affect her.

She crept into Van Oudijck's bedroom; the doors were always left open for coolness and only a screen separated the bedroom from the office. She peeked around the screen. And she saw the old princess more excited than any Javanese woman she had ever seen. The radèn-aju was beseeching Van Oudijck in Malay; he was assuring her in Dutch that what she asked was impossible. Léonie listened more closely. And she heard the old princess imploring the resident to show mercy to her second son, the regent of Ngadjiwa. She entreated Van Oudijck to remember her husband, the pangéran, whom he had loved as a father, who had loved him as a son, with a mutual affection more intense than that of an "elder and younger brother." She implored him to think of their illustrious past, of the glory of the Adiningrats, always loyal friends of the Company, its allies in war, its most faithful vassals in peace. She implored him not to decree the downfall of their race, on which doom had descended since the pangéran's death, driving it into an abyss of fatal destruction. She stood before the resident like Niobe, like a tragic mother, flinging up her arms in the vehemence of her protestations, while tears poured from her somber eyes, and only the wide mouth, painted with brown *sirih* juice, was like the grimace of a mask. But from this grimace issued the fluent phrases of protestation and supplication, and she wrung her hands in entreaty and beat her breast in contrition.

Van Oudijck answered in a firm but gentle voice, telling her that certainly he had loved the old pangéran most sincerely, that he respected the old race highly, that no one would be better pleased than he to uphold their lofty position. But then he became more severe and asked her whom the Adiningrats had to blame for the fate that was now pursuing them. And with his eyes looking into hers, he said that it was she! She fell back, flaring up with rage, but he repeated it again and yet again. Her sons were *her* children, bigoted and proud and inveterate gamblers. And it was gambling, that low passion, which was wrecking their greatness. Their race was staggering to its downfall through their insatiable greed of gain. How often did it not happen that a month went by at Ngadjiwa before the regent paid the native heads their salaries? She confessed that that was true: it was at *her* instigation that her son had taken the money from the treasury, to pay gambling debts. But she also swore that it would never happen again. And where, asked Van Oudijck, had a regent, descended from an ancient race, ever behaved as the regent of Ngadjiwa had at the races? The mother lamented: it was true, it was true; fate dogged their footsteps and had clouded her son's mind, but it would never, never happen again. She swore by the soul of the old pangéran that it would never happen again, that her son would win back his dignity. But Van Oudijck grew more vehement and reproached her for not having exercised a good influence over her sons and nephews, for being the evil genius of her family, because a demon of gambling and greed had her fast in its claws. She began to shriek with anguish—she, the old princess, who looked down upon the resident, the Hollander without birth or breeding—shrieking with anguish because he dared to speak like this and was entitled to do so. She flung out her arms, she begged for mercy, she begged him not to urge her son's dismissal by the government, which would act as the resident suggested, which would follow the advice of such a highly esteemed official; she begged him to have pity and show patience a little longer. She would speak to her son, Sunario would speak to his brother, they would bring him back to his senses, which had been bewildered by drink and gambling and women. Oh, if the resident would only have pity, if he would only relent! But Van Oudijck remained inexorable. He had shown patience far too long. It was now exhausted. Since her son, at the instigation of the *dukun,* relying on his *djimat,* had resisted him with his insolent silence, which, as he firmly believed, made him invulnerable to his enemies, he would prove that he, the spokesman of the government, the representative of the queen, was the stronger, *dukun* and *djimat* notwithstanding. There was no alternative: his patience was at an end, his love for the pangéran did not allow further indulgence, his feeling of respect for their race was not such that he could transfer it to an unworthy son. It was settled: the regent would be dismissed.

The princess had listened to him, unable to believe his words, seeing the abyss yawn before her. And, with a yell like that of a wounded lioness, with a scream of pain, she pulled the jeweled hairpins from her bun, and her long gray hair fell streaming about her face. She tore open her satin *kabaja,* beside herself with anguish, and threw herself at the feet of the European, took firm hold of his foot with her two hands, planted it, with a movement which made Van Oudijck stagger, on her bowed neck, and cried aloud, screamed that she, the daughter of the sultans of Madura, would forever be his slave, swore that she would be nothing but his slave, if only he would have mercy on her son this time and not plunge her house into the abyss of shame which she saw yawning around her. And she clutched the European's foot, as though with the strength of despair, and held that foot, like a yoke of servitude, with the sole and heel of the shoe pressed upon her flowing gray hair, upon her neck bowed to the floor. Van Oudijck trembled with emotion. He realized that this high-spirited woman would never humble herself like that, with evident spontaneity, to the lowest depths of humiliation that she could conceive, would not resort to the most vehement utterance of actual grief that a woman could ever display, with her hair unbound and the ruler's foot planted on her neck, if she had not been shaken to the very depths of her soul, if she did not feel desperate to the pitch of self-destruction. And he hesitated for a moment. But only for a moment. He was a man of considered principles, of fixed, a priori logic, immovable when he had come to a decision, wholly inaccessible to impulse. With the utmost respect, he at last released his foot from the princess's clinging grasp. Holding out both hands to her, with visible compassion, visible emotion, he raised her from the floor. He made her sit down, and she fell into a chair, broken, sobbing aloud. For a moment, perceiving his gentleness, she thought that she had won. But when he calmly but decidedly shook his head in denial, she understood that it was over. She panted for breath, half swooning, her *kabaja* still open, her hair still unbound.

At that moment Léonie entered the room. She had seen the drama enacted before her eyes and felt a thrill of artistic emotion. She experienced something like compassion in her barren soul. She approached the princess, who flung herself into her arms, woman seeking woman in the unreasoning despair of that inevitable doom. And Léonie, turning her beautiful eyes on Van Oudijck, murmured a single word of intercession and whispered:

"Give in! Give in!"

And for the second time Van Oudijck wavered. Never had he refused his wife anything, however costly, for which she asked. But this meant the sacrifice of his principle never to reconsider a decision, always to persist in what he had resolved should happen. In this manner he had always controlled the future; thus things always happened as he willed, and he had never shown any weakness. He answered that it was impossible.

In his obstinacy, he did not divine the sacred moments in which a man must not insist upon his own will, but must piously surrender to the pressure of the hidden forces. These moments he did not respect, acknowledge, or recognize; no, never. He was a man with a clear, logically deduced, simple, masculine sense of duty, a man of a plain and simple life. He would never know that, lurking under the simple life, there are all those forces which together make the omnipotent hidden force. He would have laughed at the idea that there are nations that have a greater control over that force than the Western nations have. He would shrug his shoulders—and continue on his way—at the mere supposition that among the nations there are a few individuals in whose hands that force loses its omnipotence and becomes an instrument. No experience would teach him that. Perhaps for an instant he would be nonplussed, but immediately afterwards he would grasp the chain of his logic in his virile hand and line up the iron actualities together. . . .

He saw Léonie lead the old princess from his office, bowed and sobbing.

A deep emotion, an utterly agitating compassion, brought tears to his eyes. And before those tearful eyes rose the vision of that Javanese whom he loved like a father.

But he did not give in.

20

Reports arrived from Ternate and Halmaheira that a terrible submarine earthquake had devastated the surrounding group of islands, that whole villages had been washed away, that thousands of inhabitants had been rendered homeless.[66] The telegrams caused greater consternation in Holland than in the Indies, where people seemed more used to the convulsions of the sea, to the volcanic upheavals of the earth. They had been discussing the Dreyfus case for months, they were beginning to discuss Transvaal, but Ternate was hardly mentioned. Nevertheless, a central committee was formed at Batavia, and Van Oudijck called a meeting. It was resolved to hold at the earliest possible date a charity bazaar in the club and the garden attached to it. Mrs. Van Oudijck, as usual, delegated everything to Eva Eldersma and did not trouble herself at all.

For a fortnight Labuwangi was filled with excitement. In this silent little town, full of Eastern slumber, a whirlwind of tiny passions, jealousies, and enmities began to rise. Eva had her club of faithful adherents, the Van Helderens, the Doorn de Bruijns, the Rantzows, with which all sorts of tiny sets strove to compete. One was not on speaking terms with the other, this one would not take part because that one did, another insisted on taking part only because Mrs. Eldersma must not think that she was everybody, and this one and that one and the other considered that Eva was much too pretentious and need not fancy that she was the most important woman in the place because Mrs. Van Oudijck left everything to her. Eva, however, had spoken to the resident and declared that she was willing to organize everything, provided she received unlimited authority. She had not the slightest objection to his appointing someone else to set the ball rolling, but, if he appointed her, unlimited authority was an express condition, for to take twenty different tastes and opinions into account would mean that one would never get anywhere. Van Oudijck laughingly consented, but impressed upon her that she must not make people angry and that she must respect everyone's feelings and be as conciliatory as possible, so that the charity bazaar might leave pleasant memories behind. Eva promised; she was not quarrelsome by nature.

To get a thing done, to set a thing going, to put a thing through, to employ her artistic energies was her great delight; it was life to her, and was the only consolation in her dreary life in the Indies. For, though she had grown to love and admire many things in Java, the social life of the country, save for her little clique, lacked all charm for her. But now to prepare an entertainment on a large scale, the fame of which would reach as far as Surabaja, flattered alike her vanity and her love of work. She sailed through every difficulty and, because people saw that she knew best and was more practical than they, they gave way to her. But, while she was busy evolving her fancy booths and *tableaux vivants* and while the bustle of the preparations occupied the leading families of Labuwangi, something seemed also to occupy the soul of the native population, but something less cheerful than charitable entertainment. The chief of police, who brought Van Oudijck his short report every morning, usually in a few words—that he had made his rounds and that everything was quiet and orderly—had had longer conversations with the resident of late, seemed to have more important things to communicate. The *oppassers* whispered more mysteriously outside the office, the resident sent for Eldersma and Van Helderen, the secretary wrote to Ngadjiwa, to Vermalen the assistant resident, to the commander of the garrison, and the *controleur-kotta* patrolled the town with increased frequency and at unaccustomed hours. Because they were so busy, the ladies perceived little of these mysterious doings, and only Léonie, who took no part in the preparations, noticed in her husband an unusual silent concern. She was a quick and keen observer, and because Van Oudijck, who was accustomed to mentioning business at home, had been silent the last few days, she suddenly asked where the regent of Ngadjiwa was, now that he had been dismissed by the government at Van Oudijck's insistence, and who was going to replace him. He made a vague reply, and she took alarm and became anxious. One morning, passing through her husband's bedroom, she was struck by the whispered conversation between Van Oudijck and the chief of police, and she stopped to listen, with her ear against the screen. The conversation was muffled because the garden doors were open. The *oppassers* were sitting on the steps; a couple of gentlemen who wished to speak to the resident were walking up and down the side verandah, after writing their names on the slate which the chief *oppasser* brought in to the resident. But they had to wait, because the resident was engaged with the chief of police. . . .

Léonie listened, behind the screen. And she turned pale at the sound of a word or two which she overheard. She returned silently to her room, feeling frightened. At lunch she asked if it would be really necessary for her to attend the feast, because she had had such a toothache lately and she wanted to go to Surabaja, to the dentist. It would probably mean a few days because she had not been to the dentist for a long time. But Van Oudijck, sterner than usual in his somber mood of secret concern and silence, told her that it was impossible, that on an occasion like that she simply had to be present as the resident's wife. She pouted and sulked and held her handkerchief to her mouth, so that Van Oudijck became distressed. Because of this unusual agitation she did not sleep that afternoon, did not read, did not dream. She was frightened, she wanted to get away. And at tea, in the garden, she began to cry, said that the toothache was making her head ache, that it was making her quite ill, that it was more than she could bear. Van Oudijck, distressed and nervous, was touched; he could never endure to see her in tears. And he gave in, as he always did to her, where her personal affairs were concerned. Next day she went off to Surabaja, stayed at the resident's, and really did have her teeth attended to. It was always a good thing to do, once a year or so. This time she spent about five hundred guilders on the dentist.

After this, incidentally, the other ladies also seemed to guess something of what was happening at Labuwangi behind a haze of mystery. For Ida van Helderen, the tragic white *nonna*, her eyes starting out of her head with fright, told Eva Eldersma that her husband and Eldersma and the resident too were fearing a rebellion of the population, incited by the regent and his family, who would never forgive the dismissal of the regent of Ngadjiwa. The men, however, were noncommittal and reassured their wives, but a dark swirling tide continued to stir under the apparent calmness of their provincial life. And gradually the gossip leaked out and alarmed the European inhabitants. Vague paragraphs in the newspapers, commenting on the dismissal of the regent, contributed to their alarm.

Meanwhile the bustle of preparation for the feast went on, but people no longer put their hearts into it. They led a hectic, restless life and were becoming nervous and ill. At night they locked and bolted their houses, had weapons ready, and they woke suddenly in terror, listening to the noises of the night. And they condemned Van Oudijck's hastiness when, after the scene at the races, he had been unable to restrain his patience any longer and had not hesitated to recommend the dismissal of the regent, whose house was firmly rooted in the soil of Labuwangi, who was one with Labuwangi.

The resident had ordered for the population a *pasar malam* on the *alun-alun,* to last for a few days, coinciding with the bazaar. There would be a people's fair, many little stalls and booths, and the *Komedie-Stambul,* with plays drawn from the *Arabian Nights.*[67] He had done this in order to give the Javanese a treat that they would value greatly, while the Europeans were enjoying themselves in their own way. It was now a few days before the fair, and on the day prior to the opening it so happened that the *kumpulan* was to be held in the *kabupatèn*. The anxiety, activity, and general nervousness filled the otherwise quiet little town with an emotion that made people almost ill. Mothers sent their children away and were themselves undecided what to do. But the fair made people stay. How could they avoid going to the fair? There was so seldom any amusement. But . . . if there really were an uprising! And they did not know what to do, whether to take the vague menace seriously, or make light of it.

The day before the *kumpulan* Van Oudijck asked for an interview with the radèn-aju pangéran, who lived with her son. His carriage drove past the stalls and booths in the *alun-alun* and through the triumphal arches of the *pasar malam,* which had been made of bamboo stalks curving toward each other, with a narrow strip of bunting waving in the wind, a manner of decoration that in Javanese is known as "rippling." That evening was to be the first evening of the fair. Everyone was busy with the final preparations, and, in the bustle of hammering and arranging, the natives sometimes neglected to squat when the resident's carriage passed and they paid no attention to the golden *pajong* which the *oppasser* on the box held in his hands like a furled sun. But, when the carriage turned by the flagstaff and up the drive leading to the *kabupatèn* and they saw that the resident was going to the regent, groups huddled together and spoke in eager whispers. They crowded at the entrance to the drive and stared. But the natives saw only the empty *pendoppo* looming beyond the shadow of the *waringins*, with the rows of waiting chairs. The chief of police, suddenly passing on his bicycle, caused the groups to break up as though by instinct.

The old princess was awaiting the resident on the front verandah. Her dignified features wore a serene expression and betrayed no trace of all that was raging within her. She motioned the resident to a chair and the conversation opened with a few ordinary phrases. Then four servants approached in a crouching posture: one with a bottle stand, the second with a tray full of glasses, the third with a silver ice bucket filled with ice, while the fourth, without carrying anything, salaamed. The princess asked the resident what he would drink; he replied that he would like a whisky and soda. The fourth servant came crouching through the other three to prepare the drink, poured in the measure of whisky, opened the bottle of *ajer-blanda* with a report as of a gun, and dropped into the tumbler a lump of ice the size of a small glacier. Not another word was said. The resident waited for the drink to grow cold, and the four servants crouched away. Then at last Van Oudijck said something and asked if he might speak to her in confidence, if he could say what he had on his mind. She begged him, civilly, to do so. And in his firm but hushed voice he told her, in Malay, in very courteous sentences, full of friendliness and flowery politeness, how great and exalted his love had been for the pangéran and still was for that prince's glorious house, although he, Van Oudijck, to his intense regret, had been obliged to act counter to that love, because his duty commanded him so to act. And he asked her —presuming that it was possible for her, as a mother—to bear him no grudge for this exercise of his duty; he asked her, on the contrary, to show a motherly feeling for him, the European official who had loved the pangéran as a father, and to cooperate with him, the official—she, the mother of the regent—by employing her great influence for the happiness and welfare of the population. Because of his piety and his abstract concern for things invisible, Sunario had a tendency to forget the actual realities that were before his eyes. Well, he, the resident, was asking her, the powerful, influential mother, to cooperate with him in ways that Sunario overlooked, to cooperate with him in love and unity. And, in his elegant Malay, he opened his heart to her entirely, describing the turmoil which for days on end had been seething among the people like an evil poison which could only make them wicked and drunk and would probably lead them to things, to acts, which were bound to have lamentable results. He made her feel his unspoken threat that the government would be the stronger, that a terrible punishment would be meted out to all those who would be proven guilty, high and low alike. But his language remained exceedingly cautious and his speech respectful, as of a son addressing a mother. She, though she understood him, valued the tactful grace of his manner, and the flowery depth and earnestness of his language made him rise in her esteem and almost surprised her . . . this from a low Hollander, without birth or breeding.

But he continued. He did not tell her what he knew, that she was the instigator of this obscure unrest. He excused that unrest, said that he understood it, that the population shared her grief for her unworthy son, himself a scion of the noble race, and that it was only natural that the people should sympathize deeply with their old sovereign, even though the sympathy was ignorant and illogical. For the son *was* unworthy; the regent of Ngadjiwa had proved himself unworthy and what had happened could not have happened otherwise.

His voice, for a moment, became severe, and she bowed her gray head, remained silent, seemed to agree. But then his words became gentler again, and once more he asked for her cooperation, asked her to use her influence. He trusted her completely. He knew that she held high the traditions of her family, loyalty to the Company, unimpeachable loyalty to the government. Well, he asked her to direct her power and influence, to use the love and reverence that the people bore her in such a way that she, together with him, would silence what was seething in the darkness; that she would move the thoughtless to reflection; that she would assuage and pacify what was secretly threatening, thoughtlessly and frivolously, the firm and dignified authority of the government. And, while he flattered and threatened her in one breath, he felt that she —although she spoke hardly a word and merely punctuated his words with her repeated *saja*—he felt that she was falling under his stronger influence, the influence of the man of tact and authority, and that he was giving her food for thought. He felt that, while she reflected, her hatred was subsiding, her vindictiveness was losing its force, and that he was breaking the energy and the pride of the ancient blood of the Maduran sultans. Despite his flowery speech, he allowed her to catch a glimpse of utter ruin, of terrible penalties, of the undeniably greater power of the government. And he brought her back to the old pliant attitude of yielding before the might of the ruler. He reminded her that, despite her impulse to rebel and throw off the hated yoke, it was better to be calm and reasonable and to adapt herself placidly to things as they were. She nodded her head softly in assent, and he felt that he had conquered her. And this aroused a certain pride within him.

Now she also spoke and gave the required promise, saying in her broken, tearful voice, that she loved him as a son, that she would do what he wished and would assuredly use her influence, outside the *kabupatèn,* in the town, to still these menacing troubles. She denied her own complicity and said that the unrest arose from the unreflecting love of the people, who suffered with her, because of her son. She now echoed his own words, save that she did not speak of unworthiness. For she was a mother. And she repeated once again that he could trust her, that she would act according to his wish. Then he informed her that he would come to the *kumpulan* next day, with his subordinates and with the native headmen, and he said that he trusted her so completely that all of them, the Europeans, would be unarmed. He looked her in the eyes. He threatened her more by saying this than if he had spoken of arms. For he was threatening her—without a threatening word, merely by the intonation of his Malay speech—with the punishment, with the vengeance of the government, if even the slightest harm were to come to the least of its officials.

He had risen from his seat. She also rose, wrung her hands, entreated him not to speak like that, entreated him to have the fullest confidence in her and in her son. She sent for Sunario. The regent of Labuwangi entered, and Van Oudijck again repeated that he hoped for peace and reason. He felt that she, the mother, was omnipotent in the *kabupatèn.* The regent bowed his head, agreed, promised, even said that he already had taken measures, that he had always regretted this excitement of the populace, that it grieved him greatly, now that the resident had noticed it, in spite of his, Sunario's, attempts at pacification. The resident did not go further into this insincerity. He knew that the discontent was fanned from the *kabupatèn,* but he knew also that he had won. Once more, however, he impressed upon the regent his responsibility, if anything happened in the *pendoppo,* next day, during the *kumpulan.* The regent entreated him not to think of such a thing. And now, to part on friendly terms, he begged Van Oudijck to sit down again. Van Oudijck resumed his seat. In doing so, he knocked as though by accident against the tumbler, all frosted with the chill of the ice, which he had not yet put to his lips. It fell clattering to the ground. He apologized for his clumsiness. The radèn-aju pangéran had remarked his movement and her old face turned pale. She said nothing, but beckoned to an attendant. And the four servants appeared again, crouching along the floor, and mixed a second whisky and soda. Van Oudijck at once lifted the glass to his lips.

There was a painful silence. To what degree the resident's movement in upsetting the glass was justified would always remain a question. He would never know. But he wished to show the princess that, when coming here, he was prepared for anything, *before* their conversation, and that, *after* this conversation, he meant to trust her utterly and completely, not only in respect of the drink she offered him, but next day, at the *kumpulan,* where he and his officials would appear unarmed, because of their respect for her influence, for her desire to do good, which would bring peace and tranquillity to the people. And, as though to show him that she understood him and that his confidence would be wholly justified, she stood up and whispered a few words to an attendant whom she had beckoned to her. The Javanese disappeared and soon returned, crouching all the way through the front verandah, carrying a long object in a yellow case. The princess took it from him and handed it to Sunario, who took a walking stick from the yellow silk case and offered it to the resident as a token of their fraternal friendship. Van Oudijck accepted it, understanding the symbol. For the yellow silk case was of the color and the material of authority, yellow or gold, and silk; the stick was from wood that served as a protection against snakebites and bad luck; and the heavy knob was wrought of the metal of authority, gold, in the form of the ancient sultan's crown. This stick, offered at such a moment, signified that the Adiningrats submitted anew and that Van Oudijck could trust them.

And when he took his leave, he was very proud of himself. By exercising tact, diplomacy, and knowledge of the Javanese, he had won; he would have allayed the rebellion merely by force of words. That would be a fact.

That was so, that would be so: a fact. On that first evening of the *pasar malam*, lit gaily with a hundred paraffin lamps, smelling invitingly of cooking, packed with the colorful crowd of the celebrating populace —that first evening was only meant for fun, and the people discussed with one another the long and friendly visit that the resident had paid to the regent and his mother, for they had seen the carriage with the *pajong* waiting a long time in the drive, and the regent's attendants had told of the present of the walking stick.

That was right. The fact existed and had happened as Van Oudijck had planned it in advance and compelled it to happen. And that he should be proud of this was human. But what he had not compelled or planned in advance was the hidden forces, which he never divined, whose existence he would deny, always, in his simple, natural life. What he did *not* see and hear and feel was the very hidden force that, though it had indeed subsided, was yet smouldering like a volcanic fire under the apparently peaceful meadows of flowers and amity and peace. This was the hatred that would have a power of impenetrable mystery, against which he, the European, was unarmed.

21

Van Oudijck was fond of certain effects. He did not say much about his visit to the *kabupatèn* that day, nor in the evening, when Eldersma and Van Helderen came to speak to him about the *kumpulan* to be held the next morning. They felt more or less uneasy and asked if they should go armed. But Van Oudijck very firmly and decidedly forbade them to take arms with them and said that no one was allowed to do so. The officials gave in, but nobody felt comfortable. The *kumpulan*, however, took place in complete peace and harmony. There were only more people moving about among the booths of the *pasar malam*, and there were more police near the ornamental arches, with the rippling strips of bunting. But nothing happened. At home the wives were anxious and felt relieved when their husbands returned safely. And Van Oudijck had achieved what he wanted. He paid a few visits, feeling sure of his grip on things, relying on the radèn-aju pangéran. He reassured the ladies and told them to think of nothing now except the fair. But they didn't trust things. Some families bolted all their doors at night and remained in the middle gallery with their visitors and children and *babus*, armed, listening, on their guard.

After his father had spoken to him in an outburst of confidence, Theo played a practical joke with Addy. One evening the two of them went to the houses of those whom they knew to be most frightened and made their way onto the front verandah and shouted to have the doors opened, and they could hear the cocking of firearms in the middle galleries. They had a lot of fun that night.

Then at last the fair took place. Eva had organized a series of three *tableaux* from the Arthurian legends on the stage of the club: Vivian and Guinevere and Lancelot. In the middle of the garden was a Maduran proa, fitted out like a Viking's ship, in which iced punch was served. A nearby sugar factory, always ready for fun, had provided a complete Dutch *poffertjes* stall,[68] as a nostalgic memory of Holland, with the ladies dressed as Frisian farmers' wives and the employees of the factory as cooks. The excitement about Transvaal was represented by a Majuba Hill with ladies and gentlemen in fantastic Boer costumes. Nothing referred to the tremendous seaquake at Ternate, although one half of the receipts was destined for the devastated districts. Under the glowing festoons of the Chinese lanterns slung across the gardens, a great sense of fun prevailed, coupled with a readiness to spend lots of money, especially on behalf of Transvaal. But despite the merriment there was an undertone of fear. Small groups were formed, peering anxiously at the road outside, where Indos, Javanese, Chinese, and Arabs stood around the steaming portable kitchens. And while drinking a glass of champagne or eating a plate of *poffertjes*, people tried to hear what was going on in the *alun-alun*, where the *pasar malam* was in full swing. When Van Oudijck appeared with Doddy, greeted by the Dutch national anthem, generously distributing money, he was constantly asked whispered questions. And when they noticed that Mrs. Van Oudijck was not coming, people began to ask one another where she was. She had a terrible toothache, people said; she had gone to Surabaja to see the dentist. They did not think it nice of her; they did not like her when they did not see her. She was much discussed that evening, and the most horrible scandals were told about her. Doddy took her place in the Madura proa as a saleswoman, and Van Oudijck, with Eldersma, Van Helderen, and a couple of controllers from other districts, went round and treated his personnel. When people asked him mysterious questions, with anxious glances at the road, with ears pricked toward the *alun-alun*, he reassured them with a majestic smile: nothing was going to happen, he pledged his word on it. They considered him too trusting and sure of himself, but the jovial smile under his thick mustache was comforting. He urged all who lived in the good town of Labuwangi to think of nothing but enjoyment and charity. And, when suddenly the regent, Radèn Adipati Sunario, and his wife, the young radèn-aju, appeared at the entrance and paid for bouquets, programs, and fans with a hundred-guilder note, the tension relaxed throughout the garden. Everybody soon knew about the hundred-guilder note. And they all breathed again, realizing that there was now no occasion for anxiety, that there would be no insurrection that night. They made much of the regent and his smiling young wife, who glittered with her beautiful jewels.

Out of sheer relief and relaxation of their tense anxiety, out of sheer craziness, they spent more and more money, trying to compete with the few wealthy Chinese—those dating from before the opium monopoly, owners of the white marble and stucco palaces—who, with their wives in embroidered gray and green Chinese robes, with their shiny hair covered with flowers and precious stones and smelling strongly of sandalwood, scattered *rijksdaalders* everywhere.[69] Money flowed like water, tinkled like silver drops into the collection boxes of the delighted saleswomen. The fair was a success. When finally Van Oudijck, little by little, here and there, said a word to Doorn de Bruijn, to Rantzow, to the officials from other residencies, about his visit, about his interview with the radèn-aju pangéran—assuming an air of humility and simplicity, but nevertheless, despite himself, beaming with happy pride, with delight in his triumph—then he made his greatest impression.

The story spread throughout the garden, about the tact and the cleverness of the resident, who had prevented an insurrection with just a few words. He was feted. He filled every glass with champagne, he bought up every fan, he bought all the unsold tickets of the raffle. People adored him; it was his greatest moment of success and popularity. And he joked with the ladies and flirted with them.

The party went on until daylight, until six o'clock in the morning. The merry cooks were drunk and danced around their *poffertjes* stove. And, when Van Oudijck went home at last, he felt pleased with himself, strong, happy. He felt like a king in his little world, like a diplomat, and loved by all whose quiet and peace he had assured. That evening made him rise in his own estimation and he valued himself more highly than he ever had before. Never had he felt as happy as he felt now.

He had sent the carriage away and he walked home with Doddy. A few early salesmen were going to the *pasar*. Doddy, worn out and half asleep, trudged along on her father's arm . . . until someone passed very close to her; feeling rather than seeing, she suddenly shuddered. She looked up. The figure had passed. She looked round and recognized the back of the *hadji*, hurrying away. . . .

She turned cold and felt as though she would faint. But then, wearily, as if walking in her sleep, she thought that she was dreaming, dreaming about Addy, about Patjaram, about the moonlit night under the *tjemaras*, where the white *hadji* had startled her at the end of the avenue. . . .

22

Eva Eldersma was in a more listless and dejected mood than she had ever experienced in the Indies. After all her efforts, after the fuss and the success of the fair, after the shuddering fear of an uprising, the little town went back to sleep again, as though well content to be able to slumber as usual. It was December and the heavy rains had begun as usual, on the fifth of the month: the rainy monsoon invariably began on St. Nicholas Day. The clouds that for the past month, continually swelling, had piled themselves up on the low horizon, moved like curtains, like water-laden sails higher against the skies, and were torn open as if by a sudden fury of distantly flashing electricity, pouring and lashing down as though this wealth of water could no longer be contained, now that the swollen sails had been ripped apart, as though all their wanton abundance came streaming down from a single rent. During the evening, Eva's front verandah was invaded by a crazy swarm of insects which, drunk with light, rushed upon their destruction in the lamps, as in an apotheosis of fiery death, filling the lamp chimneys and strewing the marble tables with their fluttering, dying bodies. Eva inhaled a cooler air; but a mist of damp, arising from earth and leaves, soaked the walls, seemed to ooze from the furniture, dimmed the mirrors, stained the silk hangings, and covered boots and shoes with mildew, as if nature's frenzied downpour were bent on the ruin of all that was fine and delicate, sparkling and graceful in human achievement. But trees, foliage, and grass came to life and expanded and rioted luxuriantly upward, in a thousand shades of fresh green, and in the reviving glory of verdant nature, the crouching human community of open villas, wet and humid with fungi, all the whiteness of the stuccoed pillars and flowerpots turned to a moldy green.

Eva watched the slow and gradual spoiling of her house, her furniture, her clothes. Day by day, inexorably, something was spoilt, something rotted away, something was covered with mildew or rust. And nothing of the aesthetic philosophizing which she had used at first to teach herself to love the Indies, to appreciate the good in the Indies, to seek also in the Indies for the external line of beauty and the inward beauty of the soul, none of it was able to withstand the streaming water, the cracking of her furniture, the staining of her frocks and gloves, the damp, mildew, and rust that ruined the exquisite environment that she had designed and created all around her, as a comfort, to console her for living in the Indies. All her logic, all her reasoning for making the best of things, of finding something after all that was attractive and beautiful in this land of overpowering nature, and of people eager for money and positions—all this failed her and came to naught, now that she was every moment irritated and angered as a housewife, as an elegant woman, an artistic woman. No, it was impossible in the Indies to surround one's self with taste and elegance. She had been here for only two years and she was still able to put up a fight for her Western culture, but she also understood better than before why men let themselves go after their busy day at work, or women after their housekeeping.

True, the servants with their soundless movements, working with gentle hands, willing, never impertinent, she preferred far more than the noisy, banging maids in Holland, and yet she felt that there was in her household an Eastern antagonism to her Western ideas. It was always a struggle not to surrender to lassitude, to let the grounds go wild, which invariably displayed in the back the dirty laundry of the servants and which were covered with half-eaten mangoes; to let the paint peel on the house that was too large, too open, too much exposed to wind and weather to be cared for with Dutch cleanliness; to get into the habit of sitting and rocking in *sarong* and *kabaai,* with bare feet in slippers, because it was really too hot and too sultry to put on a dress or robe which would only get soaked from perspiration. It was for her sake that her husband always dressed for dinner in a black jacket and stiff collar, but when she saw his tired face that was more and more etched with that overtired office look above that stiff collar, she told him not to bother to dress up next time after his second bath, and allowed him to dine in a white jacket, or even in pajamas. She thought that terrible, unspeakably dreadful, and it shocked all her ideas of propriety, but really, he was too tired and it was too sultry and oppressive for her to expect anything more from him. And she, after only two years in the Indies, understood more and more easily that letting things go—in dress, in body, and in soul—now that every day she lost something more of her fresh, Dutch blood and her Western energy, now that she had to admit that in the Indies people worked perhaps harder than in any country, but that they did so for only one reason: position, money, retirement, pension . . . and then home, back home to Europe.

True, there were others, born in the Indies, who had left only once, for barely a year, who didn't want anything to do with Holland, who adored their land of sunshine. She knew that the De Luces were like that, and there were others as well. But in her own circle of civil servants and planters everyone had the same object in life: position, money . . . and then off, off to Europe. Everyone counted the years of work still ahead of him. Everyone looked to the future for the illusion of that European retirement. Occasionally someone like Van Oudijck—who perhaps loved his work for its own sake and because it suited his nature—feared retirement because it meant vegetating. But Van Oudijck was an exception. The majority worked only in the civil service and on the plantations for the sake of future retirement. Her husband, for instance, worked like a slave to become assistant resident and to retire after a few years in rank, slaved and toiled for his illusion of rest. Well, she felt her own energy leaving her with every drop of blood that she felt flowing more sluggishly through her weary veins. And in these early days of the wet monsoon, when the gutters of the house incessantly spewed forth streams of water that irritated her with the clatter, while she watched the gradual ruin of the material things that she had selected with so much taste as her artistic consolation for the Indies, she experienced a worse mood of listlessness and dejection than she had ever gone through before. Her child was still too small to mean much to her, to be a kindred spirit. Her husband did nothing but work. He was a kind and thoughtful husband to her, a sweet man in every way, a man of great simplicity whom she might have accepted precisely for that simplicity, because of the quiet serenity of his smiling, fair Frisian face and his substantial broad shoulders, after one or two excited, juvenile romances of enthusiasm and misunderstanding and soulful discussion, romances dating from her girlhood. She, who was herself neither simple nor serene, had looked for the simplicity of life in a simple romance. But his qualities failed to satisfy her. Now especially, when she had been in the Indies for a while and was suffering defeat in her contest with the country that did not harmonize with her nature, his serene conjugal love failed to satisfy her.

She was beginning to feel unhappy. She was too versatile a woman to find all her happiness in her little boy. He did fill part of her life with the minor cares of the present and the thought of his future. She had even worked out a plan on how to raise him, but it did not occupy her entire life. And a longing for Holland overwhelmed her, a longing for her parents, a longing for the beautiful, artistic home where there were always painters to meet, writers, musicians, the artistic *salon*—an exception in Holland—that gathered for a brief moment the artistic elements which in Holland usually remained isolated.

The vision passed before her eyes like a vague and distant dream, while she listened to the approaching thunder that filled the air, sultry to the point of bursting, while she gazed at the downpour that followed. Here she had nothing. Here she felt out of place. Here she had her little clique of adherents, who collected around her because she was cheerful, but she did not find a more profound sympathy, or a more intimate conversation . . . except with Van Helderen. And with him she meant to be careful, so as to give him no illusions.

There was only Van Helderen. And she thought of all the other people around her in Labuwangi. She thought of people, people everywhere. And, because she felt pessimistic these days, she found in all of them the same egoism, the same complacency, the same unattractiveness, the same self-absorption: she could hardly express it to herself, distracted as she was by the terrific force of the pelting rain. But she found in everybody conscious and unconscious traits of unpleasantness, even in her faithful adherents, in her husband, and in the men, the young wives, girls, young men around her. Everybody lived for themselves. No one was sufficiently in tune with himself to care about others. She disapproved of this in one, hated that in another, a third and a fourth she condemned entirely. This critical attitude made her despondent and melancholy, for it was against her nature. She preferred to like people.

She liked to be one, in spontaneous harmony, with a number of people: originally she had a profound love for people, for humanity. Important issues moved her. But nothing that she felt found any rapport. She found herself empty and alone, in a country, a town, an environment where everything, large and small, offended her soul, her body, her character, her nature. Her husband worked. Her child was adapting more and more to the Indies. Her piano was out of tune.

She stood up and tried the piano, with long runs that ended in the *Feuerzauber* of Wagner's *Walküre*. But the roar of the rain was louder than her playing. When she got up again, feeling desperately dejected, she saw Van Helderen standing before her.

"You startled me," she said.

"May I stay for lunch?" he asked. "I am all by myself at home. Ida has gone to Tosari[70] for her malaria and has taken the children with her. She went yesterday. It's an expensive business. I don't know how I'm going to make it this month."

"Send the children to us after they've had a few days in the hills."

"Won't they bother you?"

"Of course not. I'll write to Ida."

"It's really very nice of you. It would certainly make things easier for me."

She laughed dully.

"Aren't you well?" he asked.

"I feel deadly," she said.

"How do you mean?"

"I feel as if I were dying by inches."

"Why?"

"It's terrible here. We've been longing for the rains, and, now that they've come, they are driving me crazy. And . . . I don't know, I can't stand it here any longer."

"Where?"

"In the Indies. I taught myself to see the good, the beautiful in this country, but it's no use. I can't go on with it."

"Go to Holland," he said, gently.

"My parents would be glad to see me. It would be good for my boy, because he's forgetting more and more Dutch every day. I had started to teach him so conscientiously, and he speaks Malay, or worse even, he speaks like a *sinjo*. But I can't leave my husband here. He would have nothing here without me. At least, I think so. Perhaps it's not so at all."

"But, if you fall ill. . . ."

"Oh, I don't know. . . ."

She was overwhelmed by an unusual fatigue.

"Perhaps you're exaggerating!" he began cheerfully. "Come, perhaps you're exaggerating! What's upsetting you, what's making you so unhappy? Let's make a list."

"A list of my misfortunes? Very well. My garden is a swamp. Three chairs on my front verandah are splitting to pieces. White ants devoured my beautiful Japanese mats. A new silk dress suddenly has stains all over it, for no reason that I can make out. Another is all unraveled, simply with the heat, I believe. To say nothing of various minor miseries of the same order. To console myself I took refuge in the *Feuerzauber*. My piano was out of tune, I believe there are cockroaches walking among the strings."

He laughed a little.

"We're idiots here," she continued, "we Europeans in this country! Why do we bring all the paraphernalia of our costly civilization with us, considering that it will never last? Why don't we live in a cool bamboo hut, sleep on a mat, dress in a *kain pandjang* and a chintz *kabaai*, with a scarf over our shoulders and a flower in our hair? All your civilization by which you propose to grow rich . . . it's a Western idea, which fails in the long run. Our whole administration . . . it's so tiring in the heat. Why —if we must be here—don't we live simply and plant paddy and live on nothing?"

"You're talking like a woman," he said, with another little laugh.

"Possibly," she said. "Perhaps I don't mean quite all I say. But what I feel here, opposing me, opposing all my Western notions, is a force that is antagonistic to me . . . that is certain. I am sometimes frightened. I always feel . . . that I am on the point of being conquered, I don't know by what, by something out of the ground, by a force of nature, by a secret in the soul of these black people, whom I don't know. . . . I feel particularly afraid at night."

"You're overwrought," he said, tenderly.

"Possibly," she replied wearily, seeing that he did not understand her and she was too tired to go on explaining. "Let's talk about something else. That table-turning was very strange."

"Very," he said.

"The other day, the three of us: Ida, you, and I. . . ."

"It certainly was very strange."

"Do you remember the first time? Addy de Luce: it seems to be true about him and Mrs. Van Oudijck. . . . And the insurrection . . . the table foretold it."

"May we not have suggested it unconsciously?"

"I don't know. But to think that we were all playing fair and that that table should go tapping and talking to us by means of an alphabet."

"I shouldn't do it often, Eva, if I were you."

"No, I can't explain it. And yet it's already beginning to bore me. One grows so accustomed to the incomprehensible."

"Everything's incomprehensible."

"Yes . . . and everything's a bore."

"Eva," he said, with a soft, reproachful laugh.

"I give up the fight. I shall just sit in my rocking chair . . . and look at the rain."

"There was a time when you used to see the beautiful side of my country."

"Your country? Which you would be glad to leave tomorrow to go to the Paris Exhibition."

"I've never seen anything."

"How humble you are today."

"I am sad, because of you."

"Oh, please don't."

"Play something. . . ."

"Here, have your gin-and-bitters. Help yourself. I'll play on my out-of-tune piano, it will sound as melodious as my soul, which is also confused. . . ."

She went back to the middle gallery and played something from *Par-*

sifal. He remained sitting outside and listened. The rain was pouring furiously. The garden was flooded. A violent clap of thunder seemed to split the world asunder. Nature was supreme; compared to her gigantic manifestation, the two people in that damp house were diminished, his love was nothing, her melancholy was nothing, and the mystic music of the Grail was like a children's song compared to the echoing mystery of that thunder, wherewith fate itself seemed to sail with heavenly cymbals over these creatures drowned in the deluge.

23

Van Helderen's two children, a boy and girl of six and seven, were staying at Eva's, and Van Helderen came regularly once a day for a meal. He never mentioned his intense feeling anymore, as though unwilling to disturb the pleasant intimacy of their daily encounters. And she accepted his daily visits, was powerless to keep him at a distance. He was the only man in her immediate circle with whom she could speak and think aloud, and he was a comfort to her in these days of dejection. She did not understand how she had come to this, but she gradually lapsed into an absolute apathy, a kind of annihilating state of thinking that nothing was necessary. She had never been like this before. Her nature was lively and cheerful, seeking and admiring the beautiful in poetry and music and painting, things that, from her early childhood, from her childish books, she had seen about her and had felt and discussed. In the Indies she had gradually come to lack everything of which she felt a need. In her despair she succumbed to a sort of nihilism, as if to ask: What is the reason of anything, why the world and the people in it and the mountains, why all this insignificant whirling of life?

And then, when she read of the social movements, of the great social problems in Europe, of the increasingly urgent Indo question in Java, she thought to herself: Why should there be a world, if man eternally remains the same, small and suffering and oppressed by all the misery of his humanity.

She did not see the purpose of it all. Half of mankind was suffering poverty and struggling upwards out of that darkness . . . to what? The other half was stagnating stupidly and dully amid its riches. Between the two was a scale of gradations from bitter poverty to dismal wealth. Over them arched the rainbow of eternal illusions: love, art, the great questions of justice, peace, and an ideal future. . . . She felt that it was much ado about nothing; she failed to see the purpose and she thought to herself: Should it be this way and why the world, and why poor humanity. . . ?

She had never felt like this before, but there was no struggling against it. Gradually, from day to day, the Indies were making her so, making her sick at heart. Frans van Helderen was her only consolation. The young controller, who had never been to Europe, who had received all his education at Batavia, who had passed his examinations at Batavia, with his distinguished manners, his supple courtesy, his strange, enigmatic nationality, had grown dear to her because of his almost exotic development. She told him how she delighted in this friendship, and he no longer replied by offering his love. There was too much charm about their present relation. There was something idealistic about it, which they both needed. In their everyday surroundings that friendship shone before them like some exquisite glory of which they were both proud. He often called to see her, especially now that his wife was at Tosari, and at twilight they would walk to the lighthouse which stood by the sea like a small Eiffel Tower. These walks were much talked about, but they paid no attention. They sat down on the foundation of the lighthouse, looked out to sea, and listened to the distance. Ghostly proas, with sails like nightbirds, floated into the canal, with the droning song of the fishermen. A melancholy of resignation, of a small world and small people, hovered beneath the skies filled with twinkling stars, where gleamed the mystic diamonds of the Southern Cross or the Turkish crescent of the horned moon. And, above that melancholy of the droning fishermen, of precarious proas, of small people at the foot of the little lighthouse, drifted a fathomless immensity of the skies and the eternal stars. And from that immensity drifted the unutterable, as if it were the superhumanly divine, wherein all that was small and human sank and melted away.

"Why attach any value to life when I may die tomorrow?" thought Eva. "Why all this confusion and turmoil of mankind, when tomorrow everything may have ceased to exist?"

And she put the question to him. He replied that each person was not living for oneself and the present age, but for all mankind and for the future. But she laughed bitterly, shrugged her shoulders, thought him banal. And she thought herself banal too, to think such things that had so often been thought before. But notwithstanding her self-criticism, she continued under the obsession of the uselessness of life when everything might be dead tomorrow. And a humiliating littleness, as of atoms, overcame both of them, as they sat there, gazing into the spaciousness of the skies and the eternal stars.

Yet they loved those moments, which were everything in their lives, for, when they did not feel their pettiness too keenly, they spoke of books, music, painting, and the big important things of life. And they felt that, in spite of the circulating library and the Italian opera at Surabaja, they were no longer keeping up with things. They felt that the great and important things were far removed from them. And both of them were seized with a longing for Europe, so they wouldn't have to feel so insignificant anymore. They would both have liked to get away, to go to Europe, but neither of them was able. Their petty, daily life held them captive, but then, almost spontaneously, in mutual harmony, they spoke of what represented soul and being and all the mystery thereof.

All the mystery. They felt it in the sea, in the sky, but they also quietly sought it in the tapping of the leg of a table. They did not understand how a soul or spirit could reveal itself by means of a table on which they put their hands in all seriousness and which, by what streamed through them, was transformed from dead to living matter. But, when they did put their hands on it, the table lived and they were forced to believe. The letters that were tapped out were often confused, deriving from some strange alphabet, and the table, as though directed by a mocking spirit, constantly showed a tendency to tease and confuse, to stop suddenly or to be coarse and indecent. Together they read books on spiritualism and did not know whether to believe or not.

These were quiet days of quiet monotony in the little town swept by the rustling rain. Their life seemed unreal, like a dream that rose through the rain like a mist. And it was like a sudden awakening for Eva when, one afternoon, walking outside in the damp avenue, waiting for Van Helderen, she saw Van Oudijck coming in her direction.

"I was just on my way over," he cried, excitedly. "I was just coming to ask a favor. Will you help me once more?"

"With what, Resident?"

"But first, tell me: Aren't you well? You're not looking very fit lately."

"It's nothing serious," she said. "It'll pass. What can I help you with, Resident?"

"There's something to be done, and we can't manage without you. My wife herself was saying this morning, better ask Mrs. Eldersma."

"But tell me what it is."

"You know Mrs. Staats, the stationmaster's widow. The poor woman has been left without a thing, except for her five children and some debts."

"He committed suicide, didn't he?"

"Yes, it's very sad. And we really must help her. It'll need a lot of money. Sending round a subscription list won't do much. People are very generous, but they've already made such sacrifices lately. They went mad at the fair. They can't do much for the moment, because it's the end of the month. But early next month, in the first week of January, perhaps a play from your Thalia society. You know, nothing elaborate, a couple of drawingroom things and no expenses. Seats at a guilder and a half, two guilders and a half, perhaps, and, if *you* get it going, the hall will be full, people will come over from Surabaja. You must help me; you will, won't you?"

"But, Resident," said Eva, wearily, "we've just had those *tableaux-vivants*. Don't be angry with me, but I don't care to be always acting."

"Yes, yes, you must this time," Van Oudijck insisted, a little imperiously, greatly excited about his plan.

She became peevish. She liked her independence, and particularly during these days of dejection she was too disconsolate and too much confused to accede at once with good grace to his authoritative request.

"Really, Resident, I can't think of anything this time," she answered, curtly. "Why doesn't Mrs. Van Oudijck do it herself?"

She was startled when she made this peevish remark; walking beside her, the resident lost his composure and his face clouded over. The animated, cheerful expression and the jovial smile around his thick mustache suddenly disappeared. She saw that she had been cruel and felt sorry about it. And for the first time she suddenly saw that though in love with his wife, he did not approve of her withdrawing herself from everything. She saw that it hurt him. It was as though this side of his character was becoming clearer to her, seeing it plainly for the first time.

He did not know what to reply; while looking for his words, he remained silent.

Then she said, sweetly, "Don't be angry, Resident. It wasn't nice of me. I know that that sort of business bores Mrs. Van Oudijck. I am glad to relieve her of it. I will do anything you wish."

She was nervous and her eyes filled with tears.

He was smiling now and was scrutinizing her face.

"You're so nervous lately. But I knew that you had a good heart, and wouldn't leave me in the lurch, and would consent to help that good old Mother Staats. But nothing fancy, madam, no expense, no new scenery. Just your wit, your talent, your beautiful French or Dutch, whichever you prefer. We're proud of all that here in Labuwangi, you know; and all those marvelous things you do for us for free is quite enough to make the performance a success. But you're nervous, dear lady. Why are you crying? Aren't you well? Tell me, is there anything I can do for you?"

"Don't work my husband so hard, Resident. I never see him anymore."

He made a gesture to show that he couldn't do much about that.

"It's true," he admitted. "There's an awful lot to do. Is that the problem?"

"And make me see the good side of the Indies."

"Is *that* it?"

"And a lot besides."

"Are you becoming homesick? Don't you care for the Indies any longer, don't you care for Labuwangi, where all of us admire you so much? . . . You misjudge the Indies. Try to see the good side of it."

"I have tried."

"Is it no use?"

"No."

"You are too sensible not to see the good things here."

"You are too fond of it to be impartial. And I don't know how to be impartial. But tell me the good things."

"What shall I begin with? The satisfaction of being able, as an official, to do good for the country and the people. The wonderful sense of working for this country and this people, the hard work that fills a man's life out here. . . . I'm not speaking about the paperwork your husband has to do, because he is a secretary. But I'm speaking of later on, when he becomes an assistant resident!"

"It will be so long before that happens!"

"Well, then, the ample way we live here."

"The white ants gnaw everything."

"That's a poor joke, madam."

"Very possibly, Resident. Everything is out of tune with me, inside and out: my wit, my piano, and my poor soul."

"Nature, then?"

"I don't feel it at all. Nature is conquering me and devouring me."

"Your own activities?"

"My activities? One of the good things in the Indies?"

"Yes. To inspire us practical people once in a while with your wit."

"Resident! You're paying me compliments! Is this all on account of the play?"

"And to do good for Mother Staats by using that wit of yours?"

"Couldn't I do good in Europe?"

"Certainly, certainly," he said curtly. "Go to Europe, by all means. Go and live at The Hague, join the Charity Organization . . . with a collection box at your door and a *rijksdaalder* . . . how often?"

She laughed: "Now you're becoming unfair. They do a lot of good in Holland too."

"But we're doing it for *one* poor soul; would that ever happen in Holland? And don't tell me that there's less poverty here."

"Well?"

"Well, then, there is a great deal of good to be done here. Your material and moral work for others. Don't let Van Helderen get too much smitten with you, madam. He's a charming fellow, but he puts too much literature into his monthly reports. I see him coming and I must be off. So I can rely on you?"

"Absolutely."

"When shall we have the first meeting, with the committee and the ladies?"

"Tomorrow evening, Resident, at your house?"

"Fine. I will send the subscription lists around. We must make a lot of money."

"We'll do our best for Mother Staats," she said, gently.

He shook her hand and went away. She felt limp and did not know why.

"The resident has been warning me about you, because you're too literary!" she teased Van Helderen.

She sat down on the front verandah. The skies burst asunder; a white curtain of rain came down in straight folds of water. A plague of locusts came hopping along the verandah. In the corners a cloud of tiny flies hummed like an Aeolian harp. Eva and Van Helderen placed their hands on the little table and it jerked one of its legs while the beetles buzzed around them.

24

The subscription list went around. The plays were rehearsed and performed in three weeks' time, and the committee handed the resident a sum of nearly fifteen hundred guilders for Mother Staats. Her debts were paid, a little house was rented for her, and she was set up in a small dress shop which Eva stocked from Paris. All the ladies in Labuwangi placed an order with Staats, and in less than a month not only was the woman saved from utter ruin, but her life had returned to normal, her children were going to school again, and she was enjoying a pleasant livelihood. All this had happened so swiftly and unostentatiously, the subscriptions were so substantial, and the ladies so readily ordered a dress or a hat which they did not need, that Eva was astounded. And she had to confess to herself that the egoism, the self-absorption, the unlovable qualities that she had often observed in their social life—in their conversation, intrigue, and gossip—had suddenly been thrust into the background by a common talent for doing the right thing, doing it simply because it had to be done, because there was no question about it, because the woman had to be helped. Roused from her depression by the bustle of the rehearsals, stimulated to brisk action, she appreciated the better, finer side of her environment and wrote so enthusiastically of it to Holland that her parents, to whom the Indies was a blank book, smiled. But, although this episode had awakened a soft and gentle and appreciative feeling in her, it was only an episode, and she returned to being the same person again when the emotion of it was over. And despite the fact that she felt the disapproval of Labuwangi around her, she continued to find the main interest of her life in Van Helderen's friendship.

For there was so little else. Her little circle of the faithful, which she had gathered round her with so many illusions, whom she invited to dinner, for whom her doors were always open: What did it actually amount to? She now accepted the Doorn de Bruijns and the Rantzows as indifferent acquaintances, but no longer as friends. She suspected Mrs. Doorn de Bruijn of insincerity, Dr. Rantzow was too bourgeois, too vulgar for her, and his wife was an insignificant German *Hausfrau*. True, they joined in the table-turning, but they relished the absurd ineptitudes, the indecent conversation of the mocking spirit. She and Van Helderen took the whole thing seriously, though she also thought the table rather comical. And so there was no one left but Van Helderen to interest her.

But Van Oudijck had won her admiration. She had suddenly obtained a glimpse of his character; though it entirely lacked the artistic charm which had hitherto exclusively attracted her in men, she saw the line of beauty also in this man, who was not at all artistic, who had not the least conception of art, but who had so much that was beautiful in his simple, manly notion of duty and in the calmness with which he endured the disappointment of his domestic life. For Eva saw that, though he adored his wife, he did not approve of Léonie's indifference to all the interests on which his own life was built. If he saw nothing more, if he was blind to all the rest that went on in his family life, it was this disappointment that was his secret pain, to which he was not blind, down deep in himself.

And she admired him; her admiration was like a revelation that art is not always paramount in life. She suddenly understood that the exaggerated worship of art in our time was a disease, a disease from which she herself had suffered, and was still suffering from. For what was she, what did she do? Nothing. Her parents, both of them, were great artists, true artists; their house was like a temple, and their bias was comprehensible and pardonable. But what about her? She played the piano pretty well, that was all. She had a few ideas, some taste; that was all. But in her day she had raved about things with other young girls, and she now remembered that silly adoration, of exchanging letters full of cheap philosophy and written in a derivative modern style. And thus, despite her depression, her thought processes carried her a step further and she underwent a certain development. For it seemed incredible that she, the child of her parents, should not always place art above everything else.

And she had in her that tension between seeking and thinking in order to find her way, now that she was quite lost in a country alien to her nature, among people whom she looked down on, without letting them know it. She strove to find what was good in the country, in order to make it her own and cherish it; she was glad to find among the people those few who roused her sympathy and her admiration, but whatever was good remained incidental to her, a few people remained exceptional, and, despite all her searching and thinking, she did not find her way and retained the moodiness of a woman who was too European, too artistic—despite her self-knowledge and consequent denial of her artistic capacity—to live quietly and contentedly in a provincial Javanese town, with a husband wrapped up in his office work, in a climate that upset her health, amid natural surroundings that overwhelmed her, and among people whom she disliked.

During the most lucid moments of this play and counterplay, it was the obvious fear, the fear that she felt most clearly of all, the fear that she felt slowly approaching, she knew not whence, she knew not whither, but hovering over her head, as with the thousand veils of a fate gliding through the sultry, rain-laden skies. . . .

During these moods she had refrained from gathering her little clique around her, for she herself did not care to take the trouble to ask them, and her friends did not understand her well enough to look her up. They missed the cheerfulness in her which had attracted them at first, and now envy and hostility came to the fore,[71] and people began to talk about her: she was affected, pedantic, vain, proud; she was pretentious and always wanted to be the first in the town; she behaved as though she were the resident's wife and ordered everyone about. She wasn't really pretty, she had an impossible way of dressing, her house was preposterously arranged. And then there was her relationship with Van Helderen, their evening walks to the lighthouse. Ida heard about it in Tosari, from the gossip in the small poky hotel where the guests were bored when they were not going on excursions, and so sat around on the small verandahs, almost in each other's laps, peeking into one another's rooms, listening at the thin partitions. Ida heard about it in Tosari and it was enough to arouse in her the white-*nonna* instincts and induce her to suddenly, without explanation, remove her children from Eva's charge. When he went up for the weekend, Van Helderen asked his wife for an explanation, asked her why she insulted Eva by taking the children away, without a reason, bringing them back to the hotel, and thus greatly increasing the bill. Ida made a scene, yelled, and had hysterics, which rang through the little hotel, made all the guests prick up their ears, and, like a gale, whipped the cackling chatter into a storm. And, without further explanation, Ida broke with Eva.

Eva withdrew into herself. Even in Surabaja, where she went to do some shopping, she heard the gossip and backbiting. She became so sick of her world and her people that she quietly withdrew from society. She wrote Van Helderen not to come anymore. She entreated him to patch things up with his wife. She stopped seeing him. And now she was completely alone. She felt that she was not in the mood to find comfort from anyone around her. There was no sympathy or understanding to be found in the Indies for moods such as hers. And so she withdrew. Her husband was working hard, as usual, but she devoted herself more zealously to her little boy, she immersed herself in her love for her child. She withdrew into her love for her house. This was a life of never going out, of never seeing anyone, of never hearing any music other than her own. This was seeking comfort in her house, her child, and her books. This was the personality that she had become after her early illusions and aspirations. She now constantly felt the longing for Europe, for Holland, for her parents, for people of artistic culture. And now it developed into hatred for the country that she had at first seen in the overwhelming grandeur of its beauty, with its majestic mountains and the soft mystery in its nature and people. Now she hated nature and humanity, and their mystery terrified her.

She now filled her life with nothing but her child. Her boy, little Onno, was three years old. She would guide him, make a man of him. From the day he was born she had had vague notions of seeing her son become a great artist, by preference a writer, famous throughout the world. But she had learnt a lot since then. She felt that art could not always be supreme. She felt that there were higher things which, when she was depressed, she denied, but which were there nevertheless, radiant and great. They had to do with shaping the future with, above all, peace, justice, and brotherhood. Oh, the great brotherhood of the poor and the rich which now, in her loneliness, she thought to be the highest ideal to work for, the way sculptors work on a monument. Justice and peace would follow, but brotherhood had to be established first, and she wished her son to work for this. Where? In Europe? In the Indies? She did not know. She saw it in Europe rather than in the Indies. And in the Indies the inexplicable, the enigmatical, the fearful was always in her thoughts. How strange it was, how strange. . . . She was a woman made for ideals. Perhaps this by itself was the simple explanation of what she felt and feared in the Indies.

"Your impressions of the Indies are completely wrong," her husband would say. "Quiet? You think it's quiet here? Why should I have to work so hard here if things were quiet in Labuwangi? We have hundreds of interests at heart, of Europeans and Javanese alike. Agriculture is studied as eagerly in this country as anywhere.

The population is increasing steadily. . . . Declining? A colony where there's always so much going on? That's one of Van Helderen's imbecile notions. Speculative ideas, completely out of the blue, which you just mouth after him. . . . I can't understand the way you see the Indies nowadays. . . . There was a time when you saw all that was beautiful and interesting here. That time seems to be past. Perhaps you should go home to Holland. . . ."

But she knew that he would be very lonely without her, and for this reason she refused to go. Later, when her boy was older, she would *have* to go. But by then Eldersma would certainly have become an assistant resident. At present he still had seventeen controllers and secretaries above him. It had been going on like this for years, that looking toward promotion in the distant future. It was like yearning after a mirage. He never even considered becoming a resident. Assistant resident for a couple of years, and then to Holland, retired. . . . She thought it a miserable existence, slaving one's self to death like that for Labuwangi. . . .

She was down with malaria and her maid, Saina, was giving her a massage, kneading her aching limbs with supple fingers.

"It's a nuisance, Saina, when I'm ill, for you to stay in the *kampong*. You'd better move here tonight with your four children."

Saina thought it troublesome, a great *susa*.

"Why?"

So Saina explained. Her cottage had been left to her by her husband. She was attached to it, though it was in bad shape. Now that it was the rainy season, the rain often came in through the roof, and then she was unable to cook and the children had to go without food. To have it repaired was difficult. She had a *ringgit* a week from the *njonja*. Sixty cents of that went for rice. Then there were a few cents daily for fish, coconut oil, *sirih*, a few cents for fuel. . . . No, repairs were out of the question. She would be much better off with the *kandjeng njonja*, much better off on the estate. But it would be a *susa* to find a tenant for the cottage, because it was so wrecked, and the *njonja* knew that you could not leave a house empty in the *kampong*, there was a heavy fine for that. . . . So she would rather go on living in her damp cottage. She could stay at night and sit up with the *njonja*, her eldest girl would look after the little ones.

And, resigned to her small existence of little miseries, Saina passed her supple fingers, with a firm and gentle pressure, over her mistress's ailing limbs.

And Eva thought it heart-rending, this living on a *rijksdaalder* a week, with four children, in a house that let in the rain, so that it was impossible to cook there.

"Let me look after your second daughter, Saina," said Eva, a couple of days later.

Saina hesitated and smiled; she'd rather not, but dared not say so.

"Yes," Eva insisted, "let her come here. You'll see her all day long, and she can sleep in *kokkie's* room. I shall get her some clothes, and all she'll have to do is to make sure that my room is tidy. You can teach her that."

"So young still, *'nja*, she's only ten."

"No, no," Eva insisted, "let me do this to help you. What's her name?"

"Mina, *'nja*."

"Mina? That won't do," said Eva. "That's the *djait's* name. We'll find another for her."

Saina brought the child, who was very shy, with a streak of *bedak* on her forehead, and Eva dressed her prettily. She was a very attractive child, with a soft brown, downy skin, and looked charming in her new clothes. She carefully stacked the *sarongs* in the closet and put fragrant white flowers between them. They had to be replaced with fresh ones every day. For a joke, because she arranged the flowers so prettily, Eva called her Melati.

Two days later, Saina crouched down before her *njonja*.

"What is it, Saina?"

Could the little girl come back to the damp cottage in the *kampong*.

"Why?" asked Eva, in amazement. "Isn't your little girl happy here?"

Yes, she was, said Saina bashfully, but she preferred the cottage. The *njonja* was very kind, but little Mina would rather be in the cottage.

Eva was angry and let the child go home, with the new clothes that Saina took with her as a matter of course.

"Why wasn't the child allowed to stay?" Eva asked of the *latta* cook.

Kokkie at first dared not say.

"Come, why wasn't she, *kokkie*?" asked Eva, insisting.

"Because the *kandjeng* called the little girl Melati. . . . Names of flowers and fruits . . . are given only . . . to dancing girls," explained the *kokkie*, mysteriously.[72]

"But why didn't Saina tell me?" asked Eva, greatly incensed. "I had no idea!"

"Too shy," said the *kokkie*, by way of excusing Saina. "*Minta ampon, 'nja.*"[73]

These were trivial incidents in the daily domestic life, little episodes of her housekeeping, but they embittered her, because she felt that they represented a gap that would always exist between her and the people and things of the Indies. She did not know the country, she would never know the people.

And the minor disappointment of those episodes filled her with just as much bitterness as had the greater disappointment of her illusions, because her life, amid the daily trivialities of her housekeeping, was itself becoming more and more trivial.

The early hours of the day were often cool, washed clean by the abundant rains, and the young sunshine of those morning hours evoked from the earth a tender haze, a blue softening of every hard line and color so that the Lange Laan, with its villa residences and fenced gardens, seemed to be surrounded with the vagueness and beauty of a dream avenue. The dream columns rose insubstantially, like a vision of pillared tranquillity, the lines of the roofs acquired distinction in their indefiniteness, and the hues of the trees and the outlines of their leafy tops were etherealized into tender pastels of misty rose and even mistier blue, with a single brighter gleam of morning yellow and a distant purple streak of dawn. And upon this morning world fell a cool dew, like a fountain that rose from the drenched ground and fell back in pearly drops in the childlike gentleness of the first sunbeams. It was as though every morning the earth and her people were newly created, as though mankind were newly born to a youth of innocence and paradisiacal unconsciousness. But the illusion of the dawn lasted for only a minute, barely a few moments: the sun, rising higher in the sky, shone forth from the virginal mist, unfurling boastfully its proud halo of piercing rays, pouring down its burning gold, full of godlike pride because it was reigning over its brief moment of the day. For the clouds were already mustering, grayly advancing, like battle hordes of dark phantoms, pressing eerily onward: deep bluish-black and heavy lead-gray phantoms, overmastering the sun and crushing the earth under white torrents of rain. And the evening twilight, brief and hurried, let fall veil upon veil of crêpe, like an overwhelming melancholy of earth, nature, and life, in which they forgot that paradisiacal moment of the morning. The white rain rustled down like an inundating tide of melancholy; the road and gardens were dripping, drinking up the falling torrents until they shone like marshy pools and flooded meadows in the dusky evening. A chill, spectral mist vaporized with a slow movement as of ghostly draperies that hovered over the pools, and the chilly houses, sparsely lit with smoking lamps, round which clouds of insects swarmed, dying everywhere with singed wings, enclosed an even chillier sadness, an overshadowing fear of the menacing world out of doors, of the omnipotent cloud hordes, of the boundless immensity that came whispering on the gusty winds from the far-off unknown, high as the heavens, wide as the firmament, against which the open houses appeared unprotected, while the inmates were small and petty, for all their civilization and science and soulful feelings, small as wriggling insects, insignificant, at the mercy of the game the giant mysteries played, rushing in from the distance.

Léonie van Oudijck, on the partially lit back verandah of the residency, was talking to Theo in a soft voice. Urip squatted beside her.

"It's nonsense, Urip!" she said, irritated.

"It isn't, *kandjeng*," said the maid. "It's not nonsense. I hear them every evening."

"Where?" asked Theo.

"In the *waringin* tree behind the house, high up, in the top branches."

"They're *luaks*," said Theo.[74]

"Not *luaks, tuan*," the maid insisted. "*Massa*, as if Urip didn't know how wild cats mewed! Kriow, kriow: that's how they sound. What we hear every night are the *pontianaks*.[75] It's the little children crying in the trees. The souls of the little children, crying in the trees."

"It's the wind, Urip."

"*Massa, kandjeng*, as if Urip couldn't hear the wind! Boo-ooh: that's how the wind goes, and then the branches move. But this is the little children, moaning in the top boughs, and the branches don't move then. This is *tjelaka, kandjeng*."

"And why should it be *tjelaka*?"

"Urip knows but dares not tell. *Tentu*, the *kandjeng* will be angry."

"Come, Urip, tell me."

"It's because of the *kandjeng tuan*, the *kandjeng residèn*."

"Why?"

"The other day the *pasar malam* in the *alun-alun* and the *pasar malam* for the *orang blanda*, in the *kebon kotta*."

"Well, what about it?"

"The day wasn't well chosen, according to the *petangans*. It was an unlucky day. . . . And with the new well. . . ."

"What about the new well?"

"There was no *sedeka*.[76] So no one uses the new well. Everyone fetches water from the old well, even if that water isn't very good. Because from the new well the woman rises with the bleeding hole in her breast. . . . And Miss Doddy. . . ."

"What about her?"

"Miss Doddy has seen the white *hadji* going by! The white *hadji* is not a good *hadji*. He's a ghost. . . . Miss Doddy saw him twice: in Patjaram and here. . . . Listen, *kandjeng*!"

"What?"

"Don't you hear? The children's little souls are moaning in the top branches. There's no wind blowing at this moment. Listen, listen, that's not *luaks!* The *luaks* go kriow, kriow, when they're in heat! These are the little souls!"

All three listened. Léonie pressed closer to Theo. She looked deathly pale. The roomy back verandah, with the table always set, stretched away in the dim light of a single hanging lamp. The puddly back garden gleamed wet out of the darkness of the *waringins,* full of pattering drops but motionless in the impenetrable masses of their velvety foliage. And an inexplicable, barely noticeable moaning, like a gentle mystery of little tormented souls, whimpered high above their heads, as though in the sky or in the topmost branches of the trees. Now it was a short cry, then a moan as of a little sick child, then a soft sobbing as of tortured little girls.

"What kind of animal can that be?" asked Theo. "Is it a bird or insects?"

The moaning and sobbing was very distinct. Léonie looked white as a sheet and was trembling all over.

"Don't be so scared," said Theo. "Of course they're animals."

But he himself was white as chalk, and, when they looked at each other, she understood that he too was afraid. She clutched his arm and pressed up against him. The maid squatted low, humbly, as though accepting all fate as an inexplicable mystery. She would not run away. But the eyes of the white man and woman held only one idea, the idea of escaping. Suddenly, both of them—the stepmother and the stepson who were bringing shame upon the house—were afraid, with a single fear, afraid as if punishment threatened. They did not speak; they said nothing to each other, but huddled together, understanding each other's trembling: two white children of this mysterious soil of the Indies, who from childhood had breathed the mysterious air of Java and had unconsciously heard the vague, stealthily approaching mystery like an accustomed music, a music that they had not noticed, as though mystery were an accustomed thing. And while they were like that, trembling and looking at each other, the wind rose, bearing away with it the secret of the tiny souls, bearing away with it the little souls themselves. The branches swayed angrily and the rain began to fall once more. A quivering chill came up, filling the house; a sudden draft blew out the lamp. And they remained in the dark a little longer—she, despite the openness of the verandah, almost in the arms of her stepson and lover, the maid crouching at their feet. But then she freed herself from his arms, freed herself from the black oppression of darkness and fear, filled with the rustling of the rain; the wind was cold and shivery, and she staggered indoors, on the verge of fainting. Theo and Urip followed her. The middle gallery was lighted. Van Oudijck's office was open. He was working. Léonie stood irresolute, with Theo, not knowing what to do. The maid disappeared, muttering. It was then that Léonie heard a whizzing sound, and a small round stone flew through the gallery and fell somewhere. She screamed and, behind the screen that divided the gallery from the office where Van Oudijck sat at his desk, she flung herself once more into Theo's arms, abandoning all her caution. They stood shivering in each other's arms. Van Oudijck had heard her; he got up and came from behind the screen. His eyes blinked, as though tired from working. Léonie and Theo had recovered themselves.

"What is it, Léonie?"

"Nothing," she said, not daring to tell him of the little souls or of the stone, afraid of the threatening punishment.

She and Theo stood there like criminals; both were white and trembling. Van Oudijck, his mind still on his work, did not notice anything.

"Nothing," she repeated. "The mat is frayed and . . . and I nearly stumbled. But there was something I wanted to tell you, Otto."

Her voice shook, but he did not hear it, blind to what she did, deaf to what she said, still absorbed in his papers.

"What's that?"

"Urip has suggested that the servants would like to have a *sedeka*, because a new well has been built in the grounds. . . ."

"The well that is two months old already?"

"They don't use the water."

"Why not?"

"They are superstitious, you know; they won't use the water unless there has been a *sedeka*."

"Then it ought to have been done at once. Why didn't they tell Kario to ask me? I can't think of all that nonsense myself. But I would have given them the *sedeka* at the time. Now it's like mustard after a meal. The well is two months old."

"It would be a good thing all the same, Papa," said Theo. "You know what the Javanese are like. They won't use the well as long as they've not had a *sedeka*."

"No," said Van Oudijck, unwillingly, shaking his head. "To give a *sedeka* now would make no sense. I would have done so gladly, but now, after two months, it would be absurd. They should have asked me then."

"Please, Otto," Léonie entreated. "Let's give them the *sedeka*. You'll please me if you do."

"Mamma half promised Urip," Theo insisted gently.

They stood before him like petitioners, trembling and white in the face. But he, weary and thinking of his papers, was seized with a stubborn unwillingness, though he was seldom able to refuse his wife anything.

"No, Léonie," he said, decidedly. "And you should never promise things you're not certain about."

He turned away, went round the screen, and sat down to his work.

They looked at each other, the mother and the stepson. Slowly, aimlessly, they moved away to the front verandah, where a moist, dripping darkness drifted between the stately pillars. They saw a white form coming through the puddly garden. They started, for they were now afraid of everything, and at the sight of every shape they thought of the chastisement that would overtake them like a strange thing, as long as they remained in the parental house that they had covered with shame. But when they looked more closely, they saw it was Doddy. She had come home, and, trembling all the while, said that she had been with Eva Eldersma. Actually, she had been walking with Addy de Luce, and they had found shelter from the rain in the *kampong*. She was very pale and trembling, but on the dark verandah Léonie and Theo did not notice it; nor did Doddy see that her stepmother and Theo were pale. She was trembling like that because in the garden—Addy had brought her to the gate—stones had been thrown at her. It must have been some impudent Javanese who hated her father and his house and household. But on the dark verandah, where she saw her stepmother and brother sitting silently side by side, as though in despair, she suddenly felt—she did not know why—that it had not been an impudent Javanese. . . .

She sat down next to them, without a word. They looked out at the damp, dark garden, under the wide night that hovered over it as if with wings of a gigantic bat. And in the mute melancholy that drifted like a gray twilight between the stately white pillars, all three—Doddy singly, but the stepmother and stepson together—felt frightened to death and crushed by the strange thing that was about to happen to them. . . .

26

And, despite their anxiety, the two sought each other all the more, feeling themselves now bound by indissoluble bonds. In the afternoon he would steal to her room; despite their anxiety, they lost themselves in wild embraces and then remained close together.

"It must be nonsense, Léonie," he whispered.

"Yes, but then what *is* it?" she murmured in return. "After all, I heard the moaning and heard the stone whizz through the air."

"And then?"

"What?"

"If it *is* something . . . suppose it is something that we can't explain."

"But I don't believe in it!"

"Nor I. . . . Only. . . ."

"What?"

"If it's something . . . *if* it's something that we can't explain, then. . . ."

"Then what?"

"Then . . . it's not because of *us!*" he whispered, almost inaudibly. "Urip said so herself. It's because of Papa!"

"That's ridiculous. . . ."

"I don't believe in that nonsense either."

"The moaning . . . that's like animals."

"And that stone . . . one of the servants, somebody who imagines himself . . . or who has been bribed. . . ."

"Bribed? By whom?"

"By . . . by the regent. . . ."

"Come on, Theo!"

"Urip said the moaning came from the *kabupatèn.* . . ."

"What do you mean?"

"And that they wanted to torment Papa from there. . . ."

"To torment him?"

"Because the regent of Ngadjiwa has been dismissed."

"Urip said that. . . ?"

"No, *I* do. Urip said that the regent has occult powers. That's nonsense, of course. The fellow's a scoundrel. He has bribed people . . . to pester Papa."

"But Papa doesn't notice anything. . . ."

"No. . . . We won't tell him, either. . . . That's the best thing to do. . . . We must ignore it."

"And the white *hadji*, Theo, the one Doddy saw twice. . . . And, when they do table-turning at Van Helderen's, Ida sees him too. . . ."

"Oh, another accomplice of the regent, of course!"

"Yes, I expect that's true. . . . But it's still horrible, Theo. . . . I'm so scared!"

"Because of that nonsense? Come on!"

"If it is something, Theo . . . it has nothing to do with *us?*"

He laughed.

"What next? What could it have to do with us? I tell you, it's a practical joke of the regent's. . . ."

"We shouldn't see each other anymore."

"No, no, I love you, I'm crazy about you!"

He kissed her fiercely. They were both afraid. But he bragged:

"Come, Léonie, don't be so superstitious."

"When I was a child, my *babu* told me. . . ."

She whispered a story in his ear. He turned pale.

"Léonie, what nonsense!"

"Strange things happen here. . . . If they bury something belonging to you, a handkerchief or a lock of hair, they are able—simply by witchcraft—to make you ill and pine away and die . . . and not a doctor can tell what the illness is. . . ."

"That's nonsense!"

"It's true!"

"I didn't know you were so superstitious!"

"I never thought of it before, but lately I do. . . . Theo, *can* there be anything?"

"There's nothing . . . but kissing."

"No, Theo, don't; be quiet, I'm scared. . . . It's quite late. It gets dark so quickly. Papa is up already, Theo. Go away now, Theo . . . through the boudoir. I want to take my bath quickly. I'm frightened nowadays when it gets dark. There's no twilight, with the rains. The evenings come so suddenly. . . . The other day, I hadn't told them to bring a light to the bathroom . . . and already it was so dark . . . at half past five . . . and two bats were flying all over the place. I was so scared that they would get stuck in my hair. . . . Quiet. . . . Is that Papa?"

"No, it's Doddy. She's playing with her cockatoo."

"Go away now, Theo."

He went through the boudoir and walked into the garden. She got up, put a kimono over the *sarong* which she had knotted loosely under her arms, and called Urip.

"*Bawa barang mandi!*"[77]
"*Kandjeng!*"
"Where are you, Urip?"
"Here, *kandjeng.*"
"Where were you?"
"Here, outside the garden door, *kandjeng.* . . . I was waiting," said the girl, meaningfully, implying that she was waiting until Theo had gone.
"Is the *kandjeng tuan* up?"
"*Suda* . . . had his bath, *kandjeng.*"
"Then get my things. . . . Light the little lamp in the bathroom. . . . Yesterday the glass was broken and the lamp was not filled. . . ."
"The *kandjeng* never used to take a bath with the light on. . . ."
"Urip . . . has anything happened . . . this afternoon?"
"No, everything has been quiet. . . . But, when the night comes! . . . All the servants are frightened, *kandjeng.* . . . The *kokkie* says she won't stay. . . ."
"Oh, what a *susa!* . . . Urip, promise her five guilders . . . as a present . . . if she stays. . . ."
"The *spen* is frightened too, *kandjeng.*"
"Oh, what a *susa!* . . . I've never had such *susa*, Urip. . . ."
"No, *kandjeng.*"
"I've always been able to arrange matters so well. . . . But these things . . . !"
"*Apa bolè buat, kandjeng?*"[78] . . . Things are stronger than men. . . ."
"Couldn't it really be *luaks* . . . and a man throwing stones?"
"*Massa, kandjeng!*"
"Well, bring my things. . . . Don't forget to light the lamp. . . ."
The maid left the room. Dusk was already sifting from the air, shrouded with rain. The great house stood still as death in the night of its giant *waringins*. The lamps had not been lit yet. On the front verandah, Van Oudijck, by himself, lay in his pajamas in a wicker chair, drinking tea. In the garden the dense shadows were gathering like strips of immaterial velvet falling heavily from the trees.
"*Tukan lampu!*" called Léonie.
"*Kandjeng?*"
"Come on, light the lamps! Why are you so late? Light the lamp in my bedroom first. . . ."
She went to the bathroom. She went past the long row of *gudangs* and servants' rooms which shut off the garden in the back. She looked up at the top branches of the *waringins* where she had heard the little souls moaning. The branches did not move; there was not a breath of wind,

the air was sultry and oppressive with a threatening storm, with rain too heavy to fall. Urip was lighting the little lamp in the bathroom.

"Have you brought everything, Urip?"

"*Saja, kandjeng.*"[79]

"Haven't you forgotten the big bottle with the white *ajer wangi?*"

"Isn't this it, *kandjeng?*"

"Yes, that's right. . . . But in the future give me a finer towel for my face. I'm always telling you to give me a finer towel. I hate these coarse ones. . . ."

"I'll go get one."

"No, no! Stay here, stay and sit by the door."

"*Saja, kandjeng.*"

"And you must have the keys inspected by a *tukan besi.* We can't lock the bathroom door. . . . That's crazy, when there are visitors."

"I'll do it tomorrow."

"Mind you don't forget."

She shut the door. The maid squatted down outside the closed door, patient and resigned under the big and little things of life, knowing nothing but loyalty to her mistress, who gave her pretty *sarongs* and advances as often as she wanted them.

In the bathroom the little nickel lamp gleamed faintly over the green marble of the wet floor, over the water brimming in the square, cement cistern.

"I think I'll do this earlier," thought Léonie.

She removed her kimono and *sarong* and, naked, she glanced in the mirror at her soft, milky white shape, the curves of a woman who loved love. Her blond hair shone golden, and a pearly luster spread from her shoulders over her chest and vanished in the shadow of her small, round breasts. She lifted her hair, admiring herself, examining herself, to see if a wrinkle was folding, feeling whether her flesh was hard and firm. One of her hips curved out because she was leaning on one leg, and the long line of a white lit curve caressed along thigh and knee, ebbing away at the arch of her foot. But she gave a start as she stood thus absorbed in admiration: she had meant to hurry. She quickly tied her hair into a knot, covered herself with a lather of soap, and, taking the *gajong,* poured the water over her body. It flowed heavily over her in long smooth streams, and as marble she shone, polished shoulders, breasts, and hips, in the light of the little lamp. She wanted to hurry even more and looked up at the window to see if the bats would fly again. . . . Yes, she would bathe earlier in the future. It was already dark outside.[80]

She dried herself hurriedly, with a rough towel. She quickly rubbed herself with the white ointment that Urip always prepared, her magic elixir of youth, suppleness, and firm whiteness. At that moment, she saw on her thigh a small red spot. She paid no attention to it, thinking that there must have been something in the water, a tiny leaf, a dead insect. She rubbed it off. But, while she was rubbing herself, she saw on her chest two or three larger spots, a dark vermilion. She turned suddenly cold, not knowing what it was, not understanding. She rubbed herself again, and she took the towel whereon the spots had left something foul like thick blood. She shivered from head to foot. And suddenly she saw. The spots came from the corners of the bathroom—how and where she did not see—first small, then larger, as if spat out by a drooling *sirih* mouth. Deathly cold, she screamed. The spatters, thicker, became full, like purple globs spewed at her. Her body was befouled and filthy with a grimy, dribbling red. One spatter hit her in the back. . . .

The slimy spittle slithered on the greenish white of the floor and floated on the water that had not yet run off. It also fouled the water in the cistern where it dissolved into filth. She was all red, befouled, as though defiled by a shame of filthy vermilion that invisible *sirih* mouths hawked and spat at her from the corners of the room, aiming at her hair, her eyes, her breasts, her lower belly. She screamed and screamed, driven crazy by what was happening. She threw herself at the door, tried to open it, but there was something wrong with the handle. The door wasn't locked, nor was it bolted. The spitting continued on her back, and the red dripped from her buttocks. She screamed for Urip and heard the girl on the other side of the door, pulling and pushing.

At last the door yielded. And, desperate, mad, crazed, insane, naked, and befouled, she threw herself into her maid's arms. The servants came running up. She saw Van Oudijck, Theo, and Doddy coming from the back verandah. In her utter madness, with her eyes staring wildly, she felt ashamed not of her nudity but of her defilement. The maid had snatched the kimono, also besmirched, from the handle of the door and threw it around her mistress.

"Stay back!" Léonie yelled, desperately. "Don't get closer!" she screamed madly. "Urip, Urip, take me to the swimming pool! A lamp, a lamp . . . in the swimming pool!"

"What's going on, Léonie?"

She didn't want to say anything.

"I've . . . stepped . . . on a . . . toad!" she screamed. "I'm afraid . . . of a rash! . . . Don't come any nearer! I'm naked! . . . Stay away! Stay away! . . . A lamp, a lamp . . . a *lamp*, I tell you . . . in the swimming pool! . . .

No, Otto! Stay away! Stay away, all of you! I'm naked! Stay away! Bawa . . . la-a-ampu!"

The servants were running everywhere. One of them brought a lamp to the swimming pool.

"Urip! Urip!"

She clutched her maid.

"They've spat at me . . . with *sirih*! . . . They've spat . . . at me . . . with *sirih*! . . . They've spat . . . at me with *sirih*!"

"Hush, *kandeng*! . . . Come with me . . . to the swimming pool!"

"Wash me, Urip! . . . Urip, my hair, my eyes! O God, I can taste it in my mouth! . . .

She sobbed desperately; the maid dragged her along.

"Urip! First, look . . . *preksa* . . . if they're also spitting . . . in the swimming pool!"

The maid went in, shivering.

"There's nothing there, *kandjeng*."

"Quick then, Urip, bathe me, wash me."

She threw the kimono away. Her beautiful body became visible in the light of the lamp, as if soiled with filthy blood.

"Urip, wash me. . . . No, don't go for soap, water will do! . . . Don't leave me alone! Urip, wash me here, can't you? . . . Burn the kimono! Urip!"

She dove into the pool and swam round desperately; the maid, half naked, dove in after her and washed her.

"Quick, Urip! Quickly, only the worst places! . . . I'm scared! Soon . . . they'll be spitting here. . . . In the bedroom next, Urip! . . . Yell that nobody's to be in the garden! I am not going to put the kimono on again! Quickly, Urip, yell! I want to get out of here!"

The maid called across the garden, in Javanese.

Léonie, dripping, rose from the water and, naked and wet, flew past the servants' rooms, with the maid behind her. Inside the house, Van Oudijck, frantic with worry, came running toward her.

"Go away, Otto! Leave me alone! I am . . . naked!" she screamed.

And she rushed into her room and, when Urip had followed her, locked all the doors.

In the garden the servants huddled together, under the sloping roof of the verandah, close to the house. The thunder was muttering softly and a silent rain was beginning to fall.

27

Léonie kept to her bed for several days with nervous fever. People in Labuwangi said that the residency was haunted. At the weekly assemblies in the Municipal Garden, when the band played and the children and young people danced on the open stone floor, there were whispered conversations around the tables about the strange happenings in the residency. Dr. Rantzow was asked many questions, but could only tell what the resident had told him, what Mrs. Van Oudijck herself had told him, of being frightened in the bathroom by an enormous toad, which she had stepped on and stumbled over. The servants told more, but if one spoke about throwing stones and *sirih* spitting, another would laugh and call it all *babu* talk. And so uncertainty prevailed. Nevertheless, the papers throughout the country, from Surabaja to Batavia, contained short paragraphs of a curious nature, which were not very lucid but which suggested a good deal.

Van Oudijck did not discuss the matter with anybody, not with his wife and his children, nor with the officials or the servants. But one time he came out of the bathroom looking deathly pale, with eyes staring wildly. He went indoors quietly, however, pulled himself together, and no one noticed anything. Then he spoke to the chief of police. There was an old graveyard next to the residency grounds. This was now watched day and night, also the outer wall of the bathroom. The bathroom itself was no longer used; they took their baths instead in the one reserved for guests.

As soon as Mrs. Van Oudijck had recovered, she went to stay with friends in Surabaja. She did not return. Gradually, and without drawing attention to it, without a word to Van Oudijck, she had Urip pack up her clothes and all sorts of knickknacks she was attached to. Trunk upon trunk was sent after her. When one day Van Oudijck happened to go to her bedroom, he found it empty of all but the furniture. Numberless things had also disappeared from her boudoir. He had not noticed that the trunks had been sent, but he now understood that she would not return. He cancelled his next reception. It was December, and René and Ricus were to come from Batavia for the Christmas holidays, for a week or ten days, but he cancelled the boys' visit. Then Doddy was invited to stay in Patjaram, with the De Luce family. Although, with the instinct of a full-blooded Hollander, he did not like the De Luces, he consented. They were fond of Doddy there, and she would have a better time there than in Labuwangi. He had given up the hope that his daughter would not succumb to the Indies. Suddenly, Theo also went away. Through Léonie's influence with commercial magnates in Surabaja, he suddenly found a lucrative position in an import-export business.

Van Oudijck was left all alone in his big house. Because the *kokkie* and the *spen* had run away, Eldersma and Eva were constantly asking him over, for lunch as well as dinner. He never mentioned his house at their table and it was never discussed. What he discussed confidentially with Eldersma, as secretary, and with Van Helderen, as controller, these two never mentioned, as if it were an official secret. The chief of police, who was used to making a brief daily report—that nothing particular had happened, or that there had been a fire, or that a man had been wounded—now made long, secret reports, behind the locked doors of the office to prevent the *oppassers* outside from listening. Gradually all the servants ran away, departing stealthily in the night, with their families and belongings, leaving their homes behind in a dirty emptiness. They did not even stay in the residency. Van Oudijck let them go. He kept only Kario and the *oppassers,* and every day the prisoners tended the garden. And so it seemed that the house remained outwardly unaltered. But inside, where nothing was looked after, the dust was thick on the furniture, white ants devoured the mats, and mildew and damp spots were everywhere. The resident never went through the house, living only in his bedroom and office. His face began to wear a look of gloom, like a bitter, silent doubt. He worked more conscientiously than ever, drove his subordinates harder than before, as if he were thinking of nothing but the interests of Labuwangi. In his isolated position, he had no friend and sought none. He bore everything alone, on his own shoulders, on his own back, which stooped from approaching age, bore the heavy burden of his house, which was being destroyed. His family life broke up amidst strange happenings that escaped his police, his watchmen, his personal vigilance, and his secret spies. He discovered nothing. Nobody told him anything. No one threw any light on anything.

And the strange happenings continued. A mirror was smashed by a large stone. Calmly he had the pieces cleared away. It was not in his nature to believe in supernatural events, nor did he do so. He was secretly enraged at being unable to discover the culprits or an explanation. But he refused to believe. He did not believe when he found his bed soiled, and Kario, squatting at his feet, swore that he did not know how it had happened. He did not believe when the glass that he lifted broke into slivers. He did not believe when he heard a constant irritating hammering overhead. But his bed was soiled, his glass did break, the hammering was a fact. He investigated these facts, as punctiliously as if he were investigating a criminal case, and nothing came to light. He remained unperturbed in his relations with his European and native officials and with the regent. No one remarked anything in his behavior, and in the evenings he worked on, defiantly, at his desk, while the hammering continued and the night fell softly in the garden, as if enchanted.

On the steps outside, the *oppassers* huddled together, listening and whispering, glancing round timorously at their master, who sat writing with a frown of concentration.

"Doesn't he hear it?"

"Yes, yes, he's not deaf."

"He must hear it."

"He thinks he can find it out through *djagas*."

"They're bringing soldiers from Ngadjiwa."

"From Ngadjiwa!"

"Yes, he does not trust the *djagas*. He has written to the *tuan* major."

"To send soldiers?"

"Yes, soldiers are coming."

"Look at him frowning."

"And he just goes on working!"

"I'm frightened. I would never dare to stay if I didn't have to."

"I'm not afraid to stay, as long as he's there."

"Yes, . . . he's brave."

"He's tough."

"He's a brave man."

"But he doesn't understand it."

"No, he doesn't know what it is."

"He thinks it's rats."

"Yes, he had them look for rats upstairs, under the roof."

"Those Hollanders don't know anything."

"No, they don't understand."

"He smokes a lot."

"Yes, as much as twelve cigars a day."

"He doesn't drink much."

"No . . . only his whisky soda in the evening."

"He'll ask for it in a moment."

"No one has stayed with him."

"No. The others understood. They've all left."

"He goes to bed very late."

"Yes, he's working hard."

"He never sleeps at night, only in the afternoon."

"Look at him frowning."

"He never stops working."

"*Oppas!*"

"He's calling."

"*Kandjeng?*"

"*Bawa* whisky soda."

One of the *oppassers* got up to fetch the drink. He had everything close by, in the guests' wing, to avoid having to go through the house. The others pressed closer together and went on whispering. The moon pierced the clouds and lit up the garden and the pond as with a damp mist of silent enchantment. The *oppasser* had mixed the drink, returned, squatted, and offered it to the resident.

"Put it down," said Van Oudijck.

The *oppasser* put the glass on the desk and crept away. The other *oppassers* whispered.

"*Oppas!*" called Van Oudijck after a while.

"*Kandjeng?*"

"What did you put in this glass?"

The man trembled and shrank away at Van Oudijck's feet.

"*Kandjeng,* it's not poison, I swear it by my life, by my death. I can't help it, *kandjeng.* Kick me, kill me, I can't help it, *kandjeng.*"

The glass was a dull yellow.

"Get me another glass and pour it here."

The *oppasser* went away, trembling.

The others sat close together, feeling the contact of one another's bodies through the sweat-soaked cloth of their liveries, and stared in fear. The moon rose from its clouds, laughing and mocking like a wicked fairy; its moist and silent enchantment shone silver over the wide garden. In the distance, from the garden in the back, a plaintive cry rang out, as if a child were being strangled.

28

"And how are you, Madam? How's the depression? You like the Indies a little better today?"

His words sounded cheerful to Eva, as she saw him coming through the garden, around eight, for dinner. His tone expressed nothing more than the pleasant greeting of a man who has been working hard at his desk and who is delighted to see a pretty woman with whom he's about to dine. She was filled with surprise and admiration. There was not a hint that this was a man who was plagued all day long, in a deserted house, by strange and incomprehensible happenings. There was hardly a shadow of dejection on his wide forehead, hardly a care seemed to rest upon his broad, slightly bowed back, and the jovial smile under his thick mustache was there as usual. Eldersma came up, and Eva divined in his greeting, in the pressure of his hand, a silent freemasonry of things known, of confidences shared in common. And Van Oudijck drank his gin and bitters in a perfectly normal manner, spoke of a letter from his wife, who was probably going on to Batavia, and said that René and Ricus were staying in the Preanger[81] with friends who had a plantation there. He did not speak of the reason why they were not with him, why he had been entirely abandoned by his family and servants. In the intimacy of their circle, which now welcomed him twice a day for his meals, he had never mentioned it. And, though Eva did not ask any questions, it was making her extremely nervous. So close to the house, the haunted house, whose pillars she could see by day in the distance, gleaming through the foliage of the trees, she became more nervous every day. All day long, the servants whispered around her and peered timidly at the haunted *residinan*. At night, unable to sleep, she tried to see if she could hear anything strange, the moaning of the little children. The tropical night was so full of voices that it could only make her shudder in her bed. Through the imperious roaring of the frogs for rain and rain and more rain still, the constant croaking on the one roaring note, she heard thousands of ghostly sounds that kept her from sleeping. Through it all the *tokkès* emitted their clockwork strokes, like strange mysterious timepieces.

She thought of it all day long. Eldersma did not speak of it either, but when she saw Van Oudijck come to lunch or dinner, she had to bite her tongue to keep from asking him. And the conversation was about all kinds of things, but never about the strange happenings. After lunch, Van Oudijck went across to the residency again; after dinner, at ten o'clock, she saw him once more vanish into the haunted shadows of the garden. He calmly went back every evening, through the enchanted night, to his miserable, deserted house, where the *oppasser* and Kario sat squatting close together outside his office, and he worked until late in the night. He never complained. He pursued his enquiries carefully, all through the *kotta*, but nothing came to light. Everything continued to happen in impenetrable mystery.

"And how do you like the Indies tonight, Madam?"

It was always more or less the same pleasantry, but each time she admired his tone. Courage, robust self-confidence, a certainty in his own knowledge, a belief in what he knew for certain, all these rang in his voice. Miserable though he must feel—the man who liked domesticity and a man of cool, practical sense—in a house deserted by his own and full of inexplicable happenings, there was not a trace of doubt or dejection in his unfailing masculine simplicity. He went his way and did his work, more conscientiously than ever; he continued his investigations. And at Eva's table he always kept up an animated conversation; about promotions, about colonial politics and the new craze for having the Indies ruled from Holland by laymen who didn't know the first thing about it. And he talked with an easy, pleasant vivacity, without boasting, till Eva came to admire him more and more. But because she was a sensitive woman, it became a nervous obsession with her. And one time, during the evening, when she walked a little way with him, she asked him if it wasn't terrible, if he couldn't leave the house, if he couldn't go on tour, for a good long time. She saw his face darken at her questions. But still he answered kindly, saying that it was not so bad, even though there was no explanation, and that he was sure that he would get to the bottom of these tricks. And he added that he really should go on tour, but that he didn't because he didn't want to give the impression that he was running away. Then he lightly pressed her hand and told her not to get upset about it, and not to think or talk about it. The last words sounded like a friendly admonition. She pressed his hand once more, with tears in her eyes. And she watched him walk away, with his calm, firm step, and disappear in the night of his garden, where the enchantment had to filter in through the croaking of the frogs for rain. But standing there like that made her shiver, and she hurried indoors. And she felt that her house, her spacious house, was small and open and defenseless against the vast Indies night, which could enter from every side.

But she was not the only person obsessed by the mysterious happenings. Their inexplicable nature oppressed the entire town of Labuwangi, because they clashed so much with the quotidian. The mystery was discussed in every house, but only in a whisper, to keep the children from being frightened and in order to keep the servants from knowing that people were impressed by the Javanese conjuring, as the resident called it. And the fear and depression were making everybody ill from nervous apprehension and from listening to the night that was teeming with voices in the dark. The fear drifted down on the town in a dense, velvety grayness, and the town seemed to be hiding itself more deeply than ever in the foliage of its gardens, seemed, in these moist evening twilights, to be shrinking away altogether in dull, silent resignation, bowing before the mystery.

Van Oudijck thought it was time to take strong measures. He wrote to the major commanding the garrison at Ngadjiwa to come over with a captain, a couple of lieutenants, and a company of soldiers. That evening the officers, with the resident and Van Helderen, dined at the Eldersmas'. They hurried through their meal, and Eva, standing at the garden gate, saw them all—the resident, the secretary, the controller, and the four officers—go into the dark garden of the haunted house. The residency grounds were closed off, the house surrounded, and the churchyard watched. And only the men went into the bathroom.

They remained there all through the night. And all through the night the grounds and house remained closed off and surrounded. They came out at about five o'clock and went straight to the swimming pool and bathed. What had happened to them they did not say, but they had had a terrible night. That morning the bathroom was pulled down.

They had all promised Van Oudijck not to speak about that night, and Eldersma would not tell anything to Eva, nor Van Helderen to Ida. The officers too, on their return to Ngadjiwa, were silent. They only said that their night in the bathroom was so incredible that no one would believe their story. At last one of the young lieutenants let a hint of his adventures slip out. And a tale made the rounds—of *sirih* spitting and stone throwing, of a floor that heaved, while they struck at it with sticks and swords, and of something more, something unutterably horrible that had happened in the water. Everyone now added something to it. When the story reached Van Oudijck's ears, he hardly recognized it as an account of that terrible night, one that had been terrible enough without any additions.

Meanwhile Eldersma had written a report of the vigil they had shared, and they all signed the improbable story. Van Oudijck took the report personally to Batavia and delivered it to the governor-general. From that time it slumbered in the secret archives of the government.

The governor-general advised Van Oudijck to go to Holland on a short leave, assuring him that this leave would not influence his promotion to resident first class, which was nearly due. He refused this favor, however, and returned to Labuwangi. The only concession he allowed himself was to move into Eldersma's house until the residency had been thoroughly cleaned. But the flag continued to fly over the grounds of the residency.

On his return from Batavia, Van Oudijck often met with Sunario, the regent, on official business. And his relations with the regent remained stern and formal. Then he had a brief interview, first with the regent and afterwards with his mother, the radèn-aju pangéran. Both conversations did not last longer than twenty minutes, but it appeared that those few words had been of great importance.

For the strange happenings ceased. When everything had been cleaned and repaired, under Eva's supervision, Van Oudijck compelled Léonie to come back, because he wished to give a great ball on New Year's Day. In the morning, the resident received all his European and native officials. In the evening, the guests streamed into the brightly lit galleries from every part of the town, still inclined to shudder a little, very inquisitive, and instinctively looking around and above them. While the champagne went around, Van Oudijck himself took a glass and offered it to the regent, with a deliberate breach of etiquette. And in a tone of solemn admonition mingled with good-humored jest, he uttered these words, which were seized upon and repeated everywhere and which continued to be repeated for months throughout Labuwangi:

"Drink with an easy mind, Regent. I give you my *word of honor* that no more glasses will be broken in my house, except by accident or carelessness."

He was able to say this because he knew that, this time, he had been too strong for the hidden force, because of his simple courage as an official, as a Hollander, and as a man.

But while he drank, there was in the regent's gaze a very slight gleam of irony, intimating that, though the hidden force had not conquered, this time, it would still remain an enigma, forever inexplicable to the shortsighted Europeans. . . .

29

Labuwangi came alive again. People unanimously agreed not to discuss the strange affair with outsiders, because they understood that nobody would believe what they, in Labuwangi, believed. And the provincial town, after the mystic oppression that had made them cower during those unforgettable weeks, came to life again, as if shaking off all its obsession. Party followed party, ball upon ball, and there were concerts and theater. Everyone opened his doors to entertain friends and to make merry, in order to feel normal and natural again after the incredible nightmare. People so accustomed to a normal and tangible life, people used to the spacious and lavish material existence of the Indies—to good cooking, cool drinks, large beds, roomy houses, to everything that represents physical luxury to the European in the East— such people breathed again and shook off the nightmare, shook off the belief in strange happenings. And if it was discussed at all, they called it incomprehensible conjuring (echoing the resident) or the regent's tricks. For that he had something to do with it was certain. That the resident had threatened him and his mother with something terrible, if the strange happenings did not cease, was certain. And that, after this, normal order had been restored, was also certain. So it was conjuring. And they were now ashamed of their credulity and their fears and of having shuddered at what had looked like mysticism and was only clever tricks. And all breathed again and made up their minds to be cheerful; and entertainment followed upon entertainment.

Amid all this dissipation, Léonie forgot her irritation at having been called back by Van Oudijck. And she too *was determined* to forget the vermilion pollution of her body. But something of the terror lingered in her. She now bathed early in the afternoon, as early as half past four, in the newly built bathroom. Her second bath was always something unpleasant. And now that Theo had a job in Surabaja, she got rid of him; this too was from fear. She could not get rid of the idea that the enchantment had threatened to punish both of them, both mother and son, because they brought shame on the household. The romantic side of her perverse imagination, her rosy fancy full of cherubs and cupids, accorded this idea, inspired by her fears, a precious note of tragedy which she cherished, no matter what Theo might say. She would not go on. And it made him furious, because he was mad with love for her, because he could not forget the disgraceful delight he had enjoyed in her arms. But she steadily refused him and told him of her dread and said she was certain that the witchcraft would begin again if they loved one another, he and his father's wife. On the one Sunday that he spent in Labuwangi, her words made him red with fury. He was furious about her refusal, about the motherly attitude she now adopted, and about the fact, of which he was well aware, that she saw Addy frequently, that she often went to stay in Patjaram. Addy danced with her at parties and leaned on her chair at concerts, in the improvised residential box. True, he was not faithful to her, for it was not his nature to love one woman—he loved women wholesale—but still he was as faithful to her as he was able to be. He inspired her with a more lasting passion than she had ever felt before, and this passion roused her from her usual passive indifference. Often, while suffering and inflicting boredom, enthroned in the brilliance of her white beauty, like a smiling idol, with the languor of her Indies years gradually filling her blood until her movements had acquired that lazy indifference for anything that did not spell love and caresses, until her voice had assumed a drawling accent for any word that was not a word of passion—often she would become transfigured, by the flame that Addy shone over her, into a younger woman, livelier in company, gayer, flattered by the persistent homage of this youth who was the darling of every girl.

And she delighted in monopolizing him as much as she could, to the vexation of all the younger women, of Doddy in particular. In the midst of her passion she also took an evil delight in teasing, merely for its own sake. It gave her exquisite enjoyment, and it made her husband jealous —perhaps for the first time, for she had always been very careful—and made Theo and Doddy jealous. She aroused the jealousy of every young married woman and of every girl, and, since she, as the resident's wife, stood above them all, she had an ascendancy over all of them. And if she sometimes went too far, she delighted in winning back, with a smile, with a gracious word, the place in their affection that she had lost through her flirtations. Strange though it might seem, she succeeded. The moment they saw her, the moment she spoke, smiled, and willed herself to be amiable, she won back all she had lost and was forgiven everything. Even Mrs. Eldersma allowed herself to be conquered by the strange charm of this woman who was neither witty nor intelligent, who became only a little more cheerful, who roused herself only slightly from her boring lethargy, who triumphed only through the lines of her body, the contour of her face, the glance of her strange eyes, calm and yet full of hidden passion, and who was conscious of all her charm because she had meditated upon it since her childhood. Together with her indifference, this charm constituted her strength. Fate seemed to have no hold on her. It had indeed touched her with a strange magic, until she thought that a chastisement was about to descend upon her, but it had gone away again, drifted away. Still, she accepted the warning. She was finished with Theo and henceforth affected a motherly attitude toward him. It made him furious, especially at these parties, where she was younger, livelier, and more seductive.

His passion for her began to turn to hatred. He hated her now with all the instinct of a blond native, for that was what he really was, despite his white skin. He was his mother's son rather than his father's. Oh how he hated her now, for he had felt his fear of the punishment only for an instant, and he, he had forgotten everything by now. And his one idea was to harm her. How, he did not know yet, but he would injure her so that she might feel pain, and suffer. The process of thinking it over imparted a satanic gloom to his small, murky soul. Although he did not think about it, he felt unconsciously that she seemed to be invulnerable. He even felt that, to herself, she boasted of her invulnerability and that it made her daily more brazen and indifferent. She was constantly staying in Patjaram, for the flimsiest reason. The anonymous letters, which Van Oudijck still showed her, no longer disturbed her; she was growing accustomed to them. She returned them to him without a word; once she even forgot them, and left them lying around on the back verandah. Once Theo read them. Suddenly—due to he knew not what—suddenly he seemed to recognize certain letters, certain strokes. He remembered the hut in the *kampong* near Patjaram, made partly from bamboo, partly from crates, where he and Addy de Luce had been to see Si-Oudijck, and where he had seen papers hastily collected by an Arab. He had a vague recollection of seeing the same letters, the same strokes, on a scrap of paper on the floor. It passed vaguely and quickly as lightning through his mind. But it was no more than a flash. His small, somber soul had only room for dull hatred and shady calculations. He hated his father from instinct and innate antipathy, hated his mother because she was a *nonna*, his stepmother because she was finished with him, hated Addy and Doddy into the bargain. He hated the world because it made him work, he hated every job he had ever had, he now hated his office at Surabaja. But he was too lazy and too dense to do any harm. Rack his brains as he might, he could not discover how to harm his father, Addy, and Léonie. Everything about him was vague, turbid, dissatisfied, indistinct. His passion was only for money and a beautiful woman. Beyond that, there was nothing more in him than the dull gloom and the discontent of a fat, blond *sinjo*. And he continued to brood.

Until now, Doddy had always been instinctively fond of Léonie. But she could no longer hide from herself that what she had first thought an accident—Mamma and Addy always seeking each other with the same alluring smile, the one attracting the other across the length of the large room, as though irresistibly—was not an accident at all! And she too hated Mamma now, Mamma with her beautiful calmness, her sovereign indifference. Her own violent and passionate nature was colliding with that other nature with its milky white Creole languor, which now for the first time, because of the sheer kindliness of fate, was letting itself go as it pleased, without reserve. She hated Mamma, and her hatred caused scenes, scenes of nervous, loud tantrums contrasting with the irritating calmness of Mamma's indifference, scenes caused by all sorts of little disagreements: about a visit, a horseback ride, a dress, a *sambal* that one liked and the other did not. And Doddy wanted to have a good cry in Papa's arms, but Van Oudijck would not agree with her and said that she must show more respect for Mamma. Once, when Doddy had come to him for consolation and he reproached her for going for walks with Addy, she screamed out that Mamma herself was in love with Addy. Van Oudijck angrily ordered her out of the room. But it all agreed too closely—the anonymous letters, his wife's recent flirtations, Doddy's accusations, and what he himself had noticed at the last few parties—not to give him food for thought and even to worry him. And once he began to worry and think about it, memories suddenly darted in his mind like brief flashes of lightning: memories of an unexpected visit, of a locked door, of a moving curtain, of a whispered word, of a timidly averted glance. He pieced it all together and he quite suddenly recollected those same subtle memories in combination with others, of an earlier date. It aroused his jealousy, a husband's jealousy of the wife whom he loved as his most personal possession. This jealousy burst upon him like a gust of wind, blowing its way through his concentration at work, confusing his thoughts as he sat writing, made him suddenly run out of his office during the police cases, and made him search Léonie's room, lift up a curtain, even look under the bed.

And now he no longer consented to have Léonie stay in Patjaram, with the pretext that the De Luces should not be encouraged in the hope of getting Doddy as a wife for Addy. For he dared not speak to Léonie of his jealousy. . . . That Addy should ever get Doddy for his wife! True, there was native blood in his daughter too, but he wanted a full-blooded European as his son-in-law. He hated anything half-caste. He hated the De Luces and all the provincial, Indies, half-Solo traditions of that Patjaram of theirs. He hated their gambling, their hobnobbing with all sorts of native headmen, people whom he officially granted what was

theirs but whom he otherwise regarded as necessary tools of government policy. He hated their posing as an old Indies family and he hated
Addy: an idle youth who was supposed to be employed in the factory
but who did nothing at all, except run after every woman, girl, or maid.
To the older, industrious man, such a life was intolerable.

So Léonie had to do without Patjaram, but in the mornings she quietly went to Mrs. Van Does and met Addy in this woman's little house
while Mrs. Van Does went out peddling in a *tjikar*, with two jam pots of
inten-inten and a bundle of batik bedspreads. And in the evenings
Addy would go for a walk with Doddy and listen to her passionate reproaches. He laughed at her temper, took her in his arms till she was
panting on his chest, kissed the reproaches from her mouth until she,
mad with love, dissolved in his arms. They did not go any further, too
much afraid, especially Doddy. They strolled behind the *kampongs*, on
the *galengans* of the *sawahs*, while swarms of fireflies whirled around
them in the dark like tiny lanterns; they strolled arm in arm, they
walked hand in hand, in a state of enervating physicality, which never
went any further. They knew each other entirely with their hands, they
loved each other with their hands. When she came home again, she was
furious, raging at Mamma because she envied the calm, smiling satiety
as she lay musing, in her white peignoir, with a touch of powder on her
face, in a cane chair.

And the house, newly painted and whitewashed after the strange happenings, which were now past, the house was filled with hatred that
arose everywhere like the demoniacal bloom of that strange secret. A
hatred around that smiling woman who was too languid to hate and
only delighted in quiet teasing; a jealous hatred of the father for the son,
when he saw him too often sitting beside his stepmother, begging, despite his own hatred, for something, the father did not know what; a hatred of the daughter for the mother; a hatred that wrecked the entire
family.

How it had all happened, Van Oudijck did not know. He sadly regretted the time when he had been blind to it, when he had only seen his
wife and children in the light in which he wished to see them. That time
was past. Like the strange happenings of not so long ago, a hatred was
now rising out of life, like a pestilential vapor coming out of the ground.
And Van Oudijck, who had never been superstitious, who had worked
on coolly and calmly in his lonely house, with the incomprehensible
witchcraft all about him, who had read reports while the hammering
went on above his head and his whisky soda ochred in his glass; Van
Oudijck for the first time in his life—now that he saw the gloomy ex-

pressions of Theo and Doddy, now that he suddenly discovered his wife becoming bolder every day, sitting hand in hand with young De Luce, her knees almost touching his—became superstitious, believing in a hidden force that lurked he knew not where, in the Indies, in the soil of the Indies, in a profound mystery, somewhere, a force that wished him ill because he was a European, a ruler, a foreigner on the mysterious, sacred soil. And when he noticed this superstition within himself, something so new to him, the practical man, something so strange and incredible to him, a man of ordinary masculine simplicity, he was afraid of himself, as of incipient insanity, which he began to perceive deep down within himself.

And no matter how strong he had proved himself to be during the time of the strange happenings, when he had been able to exorcize them with a single word that threatened force, this superstition, which came as an aftermath to those events, found a weakness in him, a vulnerable spot. He was so surprised at himself that he did not understand his own mind and was afraid that he might be going mad. And yet, and yet, he still worried. His health was undermined by an incipient liver illness, and he kept on examining his jaundiced complexion. Suddenly he had the idea that he was being poisoned. The kitchen was searched, the cook subjected to a cross-examination, but nothing came to light. He realized that he had been frightened by nothing. But the doctor declared that he had an enlarged liver and prescribed the usual diet. A thing that otherwise he would have thought quite natural—an illness that occurred so frequently—now suddenly struck him as strange, a mysterious event that he worried about.

And it got on his nerves. He began to suffer from sudden fatigue when he was working, from throbbing headaches. His jealousy haunted him, and he was overcome by a trembling restlessness. He suddenly realized that, if there were now any hammering above his head, if *sirih* were now spat at him, he would not be able to stay in the house. And he began to believe in a hatred that rose slowly around him out of the hostile soil, like a plague. He believed in a force hidden in the things of the Indies, in the nature of Java, in the climate of Labuwangi, in the conjuring tricks —as he continued to call it—that sometimes makes the Javanese cleverer than the European and gives him the power, a mysterious power, not to release himself from the yoke, but to cause illness, lingering illness, to pester and harass, to play the ghost most incredibly and hideously: a hidden force, a hidden power, hostile to our temperament, our blood, our bodies, our souls, our civilization, to all that seems to us the right thing to do and be and think. It had revealed itself to him as in a sudden light; it was not the result of thought, it had unveiled itself to him as if in a dreadful revelation, which was utterly in conflict with all the logic of his methodical mode of thought. In a vision of terror he suddenly saw it before him, like the light of his approaching old age, just as old people sometimes suddenly perceive the truth. And yet he was still young and strong. And he felt that if he did not divert his maddening thoughts, they might make him ill, weak, and miserable, for ever and ever. . . .

Especially for him, a simple, practical man, this change of mental attitude was almost unbearable. What a morbid mind might have contemplated in quiet meditation struck him as a sudden terror. For it had never occurred to him that somewhere, deeply hidden in life, there might be things that were stronger than the power of the human will and intellect. Now, after the nightmare that he had so courageously defeated, it seemed to him that the nightmare had sapped his strength after all, and that it had inoculated him with every sort of weakness. It was incredible, but now, as he sat working in the evening, he would listen to the evening voices in the garden, or to the rapid rustle of a rat above his head. And then he would suddenly get up, go to Léonie's room, and look under the bed. When he at last discovered that many of the anonymous letters that persecuted him came from the pen of a half-caste who described himself as his son and was even known by his own name in the *kampong,* he felt too unsure of himself to investigate the matter, because of what might come to light—things he had himself forgotten, dating from his controllership, from the old days in Ngadjiwa. He now vacillated where he had once been certain and positive. Now he was no longer able to order his recollections of that period so positively that he could have sworn not to have a son, begotten almost unknowingly in those days. He did not clearly remember the housekeeper who had looked after him before his first marriage. And he preferred to let the whole business of the anonymous letters smoulder in the dusky shadows, rather than stir things up and inquire after them. He even had money sent to the native who called himself his son, so that the fellow might not abuse the name he had arrogated while demanding contributions all over the *kampong:* chickens and rice and clothes, things that Si-Oudijck exacted from ignorant *dessa* folk, whom he threatened with the vague anger of his father, the *kandjeng* in Labuwangi. And Van Oudijck sent him money so that the threat of that power could no longer be used. It was weak of him: he would never have done it in the old days. But now he had an inclination to hush things up, to gloss things over, to be less stern and severe and rather to muffle with half-measures anything that was too sharp. Eldersma was sometimes amazed when he saw the resident, who used to be so firm, hesitate, when he saw him yielding in matters of business, in differences with land tenants, as he would never have done before. And at the office, things would have become very lax if Eldersma had not taken the work out of Van Oudijck's hands and given himself even more to do than he already had. It was generally stated that the resident was ill. And, indeed, his skin was yellow, his liver was painful, and the least thing grated on his nerves. It made for a neurotic household, what with Doddy's temper tantrums and Theo's jealousy and hatred, for Theo was back home again since he had given up in Surabaja. Only Léonie continued triumphant, ever beautiful, white, calm, smiling, contented, happy because of Addy's lasting passion, because she knew how to enthrall him, she the sorceress of love, savant of passion. Fate had warned her and she kept Theo at a distance, but, for the rest, she was happy and contented.

Then suddenly the position in Batavia became vacant. The names of two or three residents were mentioned, but Van Oudijck had the best chance. And he worried about it, was afraid of it: he did not care for Batavia as a residency. He would not have been able to work there as he worked here, in Labuwangi, where he had zealously devoted himself to fostering many different aspects of agriculture and population. He would rather have been appointed to Surabaja, where there was plenty going on, or to one of the "Principalities," where his tact in dealing with the native princes would have been turned to good purpose. But Batavia! For a resident, it was the least interesting of all districts. It was the least flattering assignment for someone in the position of resident, because of the arrogant atmosphere of the place, the close contact with the governor-general and the highest officials, so that a resident, who was almost supreme anywhere else, was in Batavia just another high official among the many members of the Council and the host of directors. And it was much too close to Buitenzorg, with its arrogant secretariat, whose bureaucracy and red tape were always in conflict with the realistic practices of the residents themselves.

The prospect of being appointed unsettled him, and harassed him with the thought of having to leave Labuwangi in a month and of selling his furniture. It would break his heart to leave Labuwangi. In spite of all that he had gone through, he loved the town, and especially his district. During all those years, he had left traces of activity throughout the area, traces of his devoted labor, his ambition, and his affection. And now, within the month, he would have to transfer all this to a successor, to tear himself away from everything that he had so lovingly cherished and fostered. It filled him with a somber melancholy. It did not matter to him that a promotion would bring him closer to his pension. That future of doing nothing, with the boredom of approaching old age, was a nightmare to him. And his successor might change everything and would disagree with him on every single point.

Finally, the chance of promotion became such a morbid obsession that, improbable as it might seem, he wrote to the director of the civil service and to the governor-general, begging them to leave him in Labuwangi. Little of what these letters contained was leaked. He did not mention them, either to his family or to his colleagues, so that, when a younger, second-class resident was appointed resident of Batavia, people said that Van Oudijck had been passed over, because they didn't know that this had happened at his own request. And, in looking for a cause, they stirred up the old gossip about the dismissal of the regent of Ngadjiwa and the strange things that happened thereafter, though neither gave a satisfactory answer to why the government had failed to promote Van Oudijck.

It granted Van Oudijck a strange kind of peace, a peace due to lassitude, to letting himself go, to being stuck in his familiar Labuwangi, to not having to be transferred, old Indies hand that he was, to Batavia, where things were so much different. When, at his last audience, the governor-general had spoken to him about going to Europe on leave, he had felt afraid of Europe, afraid of no longer feeling at home there, and now he felt a similar fear for Batavia. And yet he was well aware of the fake Western humbug of Batavia, was well aware that the capital of Java only pretended to be very much European while in reality this was only partly true. Unknown to his wife, who regretted the lost illusion of Batavia, he chuckled at the thought that he had succeeded in remaining in Labuwangi. And yet, though he might chuckle at it, he felt changed nevertheless, aged, diminished, felt that he was no longer aspiring along that ascending line—the prospect of constantly winning a higher place in society—which had always been his life's ambition. What had become of his ambition? What had lessened his love of authority? He put it all down to the influence of the climate. It would certainly be a good thing to refresh his blood and his mind in Europe, to spend a couple of winters there. But the idea immediately evaporated, because of his lack of resolution. No, he did not want to go to Europe. It was the Indies that he loved. And he gave in to long periods of musing, while lying in a long chair, enjoying his coffee, enjoying the comfortably light clothing he now wore, the gentle weakening of his muscles, the aimless drowsiness of his thoughts. The only thing that was still sharp in this drowsy mood was his ever-increasing suspicion, and every so often he would suddenly wake from his languor and listen to the vague sounds, the soft suppressed laughter which he seemed to hear in Léonie's room, just as, at night, apprehensive of ghosts, he listened to the muffled sounds in the garden and to the rats scurrying above his head.

30

Addy was sitting with Mrs. Van Does on the little verandah in the back when they heard a carriage rattle up in front of the house. They smiled at each other and rose from their seats.

"I shall leave you to yourselves," said Mrs. Van Does.

And she disappeared, to drive around the town in a *dos-à-dos,* doing business with her friends.

Léonie entered.

"Where is Mrs. Van Does?" she asked, for she always behaved as though it were the first time. It was her great charm. He knew this, and answered:

"She has just gone out. She will be sorry to have missed you."

He spoke like this because he knew that she liked it, the polite beginning each time, in order to preserve most of all the freshness of their affair.

They sat down side by side on a settee in the little closed middle gallery. The settee was covered with cretonne that had a pattern of garish flowers. On the white walls hung a few cheap fans and *kakemonos,*[82] and on either side of a small mirror stood a console table with imitation bronze statues on them: two nondescript knights, each with one leg forward and a spear in his hand. Through the glass door the small, musty back verandah could be seen, with its damp, yellow-green pillars, its flowerpots, also yellow-green, with a few withered rosebushes. Behind this was the damp, neglected little garden with a couple of skinny coconut palms, their leaves hanging down like broken feathers.

He took her in his arms and drew her to him, but she gently pushed him away.

"Doddy is becoming unbearable," she said. "Something's got to be done about it."

"How so?"

"She's got to leave the house. She is so irritable that I can't put up with her anymore."

"You tease her, you know."

She shrugged her shoulders, displeased with a recent scene with her stepdaughter.

"I never used to tease her. She loved me and we got on all right. Now she flies off the handle about anything. It's your fault. Those everlasting evening walks, which lead to nothing, upset her."

"Perhaps it's just as well that they lead to nothing," he murmured, with his little laugh of the tempter. "But I can't stop seeing her, you know; it would make her unhappy. And I can't bear to see a woman unhappy."

She laughed scornfully.

"Yes, you're so good-natured. You'd spread your favors everywhere just because you're so kindhearted. Anyway, she'll have to go."

"Where to?"

"Don't ask such silly questions!" she exclaimed, angrily, roused out of her usual indifference. "She'll have to go, somewhere or other, I don't care where. You know that once I've said something, it happens. And this is going to be done."

"You're angry. It doesn't become you. . . ."

Still miffed, she first refused to let him kiss her, but, since he did not like bad moods and was well aware of the irresistible power of his comely Moorish virility, he overpowered her with rough, smiling violence and held her so tight that she could not move.

"Stop being angry now."

"No, I won't. I hate Doddy."

"The poor girl has done you no harm."

"Possibly."

"On the contrary, you tease her."

"Yes, because I hate her."

"Why? You're not jealous, are you?"

She laughed out loud.

"No! That's not like me."

"Then why?"

"What does it matter to you? I don't know myself. I hate her. I love tormenting her."

"Are you just as bad as you are beautiful?"

"What do you mean: bad? How do I know? I'd like to torment you too, if I knew how."

"And I'd give you a good spanking.'

Again she laughed.

"Perhaps it would do me good," she admitted. "I seldom lose my temper, but Doddy . . . !"

She tensed her fingers and, suddenly calmer, she nestled against him and put her arms around his body.

"I used to be very indifferent," she confessed. "But lately I'm much more nervous, after that scare in the bathroom. After they spat at me with *sirih*. Do you think they were ghosts? I don't. It was some practical joke of the regent's. Those awful Javanese know all sorts of things. . . .

But since that time I have, as it were, lost my footing. Do you know what I mean? . . . It used to be so great. I wouldn't let anything bother me. But after having been sick like that, I seem to have changed, become more nervous. One day, when Theo was angry with me, he said that I've been hysterical since then . . . and I never used to be. I don't know, maybe he's right. But I have certainly changed. . . . I care less about people, and I think I'm becoming more flagrant. . . . The gossip is getting nastier too. . . . Van Oudijck irritates me, snooping around like that. He's beginning to notice something. . . . And Doddy, Doddy! . . . I'm not jealous, but I can't stand those evening walks with you. . . . You have to give it up, do you hear, walking with her. I won't have it, I won't have it. . . . And everything bores me here, in Labuwangi. What a miserable, monotonous life! . . . Surabaja's a bore too. . . . So's Batavia. . . . It's all so dumb, people never think of anything new. . . . I would like to go to Paris. I think that I would be able to enjoy myself there."

"Do I bore you, too?"

"You?"

She stroked his face with her hands, stroked his chest and all the way down his legs.

"I'll tell you what I think of you. You're a pretty boy, but you're too good-natured. That irritates me too. You kiss anybody who wants to be kissed by you. In Patjaram, you are always pawing everybody, including your old mother and your sisters. I think that's awful."

He laughed.

"You're becoming jealous!" he exclaimed.

"Jealous? Am I really getting jealous? That'd be terrible. I don't know, I don't think I am. I don't want to be. After all, I believe there's something that will always protect me."

"A devil. . . ."

"Possibly. *Un bon diable.*"

"Are you taking up French?"

"Yes. Because of Paris. . . . There's something that protects me. I firmly believe that life can't hurt me, that nothing can touch me."

"You're becoming superstitious."

"I always was. Perhaps I've become more so. . . . Tell me, have I changed lately?"

"You're more nervous."

"Not so indifferent as I was?"

"You're more fun, more amusing."

"Was I a bore before?"

"You were a little quiet. You were always beautiful, delicious, divine
. . . but rather quiet."

"Perhaps because I paid more attention to people then."

"Don't you now?"

"No, not now. They talk about me anyway. . . . But tell me, haven't I
changed more than that?"

"Yes, you have. You're more jealous, more superstitious, more nervous. . . . What more do you want?"

"Physically, have I changed physically?"

"No."

"Don't I look older? . . . Am I not getting wrinkled?"

"You? Never."

"Listen, I think that I still have quite a future ahead of me, something
very different. . . ."

"In Paris?"

"Perhaps. . . . Tell me, am I not too old?"

"For what?"

"For Paris. . . . How old do you think I am?"

"Twenty-five."

"You're joking. You know perfectly well that I'm thirty-two. Do I
look thirty-two?"

"Not at all. . . ."

"Tell me, don't you think that this is an awful country? . . . Have you
ever been to Europe?"

"No."

"I was there from when I was ten to fifteen. . . . When you get down to
it, you're a brown *sinjo* and I'm a white *nonna*. . . ."

"I love my country."

"Yes, because you think that you're a Solo prince. . . . That's your
Patjaram nonsense. . . . I hate the Indies, I can't stand Labuwangi. I want
to get out. I want to go to Paris. . . . You're coming with me?"

"No. I will never go. . . ."

"Even when you know that there are hundreds of European women
you haven't had yet?"

He looked at her. Something in her words and in her voice struck
him: a crazy hysteria, which he had never noticed before, when she had
always been the quietly passionate mistress, her eyes half closed, who
always wanted immediately to forget everything and become proper
again. Something in her repelled him. He loved the soft, pliant surrender
of her caresses, the smiling indolence that she used to display, but not

these half-crazed eyes and purple mouth which seemed ready to bite. She seemed to feel it, because she suddenly pushed him away and said brusquely:

"You bore me. . . . I know you by now. . . . Go away. . . ."

But he didn't want that. He didn't like a futile *rendez-vous* and he now embraced her and asked. . . .

"No," she said, curtly. "You bore me. Everyone bores me here. Everything bores me."

On his knees, he encircled her waist and drew her to him. Smiling a little, she became slightly more yielding and rumpled his hair nervously. A carriage pulled up in front of the house.

"Listen!" she said.

"That's Mrs. Van Does. . . ."

"She's back early. . . ."

"She probably didn't sell anything."

"Then it'll cost you some money. . . ."

"Probably. . . ."

"Do you pay her much. For us getting together?"

"What difference does it make? . . ."

"Listen," she said again, more attentively.

"That's not Mrs. Van Does. . . ."

"No. . . ."

"It's a man's footstep. . . ."

"It wasn't a *dos-à-dos*, either; it was much too noisy."

"It's probably nothing," she said. "Somebody at the wrong house. Nobody ever comes here."

"The man's going round," he said, listening.

They both listened for a moment. And then, suddenly, after two or three strides through the narrow little garden and along the little verandah in the back, Van Oudijck appeared outside the closed glass door, visible through the curtain. And he had pulled the door open before Léonie and Addy could change their position, so that Van Oudijck saw them both, her sitting on the couch and him kneeling before her, while her hand still lay, as though forgotten, on his hair.

"Léonie!" roared her husband.

Because of the shock of surprise, blood stormed through her veins, and in one moment she saw the entire future: his anger, the trial, the divorce, the money that her husband would give her, all in one whirling vision. But, as if compelled by her nervous will, the rush of blood subsided and she remained quietly sitting there, her terror showing for just one more moment in her eyes, before she turned them on Van Oudijck.

Pressing her finger softly on Addy's head, she suggested to him to remain in the same position, to remain kneeling at her feet, and she said, as though self-hypnotized, and listening in astonishment to her own slightly husky voice:

"Otto. . . . Adrien de Luce is asking me to put in a good word for him. . . . with you. . . . He is asking . . . for Doddy's hand. . . ."

All three remained motionless, all three under the influence of these words, of this notion which had come . . . even Léonie herself did not know from where. And, sitting rigid and erect like a sibyl, still with that gentle pressure on Addy's head, she repeated:

"He is asking . . . for Doddy's hand. . . ."

She was still the only one to speak. And she continued:

"He knows that you have some objections. He knows that you do not care for his family . . . because they have Javanese blood in their arteries."

She was still speaking as though someone else were speaking inside her, and she had to smile at that word "arteries," she did not know why: perhaps because it was the first time in her life that she had used the word, in conversation.

"But," she went on, "there are no financial problems if Doddy goes to live in Patjaram. . . . And the children have loved each other . . . for so long."

She was still the only one that was speaking.

"Doddy has been highstrung for a long time, almost ill. . . . It would be a crime, Otto, not to consent."

Gradually her voice became more musical and the smile came on her lips, but her eyes remained hard as steel, as though she were threatening Van Oudijck with her anger if he refused to believe her.

"Come," she said, very gently, very kindly, patting Addy's head softly with her trembling fingers. "Get up . . . Addy . . . and go to . . . Papa."

He rose, mechanically.

"Léonie, what were you doing here?" asked Van Oudijck, hoarsely.

"Here? I was with Mrs. Van Does."

"And he?" pointing at Addy.

"He? . . . He happened to be calling. . . . Mrs. Van Does had to go out. . . . Then he asked if he could speak to me. . . . And then he asked me . . . for Doddy's hand. . . ."

All three were again silent.

"And you, Otto?" she now asked, more harshly. "What brought you here?"

He looked at her sharply.

"Is there anything you want to buy from Mrs. Van Does?"

"Theo told me you were here. . . ."

"Theo was right. . . ."

"Léonie. . . ."

She rose, and, with her eyes hard as steel, she intimated to him that he *must* believe her, that she *insisted* on his believing her.

"In any case, Otto," she said, once more gentle and sweet, "don't leave Addy any longer in his uncertainty. And you, Addy, don't be afraid . . . and ask Papa for Doddy's hand. . . . I have nothing to say where Doddy is concerned . . . as I told you."

They now stood facing one another, in the narrow middle gallery, breathing with difficulty, oppressed by their accumulated emotions. Then Addy said:

"Resident, I ask you . . . for your daughter's hand."

A *dos-à-dos* pulled up at the front of the house.

"That's Mrs. Van Does," said Léonie hurriedly. "Otto, say something before she comes. . . ."

"All right," said Van Oudijck, somberly.

He got out the back before Mrs. Van Does entered and did not see the hand Addy held out to him. Mrs. Van Does came in trembling, followed by a *babu* carrying her bundle, her merchandise. She saw Léonie and Addy standing rigidly and hypnotized.

"That was the *residèn*'s carriage!" stammered the Indies woman, white as a sheet. "Was it the *residèn*?"

"Yes," said Léonie, calmly.

"*Astaga!* What happened?"

"Nothing," said Léonie, laughing.

"Nothing?"

"Or rather, something did happen."

"What?"

"Addy and Doddy are. . . ."

"What?"

"Engaged!"

And she burst out laughing with uncontrollable mirth about the madness of life and took Mrs. Van Does, who stood there nonplussed, and spun her around and kicked the bundle out of the *babu*'s hands, so that a parcel of *batik* bedspreads and table runners fell to the ground and a small jar full of glittering crystals rolled away and broke.

"*Astaga!* . . . My diamonds!"

One more kick of glee, and the table runners flew left and right and the diamonds glittered among the legs of the tables and chairs. Addy, his eyes still filled with terror, crawled about on his hands and knees, trying to collect them.

Mrs. Van Does repeated:

"Engaged?"

31

Doddy was thrilled, in seventh heaven, delighted, when Van Oudijck told her that Addy had asked for her hand in marriage. And when she heard that Mamma had spoken up for her, she embraced Léonie wildly, with the emotional spontaneity of her temperament, once more surrendering to the attraction that Léonie had had for her for years. She immediately forgot everything that had annoyed her about the excessive intimacy between Mamma and Addy, when he used to hang over her chair and whisper to her. She had never believed what she had heard now and then, because Addy had always assured her that it wasn't true. And she was ever so happy that she was going to live with Addy, he and she together in Patjaram. For Patjaram was her ideal of what a home should be. The big house, full of sons and daughters and children and animals, who were all subjected to the same kindness and cordiality and boredom, while behind those sons and daughters shone the halo of their Solo heritage. The big house built onto the sugar factory was to her the ideal residence, and she felt part of all its little traditions: the *sambal,* crushed and ground by a *babu* squatting behind her chair while she ate, represented to her the supreme indulgence of the palate; the races at Ngadjiwa, attended by the languid *lengang-lengang* procession of all those women,[83] with the *babus* behind them, carrying the handkerchief, the scent bottle, the binoculars, were for her the *ne plus ultra* of elegance. She loved the old dowager radèn-aju, and she had given herself to Addy entirely, without reserve, from the first moment she saw him, when she was a little girl of thirteen and he a boy of eighteen. It was because of him that she had always resisted when Papa wanted to send her to Europe, to a boarding school in Brussels; because of him she had never cared for any place except Labuwangi, Ngadjiwa, or Patjaram; because of him she was prepared to live and die in Patjaram.

It was because of him that she had felt all the little jealousies when her girl friends told her that he was in love with this one or carrying on with that one; because of him she would always know those jealousies great and small, her whole life long. He would be her life, Patjaram her world, sugar her interest, because it was Addy's interest. Because of him she would long for many children, a lot of children, who would be really brown—not white, like Papa and Mamma and Theo—but brown, because her own mother was brown. She herself was a delicate brown, while Addy was a beautiful bronze color, a Moorish brown, and, after the example set in Patjaram, her children, her numerous children, would be brought up in the shadow of the factory, their interests determined by sugar, so they would plant the fields later on, when they grew up, and mill the sugar cane and restore the fortunes of the family to their former brilliance. And she was as happy as a girl in love could imagine herself to be, seeing her ideal, Addy and Patjaram, so closely attainable. She never had an inkling how her happiness had come about, through what Léonie had said, almost unconsciously, as though by auto-suggestion, at the very last moment. Oh, now she didn't have to look for the dark corners or dark *sawahs* with Addy. Now she was constantly kissing him in broad daylight, leaned radiantly against him, feeling his warm, virile body which was hers and would soon be hers entirely. Now her eyes desired him, for all to see, because she no longer had the strength of chastity to hide her feelings from others; now he was hers, hers.

And he, with the good-natured surrender of a young sultan, let her caress his shoulders and knees, let her kiss him and stroke his hair, allowed her arm around his neck, accepting it all as a tribute due to him because he was used to the tributes of love that women had always paid him, he who had been fondled and caressed from the time he was a little chubby boy, from the time when he was carried by Tidjem, his *babu*, who was in love with him ever since he used to romp in a *tjelana monjèt* with little sisters and cousins, all of whom were in love with him. All this tribute he accepted good-naturedly, though he was secretly surprised and shocked by what Léonie had done.... And yet, he argued, it might have happened anyway, because Doddy loved him so much. He would rather have remained unmarried. Even unmarried he would still have had all the domesticity in Patjaram that he wanted and retained his liberty to bestow, good-naturedly, abundant love upon women. And he was already ingenuously thinking that it would not do, that it would never do to remain faithful to Doddy alone, because he was really too good-natured, and women were all crazy. Doddy must get used to it later on, must learn to accept it because, after all, in Solo, in the *kraton*, it was the same thing, with his uncles and cousins....

Had Van Oudijck believed what Léonie said? He didn't know whether he did or not. Doddy had accused Léonie of being in love with Addy. When Van Oudijck had asked Theo that morning where Léonie was, his son had curtly answered:

"At Mrs. Van Does's ... with Addy."

He had glared at his son, but asked no further questions; he had simply driven straight to Mrs. Van Does's house. And he had actually found his wife with young De Luce, found him on his knees before her, but she had said so calmly:

"Adrian de Luce is asking me for your daughter's hand."

No, he himself did not know whether he believed her or not. His wife had answered so calmly and now, during the first few days of the engagement, she was so calm, smiling just as usual. . . . He now saw for the first time that strange side of her, that invulnerability, as though nothing could harm her. Did he suspect that behind this wall of invulnerability there was still the ironical feminine secrecy of her silently smouldering inner life? It was as though, because of his recent nervous suspicion, his restless mood, his superstitious prying and listening to the haunting silence, he had learned to see things that he had been blind to when still in his prime as a ruler and aloof official. And his desire to make certain of the mysteries at which he guessed became so violent in his morbid irritability, that he grew more pleasant and kinder to his son, not from the spontaneous paternal affection he had always felt for Theo, but from curiosity, to hear all that he had to say, to make Theo confess what he knew. And Theo, who hated Léonie, who hated his father, who hated Addy, who hated Doddy, who hated everybody around him, who hated life with his stubborn notions of a blond *sinjo*, who longed for money and beautiful women, who was angry because the world, life, fortune, happiness—as he pictured it in his small-minded fashion—did not come rushing up to him to fall in his arms. Theo was willing enough to squeeze out his words one by one, like drops of wormwood, silently enjoying the sight of his father's suffering. And he let Van Oudijck gradually guess that it was true after all, about Mamma and Addy.

The intimacy between father and son that had been generated by suspicion and hatred caused Theo to mention his brother in the *kampong*. He said that he knew that Papa sent Si-Oudijck money and that therefore he acknowledged that it was true. And Van Oudijck, no longer certain, no longer knowing the truth, gave in, admitted that it might be so, was giving in, admitted that it was so. Then, remembering the anonymous letters—which had only lately ceased, since Van Oudijck had been sending money to that half-caste who ventured to assume his name—he also remembered the libels that he had often read in them and that, at the time, he had always cast from him as so much filth, remembered the two names, those of his wife and of Theo, which had constantly been connected. His distrust and suspicion blazed up like flames, like an inextinguishable fire, which scorched every other thought or feeling . . . until at last he was no longer able to restrain himself and spoke to Theo about it openly. He did not trust Theo's indignation and denial. And he now trusted nothing and nobody, he distrusted his wife and children and his officials, he distrusted his cook. . . .

32

Like a bolt of lightning, the rumor ran through Labuwangi that Van Oudijck and his wife were going to be divorced. Léonie went to Europe very suddenly, really without anyone's knowing why, and without taking leave of anybody. It caused a great scandal in the little town, people talked of nothing else and talked of it even as far away as Surabaja, as far away as Batavia. Only Van Oudijck didn't say a word about it. Perhaps his back was a little more bowed, but he went his way, working on, leading his ordinary life. He had abandoned his principles and assisted Theo to obtain a job in order to be rid of him. He preferred to have Doddy staying in Patjaram, where the De Luce women would help her with her trousseau. He wanted Doddy to get married as quickly as possible in Patjaram. In his great, empty house, he now longed for nothing but solitude, for a vast, cheerless solitude. He no longer had the table laid for him; they brought him a plateful of rice and a cup of coffee in his office. He felt ill, his zeal lessened, a dull indifference gnawed at him. He delegated all the work, all the district to Eldersma, and when Eldersma, after not sleeping for weeks, half-crazy with nervous strain, told the resident that the doctor wanted to send him to Europe, Van Oudijck lost all his courage. He said that he too felt ill and done for. And he applied to the governor-general for leave and went to Batavia. He said nothing about it, but he felt certain that he would never return to Labuwangi. And he went away quietly, without a glance at what he was leaving behind him, his accomplishments that he had once so lovingly strived for. The administration remained in the hands of the assistant resident at Ngadjiwa. It was generally believed that Van Oudijck wished to see the governor-general about certain questions of importance but suddenly the news arrived that he wanted to retire. Nobody believed it at first, but the report was confirmed. Van Oudijck did not return.

He had gone, without once looking back, with a strange indifference, an indifference that had gradually corrupted the very marrow of this once so robust and practical man. He felt this indifference toward Labuwangi which he had thought himself incapable of leaving except with the greatest regret, when there had been the question of his promotion to resident first class, and he felt this indifference toward his domestic circle, which no longer existed. His soul was filled with a gradual blight, it was withering and dying. It seemed to him that all his powers were melting away in the lukewarm stagnation of this indifference. He vegetated for a while in his hotel in Batavia, and it was generally assumed that he would go to Europe.

Eldersma had already gone, seriously ill, and Eva had been unable to accompany him with the little boy, because she had come down with a bad attack of malaria. When she was more or less on her feet again, she sold her furnishings, intending to go to Batavia to stay there for three weeks with friends until her boat sailed. She left Labuwangi with mixed feelings. She had suffered much there, but she had also thought about many things, and she had cherished a deep feeling for Van Helderen, a pure radiant feeling which, she was sure, could only shine forth once in a lifetime. She took leave of him as if of an ordinary friend, in the presence of others, with no more than an ordinary handshake. But she felt so depressed about that mere handshake, that commonplace farewell, that tears rose to her eyes. That evening, left to herself, she did not weep, but sat in her room at the hotel, staring silently in front of her for hours. Her husband was gone, ill, and she did not know how he would be when she saw him again, that is, if she would ever see him again at all. To be sure, after her years in the Indies, Europe's shores bid her a warm welcome, beckoned her with its cities, its culture, its art; but she was afraid of Europe. An unspoken fear lest she should have lost ground intellectually made her almost dread her parents' home, where she would be in a month's time. She trembled at the thought that people would consider her colonial in her manners and ideas, in her speech and dress, in the education of her child. And despite her bravura as a smart and cultured woman, it made her feel shy in anticipation. She certainly no longer played the piano as well as she used to and she would not dare play in The Hague. Perhaps it would be a good thing to stay in Paris for a couple of weeks and reacquaint herself with the world, before showing herself in The Hague. . . .

But Eldersma was too ill. . . . And what would they think of him, her husband, so much changed, her once robust Frisian husband, now tired out, worn out, yellow as parchment, careless of his appearance, muttering gloomily when he spoke? . . . But a gentle vision of a refreshing German landscape, of Swiss snows, of music in Bayreuth, of art in Italy, dawned before her staring gaze, and she saw herself reunited with her sick husband, no longer united in love but united under the yoke of the life that they had once shouldered together. . . . Then there was the education of her child! Oh, to save her child, from the Indies! And yet he, Van Helderen, had never been out of the Indies. But then he was himself, he was an exception.

She had said goodbye to him. . . . She must make up her mind to forget him. Europe was waiting for her, and her husband, and her child. . . .

Two days later, she was in Batavia. She hardly knew the city, she had been there once or twice, years ago, when she first came out. In Labuwangi, in that little outlying district, Batavia had gradually become glorified in her imagination as an essentially Eurasian capital, a center of Eurasian civilization, a dim vision of stately avenues and squares, surrounded by great, wealthy, porticoed villas, thronged with smart carriages and horses. She had always heard so much about Batavia. . . .

She was now staying with friends. The husband was at the head of a big commercial firm, and the house was one of the finest villas on the Koningsplein.[84] And she was at once strangely impressed by the funereal character, by the deadly melancholy of this great city of villas, where thousands of varied lives were waging a silent, feverish battle for a future of moneyed repose. It seemed as if all those houses, gloomy despite their white pillars and their grand facades, were frowning like faces careworn with troubles which they sought to hide behind a pretentious display of broad leaves and clustering palms. The houses, however much exposed amidst their pillars, however apparently invitingly open, remained closed; the occupants were never seen. Only in the mornings —when she did her errands in the shops on Rijswijk and Molenvliet which, with a few French names, tried to give the impression of a southern shopping center, of European luxury—did Eva see the exodus to the Old Town of the white men with white complexions, dressed in white, with blank stares, blank from brooding anxieties, with a distant blank gaze fixed upon a future that they had figured with so many years or decades—so much made, in this year or that, and then, away, away home, from the Indies to Europe. It seemed as if it were not malaria that was undermining them, but another fever. And she felt clearly that it was undermining their bodies and souls that had never acclimated, as though they were trying to skip that day for tomorrow, or the day after, days that brought them a little nearer to their goal, because they were secretly afraid that they would die before that goal was reached. The exodus filled the trams with its white burden of mortality. Many, already well off, but not yet rich enough for their purposes, drove in their *mylords* and buggies to the Harmonie Club, where they took the tram to spare their horses.

And in the Old Town, in the old, aristocratic houses of the first Dutch merchants, which were built like they were in Holland, with oak staircases leading to upper floors which now, during the eastern monsoon, were close with a dense, oppressive heat, like something tangible that stifled the breath, the white men were bent over their work, forever seeing between their thirsty glance and the white desert of their papers the bedewed mirage of the future, the refreshing oasis of their materialistic illusion: to make within a certain amount of time a certain amount of money and then gone, gone ... to Europe.... And in the city of villas, around the Koningsplein and along the green avenues, the women hid themselves, the women remained unseen, the whole livelong day. The hot day passed, the time of beneficent coolness came, the time from half-past five to seven. The men returned home worn out, and they rested, and the women, tired of their housekeeping, their children, and of nothing at all, of a life of doing nothing, a life without any interest, tired of the deadliness of their existence, the women rested beside the men. That hour of beneficent coolness meant rest, rest after the bath, in undress, around the tea table; a short momentary rest, for the fearsome hour of seven was at hand, when it was already dark, when one had to go to a reception. A reception meant dressing in stuffy European clothes, meant a brief but dreadful display of European drawing-room manners and social graces, but it also meant meeting this person and that and striving to advance yet one more step toward the mirage of the future: money and ultimate rest in Europe. And after the city of villas had been prostrate beneath the sun all day, as if dying and deserted—with the men away in the Old Town and the women hidden in their houses—a few carriages now passed one another in the dark, round the Koningsplein and along the green avenues, a few European-looking people, going to a reception. But, around the Koningsplein and in the green avenues all the other villas persisted in this funereal desolation and remained filled with gloomy darkness, the house where the party was being given shone with lamps among the palm trees. And for the rest, the deadliness lingered everywhere, and everywhere the somber brooding hung over the houses wherein the tired people were hiding, the men exhausted from work, the women exhausted from doing nothing....

"Wouldn't you like to go for a drive, Eva?" asked her hostess, Mrs. De Harteman, a little Dutch woman, white as wax and always worn out by her children. "But I'd rather not come with you, if you don't mind. I'd rather wait for Harteman. Otherwise there'd be nobody at home. Why don't you go, with your little boy."

So Eva, with her little fellow, went for a drive in the De Hartemans' carriage. It was the cool hour of the day, before darkness set in. She met two or three carriages: Mrs. This and Mrs. That, who were known to drive in the afternoon. In the Koningsplein she saw a lady and gentleman walking: the So-and-Sos, who always went for a walk, as all Batavia knew. She met no one else. No one. At that beneficent hour, the

city of villas remained as desolate as a city of the dead, as a vast mauso-
leum amid green trees. And yet it was a comfort, after the overwhelming
heat, to see the Koningsplein expanding like a gigantic meadow, where
the parched grass was turning green with the first rains, while the houses
were so lost in the distance very far away in their hedged-in gardens,
that it seemed as if one were in the country, amid woods and fields and
pastures, with the big sky overhead which gave air to the lungs as if, for
the first time that day, they were breathing in oxygen and life. That big
sky displayed every day a different wealth of colors, an excess of sunset
fires, a glorious death of the scorching day, when the sun seemed to
burst into torrents of gold among the lilac threatening rainclouds. And
it was so spacious and so delightful, it was such an immense comfort
that it actually made up for the day.

But there was no one to see it except the two or three people who were
known in Batavia to go driving or walking. A violet twilight rose, and
then the night lowered its heavy shadow and the city, which had been
like death all day, with its frown of brooding gloom, dropped wearily
asleep, like a city of worry. . . .

It used to be different, said old Mrs. De Harteman, the mother-in-law
of Eva's friend. They were no longer there, the pleasant houses with
their Indies hospitality, their inviting tables, their sincere and cordial
welcomes. The colonist's character seemed to have changed, saddened
by the vicissitudes of chance, by the disappointment of not quickly
achieving his goal, his material goal of wealth. And, thus embittered, it
seemed that his nerves became also frayed, just as his soul saddened and
his body weakened so that he no longer could withstand the destructive
climate. . . .

And Eva did not find Batavia the ideal city of Eurasian civilization
that she had pictured in eastern Java. In this great center of worry about
money, of desire for money, every trace of spontaneity had vanished
and life dozed off into an everlasting seclusion in the office or at home.
People never saw each other except at receptions, any other conversation took place over the telephone.[85]

The abuse of the telephone for domestic purposes killed the intimacy
among friends. People no longer saw one another, they no longer had
any need to dress and send for the carriage, because they chatted over
the telephone, in *sarong* and *kabaai*, in pajamas, almost without stirring
a limb. The telephone was close at hand and it rang constantly on the
back verandah. People called each other for nothing, or just for the fun
of it. Young Mrs. De Harteman had an intimate friend, a young woman
whom she had never seen, but whom she telephoned daily, for half an

hour at a time. She sat down when she talked, so it did not tire her. And she laughed and joked with her friend, without having to dress and without moving. She did the same with other friends; she visited them by telephone. She did her shopping by telephone. In Labuwangi Eva had not been used to this endless jangling and ringing, which killed all conversation, which on the back verandah revealed only one half of a dialogue—the answer being inaudible to anyone sitting away from the instrument—in the form of an incessant, one-sided jabbering. It got on her nerves and drove her to her room. And, amid the boredom of this life, full of care and inward brooding for the husband and penetrated by the chatter of the wife's telephone conversations, Eva would be surprised to hear suddenly of a special excitement: a fancy fair or rehearsals for an amateur opera performance.

She attended one of these rehearsals during her visit and was astonished by what was really a very good performance, as if those musical amateurs had put the strength of despair into it, to dispel the tedium of the Batavian evenings. For the Italian opera had left, and she had to laugh at the heading "Amusements" in the newspaper, the *Javabode*, because those amusements were as a rule limited to a choice of three or four meetings of shareholders. This too used to be different, said old Mrs. De Harteman, who remembered the excellent French opera of twenty-five years ago which, to be sure, cost thousands, but for which the thousands were always available. No, people no longer had the money to amuse themselves at night. They sometimes gave a very expensive dinner, or else went to a meeting of shareholders. Eva came to feel that Labuwangi was a much livelier place. True, she had largely been responsible for that liveliness at the instigation of Van Oudijck, who was glad to make the capital of his district a pleasant, cheerful little town. And she came to the conclusion that, after all, she preferred a small, provincial place, with a few cultured, agreeable European inhabitants—provided that they got along with each other and did not quarrel too much in their narrow lives—to this pretentious, pompous, dreary Batavia. Only the military element had some life in it. Only the officers' houses were lit up in the evening. Apart from that, the city lay as though moribund, the whole long hot day, with its frown of care, with its invisible population of people looking to the future: a future of money and, perhaps even more so, a future of rest in Europe.

She longed to get away. Batavia suffocated her, notwithstanding her daily drive round the spacious Koningsplein. She had only one wish left, the sad wish of saying goodby to Van Oudijck. Though she had the temperament of a smart and artistic woman, she had, strangely enough, appreciated and felt the fascination of his character, the character of a simple and practical man. Perhaps for one fleeting moment she had felt something for him, deep down within herself: a friendship that was the opposite of her friendship with Van Helderen, an appreciation of his fine human qualities rather than a feeling of Platonic communion of souls. She had felt a sympathetic pity for him in those strange, mysterious days, for the man who lived alone in his enormous house when the strange events had closed in on him from everywhere. She had felt intensely sorry for him when his wife, as if tossing away her exalted position, had left in an insolent mood, arousing a storm of scandal, without anyone's ever knowing exactly why. His wife, who had once been so correct, notwithstanding all her depravity, but who had been gradually devoured by the canker of the mysterious things until she was no longer able to restrain herself, and bared the innermost secrets of her profligate soul with cynical indifference. The red *sirih* spittle that ghosts had spat at her naked body had affected her like a sickness, had eaten into the very marrow of her bones, like a disintegration of her soul which might finally be her undoing when she would slowly waste away. What people now said about her, about how she lived in Paris, was so unutterably depraved that it could only be whispered.

Eva heard about it in Batavia, amid the gossip at the evening parties. And when she asked about Van Oudijck, where he was staying, whether he would soon be going to Europe after his unexpected resignation—something that had surprised the entire official world—they were unable to tell her, asked one another if he were no longer at the Hotel Wisse,[86] where he had been seen only a few weeks ago, lying on his chair on the little verandah, with his legs spread, staring straight ahead of him without moving. He had hardly gone out at all, had his meals in his room as if he—the man who had always been accustomed to dealing with hundreds of people—had become loath to meet anyone. At last Eva heard that Van Oudijck was living in Bandung.[87] Because she had to pay some farewell visits, she went to the Preanger. But he was not to be found in Bandung. The proprietor of the hotel was able to tell her that Van Oudijck had stayed a few days at his place, but had since gone, he did not know where.

Then at last, by accident, she heard from a man whom she met at dinner that Van Oudijck was living near Garut.[88] She went to Garut, glad to have found a trace of him. In her hotel in Garut people were able to tell her where he lived. She didn't know if she should first write him to announce her visit. Something seemed to warn her that if she did, he would make some excuse and that she would never see him. And now that she was about to leave Java for good, she wanted to see him, out of sympathy and curiosity. She wished to see for herself how he looked, to get out of him why he had so suddenly sent in his resignation, thrown away his enviable position in life, a position instantly occupied by the next man pushing behind him, in the great rush for promotion.

So the next morning, very early, without sending him word, she drove away in a carriage belonging to the hotel. The proprietor had explained to the coachman where he was to go. And she drove a very long way, along Lake Lellès,[89] the somber sacred lake with the two islands containing the ancient tombs of saints, while above it hovered, like a dark cloud of desolation, an ever circling flock of enormous *kalongs*,[90] gigantic black bats, flapping their demon wings and screeching their cry of despair, wheeling round and round incessantly: a black, funeral swirl against the infinite blue sky, as though they, the demons who had once dreaded light, had triumphed and no longer feared the day, because they obscured it with the shadow of their somber flight. It was oppressive; the sacred lake, the sacred tombs, and, above them, a horde as of black devils in the deep blue sky, because it seemed that a part of the mystery of the Indies was suddenly revealed, no longer hiding itself behind a vague, impalpable presence, but actually visible in the sunlight, rousing dismay with its menacing victory. Eva shivered, and when she looked up it seemed that the black multitude of saber wings would slash down, on her. But the shadow of death between her and the sun only whirled dizzily around, high above her head, and only uttered its despondent cry of triumph. . . . She drove on, and the plain of Lellès lay green and smiling before her. And that second of revelation had already passed, there was nothing now but the green and blue luxuriance of the Javanese landscape; the mystery was already hidden away among the delicate, waving bamboos or merged in the azure ocean of the sky.

The coachman was driving slowly up a steep hill. The liquid *sawahs* rose in terraces upwards like mirrored stairs, pale green, with carefully planted blades of paddy and then, suddenly, it changed to an avenue of ferns: gigantic ferns, waving their fans on high, with great fabled butterflies fluttering among them. And between the diaphanous foliage of the bamboos appeared a small house, built half of stone, half of wattled bamboo, surrounded by a little garden containing a few white pots of roses. A very young woman in *sarong* and *kabaai*, with cheeks gleaming like pale gold and coal-black eyes peering inquisitively, looked in surprise at the carriage, which was approaching very slowly, and fled indoors. Eva got out and coughed. And she suddenly caught a glimpse of Van Oudijck's face, peering round a screen in the small middle gallery. He disappeared at once.

"Resident!" she called, as sweetly as possible.

But no one appeared and she became apprehensive. She dared not sit down nor did she want to go away. But around the corner of the house peeped a little face, two little brown faces, the faces of very young *nonna* girls, and vanished again, giggling. Eva heard excited, very nervous whispering inside.

"Sidin! Sidin!" she heard somebody call.

She smiled, a little more courageously, and stayed and walked around the little front verandah. And at last there came an old woman, not perhaps so very old in years, but old because of her wrinkled skin and her eyes that had grown dim, wearing a colored chintz *kabaai* and dragging her slippers. Beginning with a few words of Dutch and then taking refuge in Malay, smiling politely, she requested Eva to be seated and said that the resident would be there in a moment. She herself sat down, smiled, did not know what to talk about, did not know what to answer when Eva asked her about the lake, about the road. She was more comfortable getting syrup and iced water and wafers. She did not talk, but only smiled and looked after her visitor. When the young *nonna*-faces peeped around the corner, the old woman angrily stamped her slippered foot and scolded them, and they disappeared again, giggling and running away with an audible patter of little bare feet. Then the old woman smiled again with her eternally smiling, wrinkled face and looked at the lady timidly, as though apologizing. It took a long time before Van Oudijck appeared.

He welcomed Eva effusively, excused himself for keeping her waiting. It was obvious that he had shaved himself in a hurry and put on a clean white suit. And it was obvious that he was glad to see her. The old woman left, with her eternal smile of apology. In that first cheerful moment, Van Oudijck seemed to Eva exactly the same as usual, but when he had calmed down and taken a chair and asked her whether she had heard from Eldersma and when she herself was going to Europe, she saw that he had grown old, that he was an old man. It did not show in his figure, which, in his well-starched white suit, still preserved something of the broad, soldierly appearance, a sturdy build, with only the back a little more bowed, as though bearing a burden. But it showed in his face, in the dull, indifferent glance, in the deep furrows of the care-worn forehead, in the color of his skin, which was dry and yellow, while the thick mustache, that still framed the jovial smile once in a while, was quite gray. His hands shook nervously. And he listened without inter-rupting while she told him what people had said in Labuwangi, betray-ing a lingering curiosity about the people there, about the district of which he had been so fond. She discussed it all vaguely, glossing over things, putting the best face on them and, especially, saying nothing about the gossip: that he had taken French leave, that he had run away, nobody quite knew why.

"And you, Resident," she asked, "are you going to Europe too?"

He stared in front of him and laughed painfully before replying. At last he said, almost shyly:

"No, I don't think I'll go home. You see, I've been somebody here in the Indies, and I'd be nobody over there. I'm also a nobody now, but I feel that the Indies have become my country. It has gotten the upper hand, and I belong to it now. I no longer belong to Holland, and I have nothing and nobody in Holland that belongs to me. I'm finished, it's true, but still I'd rather drag out my existence here than over there. In Holland I would not be able to stand the climate anymore, or the people. Here the climate suits me, and I have withdrawn from society. I have helped Theo for the last time, and Doddy is married. And the two boys are going to Europe, to school. . . ."

He suddenly bent toward her and, in a changed voice, he almost whis-pered, as though about to make a confession:

"You see, if everything had been normal, then . . . then I should not have acted as I did. I have always been a practical man, and I was proud of it and proud of living the normal life, my own life, which I lived ac-cording to principles that I thought were right, until I had reached a high position in society. I've always been like that, and things went well. While others worried about their promotion, I passed five of them at a time. It was all plain sailing for me, at least in my official career. I was not so lucky in my private life, but I have never been weak enough to break down with grief. A man has so much outside his domestic life. And yet I was always very fond of my family. I don't think it was my fault that everything went as it did. I loved my wife, I loved my children, I loved my home, I loved the place where I was husband and father. But that feeling in me was never fully satisfied. My first wife was a *nonna* whom I married because I was in love with her. Because she couldn't get to me with her whims, things became impossible after a few years. I was perhaps even more in love with my second wife. I'm fairly simple about things like that. But I was never allowed to have a pleasant home, a sweet woman, children climbing on your knees and growing up into men and women who owe their lives to you, their existence, owe to you everything they are. I would have liked that. But as I said, though I missed it, I didn't let it get to me. . . ."

He was silent for a moment and then continued in an even more mysterious whisper:

"But *that*, you see, the thing that happened . . . I never understood, and it's *that* which brought me to where I am. That . . . all that . . . was against life, reality, logic . . . all that"—he struck the table with his fist—"that damned nonsense, which . . . which happened all the same . . . that's what did it. I fought it, but I wasn't strong enough for it. There was no match for it. . . . I know: it was the regent. When I threatened him it stopped. . . . But, my God, Madam, tell me *what* was it? Do you know? No, you don't, do you? Nobody knew and nobody knows. Those terrible nights, those inexplicable noises above my head, that night in the bathroom with the major and the other officers! It wasn't a hallucination: we saw it, we heard it, we felt it, it spat at us, the whole bathroom was full of it! It is easy for people who didn't go through it to deny it. But I . . . and all of us . . . we saw it, heard it, and felt it! And nobody knew what it was. . . . And I have felt it ever since. It was all around me, in the air, under my feet. . . . You see," he whispered, very softly, "that—and that alone—did it. That made it impossible for me to stay there. It struck me dumb, turned me into an idiot in the midst of my normal life, despite my good sense and logic which suddenly appeared to me as a wrong theory of life, as the most abstract speculation, because, right in the middle of it, things happened that belonged to another world, things that escaped me and everybody else. That, that alone, did it! I was no longer myself. I no longer knew what I was thinking, what I was doing, what I had done. Everything collapsed in me. That miserable thing in the *kampong* is no child of mine: I'll bet my life on it. And I . . . I believed it. I sent him money. Do you understand me? I don't suppose you do. No one can understand it, that strange, unnatural business, if you haven't experienced it, in your flesh and in your blood, till it finds its way into your marrow. . . ."

"I think that I also experienced it once," she whispered. "When I was walking with Van Helderen by the sea, and the sky was so huge and the night so deep, or the rains came rustling from so very far away and then came down . . . or when the nights, silent as death and yet brimful of sounds, quivered around you, always with a music that no one could grasp and you could barely hear. . . . Or simply when I looked into the eyes of a Javanese, when I spoke to my *babu* and it seemed as though nothing of what I said got through to her and as if what she answered concealed her real, secret answer. . . ."

"That's another thing," he said. "I don't understand that. As far as I was concerned, I knew the Javanese through and through. But perhaps every European feels it in a different way, according to his nature and his temperament. To one it is perhaps the dislike for the country he feels from the very beginning, that it attacks his materialistic soft spot, and keeps on fighting him . . . whereas the country itself is so full of poetry and, I would almost say, mysticism. For somebody else it is the climate, or the character of the native, or whatever you want, that is hostile and incomprehensible. To me . . . it was the facts that I could not understand. And until then I had always been able to understand a fact . . . at least, I thought so. Now it appeared to me as if I no longer understood anything. . . . That's how I became a bad official and I realized that it was all over. And I simply quit. And now I'm here and here I mean to stay. And do you know the strange part of it? Perhaps I have at last . . . found a family here. . . ."

The little brown faces were peeping round the corner. And he called to them, lured them in a friendly manner, with a broad fatherly gesture. But they pattered away again, audibly, on their bare feet. He laughed.

"They're very shy, those little monkeys," he said. "They're Lena's little sisters, and the woman you saw a little while ago is her mother."

He was silent for a moment, as if she was bound to understand who Lena was: the very young woman, with the gold washed cheeks and the coal-black eyes, whom she had seen for only a fleeting glimpse.

"And then there are some little brothers, who go to school in Garut. Well, you see, that's my family now. When I got to know Lena, I adopted the whole family. It costs me a lot of money, because I have my first wife in Batavia, my second in Paris, and René and Ricus in Holland. It costs me enough. And now my new little family here. But now at least I have one. . . . It's a typical Indies mess, you'll say: a quasi-marriage with the daughter of a coffee overseer, with the old woman and the little brothers and sisters included in the bargain. But I'm even doing some good. The family doesn't have a nickel and I'm helping them. And Lena is a sweet child, the comfort of my old age. I can't live without a woman, and it all sort of happened by itself. . . . And it works very well. I vegetate here, drink good coffee, and they take good care of the old man. . . ."

He was silent again, and then continued.

"And you . . . you're going to Europe? Poor Eldersma! I hope he'll be better soon. It's all my fault, isn't it? I worked him too hard. But that's the way it is in the Indies. We all work too hard here, until we stop working altogether. And you're going . . . in a week? How glad you will be to see your father and mother and to hear good music. I am still grateful to you. You did a lot for us—you represented poetry in Labuwangi. This poor country. How they swear at it. It's not the fault of the country that we freebooters invaded it, barbarian conquerors, who only want to grow rich and get out. And if they don't get rich, they swear at it: at the heat, which God gave it from the beginning; at the lack of nourishment for mind and soul, the mind and soul of the freebooter! This poor country must think, 'Why didn't you stay away!' And you . . . you didn't like the Indies either."

"I tried to grasp the poetry of it. And now and then I succeeded. For the rest, it's my own fault, Resident, and not the fault of this beautiful country. Like your freebooter, I should have stayed away. All the depression, all the melancholy I suffered in this beautiful land of mystery, is my own fault. I don't swear at the Indies, Resident."

He took her hand almost with emotion, almost with a gleam of moisture in his eyes.

"I thank you for saying that. Those words are like you, the words of a sensible, cultivated woman, who doesn't rave and rant, as a silly Dutchman would who didn't find here exactly what corresponded with his petty ideal. You have suffered a lot here, I know. You were bound to. But it was not the fault of the country."

"It was my own fault, Resident," she repeated, with her soft, smiling voice.

He thought her adorable. That she did not burst out into imprecations, that she did not fly into ecstasy because she was leaving Java in a few days, gave him a sense of comfort. And when she rose to go, saying that it was getting late, he felt very sad.

"And so I shall never see you again?"

"I don't think that we shall be coming back."

"It's goodbye forever, then!"

"Perhaps we shall see you in Europe."

He made a gesture of denial.

"I am very grateful to you that you came to visit an old man. I'll ride with you to Garut."

He called out something to the house, where the women were keeping out of sight and the little sisters were giggling. He got into the carriage with her. They drove down the avenue of ferns, and suddenly they saw the sacred lake of Lellès, overshadowed by the circling swirl of the *kalongs* flapping around and around.

"Resident," she whispered, "I feel it here. . . ."

He smiled.

"They're only *kalongs*," he said.

"But in Labuwangi . . . perhaps it was only a rat."

He frowned for a moment, but then he smiled again, with the jovial smile under his thick mustache, and he looked up curiously.

"What?" he said, softly. "Really? Do you feel it here?"

"Yes."

"Well, I don't. It's something different with everybody.'

The gigantic bats shrilled their triumph with shrieks of desolation. The little carriage drove on and passed a small railroad stop. And, in what was otherwise such a lonely region, it was strange to see a whole populace, a swarm of motley Sundanese, streaming toward the little station, eagerly looking at a slow train that was approaching, belching black clouds of smoke amidst the bamboos. All their eyes were staring crazily, as though they expected salvation at first glance, as though their first impression would be a treasure for their souls.

"That's a train full of new *hadjis*," said Van Oudijck. "They're all pilgrims who have just returned from Mecca."

The train stopped, and from the long third-class carriages, solemnly, slowly, very devoutly, and conscious of their dignity, the *hadjis* alighted, in their rich white and yellow turbans, their eyes gleaming with pride, their lips pursed with conceit, in brand new shiny coats and gold and purple *samars* which fell in stately folds to just above their feet. And, humming with rapturous excitement, sometimes with a rising cry of ecstasy, the waiting multitude pressed closer and stormed the narrow doorways of the long railway coaches. . . . The *hadjis* solemnly alighted. And their brothers and friends vied with one another to grasp their hands and the hems of their gold and purple *samars* and kissed that sacred hand or that sacred garment, because it brought them something of Mecca the Holy. They fought, they crowded around the *hadjis*, to be the first to give the kiss. And the *hadjis*, conceited and assured, seemed unaware of the struggle, maintaining a peaceful dignity and a solemn stateliness amid the struggle, amid the billowing, buzzing multitude, and surrendered their hands and the hems of their garments to the fanatical kiss of all who approached.

And in this land of profound, secret, slumbering mystery, in these people of Java, which, as always, hid itself in the secrecy of its impenetrable soul, suppressed indeed but visible, it was strange to see rising to the surface an ecstasy, to see an intoxicated fanaticism, to see a part of that impenetrable soul revealed in its deification of those who had beheld the Prophet's tomb, to hear the soft humming of a religious rapture, to hear, suddenly, unexpectedly, a shout of glory, not to be suppressed, quavering on high, a cry that instantly sank again, drowned in the hum, as though fearful itself, because the sacred era had not yet arrived. . . .

And Van Oudijck and Eva, on the road behind the station, slowly driving past the busy multitude which still buzzed around the *hadjis*, respectfully carrying their luggage, obsequiously offering their little carts—Van Oudijck and Eva suddenly looked at each other, and, though neither of them cared to express it in words, they told each other, with a glance of understanding, that they felt *it*, that they felt *that*, both of them, both together this time, in the midst of this fanatical multitude. . . .

They both felt it, the unutterable, that lurks in the ground, that hisses under the volcanoes, that slowly draws near with the far-traveled winds, that rushes onward with the rain, that rattles by in the heavy, rolling thunder, that is wafted from the far horizon of the boundless sea, that flashes from the black mysterious gaze of the secretive native, that squats in his heart and cringes in his humble *hormat*, that gnaws like a poison and a hostile force at the body, soul, and life of the European, that silently attacks the conqueror and saps his energies, causing him to pine and perish, sapping his energies very slowly, so that he wastes away for years, and in the end he dies of it, perhaps by a sudden, tragic death: they both felt it, both felt the unutterable. . . .

And in feeling it, together with the sadness of their leave-taking, which was so near at hand, they failed to see amid the waving, billowing, buzzing multitude that reverently hustled the yellow and purple dignity of the *hadjis* returned from Mecca, they failed to see that one tall white *hadji* rising above the crowd and peering with a grin at the man who, no matter how he had lived his life in Java, had been weaker than That. . . .

Notes

Throughout the text and notes, the spelling of Indonesian or Javanese words, as well as place names, follows the traditional Dutch. Not only is it appropriate to the age when these texts were written, but it will also aid a student of this literature in finding other sources pertaining to this genre. All secondary literature will have this spelling, including dictionaries, atlases, and other references. For those who wish to follow the modern orthography of Bahasa Indonesia, the following changes should be noted: the old spelling tj [tjemar] is now c [cemar]; dj [djeroek] is now j [jeruk]; ch [chas] is now kh [khas]; nj [njai] is now ny [nyai]; sj [sjak] is now sy [syak]; and oe [soedah] is now u [sudah]. Only the latter change was adopted because the diphthong [oe] is not familiar to readers who do not know Dutch.

INTRODUCTION

1   Biographical information was mainly derived from the following sources: Henri van Booven, *Leven en werken van Louis Couperus* (1933; reprint ed. The Hague: Bzztôh, 1981); H. W. van Tricht, *Louis Couperus: Een verkenning* (The Hague: Bert Bakker-Daamen N.V., 1965); Albert Vogel, *Louis Couperus* (1973; 2d. rev. ed., Amsterdam: Elsevier, 1980); F. L. Bastet, *Een zuil in de mist. Van & over Louis Couperus* (Amsterdam: Querido, 1980). They are referred to throughout the text and are subsequently only identified by author and page number.

2   P. N. Furbank, *E. M. Forster: A Life* (New York: Harcourt Brace Jovanovich, 1978). Pagination is bothersome. This edition is really two volumes, printed together, but with separate pagination. The reference here is to 2:221.

3   Furbank, 2:131.

4   Any translations that are not from the present edition of *The Hidden Force* are mine. I've tried to keep some of the idiosyncracies of Couperus's style, though it is not always feasible. Couperus's infamous series of three periods—to indicate breaks in thought or conversation or simply to indicate fragments—have been kept. If possible, his peculiar syntax has been retained, although this too is often impossible in English. As to his ubiquitous neologisms, some attempt has been made to approximate them, but for the most part they have been avoided. In this particular quote, the final verb "flappered" is my attempt to translate Couperus's neologism *zwapperden*, probably a combination of *zwalpen* and *flappen*.

5   Henry Adams, *The Education of Henry Adams*, ed. Ernest Samuels (Boston: Houghton Mifflin, 1974), p. 9.

6   Mario Praz, *The Romantic Agony*, trans. Angus Davidson (1933; reprint ed., Cleveland: World Publishing Company, 1956); Jean Pierrot, *The Decadent Imagination, 1880–1900*, trans. Derek Coltman (Chicago: University of Chicago Press, 1981).

7   Richard Gilman, *Decadence: The Strange Life of an Epithet* (New York: Farrar, Straus and Giroux, 1979), pp. 160, 92.

8   All these terms and phrases are from ibid., pp. 10–12.

9   Quoted in ibid., p. 98.

10 Gilman also, rather surprisingly, subscribes to this dichotomy of the "feminine" East and the "masculine" West; see pp. 48–49.

11 Praz, pp. 200–202.
12 Vogel, p. 117.
13 Katherine Mansfield, *Novels and Novelists* (New York: Alfred A. Knopf, 1930), p. 131. Her two reviews of Couperus's work are on pp. 127–31 and pp. 213–17.
14 See Vogel, p. 63.
15 Tricht, pp. 69–70; compare 3:43–44 of Couperus's collected works.
16 Vogel, p. 58.
17 Booven, pp. 109–10.
18 Among others who mention Couperus's extraordinary speed of composition and pristine manuscripts is Kees Fens. See the introduction to his anthology of Couperus: *Zo ik iéts ben* (Boekenweek geschenk, 1974), pp. 5–6.
19 Tricht, pp. 8–9; also Bastet, pp. 77–88.
20 Praz, pp. 332–35, pp. 318–26; Pierrot, pp. 132–34.
21 For instance, in Booven's biography of Couperus, which is the earliest one, no mention is made of homosexuality.
22 See Tricht, pp. 73–84, 139–40; Vogel, p. 253; Bastet, pp. 89–126.
23 Booven, p. 142; Vogel, p. 84.
24 Praz, pp. 383, 182; on p. 411 n. 186, Praz mentions Couperus's novel.
25 Tricht, p. 86.
26 Vogel, p. 123.
27 Ibid., pp. 91, 100–101. Compare Pierrot, pp. 130–31; for instance, he notes that "sexual love is condemned, because it debases man" (p. 130).
28 Vogel, pp. 79–80, 100–101.
29 In a letter from 1903, in "Louis Couperus als briefschrijver," *Maatstaf* 11, nos. 3–4 (1963): 195. (This special issue of *Maatstaf* contained a selection of Couperus's letters, as well as essays on his work.)
30 In a letter from 1903, ibid., p. 173.
31 Ibid., p. 195.
32 Pierre H. Dubois, "Werd Couperus onderbetaald?" ibid., pp. 233–48, esp. pp. 241–42.
33 In a letter from 1900, printed in Bastet, p. 86; the same phrase is in a letter from 1901, printed in the special issue of *Maatstaf* 11, nos. 3–4 (1963): 190.
34 Dubois in "Werd Couperus onderbetaald?" pp. 240–41.
35 Tricht, p. 157; also *Maatstaf*, p. 147.
36 See the letters from 1907 and 1909 in *Maatstaf*, pp. 206–9.
37 Edmund Gosse reports that Couperus had "trouble with the English booksellers. 'They say I am improper! What do they mean by improper? We Continentals find you so difficult to understand.' " Gosse made some amusing mistakes. He wrote, for instance, that Couperus "earned his livelihood by teaching," while Couperus hated the very notion, and that *The Books of the Small Souls*, a realistic novel about The Hague society, "was placed in the world of ancient Egypt." Edmund Gosse, "Louis Couperus: A Tribute and a Memory," in Sir Edmund Gosse, *Silhouettes* (New York: Scribner's, 1925), pp. 259–67. For Katherine Mansfield, see n. 13. William Plomer's essay on Couperus's *The Hidden Force* was recently reprinted in an American edition: William Plomer, *Electric Delights*, ed. Rupert Hart-Davis (Boston: David Godine, 1978), pp. 58–65. The piece seems to be from 1945. I have not been able to trace whatever it was that Powys wrote; the assertion was made by Booven, p. 252. Examples of unacknowledged bowdlerization can be found in the English transla-

tion of *Van oude mensen de dingen die voorbijgaan*, published incorrectly in English as *Old People and the Things that Pass* in New York in 1918 and in London in 1919. This translation was reprinted without revision in 1963 as *Old People and the Things that Pass* (London: Heinemann, 1963), in the "Bibliotheca Neerlandica" series. On pp. 139–45, one will find several sentences left out, including the phrase "cerebral onanism" which perfectly characterizes Anton Dercksz. This phrase is almost an exact replica of what Huysmans wrote about the art of the French painter Moreau; see Gilman, p. 100. For a very useful listing of translations of Couperus's work, see Booven, pp. 274–89.

38 Gosse, p. 267.

39 Ibid., p. 266.

40 It is not entirely clear what precisely was the cause of death; see Bastet, pp. 183–85.

41 Quoted by Bastet, pp. 166–67.

42 Cicero's exposition is to be found especially in *Brutus* or *De Claris Oratoribus* and *De Oratore*. Arnold's phrase is from his essay, "The Literary Influence of Academies." This was reprinted in a recent edition: Matthew Arnold, *Essays in Criticism: First Series*, ed. Sister Thomas Marion Hoctor (Chicago: University of Chicago Press, 1968), p. 43; see also pp. 44, 50. Ernst Robert Curtius's definition is from his seminal 1948 study, *European Literature and the Latin Middle Ages*, trans. Willard R. Trask (1953; reprint ed., Princeton: Princeton University Press, 1973), p. 67. For Hocke, see Gustav René Hocke, *Manierismus in der Literatur: Sprach-Alchimie und esoterische Kombinationskunst* (Reinbek bei Hamburg: Rowohlt Verlag, 1959), pp. 12–13.

43 Praz, p. 20.

44 Walter de la Mare, *Pleasures and Speculations* (London: Faber and Faber, 1940), p. 100.

45 P. H. Ritter, Jr., "Over de stijl van Louis Couperus," in *Louis Couperus* (Amsterdam: de samenwerkende uitgevers, 1952), p. 69.

46 See ibid., pp. 54–55, 72–73.

47 Vogel, p. 160.

48 Henri Borel, quoted by Bastet, p. 144; Bastet describes Couperus's reading at length (pp. 127–48); see also Vogel, pp. 179–84.

49 A. Baudisch, *Het probleem van de "Stille Kracht"* (Weltevreden: G. Kolff, 1926), pp. 13, 61–70, 112.

50 Javanese mysticism is a large topic. In the selected texts given below one will find my argument corroborated. For contemporary mysticism and religion, see Niels Mulder, *Mysticism and Everyday Life in Contemporary Java* (Singapore: Singapore University Press, 1978) and his more recent article "*Abangan* Javanese Religious Thought and Practice," in *Bijdragen tot de Taal-, Land- en Volkenkunde* 139 (1983): 260–67; and Clifford Geertz, *The Religion of Java* (1960; reprint ed., Chicago: University of Chicago Press, 1976). For a survey of and the background for the bewildering variety of mystical groups, see Harun Hadiwijono, *Man in the Present Javanese Mysticism* (Baarn: Bosch and Keuning, 1967). For examples of more popular encounters with Javanese magic and mysticism by foreigners, see H. W. Ponder, *Javanese Panorama* (London: Seeley, Service and Co., 1942), pp. 100–121; and Nina Epton, *Magic and Mystics of Java* (London: Octagon Press, 1974), pp. 173–87. For a study of Malay superstitions, see W. W. Skeat, *Malay Magic: An Introduction to the Folklore and Popular Religion of the Malay Peninsula*

(1900; reprint ed., London: Frank Cass and Co., 1965). For a recent and critical assessment of Skeat, see Robert L. Winzeler, "The Study of Malay Magic," *Bijdragen tot de Taal-, Land- en Volkenkunde* 139 (1983): 435–58.

51   Mulder, p. 5; Hadiwijono, p. 236.

52   Mulder, pp. 23–25, 33–34, 17.

53   W. B. Yeats, *Essays and Introductions* (New York: Macmillan, 1961), p. 41.

54   The *datura* flower is *Datura fastuosa*, from the family *Solanaceae*, known in the Indies more commonly as *ketjubung*. It is a plant about three feet tall, with spiky fruits and large white or purple flowers. Flowers, seeds, and leaves are said to be poisonous. The white flowers are considered the most poisonous, and the purple ones (*ketjubung merah* or *itam*) less so. Kloppenburg-Versteegh thinks that they're not all that detrimental, but notes that the smoke of the dried flowers or dried seeds was used to put people to sleep. The smoke was blown through a hollow bamboo into a bedroom without ventilation, and the occupants would remain in a deep sleep. It is said that this method was particularly popular with thieves. The dried flowers were also smoked to counteract asthma, and the seeds were taken internally against worms. In a colonial report on native poisons (*Indische Vergiftrapporten*) it is noted that small black beetles which appeared at the onset of the monsoon were used to poison people. They were kept in glass jars and fed *ketjubung* leaves. The feces of the beetles were put in food or drink and were said to cause serious intestinal ailments. See *Indische Vergiftrapporten*, ed. M. Greshoff (The Hague: De Gebroeders Van Cleef, 1914), p. 52. See also: J. Kloppenburg-Versteegh, *Het Gebruik van Indische Planten* (1907; reprint ed., Katwijk aan Zee: Servire, 1978), p. 71.

    Elmu is more commonly spelled *ilmu* in Malay and *ngelmu* in Javanese. It is the general term for "knowledge" and in combination with other words can refer both to what we call science and to the occult sciences. For instance, *Ilmu panas* meant black magic once, but now also means thermodynamics. The word is derived from Arabic *ilm* or science that was based on divine revelation. Through European influence the word came to be applied to the Western notion of science, for instance: *ilmu bintang* is astronomy, *ilmu bahasa* is linguistics, *ilmu bumi* is geography. The occult meaning that Couperus had in mind is more noticeable in popular use, when *ilmu* generally refers to magic or mysticism. In modern Indonesian, *ilmu alik* and *ilmu gaib* mean mysticism, *ilmu batin*, occultism.

55   H. A. Van Hien, *De Javaansche Geestenwereld en De betrekking, die tusschen de geesten en de zinnelijke wereld bestaat*, 5 vols. (Semarang: G. C. T. Van Dorp; Bandoeng: Fortuna, 1896–1913).

56   Ibid., 1:13.

57   Ibid., 4:34–35. *Suru* is the Javanese word for *sirih*.

58   Compare Van Hien's discussion of *guna-guna*, ibid., 4:37–39.

59   For instance, Rob Nieuwenhuys, "De onbegrepen stille kracht," *Haagse Post,* 14 September 1974, pp. 46–49.

60   Van Hien, 1:15.

61   In a letter from 1900 Couperus stated that "de derrière van Léonie heeft in Holland veel bekijks en hoofdschuddens veroorzaakt" ("Léonie's behind has caused much attraction and head-shaking in Holland"); Bastet, p. 86. The sentence describing the *sirih* spittle dripping from her buttocks was left out of the original translation.

62   The word "Creole" did not necessarily refer to people of mixed blood who were born in the Caribbean. In Couperus's time it simply indicated people who were not born in Europe, though of European parents.

63 C. G. Jung, *Four Archetypes* (Princeton: Princeton University Press, 1970), p. 38.

64 Walter Kaufmann, "Hegel's Ideas about Tragedy," in *New Studies in Hegel's Philosophy*, ed. Warren E. Steinkraus (New York: Holt, Rinehart, Winston, 1971), p. 202.

65 Furbank, 1:96.

66 G. W. F. Hegel, *The Philosophy of History*, trans. J. Sibree (New York: Dover, 1956), pp. 272, 273.

67 Ibid., pp. 139–42. See also J. J. Bachofen, *Myth, Religion, and Mother Right*, trans. Ralph Manheim (Princeton: Princeton University Press, 1973), pp. 216–37. One will find an interpretation of the Orient similar to Bachofen's in Blake's prophetic poetry, such as "The Book of Ahania" or "The Song of Los." An interpretation of the opposition between Asia and Europe, similar to what I am proposing, can also be found in Jung's essays on oriental thought (C. G. Jung, *Psychology and the East* [Princeton: Princeton University Press, 1978], pp. 40–51, 188).

68 Carl Kerényi, *The Gods of the Greeks* (1951; reprint ed., Harmondsworth: Penguin Books, 1958), p. 221.

69 Charles Baudelaire, *Oeuvres Complètes*, Bibliothèque de la Pléiade (Paris: Gallimard, 1961), p. 285. My translation.

70 A *srimpi* or *serimpi* was a female choric dancer at a royal Javanese court, usually the courts at Solo (now Surakarta) or Djokja (now Jogya) in central Java. These dancers should not be confused with ordinary dancing girls such as *ronggèngs*. Serimpi dancers only participated in formalized dancing for the monarch and his guests. Most often they were recruited from the royal household itself and were carefully trained over a long period before they were permitted to perform. They danced to a prescribed music performed by a *gamelan* orchestra that had a specific number of instruments. The *serimpis* can only be compared to the *bedaya*, who also did choric dances—in groups of nine—at a great royal court that could afford the considerable expense of such performances. See Thomas Stamford Raffles, *The History of Java*, 2 vols. (1817; reprint ed., Kuala Lumpur: Oxford University Press, 1978), 1:340–44; J. Kunst, *Music in Java: Its History, Its Theory and Its Technique*, 2 vols. (The Hague: Martinus Nijhoff, 1973), 1:279–80; Nusjirwan Tirtaamidjaja, "A Bedaja Ketawang Dance Performance at the Court of Surakarta," *Indonesia* 3 (April 1967): 31–61; H. J. da Silva "Notes on the Royal Classical Javanese Dance-Group of the Sultanate of Jogjakarta," Program for a performance in The Hague, 1971. The last has a great deal of valuable information although, despite its English title, the text is in Dutch and Javanese.

71 J. Th. Koks, *De Indo* (Amsterdam: H.J. Paris, 1931), pp. 249–67. The life of the "Indo" was also described in a novel by Victor Ido, *De Paupers* (1912; reprint ed., The Hague: Thomas and Eras, 1978). "Victor Ido" was the pseudonym of Hans van de Wall (1869–1948) who was a Eurasian.

THE HIDDEN FORCE

Besides the texts mentioned in the notes to the Introduction, the following are used several times in this section: R. J. Wilkinson, *A Malay-English Dictionary*, 2 vols. (1901; reprint ed., London: Macmillan, 1959), hereafter referred to as "Wilkinson"; *Encyclopaedie van Nederlandsch-Indië*, 2d ed., in 4 vols, and 3 supplements (The Hague: Martinus Nijhoff, 1917–1932), hereafter referred to as *Encyclopedia of the Dutch East Indies*; Rob Nieuwenhuys, *Baren en oudgasten, tempo doeloe—een verzonken wereld: Fotografische documenten uit het oude Indië 1870–1920* (Amsterdam: Querido, 1981), hereafter referred to as *Baren en oudgasten.*

1   Lange Laan ("Long Avenue") was in reality the "Herenstraat" in Pasuruan. There is a photograph of this beautiful street in *Baren en oudgasten,* p. 160. Nieuwenhuys presents a number of fascinating pictures pertaining to *The Hidden Force* on pp. 146–66. A picture of the residency, the official lodging of the resident, or *residèn* in Malay, can be found on p. 154.

2   *Waringin* refers properly to the large fig tree, *Ficus benjamina.* It is a majestic tree, growing to a height of between forty-five and ninety feet, with a very thick trunk and a huge canopy. It is ubiquitous in Indonesia, and is considered a holy tree. This fig tree is sometimes confused with the *Ficus kurzii,* but can be easily distinguished because the *Ficus kurzii* has air roots.

3   Caladium, or *Caladium bicolor* of the *Araceae,* is a plant cultivated primarily for its showy pink leaves edged with green. It propagates from its rhizome, its leaves are shaped like arrowheads, and it requires rich soil and constant care.

4   Latania probably refers to *Latania commersonii,* also called "palm angur," which translates as the "grape palm." This tree has large, grayish, fan-shaped leaves that have deep "cuts" along the edges.

5   *Tali-api; tali* refers to anything that is a rope, string, or cord, and *api* means "fire," hence a "fire-rope." In Dutch it was called a *vuurtouw* and in English it was once called a "slow match." This was a slow-burning fuse, most often a rope soaked in a solution of saltpeter, used for lighting cigars.

6   A *sado* was a small horse-drawn carriage, with two wheels and a canopy over the space where the passengers sat. From the French *dos-à-dos.*

7   The Concordia Club was in reality the "Harmonie Club" in Pasuruan. There is a picture of it in *Baren en oudgasten,* p. 161. Such clubs were called "societies," in Dutch, *sociëteiten,* usually abbreviated to *soos.* The social life of the European community was centered on the *soos.*

8   Maduran seamen come from the island Madura that lies to the north of eastern Java, opposite the town of Pasuruan. The two islands are separated by the Straits of Madura. It is a rather sparse land of limestone hills and modest rainfall. The rain washes away whatever top soil there is, leaving a chalky soil. Madura was famous for its cattle, salt industry, and fishing fleet. The Maduran population was known for intrepid seamanship.

9   Lighthouses, so important in an island realm, were described in *Het Indische Boek der Zee,* ed. D. A. Rinkes (Weltevreden: Drukkerij Volkslectuur, 1925), pp. 189–99. Couperus may have modeled Labuwangi's lighthouse after the one in Tegal, the town on the northern coast of central Java where Couperus stayed with his brother-in-law. A photograph of this particular one in *Het Indische Boek der Zee* (p. 199), shows that it was an open structure built of steel, not very tall, and situated at the end of a long pier.

10 *Grongrong* is a Javanese word. Together with the word for wind, *angin,* it refers to a strong southern wind that blows during the east monsoon. More commonly spelled *gronggong* or *geronggang,* the word can also mean a cavity, cave, hollow, or mineshaft.

11 The *duiten* question refers to fiscal reform in the Indies during the nineteenth century. Its main objective was the standardization of methods of payment and conversion to the gold standard. There was a bewildering variety of money in existence at the time. Toward the end of the century there were, for instance, eight different

"dollars," and a plethora of other coins with values that fluctuated constantly. The *duit* was the lowest denomination. In the eighteenth century a special *duit*, minted specifically for use in the Indies, was introduced. These *duiten* (plural of *duit*) remained in circulation well into the twentieth century, although by that time they were illegal tender. In 1727, four *duiten* equaled one *stuiver*, a five-cent piece like our nickel. In 1855, legislation was passed that took *duiten* out of circulation. There was considerable opposition in that it was believed that the native population needed the *duit* because they only dealt with very small amounts of money. By the end of the nineteenth century there were six *duiten* to one *stuiver*, truly a miniscule sum. It took until 1900 (when Couperus was writing *The Hidden Force*) to enforce the removal of the *duit*. Once this goal was actively pursued (after a law was enacted in July 1899), it turned out that by March 1900 the *duit* had disappeared from circulation in Java and Madura, though it was still used in various outlying districts in Celebes and Sumatra. The change proved to be quite easy for the native population and produced few problems. Each colonial administrator was responsible for implementing the law in his district, hence Van Oudijck's interest in the problem. The complicated history of coinage and fiscal reform is clearly presented in a long article in the second volume of the *Encyclopedia of the Dutch East Indies* under the heading "muntwezen."

12   That crocodiles were believed to house the spirits of human beings was a fairly common belief all over the archipelago. One will find it in Java, Sumatra, Banka (an island where tin is found off the east coast of Sumatra), Celebes, Buru (see the novel by Beb Vuyk, *The Last House in the World*, published in this series), Borneo, and the Aru Islands. The second volume of the *Encyclopedia of the Dutch East Indies*, under the heading "krokodillen," specifically mentions that the Javanese population around Pasuruan believed they were invulnerable to attack as long as they sacrificed fruits, chickens, and other food to the reptiles. W. W. Skeat in his study of *Malay Magic*, notes that for the peninsular Malay, the crocodile could become a holy (*kramat*) animal and was then forbidden to be harmed by anyone. He relates the story of how a woman's child, who had been turned into a crocodile, instructed its mother to appease ferocious crocodiles by placing offerings of eggs, bananas, and rice on the bank of a river. See Skeat, *Malay Magic: An Introduction to the Folklore and Popular Religion of the Malay Peninsula* (1900; reprint ed., London: Frank Cass and Co., 1965), pp. 282–302.

13   *Deng-deng* (more commonly spelled *dendeng*) is something like our beef jerky, except that it is spiced. The meat is cut into thin slices, cured with salt, spiced, and dried in the sun. When used for a meal it is fried in coconut oil.

14   The house described here would appear to be an amalgamation of the two depicted in *Baren en oudgasten*, pp. 154–59.

15   The somewhat unusual syntax of Doddy's speech is an attempt to convey the peculiar Indies way of speaking.

16   Ricus, a fairly uncommon name in Dutch, was the name of Couperus's father. To give it to one of Van Oudijck's obnoxious sons would support Tricht's contention that *The Hidden Force* was the first major novel wherein the author tried to liberate himself from his father's influence.

17   The *sarong* was the "skirt" in Indonesia. It was a rectangular piece of cloth, usually of batik, about three and a half feet long and about seven feet wide. About one third of it had a pattern different from the remainder and was called the *kepala* or "head," while the rest was known as *badan* or "body." A narrow, decorated edge ran along the top, with a wider one along the bottom. The sarong was wrapped around the

body like a skirt and the *kepala* could be in the front, at the sides, or in the back. A similar piece of batiked cloth was called a *kain* or *kain pandjang* ("long cloth"). It also was about three and a half feet long, more than eight feet wide, but was decorated with a uniform design. It was also wrapped around the waist but had five pleats in front (*wiron*) which opened and closed while walking.

A *kabaai* (or *kabaja*) was a kind of blouse or jacket usually of white cotton that came halfway down the hips. It had long sleeves and was edged with lace. It was closed in front with three detachable pins, often connected with a little chain. These *kabaai* pins used to be made of silver.

A woman wore a *kutang* under the *kabaai*, a bodice of cotton that came down to the hips. It was close fitting and served both as a corset and brassiere. Both the *sarong* and the *kain* were worn over the *kutang*, covering it up to the waist, and were attached with an *udit*, a narrow, colorful strip of cotton. One usually wore slippers with this costume.

The customary colors of the *sarong* or *kain* were beige, blue, brown, and black. The traditional, abstract designs were prescribed by the monarchs of the realms of Solo (Surakarta) and Djokja. They decided which patterns were for the common people and which were appropriate for the aristocracy (*bangsawang*). The latter were called *larangan* and no one else was allowed to wear them on pain of corporal punishment. One such pattern was made up of stylized *parangs* or swords, either as *parang rusak* ("broken swords") or *parang menang* ("victorious swords").

Around the turn of the century Eurasians began to manufacture *sarongs* and *kains* that combined the traditional Javanese colors and patterns with colors and designs preferred by Europeans. The result could be very beautiful. For some fine examples of the latter see M. J. De Raadt-Apell, *De batikkerij Van Zuylen te Pekalongan* (Zutphen: Terra, 1980). Couperus's reference to a "Solo *sarong*" implies that it was the severe and traditional one in dark colors and decorated with the prescribed designs.

18   I have not been able to identify a gem called *léontine*, but it is clear from the context that it is a kind of diamond.

19   The Council of the Indies was established by the East India Company to operate as a counterforce to the authority of the governor-general. The number of members varied, but the Council had considerable power. When the Indies became a colonial empire, the authority of the Council was greatly diminished until it finally became nothing more than an advisory college without real power. By Couperus's time the Council was usually comprised of five members who met weekly with or without the governor-general. In practical terms, the governor-general remained the highest official with the greatest power and authority and paid little attention to recommendations made by this collegiate Council.

20   Van Oudijck's living beyond his means was not uncommon in the colonial Indies. As long as the colonial administrator lived in the tropics he enjoyed an ample existence with large houses, large yards, and any number of servants. When he retired to Holland and had no other private income, his pension was not sufficient to maintain such an existence. It is clear that Couperus's family felt this discrepancy keenly. See Tricht, *Louis Couperus*, p. 18.

21   Catulle Mendès (1841–1909) was a French novelist, poet, and playwright. He wrote in a dreadful purple prose, particularly in his novels, which had sensational plots, and were redolent with situations and perversions we would now call "soft porn." The novel *Zo'har* (1886) describes an incestuous relationship between a brother and

a sister. In *La première maîtresse* (*The First Mistress*, 1887) "a man is raped by a dia-
bolical woman who makes him the slave of her ghastly vampire degeneracy which
makes havoc with men." Mendès's novels were described by Praz as "all hallucination, hysteria, so deliberately, rhetorically frenzied . . . that [they become] a veritable
parody." See Praz, *Romantic Agony*, pp. 330–32. The significance of Mendès in
the present context is that he was a terrible writer of novels full of debauchery and
illicit passions that were, at best, artificial and mechanical. One may also note that
Mendès was part of the French literature of "decadence" (see Introduction).

22   The *tokkè* is a lizard of the family *Geckonidae*, generally known in English as
geckoes. The *tokkè* is the *Platydactylus guttatus* and is, in Indonesia, the largest of
the geckoes. Its skin is yellow with brown spots and, like the other common lizard in
the Indies, the *tjitjak* (*Hemidactylus fraenatus*), it makes a chirping sound. Both
lizards are ubiquitous in the tropics, live inside houses, generally near the ceiling, and
can climb and sprint across walls, ceilings, and other vertical surfaces like flies. They
feed on insects, mostly mosquitoes and flies. The presence of the *tokkè* in this novel is
not only perfectly normal, because every house in the Indies was inhabited by them,
but is also symbolically appropriate. Almost everywhere in the archipelago, these
lizards were considered oracular animals that could divine evil omens such as death,
disaster, or illness. The *tokkè* in particular was said to know what was hidden in the
future. As was mentioned in the Introduction, the peculiar combat in the garden
between the lizard and the cat foreshadows Van Oudijck's fate. See G. A. Wilken, *De
Hagedis in het Volksgeloof der Malayo-Polynesiërs* (The Hague: Martinus Nijhoff,
1891), esp. pp. 25–27, 29.

23   The cry of the Chinese vendor refers to roasted peanuts or *katjang-goreng*, where he
substitutes an "l" for an "r". *Tjina mampus* means the "Chinaman is dead."

24   Buitenzorg (now called Bogor) was the residence of the governor-general. It is a town
situated in the mountains, some eight hundred feet above sea level. It gets a great deal
of rain, but it is famous for its climate and beautiful scenery. In colonial times, the
botanical garden was renowned all over the world. "Buitenzorg" is the Dutch equivalent of the French phrase "sans-souci," i.e., "without care."

25   Batavia was the capital of the colonial Indies (now called Jakarta, it is the national
capital of Indonesia). Semarang was one of the three great ports of Java (the others
were Batavia and Surabaja) on the northern coast, almost exactly at the midpoint of
Java. Surabaja was the largest harbor in Java, also on the northern coast, but further
east of Semarang. It faces the island Madura across the Straits of Madura.
     The Principalities, the translation of *Vorstenlanden*, are two former colonial prov-
inces in central Java: Surakarta is inland; south of it, the province of Djokjakarta
faces the Indian Ocean. The volcano Mt. Merapi separates the two. Together, the
Principalities were once part of the kingdom of Mataram in central Java, and even in
colonial times they were ruled independently: Surakarta by its susuhunan (abbreviated as sunan), and Djokjakarta by its sultan. The two principalities always represented the heart and soul of Javanese culture. In 1825 they revolted against Dutch
rule under the leadership of Diponegoro. The Dutch government had to fight a large-
scale war because the revolt spread far beyond these two regions. Only in 1830 did
the Dutch succeed in restoring their authority, forcing both Djokjakarta and Surakarta to become Dutch protectorates.
     Djokjakarta means "blooming night." Surakarta is often referred to as Solo, and
its ancient name was Kartasura, which means a "city built by heroes."

26   The sugar crisis refers to the drastic reduction in the price of sugar on the world mar-

ket during the last years of the nineteenth century. Sugar cane had been raised in Java before the Europeans arrived. At first the Dutch East India Company paid little attention to this crop, but when it saw that profits were to be made, it began to build its own sugar mills in the eighteenth century. This is described in Arthur van Schendel's *John Company*, published in this series. During the last decade of the nineteenth century, European nations developed sugar-beet production, which provided them with large enough amounts of domestic sugar so that they did not have to buy the commodity abroad. That economic fact, coupled with a blight (*sereh*), drastically reduced profits in the Indies. The result of this double catastrophe was a greater scientific effort to produce the best possible cane in optimum growing conditions, and to consolidate the various commercial enterprises. When the protective measures for European beet sugar were lifted, Java was ahead of its competitors due to the forced improvements, and from 1903 to 1916 sugar was once again a profitable crop.

27   *Pangéran* was once an exalted title in the Principalities reserved for the sons of the sultan of Djokjakarta and the susuhunan of Surakarta. When the eldest legitimate son of the ruler reached maturity and had been designated by the government to be his father's successor, he received the title *pangéran adipati*.

Other aristocratic titles are frequently used in this novel. *Radèn* was a word used in Java and Madura. *Adipati*, a word derived from Sanskrit and meaning "paramount administrator," was a title conferred by the colonial government on native regents. *Radèn-aju* was the title of the wife of the *radèn*. One of the visible prerogatives of this high and noble rank was the *pajong* (or *songsong*), a parasol with different colors and circles to indicate rank (see below, note 31).

In a directive from 1820, the colonial government stipulated that the native regent was in the position of a "younger brother," while the Dutch resident was his "older brother." The regent ruled his native subjects but he did not levy taxes nor did he have legislative powers. The European resident would normally defer to his fellow ruler, but he always had the right to recommend the regent's dismissal to the governor-general and propose an alternative ruler.

That Sunario's family had connections with the island Madura is tenable. Before the arrival of the Dutch, Madura was ruled by the kingdom of Mataram (see n. 25). When the Dutch East India Company established itself, the Maduran regents were favorable to the Dutch and, because of this, received titles higher than those of their former Javanese overlords. One such title was *pangéran*, while they were also allowed to add the name *Tjakra Adining Rat*, a name their forebears once had. This must be the origin of the name Couperus gave to the regent, Sunario: i.e., Adiningrat. It was Daendels who favored the Maduran noblemen over their Javanese counterparts and granted them the right to the title of sultan. This was affirmed by Raffles during his interim administration, as well as by Van der Capellen, after restoration of Dutch authority in 1820. The title of sultan lapsed in 1847. The Dutch gradually removed more and more authority from the Maduran rulers until by the time of Couperus's novel the island was under the direct rule of the Dutch colonial administration.

The word *adiningrat* also exists in the Javanese court language spoken at the courts of Djokjakarta and Surakarta, and means "the most splendid [one] on earth." The term was added to the names of the two courts in official proclamations, indicating they were royal seats.

28   *Wajang* (*wayang*) refers to the Indonesian shadow plays which are based on episodes from the *Ramayana* and the *Mahabharata*. The principal characters of the *wajang*

kulit are flat puppets cut from leather. The *dalang*, the performer, sits behind a cloth screen. Between him and the screen hangs a lamp at about the level of his head. When the *dalang* moves the puppets by means of sticks, the lamp's illumination casts the shadows of the puppets on the transparent cloth to be seen by the audience on the other side. Couperus here refers to a *wajang kulit* puppet because they were particularly exquisite, as if made from leather filigree. The history, the variations, the large cast of characters, and the significance of *wajang* are complicated. For further reading, one may find the following texts useful: Amin Sweeney, *Malay Shadow Puppets* (London: The British Museum, 1972); James R. Brandon, *On Thrones of Gold: Three Javanese Shadow Plays* (Cambridge: Harvard University Press, 1970); Benedict R. O'G. Anderson, *Mythology and the Tolerance of the Javanese*, Monograph Series of the Modern Indonesia Project, Department of Asian Studies at Cornell University (Ithaca, 1965). Fine illustrations can be found in Clara B. Pink-Wilpert, *Das indonesische Schattentheater* (Baden-Baden: Holle Verlag, 1976).

The other major form of *wajang* is the *wajang golek*, which has three-dimensional puppets carved from wood. The best description of this can be found in Peter Buurman, *Wayang Golek* (Alphen aan de Rijn: Sijthoff, 1980).

29 The Witte Club and the Besogne Club were gathering places and watering holes for colonial officials who had retired to The Hague. One will find a description of an Indies family in the four volumes of Couperus's *The Books of the Small Souls*.

30 A *gamelan* is a Javanese orchestra. The *gamelan* emphasizes percussion instruments (such as various kinds of drums and gongs) and makes far less use of wind, string, and brass instruments than Western music does, though it does have a flute (*suling*), a violin (*rebab*), and an oboelike instrument called *selompret*. A discussion of the different instruments, of the music itself, as well as of the kind of music prescribed for special occasions, can be found in Kunst, *Music in Java*. There is also an excellent article on Indonesian music in the second volume of the *Encyclopedia of the Dutch East Indies*, under the heading "muziek en muziekinstrumenten."

A very interesting attempt to wed the *gamelan* to occidental music was made by Colin McPhee (1901–1964), a Canadian who lived most of his adult life in the United States. In the early thirties, McPhee went to Bali to explore *gamelan* music, and stayed until war broke out in 1939. The resulting composition is called "Tabuh-Tabuhan," and is identified as a toccata for orchestra. It was written in 1936 and first performed in Mexico City in the same year. McPhee wrote a book about his sojourn in Bali entitled *A House in Bali* (New York: John Day Company, 1944).

31 The *pajong* was a paper parasol that was carried by a servant behind an august person such as Surakarta's susuhunan, for instance. The parasol was painted different colors to indicate various ranks: gold for the susuhunan and the resident; for the royal consorts and princesses, yellow; white for the other members of the susuhunan's family; blue for the regent and his equals, and so on. In *Baren en oudgasten*, one will find a photograph of a Dutch resident with a servant next to him holding the golden *pajong* of his rank (p. 73). This custom was abolished by the colonial government in 1904.

32 The Chinese represented a large percentage of the foreign population in Java. At the time of this novel, most of them came from southern China and from the poorest classes. They were called *sinkehs* in Java, and worked as coolies in tin mines, as vendors, small merchants, and as commercial middlemen between the European and Javanese worlds. A great number started out as pedlars and were called *klontongs* after the rattle they used to attract attention. Most Chinese were hard workers and

very thrifty, and the result was that they often amassed a substantial sum of money and ventured into larger businesses, such as sugar factories. They chose to remain separate from both native and European societies and maintained an exclusively Chinese mode of existence, with their own religion and temples. They adhered to ancestor worship, veneration of the dead, and devotion to the family. They rarely intermarried with the Indonesians. The Chinese were also known for their passions for gambling and opium. There was always friction between the Indonesians and the Chinese because of the latter's relentless industry and acquisition of wealth. This animosity for political, economic, and social reasons has persisted to this day. For a firsthand account of the life of a poor Chinese in Malay society, see N. I. Low, *Chinese Jetsam on a Tropic Shore* (Singapore: Eastern Universities Press, 1974). For a description of Chinese graveyards in Java, see W. Walraven, *Eendagsvliegen* (Amsterdam: Oorschot, 1971), pp. 187–88.

33   The use of opium in the colonial Indies has a complicated history. A good survey can be found in the third volume of the *Encyclopedia of the Dutch East Indies*, pp. 155–67, but some general remarks may indicate the peculiar role of the colonial government in what was essentially an illicit enterprise.

Opium was known as *apiun* in Javanese and Malay, after the Arabic *afiun* and the Chinese *apian*. Opium that was ready to be smoked (referred to in Dutch with the peculiar verb *schuiven*, which means literally "to push" or "to shove," presumably derived from the sound of sucking on the opium pipe) was known in Java as *tjandu*.

Chinese coolies who smoked almost daily were able to perform heavy physical labor without noticeable adverse reactions. There was, of course, abuse of the drug and a substantial percentage of crime in Java was due to drug users trying to obtain money to support their habit. But it seems that moderate use was the norm. Although it was sometimes chewed or drunk with tea or coffee, the most common way of ingesting opium was by smoking it (in Javanese *ngudud*) in a foot-long pipe (*beduddan* in Javanese).

The greatest users were the Chinese, who sold it to their own people as well as to the Javanese. As early as the beginning of the seventeenth century, the Dutch realized there was money to be made from the opium traffic, and tried to control the import and distribution by selling exclusive rights to licensed dealers. This was far from successful. In 1833 they tried again, but smuggling persisted. In 1893 the colonial government decided to control the entire process of buying, shipping, preparing, and selling opium, a policy known as the "opium regie." For about half a century it was in the peculiar position of trafficking in narcotics and at the same time trying to control their use. The policy was first tried successfully in the island of Madura, and was introduced in Pasuruan in 1896. By 1904 it encompassed the entire archipelago.

34   Pan-Islam refers to the Muhammadans' desire to divorce themselves from Western rule and establish a global realm of Islam. The ideal was Islam's golden age in the seventh and eighth centuries when it was ruled by a single authority. In the sixteenth century this ideal was said to have been achieved once again by the Turkish sultans, though by the first two decades of the present century that supremacy was vehemently denied by orthodox groups. This dream of an omnipotent, non-Western hegemony also found its way to the Indies, though at the time Couperus was writing it was not yet politically powerful.

Couperus disliked Islam (see, for instance, 12: 437–39). Others shared his sentiment. One reason was the intransigent character of Islam, and another, its moral tyranny. Couperus preferred the Hindu element in the Indies, while E. M. Forster, for instance, was baffled by the extravagance of Hinduism and preferred the austerity of Islam. See E. M. Forster, *Abinger Harvest* (1936; reprint ed., New York: Harcourt, Brace and World, 1964), pp. 272–75.

35 The title *controleur-kota* was primarily used in Java where it referred to a Dutch official who was stationed in the capital of a district or province, though his jurisdiction usually extended beyond the town itself. *Kota* means city or town. A *controleur* or controller (though not in a fiscal sense) was in rank below the resident and assistant resident. His duty consisted of overseeing native government, of being aware of what the native population desired or objected to, and of informing his superiors of this knowledge. The controller, at least in Java, did not have judicial, legislative, or police powers, and one could say that his position was purely an advisory one.

36 *The Studio* was a famous art magazine that promoted art nouveau around the turn of the century. It championed abundance in designs, intricacies of arabesques, and stylized vegetation. Among its favorite artists was the Dutchman Toorop. See *Art Nouveau: An Anthology of Design and Illustration from "The Studio"* (New York: Dover, 1969).

37 The "royal W" refers to Queen Wilhelmina, the last Dutch monarch to nominally rule the Indies as well as Holland. Queen Wilhelmina (1880–1962) was crowned in 1898 and ruled for half a century, until 1948.

38 Solo (Surakarta) and Djokjakarta were the last two native states to be subjected by the Dutch. They once dominated a large part of Java. Ruled by its *susuhunan*, or "emperor," Solo represented what was classically and quintessentially Javanese in terms of dress, ceremony, poetry and legend, and courtly manners. Solo was also symbolic of the Dutch colonial presence. The susuhunan's palace, the *kraton*, was a completely self-sufficient, walled city. Javanese courtly life continued to exist there the way it had for centuries. But facing the kraton was the official Dutch residency where the real power resided. The susuhunan could not leave his palace without informing the Dutch resident and then only after he had obtained official permission.

39 The *kondé* is the traditional hair style for Indonesian women. It is a bun worn in the nape of the neck, fastened with pins of gold or silver, and is made by twisting strands of hair around the mass of hair that has been pushed up from every side of the head.

The *kenanga* flower is the bloom of the *Canangium odoratum*. A very tall tree, the *kenanga* grows all over the archipelago and is particularly cherished for its fragrant flowers, which are used in sachets, to adorn women's hair, and as offerings.

The *kain pandjang* is the longer sarong embellished with a single design. I assume that the "long trail" in front is the *wiron*—five long pleats in front. See note 17.

Sonket slippers (also spelled *sungkit*) were slippers embroidered with gold or silver thread. The technique is called drawn thread work, whereby short lengths of the original fabric are snipped off and replaced by gold and silver thread. "The aim of this process was to avoid the rough surface of raised embroidery" (Wilkinson, 2: 1137).

40 *Rijsttafel* is Dutch for a dinner with rice (*rijst*) as the main ingredient, which is augmented with a great variety of dishes. Properly speaking, all Indonesian dinners are *rijsttafels*, i.e., rice with some spices and a few side dishes of fish or meat, but for wealthy Indonesians and the colonial Dutch those side dishes could be innumerable, with a bewildering variety of ingredients and combinations.

Some of those traditional side dishes are mentioned on p. 101. *Sambal* is a condiment made with hot Spanish peppers (*lombok*) as a base, and with a great variety of other ingredients to make different combinations. The general term "vegetables" probably indicates the various *sajurs* (*sajurans*) or vegetable sauces. One mentioned is the *sajur lodèh*, a dish made from the young fruits of the custard-apple or soursop tree (*Annona muricata*). But the word *lodèh* refers to any number of fruits used for making *sajurs*, for instance, the young fruits of the silk cotton tree (*Ceiba pentandra*), the flower spikes of the pineapple, a kind of gourd (*Lagenaria leucantha*), and so on. Chicken, also mentioned, or *ajem*, is prepared in all sorts of ways, with any number of spices.

 Rudjak is a fruit salad with a hot sauce. One variation, *rudjak petis*, has a base made of a shrimp paste (*trassi*), *sambal ulek* (i.e., hot peppers), the Javanese version of brown sugar (*gula djawa*), tamarind fruit, pears, apples, pineapple, oranges, *manga*, and cucumber.

41 William III College was what in Dutch is called a "gymnasium," a course of secondary education. It was founded in 1860 and was located in Weltevreden, a suburb of Batavia. Its curriculum was reorganized in 1867. Split into two sections, the first became a regular HBS school modeled after its Dutch counterpart in Holland—i.e., it prepared students for the universities and other advanced education—while the other section became a preparatory school for colonial administrators. I am assuming that Couperus is referring to the latter when he speaks of "de Indische Afdeling" ("Colonial Department"), which lasted until 1913. The students' blue caps with a gold star were once a familiar object among the upper classes of Batavia.

42 Réunion was an island and French colony in the Indian Ocean between Madagascar and Mauritius. It was discovered at the beginning of the sixteenth century, taken possession of by a Frenchman in 1638, and annexed by France in 1643. It was settled by French colonists during the second half of the seventeenth century. It has, strictly speaking, no indigenous population, but a large Creole populace, descended from Europeans and Malagasy women. Réunion grew sugar cane and coffee, and cultivated the clove tree. These clove trees were imported from the Dutch East Indies by the appropriately named importer Poivre, at the risk of his life.

43 The word *sirih* refers both to the plant and to the common habit of chewing it. The plant is the *Piper betle* of the family *Piperaceae*. The tips of one or two of its leaves are torn off after they have been wiped. The wiping was done originally to prevent the user from being poisoned by a substance that could have been smeared on the leaves. These leaves are fragrant, taste bitter, and produce a red juice. A little lime is sprinkled on them, a chalky substance once derived from calcined shells. To this is added a sliver of *gambir*. This substance is manufactured from the *Uncaria gambir* plant. Its leaves are stripped and boiled down to a viscous mass, which is left to cool and harden. The better quality *gambir* is yellow or brownish yellow, the lesser ones are darker. The superior *gambir* is divided into small cubes and sold that way. The next ingredient of the *sirih* chaw is a small piece of the *pinang* nut, the fruit of the *Areca catechu* palm tree. It is also called the betel palm, which is erroneous because, properly speaking, "betel" only refers to the *sirih* plant. The lime-covered *sirih* leaves are folded around the slivers of *gambir* and *pinang* to form a little package that is put in the mouth and chewed. Sometimes a small amount of tobacco is added.

 Sirih is chewed everywhere in the archipelago by both men and women. As Raffles put it, "these stimulants are considered nearly as essential to their comfort as salt is among Europeans." The ingredients were often carried around in a special box called in Malay *tampat sirih*, in Javanese *pakinangan*. Besides the *sirih* leaves, it contained a set of small containers. When they had covers they were called *tjepuks* and contained the *gambir* and the tobacco. Those without covers were for the *pinang* nut and for the lime. If they belonged to the upper classes, these *pakinangans* were made of gold or silver and were prized possessions. Offering *sirih* to a guest was, according to Marsden, "a token of hospitality and an act of politeness. To omit it on the one hand, or reject it on the other, would be an affront."

The red saliva that results from chewing *sirih* was used in popular medicine. Prayers or charms were intoned and the red liquid was spat onto afflicted parts of the patient. The liquid obtained from boiling down the leaves was used to clean skin diseases, and finely ground *sirih* fruits were used against gum disease. Habitual chewing of *sirih* blackens the teeth and stains the mouth a bright red, but it leaves one's breath clean and fresh.

See William Marsden, *The History of Sumatra* (1783; reprint ed., Kuala Lumpur: Oxford University Press, 1966), pp. 281–83; Thomas Stamford Raffles *The History of Java*, 2 vols. (1817; reprint ed., Kuala Lumpur: Oxford University Press, 1978), 1:101; the articles "sirih" and "pinang" in the third volume of *The Encyclopedia of the Dutch East Indies*; and J. Kreemer, "Volksheelkunde in den Indischen Archipel," in *Bijdragen tot de Taal-Land-en Volkenkunde van Nederlandsch Indië* (The Hague: Martinus Nijhoff, 1914).

Sirih chewing is identical to the use of *pan* in India, where there are the same ingredients, the same implements, and the same reasons. E. M. Forster wrote a superb essay on *pan*. He notes that the British considered the use of *pan* a filthy habit, but Forster understood its real importance. "Strictly speaking, Pan is a pill, which the host administers to the guest at the conclusion of an interview; it is an internal sweetener, and thus often offered with the external attar of roses. Actually, it is a nucleus for hospitality, and much furtive intercourse takes place under its little shield" (Forster, *Abinger Harvest*, p. 320; the entire essay is on pp. 318–24).

44   *Kabupatèn* is the house of a Javanese regent.

45   Teapoy, to translate the Dutch word *knaap*, is primarily colonial usage for a small table with three legs. In British India a teapoy also referred to a tripod table. The word has nothing to do with tea, but is derived from the Hindu word for the numeral three, *tin*, and Persian *pae*, foot.

46   The war between China and Europe Couperus mentions is most likely a reference to the Boxer Uprising in China which brought European nations in armed conflict with the Chinese government. It took place in 1900–1901.

47   *Latta* (also spelled *latah, lata*) is a peculiar affliction, referred to by Wilkinson as "paroxysmal neurosis." The attacks are caused when the sufferer is startled, and this can happen from even the most trivial incident. The person will then do whatever is suggested, imitate the gestures and speech of whoever is talking, and will obey any order given, no matter how foolish it may be. Perhaps what is most unsettling is that the person suffering from *latta* is fully aware of his or her behavior. *Latta* sufferers are mostly native women. See E. H. Hermans, *Gezondsheidleer voor Nederlandsch Indië* (Amsterdam: Meulenhoff, 1925), pp. 120–21. For a more recent survey see Robert Winseler, "The Study of Malayan Latah," *Indonesia*, no. 37 (April 1984), pp. 77–104.

48   *Rambutan (Nephelium lappaceum L.)* is a common fruit in Indonesia. The tree grows very tall and can be found all over the archipelago because it does not require good soil. The fruits have a knobby red skin, and the best way to eat them is to remove the white meat from the pits. The taste is either sweet or sour-sweet. *Mangistan*

(*Garcinia mangostana L.*) is equally common and as popular as the *rambutan*. This tree is harder to grow and does not produce fruit during its first ten years. The skin of this fruit is also red, and its juicy meat is also white.

49 The Malay in this exchange can be translated as: *Buang, kokkie*, "throw it away, Cook"; *Ajo, kokkie, kluar*, "come on, Cook, outside"; *Ajo, kluar*, "come on, out"; *Alla, njonja, minta ampon, njonja, alla sudah, njonja*, "oh, Madam, I beg forgiveness, Madam, oh that's enough, Madam."

50 Sukabumi (which means "the world's pleasure") is a city in western Java, toward the southern coast, almost in a direct line south of Batavia and Buitenzorg. It was built on elevated ground more than 200 feet above sea level. It enjoys an average temperature of 75 degrees year round.

51 Opinions about the colonial Indies varied widely at the time. The colonial government had many supporters in the Indies as well as in Holland, but also a great number of vociferous critics, with Multatuli as perhaps the most brilliant and influential one. Nor were all the foreigners enchanted with the Dutch administration. Raffles, for one, was an outspoken critic, as was his colleague John Crawfurd. But another Englishman, Donald Maclaine Campbell, praised the Dutch, as did Alfred Russell Wallace. See Campbell, *Java: Past and Present*, 2 vols. (London: Heinemann, 1915), 1:xi–xii; Wallace, *The Malay Archipelago* (1869; reprint ed., New York: Dover, 1962), pp. 72–76.

52 Couperus's prediction (which he also stated in 12:461) that the Indies would revolt against the Dutch became, of course, a reality half a century later. Couperus's fear for American involvement, which, as far as I know, never took place, was shared by Multatuli before him. See *Briefwisseling tusschen Multatuli en S. E. W. Roorda van Eysinga*, ed. Mevr. Douwes Dekker (Amsterdam: W. Versluys, 1907), pp. 276, 301. Couperus offers the same sentiments about America and Japan in *Nippon* (see 12:596). In *Oostwaarts*, however, Couperus was far more positive about Dutch colonialism (see 12:244, 291, 337, 414, 460–64). His notions about Japan became reality when Japan conquered the Indies in 1942, after war had been declared on 7 December 1941.

53 The unlikely heritage of the De Luce family is based on fact. Nieuwenhuys informs us in *Baren en oudgasten* that there was indeed a princess from Solo who fell in love with a Frenchman. The European fought in the susuhunan's army against the Javanese rebel Diponegoro who had revolted against the Dutch. The real name of the Frenchman was Dézentjé. His large estate in central Java, Patjaram in the novel, was called "Ampel" in reality. He had fourteen sons and fourteen daughters with his royal wife and Nieuwenhuys notes that the close bond between the Dézentjés and the court at Solo was maintained for a long time. On p. 164, Nieuwenhuys prints a photograph of "Ampel" when it was visited by some Solo aristocrats.

54 *Adat* is the general term for native custom, law, and ritual. It was clearly distinct from European jurisprudence. It is a complex term that covers a wide variety of conditions. For a survey in English, see B. Ter Haar, *Adat Law in Indonesia* (1948; reprint ed., New York: AMS Press, 1979). For the most important Dutch scholar of *adat*, see H. W. J. Sonius, *Over Mr. Cornelis van Vollenhoven en het adatrecht van Indonesië* (Nijmegen: Katholieke Universiteit, 1976).

55 *Tableaux vivants*, costumed balls, and plays were favorite diversions for the Dutch colonialists. Couperus was particularly skilled in arranging *tableaux vivants*, at which a group of people, properly costumed, assumed a silent pose that was meant to

represent a particular scene. One will find in *Baren en oudgasten* a photograph of such a scene that Couperus had directed when he was staying with his brother-in-law in Java, plus another one wherein Couperus is part of such a scene himself.

56 *Anak* means "child," *mas* means "gold," hence "golden child." This is used to refer to a stepchild taken in by a family. Since the expression can also mean "a favorite child" it is clear that it was a pleasant situation for the child.

57 The court Javanese probably refers to what is called *Krama*, a kind of Javanese used by courtiers among themselves, or by a lower-class person addressing his social superiors. It takes a great deal of familiarity and experience to know what kinds of words and expressions are used in specific social circumstances. It is easy to make a grievous error, one that will insult a Javanese aristocrat without his ever informing you what your trespass was.

58 *Slikur*, more commonly spelled *selikur*, is similar to our card game "twenty-one." *Stoteren* refers to another card game called in Javanese *setoter*, which in turn was derived from the Dutch *stoteren*.

59 *Petangans* are almanacs that provide tables of the Javanese days, weeks, years, the significance of certain gods and spirits, astronomical information, and so on. They are meant to provide their user with the correct configuration of lucky and unlucky days for just about any activity that can be imagined. The previously mentioned study by Van Hien of *petangans* is valuable because it is difficult for a European to know this abstruse lore (*De Javaansche Geestenwereld*). An instance in the present novel when *petangans* would have been consulted is in the digging of the well in chapter 25. For their use in modern Indonesia, see Geertz, *The Religion of Java*, pp. 30–37.

60 The *Kaaba (Ka'ba)* is the square black stone in Mecca, venerated by Muhammadans, and one of the main objects of a pilgrimage or "hajj." The other one is Muhammad's tomb in Medina, in the mosque of the Prophet.

61 "Si" is a Javanese familiar title used before the name of a social equal or inferior. In Si-Oudijck's case, it would refer to a social inferior, and might be translated as "the" Oudijck, or "that" Oudijck.

62 The Brantas River is the second largest in Java. (The Solo River is the largest.) It originates on the southern border of Kediri and flows through that province toward the northern coast. One branch, the Kalimas, runs to the port of Surabaja, while the other, under the name of Polong, flows into the Straits of Madura, north of Pasuruan. The Brantas is nearly 190 miles long.

63 Oriental study in Delft meant the training to become a colonial administrator. For sixty years, from 1842 on, such training was attempted in a special institute in the city of Delft, now the seat of the Dutch equivalent of M.I.T. The curriculum took four years and led to a diploma. The problem was in deciding whether the candidates should be educated as technicians or as "Indologists," i.e., those who were knowledgeable about the variety of Indonesian cultures, languages, ethnic groups, and so on. This was resolved in 1864 when the two groups of students were separated and housed in different institutions. In September 1902, a two-year curriculum was established in Leyden that was associated with the famous university but not part of it. In 1922 the study to become a colonial administrator was recognized finally as a full-fledged academic discipline with its own faculty. From 1925 on, "Indology" was the only major area of concentration. Until 1953, three years after Indonesia's independence, a candidate could still take his doctoral exams in the subject, although by that

time no new students were accepted. See *Besturen overzee: Herinneringen van oud-ambtenaren bij het binnenlands bestuur in Nederlandsch-Indië*, ed. S. L. van der Wal (Franeker: Wever, 1977), pp. 17–41.

64   For *srimpis*, see notes 70 of the introduction.

65   A *dukun* can be a Javanese herbalist, a doctor practicing native medicine, or, as Geertz puts it, "a ceremonial specialist," if not a sorcerer. *Djimat* means an amulet or talisman for self-protection. For the *dukun* in modern Javanese society—a role not much different from that in Couperus's day—see Geertz, *The Religion of Java*, pp. 86–111.

66   Ternate is a small island off the western coast of the island of Halmaheira. Like its equally small neighbor, Tidore, the sultanate of Ternate wielded power dispropor-tionate to its size, controlled the spice trade before the Portuguese came, and became an ally of the Dutch VOC in the seventeenth century. It was the destructive rivalry be-tween Ternate and Tidore that allowed the Europeans to play off one against the other and insinuate their own authority. During the seventeenth century, Ternate ruled a vast colonial empire of islands in the southern Moluccas, where it exacted tribute and demanded obedience to its rule. The ruthless monopoly policy of the Dutch reduced Ternate, Tidore, and other Moluccan islands to indigent vassal states. See E. M. Beekman, ed., *The Poison Tree* (Amherst: University of Massachusetts Press, 1981), pp. 148–51.

Halmaheira is the largest island of the nothern Moluccas. It resembles Celebes somewhat in that it, too, is formed by four peninsulae. It lies to the east of the most northern tip of Celebes, and west of the most northern tip of New Guinea.

Indonesia is one of the most volcanic regions in the world. If one goes by the defini-tion of volcanoes as those mountains that are or were recently active, Indonesia has 78 volcanoes. But from a geological point of view there are close to 400. Related to volcanic action are earthquakes, and Indonesia has known many severe ones in its history. I have not been able, however, to identify the one Couperus is referring to, though it must have taken place between 1898 and 1900.

67   *Pasar malam* (or *malem*) is a Javanese fair that lasts for a week, and is mainly cele-brated at night.

Alun-alun is a large, usually quadrangular space covered with grass in the center of a village, town, or city. Traditionally, the *alun-alun* was outside the wall of the *kraton*, or royal palace.

Komedie-Stambul was a specific form of popular entertainment. It was neither purely native nor purely European. Folk theater as well as a kind of vaudeville, *Komedie-Stambul* had Malay texts, though it also performed works such as *Hamlet*, *The Merchant of Venice*, Dutch plays, and adaptations written by local playwrights. Of the last, the most popular were dramatized stories taken from *Thousand and One Nights*, about Ali Baba, for instance, or Aladdin. It is from these texts that it derived its name: *Stambul*, i.e., Istanbul, or Constantinople.

68   *Poffertjes* were a typical Dutch delicacy. They are small round pancakes, about the size of our dollar pancakes. They are heaped on a plate, covered with confectioner's sugar, and served with a slab of butter.

69   *Rijksdaalders* were silver coins, worth two-and-a-half guilders.

70   Tosari was the name of both a village and a sanatorium in the Tengger Mountains in east Java. It was a famous vacation spot and health resort in a mountainous region that was almost 6,000 feet above sea level. A steady temperature remained all year

within a range of 62 to 80 degrees. The air was clear and dry, and on a bright day one could see the Straits of Madura, or even the island of Madura itself. Tosari was surrounded by volcanoes. One will find more details about this once very popular town in H. J. van Mook, *Gids voor Tosari en het Tenggergebergte* (Koog aan de Zaan: Firma P. Out, 1916).

71   The sudden change in people's behavior toward Eva was something Couperus himself had experienced during his stay in Java. When he turned out not to be so docile and servile as expected, the Dutch community turned their backs on him. See the special issue on Couperus of *Maatstaf* 11, no. 3-4 (1963): p. 184.

72   Melati is a jasmine *(Jasminum sambac)*. The "dancing girls" probably refers to *ronggèngs*. These were Javanese girls who danced publicly for a fee and were also prostitutes. See the photographs in Nieuwenhuys's *Baren en oudgasten*, pp. 109-15.

73   *Minta ampon, 'nja* means "please forgive me, Madam."

74   A *luak* is civet cat *(Paradoxurus hermaphroditus)*, a carnivorous mammal that prefers to hunt at night.

75   *Pontianak* (also *kuntianak*) is a female spirit or ghost who takes on the shape of a young woman, with long beautiful hair that comes down to the ground. But the *pontianak* lacks genitalia and has instead a round opening that goes right through her body. The latter feature probably contributed to her other name, *sundel-bolong*, which in Javanese comes from *sundel*, to push up from below, and *bolong*, to have a hole. The *pontianak* laughs loudly and immoderately, behavior that was once only associated with prostitutes. One should keep in mind that the Javanese were extremely modest people and that sex and anything pertaining to it were never mentioned in public, nor alluded to. The demon was especially feared by children and women.

76   *Sedeka* is an oblation, the offering of ritual food to a deity or a spirit.

77   *Bawa* means "to bring along"; *barang* refers to anything portable, hence, in the sense intended here "things"; *mandi* is to take a bath, or refers to the bathhouse where one pours water over oneself *(siram)*, though one does not enter the water. Hence, "*bawa barang mandi*" means something like "bring my bathing things."

78   *Apa* is a Javanese interrogative; *bolè* is Javanese for "that's allowed," "you may"; *buat* is "making" or "to do." Hence: "*apa bolè buat, kandjeng*" means "what can we do about it, your ladyship?"

79   *Saja* is used here as if to mean "Yes." Its proper meaning, however, is the Sanskrit "Your humble servant," which is what Urip is really saying here. Its other general meaning is "I," the first-person pronoun. The normal way of saying "yes" is *ya*, or by simply repeating the interrogative used by the questioner in the declarative voice.

80   The description of Léonie in the nude bears a striking resemblance to one of Couperus's very early poems about a woman bathing. See "De Baadster" in Tricht, *Louis Couperus*, pp. 33–34.

81   Preanger used to be the name for a large region (one sixth of the island) in western Java. The Preanger principalities were bordered in the north by the residency Batavia, in the east by the residency Cheribon, in the west by the residency Bantam, and in the south by the Indian Ocean. The word derives from *prajangan* or *priangan*, that is to say, "the abode of spirits." It is a very volcanic terrain, having a denser concentration of volcanoes than anywhere else in the world.

82   A *kakemono* was a Japanese painting on a scroll of silk or paper, weighed down with sticks at top and bottom and hung on the wall for decoration.

83   A *"lengang-lengang* procession of all those women" is used figuratively by Couperus. *Lengang* means "to swing" one's arms, "to sway" one's hips. Hence: an undulating procession of women.

84   Koningsplein, which literally means "king's square" and is called *Gambir* in Malay, was the largest and most fashionable square in the colonial capital of Batavia, now Jakarta. It was a large space of about a square kilometer, with few trees, and some sparse grass. Colonial high society used to gather there in the evenings and parade around in their carriages. The official residence of the governor-general (who actually lived in Buitenzorg, in the mountains) was on the Koningsplein, as was the house of the resident of Batavia. Government buildings were also there, as well as clubs, consulates, and large private residences. As a boy, Couperus lived in such a luxurious dwelling here, once the most fashionable address in the capital.

85   The first telephone system in the Indies was between Batavia, Weltevreden, and Tandjong Priok (Batavia's harbor). It was established in 1883 and was expanded in 1884 to include Semarang and Surabaja. Thereafter the system kept expanding until it was gradually taken over by the government. By 1914 the government ran it completely.

86   The Hotel Wisse was a hotel in Batavia, built in the last decade of the nineteenth century. Another author in this series, P. A. Daum (see *Ups and Downs of Life in the Indies*), stayed there once, as did Couperus in 1899. There is a contemporary photograph of the hotel in E. Breton de Nijs, *Batavia: Koningin van het Oosten* (The Hague: Thomas and Eras, 1976), n.p.

87   Bandung was the main city in the Preanger residency (see n. 81), located in the mountains. It was cherished for its cool healthy climate. It was once known as the "Garden City."

88   Garut, like Bandung, was situated at an elevation of over 2,000 feet, and south of that city. It was known for its cool, dry climate, its many gardens, and the ring of volcanoes around it.

89   Lake Lellès could be reached by train from Garut. It contained several islands. One of them had the tomb of Sultan Tanuk Raja, a ruler of the ancient Javanese realm of Mataram. The tomb was built in the fifteenth century; it was shaded by a large *waringin* tree.

90   A *kalong* is a large bat that feeds on fruit. It is common in the archipelago. It belongs to the *Pteropus*, also known popularly as "flying dogs." It is brown and has a wingspread of nearly five feet. During the day the *kalongs* hang in large groups from trees they have stripped of fruits, leaves, and small twigs, while they set out at night to seek the fruit trees they prefer, particularly *manga* trees.

Glossary

adat   indigenous law, custom, ritual.

adipati   an administrative title conferred by the colonial government on native regents.

adu (or *adoh*)   a common interjection in Malay expressing disbelief.

ajem   chicken.

ajer (air) wangi   scented water, used as an eau de toilette.

ajer- (or *air-*) *blanda*   soda water.

ajo   an exclamation to encourage someone; something like "Come on" or "Let's get going."

alun-alun   originally the royal esplanade outside the palace, it also referred to palace grounds; it later came to refer to a large square space in a city used for display or sports. Now it also refers simply to a square, either in a city or a village.

ampas   refuse; in this context, whatever was left over from making sugar from sugar cane.

astaga   an exclamation of surprise and dismay. Literally, "I ask Allah for forgiveness." Similar to our "Good Lord!"

atap   thatch; a roofing material made from the leaves of various palms.

baadje   the Dutch diminutive of the Malay word *kabaja*, a kind of white cotton jacket worn by women.

babu   a female servant with various functions.

badjing   a tropical squirrel.

balèh-balèh   a bench to sleep or rest on.

bawa   to bring, to bring along, to transport.

bébé   a batik wraparound.

bedak   a powder made from rice and used for cosmetic purposes. It is most often applied to the face.

bibit   Javanese for rice seedlings.

bot'n   "No."

buang   to throw away, to discard, to get rid of.

dalem   a Javanese word for a prince, his title, or his palace. It can also mean "inner" or "within."

deng-deng (*dendeng*)   thin slices of dried meat, similar to our beef jerky.

dessa (*desa*)   Javanese for village. The other common Malay term is *kampong*.

djagas   guards.

djait   to sew; a seamstress.

djaksa   a native public prosecutor.

djati   a tall tree that produces "djati wood" or "Javanese teak."

djimat   an amulet, a talisman.

djurutulis   a scribe or copying clerk. *Djuru* referred to any trained worker, though not one trained in a handicraft.

dukun   a native doctor, herbalist, or medicine man; a man presiding over the ceremony of a *selametan*.

dupa   incense.

gajong (*gajung*)   a dipper or small bucket for taking water out of a cistern; the water is then poured over one's body when taking a bath.

galengan   little, narrow, raised dikes in rice fields.

gamelan   Javanese orchestra.

gardu   a guard; also the word for guardhouse.

gudang   warehouse or any place where goods are stored.

hadji   a Muhammadan who has made a successful pilgrimage to Mecca.

hormat   honor or respect.

inten-inten   diamonds.

kabaai (or *kabaja*)   a loose jacket worn by women which reaches just below the hips. Its front is open and has no buttons. To close it one uses the *kerosang*, three brooches connected by a small silver chain. It has long narrow sleeves. A *kabaai tjina* was worn by men, especially the Dutch, and was a loose cotton jacket with an upright collar.

kabupatèn   the house of a Javanese regent.

kain   a piece of batiked cloth similar to a sarong, but wider, and in a more traditional style.

kali   Javanese for river.

kampong   Malay for a village. In Java it can also mean a neighborhood or section of a city, or a compound (a single house). Javanese uses the term *desa* for an independent hamlet. The Dutch used *kampong* most frequently. In this novel it is also a metonym for "going native."

kandjeng   title for people of noble birth or of high rank (such as the Dutch resident). May be translated as "Your Lordship." *Kandjeng tuan* and *kandjeng residén* mean the same thing and in this text refer to Van Oudijck.

kantjil   a small deer, called mousedeer (*Tragulus pygmaeus*) indigenous to Southeast Asia. Used frequently in native folklore.

kassian   literally to feel pity, sympathy, mercy. It was a very common expression used by Dutch colonialists for anything that one felt sorry for. Comparable to the Spanish *pobrecito*.

katjang-goreng   roasted peanuts.

kebon   garden. *Kebon kotta* refers to a municipal garden.

kenanga   a tree (*Canangium odoratum*) that produces sweet, fragrant flowers, which are distilled to make perfume.

ketju   a robbery.

kluar   to go outside.

kokkie   a native cook. The word was derived from the Dutch.

kondé   a traditional hair style of Indonesian women. The hair is pulled tight and worn in a chignon in the nape of the neck.

kotta (*kota*)   town, city, fortified town.

krandjang   bamboo basket.

kraton   palace of the "emperor" or *susuhunan* in Solo.

kumpulan   a monthly meeting.

kwee kwee   a kind of cookies.

lidi broom, or *sapu lidi*   a broom made from the midrib of the long coconut-palm leaf.

lombok   strong, hot, red Spanish pepper, used for *sambals* and other condiments.

luak   the civet cat.

magang   an apprentice official in Java.

mandi room   the room where one takes a bath, not a room with a toilet.

mandur   a native overseer; from the Portuguese *mandador*.

mangistan   the fruit mangosteen (*Garcinia mangostana*).

massa (*masa*)   an exclamation of surprise, something like "I'll be. . . ."

minta ampon   "Forgive me."

njonja   Madame, Lady; a married woman of high social rank. *Njonja besar* is great lady.

nonna Javanese for an unmarried European woman; "Miss" or "Young Lady." Not to be confused with *njonja* which indicates a married woman of a certain social rank.

oppasser (abbreviated to *oppas*) a valet or an attendant. The word is Dutch, not Malay.

orang blanda (or *belanda*) a Dutchman, a European, or a Westerner. *Orang* means "person"; *blanda* means "white."

pajong the parasol used exclusively by persons of high rank or birth, to indicate their exalted status.

pangéran an exalted title for Javanese royalty in Djokja and Surakarta.

pasangrahan a word derived from Javanese, meaning a rest house or shelter for travelers.

pasar market.

pasar malam a Javanese fair that lasts for a week.

patih the assistant to a regent, or a king's chief counselor.

pending a metal belt of gold or silver.

pendoppo an open hall.

petangan a Javanese almanac used for divination.

pinter smart, clever; also educated or skilled.

pisang banana; *pisang goreng* means fried bananas.

pontianak a female demon.

preksa (*pereksa*) an investigation, an inquiry; hence, "Go investigate," "Go and take a look."

radèn a title for high Javanese nobility.

radèn-adjeng title for an unmarried female aristocrat.

ringgit the serrated edge of a coin. It could also refer to the Dutch coin *rijksdaalder* (worth two and a half guilders) or to the dollar.

rudjak a fruit salad made from various indigenous fruits and heavily seasoned with a very hot sauce.

sado a small horse-drawn carriage with two wheels.

saja "Your humble servant"; here used to say "Yes."

sajur an Indonesian vegetable sauce, usually very spicy; *sajur lodèh* is such a dish made with the young fruits of the custard apple.

samar a long, loose cloak for men.

sambal a condiment made from a base of crushed hot peppers, with a host of other ingredients; used to flavor and accompany meals.

sappis (also *sapi*) the general Javanese term for oxen.

sarong the "skirt" of the Malay, worn by both men and women. Usually batiked.

sawah (or *sawa*) an irrigated rice field.

semba a gesture of worship, honor, or respect. The hands are put together, tips touching, and then raised to the head.

sinjo a boy, either a European or the son of a European father and a native mother. Often abbreviated as *njo*.

sirih the leaves of a peppery plant which, when combined with other ingredients, are chewed like a wad of tobacco.

sonket slippers slippers embroidered with gold and silver thread.

spen a servant who functions somewhat like a butler.

suda(h) done, finished, over with.

sumpitan blowpipe.

susa(h) trouble, difficulties.

tandak to dance.

tentu   "Sure," "Absolutely."

tida (more commonly *tidak*)   the negative "No."

tjelaka (a variant spelling *tjilaka)*   misfortune, disaster, doom.

tjelana monjet   a child's pajamas. *Tjelana* means pants, *monjet* is monkey.

tjemara   a tall tree of the *Casuarinaceae*. It has blue-green, needle-like twigs which are shed, reminding one of pine trees.

tjikar   a cart drawn by oxen.

tokkè, tokè, or *tokèk*   a gecko, a tropical lizard that lives in houses.

toko   a shop, usually run by Chinese, that often contained an amazing variety of goods.

tong-tong   a large, hollowed-out block of wood that hung in the *gardu*. The guard struck the hours on it during the night.

tuan   Mister or Sir. Used particularly by the native population when addressing a European.

tukan (tukang)   a workman, in the sense of someone who knows a trade, such as carpentry. A *tukan* is not an unskilled laborer or coolie.

tukan-besi   blacksmith. *Besi* is iron.

tukan lampu   the servant who carries and cares for the lamps of a house.

ulek   Javanese for crushing something fine, "powdered," "pulverized." Said, for example, of cooking ingredients. Also a generic term for a strong condiment made with hot peppers.

wajang   Javanese puppet theater.

waringin   a tall imposing fig tree (*Ficus benjamina*), considered holy in Indonesia.

wedono   a native officer in charge of a subdistrict in central or eastern Java. The *wedono* (or *wedana*) is subordinate to the regent but superior to village chiefs.

werda   the cry of the Javanese guard in his *gardu* or guardhouse, when he challenges a suspicious person walking by at night; something like "Who goes there?"